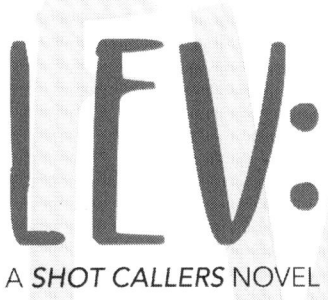

A *SHOT CALLERS* NOVEL

BELLE AURORA

LEV

Published by Belle Aurora

Copyright © 2015 Belle Aurora

First published October 2015

All rights reserved. No part of this publication may be reproduced, distributed, or transmitted in any form or by any means, including photocopying, recording, or other electronic or mechanical methods, without the prior written permission of the author, except in the case of brief quotations embodied in critical reviews and certain other non-commercial uses permitted by copyright law. For permission requests, write to the author, addressed "Request: Copyright Approval" at authorbelleaurora@hotmail.com.

License Notes
This ebook is licensed for your personal enjoyment only. This ebook may not be re-sold or given away to other people. If you would like to share this book with another person, please purchase an additional copy for each person. If you're reading this book and did not purchase it, or it was not purchased for your use only, then please return to Smashwords and purchase your own copy. Thank you for respecting the hard work of this author.

Belle Aurora is in no way affiliated with any brands, songs or musicians or artists mentioned in this book.

Paperback formatted by Buying Ham

BELLE AURORA

LEV

CHAPTER ONE

Mina

I was dying. I hadn't been surer of anything in my life.

As I sat in the alley, staring at the dirty brick wall stained with substances I'd rather not think of, I wondered if this was the place it would happen.

My stomach gave a loud growl of complaint, and rather than feeling hungry, pain consumed me. My lips quivered, and I curled in on myself, hugging my arms around my bent legs, my forehead resting on my knees. It was then, hidden away from the prying eyes of spectators, that I cried.

The warmth of the tears I shed were hardly a comfort to me. I did, however, take solace in knowing I still felt something. Anything.

I was starving, quite literally. It had been days since I ate anything. Last week, I'd become so desperate I ate from the trash. My desperation turned to regret in a matter of hours. I got sick to my stomach from the rancid food, throwing up until I was emptier than I had been before. I wouldn't be taking that risk again. It wasn't worth it.

It left me feeling more than desperation. I felt hopelessness.

Not ready to accept my fate, I realized in complete calm that I would become nothing more than a statistic if I didn't do something about my current situation.

The first item on my list: Find food.

It was late. The sounds of the city streets were quieting down, and many of the stores in my view had turned off their neons. I needed to move quickly if I had any chance of finding something to eat.

I pulled the compact mirror out of my jacket pocket and wiped the stains of the three-day-old mascara from under my eyes. I didn't need that mirror to show me I was pale and that my cheeks were sunken. I felt like a walking skeleton. Looked like one too. My collarbone protruded harshly, my shoulders were pointed, and my cheekbones looked sharp enough to cut. I hid my body under the coat I'd been given at the women's shelter, but there was no hiding my face.

Anyone could tell I was emaciated.

I wrapped my arms around myself, my body in a constant state of chill, and walked out of my alley. I didn't have to walk long before I spotted a Styrofoam container sitting on a table outside of a restaurant that had closed for the night. With my eyes on the prize, my stomach rumbled in excitement as I walked casually over to it. When I got there, I felt eyes on me. I lifted my face to see a young boy, no older than sixteen, looking back at me.

I wanted to cry as soon as I realized he looked very much like me... thin, dirty, and hungry. I knew what it felt like to be hungry. I'd been hungry for years. He eyed me a long moment before he returned his eyes to the container.

I couldn't do it. I wouldn't take it from him. And I could have. I'm a fast runner. Instead, as I felt the familiar prickling behind my eyes and nose, I jerked my chin toward to container and smiled.

He stood there, looking tired and dejected, scratching at his arm. Neither of us moved. A moment of optimism shot through me. If he wasn't going to take it, I would.

Finally, he stepped forward, and recognizing part of himself in me, he started to speak as he opened the container. "We can share."

We both looked down at our findings and my heart sank. A few stiff French fries sat in the bottom of the box, as well as the hardened crust of a sandwich and a few leaves of wilted, brown lettuce.

The boy, looking angry with himself for offering part of his slim fare, held the box out to me. And I couldn't help but smile. It was funny how people who had nothing would offer everything to those in need, and people who had comfort scarcely offered it to people who needed it.

My stomach growled angrily and I turned my smile on the boy. I lied through that smile. "No thanks. I'm not hungry."

The tilt of his brow told me he didn't believe me, but he shrugged and walked away with the box, leaving me alone to regret my decision.

God, you're stupid.

I nodded slowly to myself. I knew that already.

My numb feet took me three more blocks before I came across a sandwich bar that was closing. A man with short brown hair stacked chairs from outside the deli and brought them in before moving to close the door.

"Wait," I called, rushing over.

The man frowned down at me, his dark eyes scrutinizing my every move. "What? We're closed."

I lowered my eyes and spoke quietly. "I'm sorry to bother you, sir. I was just wondering whether you had any food that you were about to throw out." I peered up at him. "Anything would do. I'm not picky."

"You're hungry?" He scowled at me, his lip curling. "Get a job."

The door moved to close a second time and I panicked, placing my foot in the way. My eyes widened in shock at the bold move. That wasn't like me at all. The door was stopped a few inches before it shut, and the man looked down at my foot before looking back up at me and glowering. "I should beat your ass, girl. Move your foot or I'll break the fucking thing."

My lips quivered as my vision blurred. "I'm so hungry. Please," I begged. "*Please.*"

His scowl left him a moment to study my face. He opened the door another few inches before looking up and down the street. "You want food?"

I nodded enthusiastically.

He leaned back a little to leer at me. "Suck my dick and you'll get fed."

I didn't believe it possible, but I paled further then whispered, "I just want something to eat. It doesn't have to be much. I-I," I stuttered, "I don't want to do that. Please."

His scowl returned, harder than before. "Obviously not hungry enough." He jerked his chin toward the street. "Get the fuck out of here, bitch."

As he closed the door, locking it, I fell into full-fledged panic, my stomach turning violently. I threw myself at the glass door, pounding my fists against it until my knuckles throbbed sorely. My voice broke as I cried quietly, tears of regret sliding down my cheeks, "Please! I-I'm sorry! I'll do it!" But the man left my vision as he walked into the back room, turning the lights off behind him.

My shoulders shook as I sobbed in complete silence.

Angry with myself, I yelled a broken, *"I'll do it, dammit!"* and slammed my fist against the glass.

But the door remained closed. I slid down the glass door to sit on the icy-cold cement of the sidewalk, crying weakly. My head pounding, hungry, heartsick, and humiliated, my tears stopped suddenly as I closed my eyes and realized my situation was worse than I thought.

I was officially at an all-time low. But not for long. I was desperate, and desperation was a damn good motivator.

CHAPTER TWO

LEV

I stood by the door staring at my brother as he spoke to the man trembling in the chair by the solid marble desk. It didn't take much for me to recognize he was angry. That familiar bored glare told me everything I needed to know. He didn't raise his voice. He never raised his voice. That wasn't Sasha's style.

"How long we been friends, Paolo?" He spoke slowly but firmly.

The man didn't answer. There was no point in answering. Sasha wasn't friends with anyone. He merely tolerated people.

Sasha looked up at me, his light brown eyes hard. "How long we been friends with Paolo, Lev?"

My mind was quick to calculate. I answered immediately, "Three years, two months, and four days."

The moment I finished, Sasha repeated, "Three years." He stood up from his sitting position. "Two months." He moved around the desk and sat in front of the short, stocky man. "And four days." Then he scowled, lowering his voice to a hush. "That's a long time, Paolo." He made a show of removing his cufflinks and rolling up his sleeves. "So when I hear my friends are leaving me to work with Laredo, I begin to wonder if my friend was a friend at all."

Paolo blanched before straightening. "Who told you that?" He tried to scoff, but it came out a wheeze. "That's bullshit, Sash. I told you I'm taking some time off. My Vera doesn't like the hours I'm keeping. Keeps saying I don't spend enough time at home. Missing out on the kids growing up and all that shit." Then he forced a smile. "You know what they say. Happy wife, happy life."

Sasha closed his eyes, running his hand, decorated with thick silver rings, through his hair with a sigh. His cheek ticked. "I don't like liars, Paolo. You know this. You've seen what happens to liars." He squeezed his eyes shut and rolled his neck from side-to-side, working out the kinks. "Why are you lying to me?"

Then he did something stupid. He lied again. "I'm not working with Laredo. I swear to God, I'm not."

I shook my head. The man was an idiot. You didn't lie to Sasha. You didn't lie to any Leokov.

Sasha's eyes opened with a flash. He took a deep breath before laying it out there. "There was a meet this morning at Aphrodite's Kiss." Paolo blanched, but Sasha went on. "It was kind of funny, actually." The look on Sasha's face told us there was nothing funny about this situation. "Laredo told the boys that I needed to treat my staff better, or else they'd follow your lead. Said he'd welcome any and all of them with open arms."

The short man blustered, turning bright red. "W-well, he's full of shit!"

"You embarrass me," Sasha said in a calm hush.

Paolo stood when he realized it was over. It was done. He was caught. "I never wanted this, Sash. You forced my hand. I can't keep working like this. You're so fucking demanding." He panted before begging for understanding, "I had a goddamn heart attack last month! I nearly died. This job is *killing* me!"

Sasha nodded thoughtfully. The near silence in the room felt thick with the soft sounds of Paolo's wheeze. Finally, Sasha stood, and to the complete disbelief of the short man, he held out his hand. "Good luck."

Paolo, not being one to look a gift horse in the mouth, took the outstretched hand and shook it. "I'm sorry, Sash. Really, I am."

Sasha shook his hand firmly before letting go. "Me too." He added, "We'll miss you 'round here." He walked back behind his desk. "I've got a couple of things to finish up. Go down to the bar and we'll have a drink before you leave."

It was clear that Paolo couldn't believe his ears, or his luck. "Don't go to any trouble—"

But he was cut off with Sasha's firm, "I insist."

Paolo smiled then, the idiot. "Okay. I'll be there."

He turned and moved to walk out, but I stood my ground, eyeing him. The little man looked up at me. He seemed afraid.

People didn't like me.

I didn't blame them.

We stood there another moment before Sasha spoke again, gently this time. "Let the man pass, Lev."

I heard my brother, but I didn't want to listen. I didn't like Paolo.

Another moment, then again, "Move, Lev."

I stepped to the side and let the idiot pass. As soon as he was out the door, I closed it behind him and said what needed to be said. "He's a liability."

Sasha sighed as he sat. "I know." He picked up the phone, and after a short while, he spoke into the receiver. "I need you." Without another word, he hung up.

We waited in silence, and when the knock sounded, I opened the door for the tall, slim man. He wore jeans, tennis shoes, and a short-sleeved blue polo shirt. He wore glasses and looked sophisticated with his blond hair gelled back, but nothing could hide the pock-scars on his cheeks. "What's up?"

Sasha nodded toward the door, and I closed it behind us, locking it. The tall man smirked playfully. "Should I be worried? I feel like I just got called into the principal's office."

Sasha ran a hand down his face, pausing to squeeze the bridge of his nose. "Can you induce a heart attack?"

He leaned against the wall and sighed dramatically. "Well, shit. And today was such a good day."

Sasha glared at him. "Is it doable, Pox?"

Pox grinned. "Yeah, it is. It might take a while to get the dosage right. It'll take a bit of this, a bit of that. Most of the shit is illegal or off the market. When do you need it by?"

"Fifteen minutes. At max."

Pox straightened and sputtered. "You're out of your fucking mind." He shook his head in earnest. "No way. I can't do it."

I spoke up, "I know a man who deals in pharmaceuticals. The price will be high, but he can get everything you need." I added, "They deliver."

Pox turned to me slowly, blinked, and then glanced back at Sasha. "You are some scary motherfuckers." His voice was full of admiration.

I gave him the phone number and listened as Pox cursed at the absurd prices for the things he needed.

The delivery boy arrived in ten minutes. The concoction was made, dissolved, and slipped into the sixth shooter Paolo drank. The men sputtered and laughed as Paolo coughed before righting himself. Sasha smiled foxlike before calling over some of the girls.

The club turned into roaring chaos when Paolo, in the midst of getting a lap dance, suffered a heart attack. Sasha performed CPR until the ambulance arrived. Witnesses told the police that Sasha did everything he could to save Paolo.

Unfortunately, he didn't make it.

CHAPTER THREE

I didn't have much of a plan.

Okay. So I didn't have a plan at all.

After spending another fruitless night in my alley, my body was cold, chilled to the bone. I just wanted to go somewhere I'd be warm. Unfortunately, it was past midnight, and there weren't a lot of options as far as I could see.

I could go into the convenience store for a while, but they would expect me to buy something, and seeing as I had no money and looked as though I had no money, they'd turn me on my ass before I could say boo.

There was the fast food restaurant with the bright red and yellow sign, but I didn't think I could handle being engulfed in the smell of burgers and fries without bursting into tears for want.

I decided to turn and walk the opposite direction, when I noticed a group of men exit a building. They were laughing and looked happily drunk. Drunk was good. People did odd things when they were drinking.

My stomach rumbled loudly and my decision was made. I would find the tipsiest man in the club and seduce him. When he passed out, I'd take his wallet and be on my merry way. I could make a small amount of money go a long way if I had to.

I needed to eat. I felt ashamed that I would resort to low lengths to do that, but I was sick of being me. Mina was friendly, and honest, and kind. Being *me* got me nowhere. I was floating down shit creek without a paddle.

The white sign above the door read Bleeding Hearts in simple, elegant font. Steadying myself, I pushed open one side of the huge double doors and stepped inside.

A tall, bulked-up man with a crew cut and an impeccable suit looked down at me. He was not amused. "You lost?"

I shook my head before swallowing hard and muttering, "Just looking for somewhere to drink."

That changed his attitude quick enough. He opened the second set of doors and loud RnB blasted into the foyer. "We don't get a lot of ladies down here. The bar is to the right. Have a good night."

I had been called a lot of things in my life, but never a lady. I suddenly felt regretful of my reason for being here. Regardless, I walked inside and felt immediate warmth. A shiver of delight caused my skin to break out in gooseflesh.

Finally!

I could've crowed with happiness, but I had more important things to think about. Before I made my way to the bar, I was drawn to the left.

Two women with gorgeous bodies swung around provocatively on poles, dressed in nothing but little scraps of material covering their privates.

The blonde woman had glitter pasties stuck to her nipples. The redhead's nipples were pierced.

Ah. I got it then.

"We don't get a lot of ladies down here."

My cheeks turned bright pink as men hollered up at the dancing girls. My gut rolled. The bouncer must have thought I was a complete pervert.

I pulled my hair over my face to hide my flaming cheeks and found an empty bar stool in the corner of the room, hidden from light. It was the perfect place to search for the man who would help feed me.

My eyes scanned the room through the dim lighting of the club. There were too many of them. I'd have to get closer.

I stayed by my stool a while before I made my move. My heart raced as anxiety took over me. I took in a deep breath and exhaled slowly. My back ramrod straight, I would find my savior right here, in this very room.

I just didn't know what he looked like yet.

LEV

I was drawn to her immediately. Intrigue held me captive.

My brow furrowed as I watched her. What was she doing in a place like this? It was clear she didn't belong here.

By the look of her, she didn't belong quite anywhere. She was so small her black coat was at least three sizes too big, and the way she covered her face with her long dark hair was so childlike that my chest hurt.

That was new. It surprised me. I wasn't sure whether that was good or bad, but it made me take a step toward her.

I managed to spot one doe-like eye peeping through her hair as she stared openly at the girls on stage. Obviously, she hadn't come to see dancing girls. From the shock on her face, she didn't know Bleeding Hearts was a strip joint.

Reaching up, she moved to cover her face with her hair once more before she lowered her head and scurried along to the dark side of the bar. It pleased me that she chose that spot. It was the spot I normally sat. Warmth spread through my torso.

The club was almost at capacity. As news of Paolo's death carried, Sasha spread the word that he would be opening the club to friends and family. No cover charge. Drinks were on the house.

This, of course, meant that my keen eyesight would have to be keener tonight. Sasha didn't like trouble. I kept trouble from arising.

The girls behind the bar served customers, smiles pasted onto their faces, even though they would be worked to the bone. The tips would be worth the straying hands and ogling eyes.

Sasha came out from behind the door. His eyes met mine almost instantly and he jerked his chin at me in greeting. I returned it.

When I was younger, Sasha taught me it was rude to ignore a greeting. I was never any good at taking cues from other people. Conversation was painful. I didn't like to speak unless spoken to, and even then, I would rarely talk unless a question was asked.

My brother was a hard man, but he was also patient. And growing up with me was not easy, I was sure. He never raised his voice to me, even when I was told I was being unreasonable. He was kind and understanding, and he explained things to me in a way I would understand.

I was six years old when my parents realized something was wrong with me. Our family dog, Mishka, ran out into the road and was hit by car. When my father told me she hadn't survived, I simply nodded then ran upstairs to my room to process.

That was where I was found, hours later, covered in blood after slamming my head into my bedroom wall, over and over. My father rushed me to the emergency room. I'd opened the side of my head to the bone. They stitched me up, but still, I didn't cry.

When the doctor asked if this was something that happened often, my father got angry. He said there was nothing wrong with me and that it was an accident. The doctor calmly explained that he could help, but my father picked me up and took me home.

In the car, he turned to me and said, "You are my son and I love you. There is nothing wrong with you." But as the years went on, it became clear to anyone who met me that there was something wrong with me.

Although I smiled on occasion, I never laughed. I was able to remember almost every detail of every conversation I had ever had. I was smart in an abnormal way, and could calculate large sums in my mind. I did not understand or process emotion as others did. I didn't cry. And I never lied.

People called me a cyborg.

I didn't like that.

My sister, Nastasia, beat the shit out of the kids who dared to tease me. Sasha never had to raise a finger. All he would need to do was glare at them and they'd run scared.

Time went on, and Sasha helped me while Nastasia loved me unconditionally. Sasha taught me to respond to people in a casual fashion and helped me read cues. I still wasn't any good at taking prompts from people. If you didn't tell me what you were feeling, chances were I wouldn't know.

Nastasia told me there was nothing wrong with me. That it wasn't my fault I was smarter than everyone else. She said that if the rest of the world didn't have shit for brains then I wouldn't be so special, so I should be grateful.

The young woman moved amongst the crowd in a seemingly casual way, but I saw more in the way she watched the men with a hawk's eye.

She was up to something. And I would find out exactly what.

Mina

It was harder than it looked, choosing a man to seduce.

It didn't help that most of the men in the club were in their late forties and fifties and smelled like sweat combined with vodka, and that stale musty smell people got when they'd been drinking too much. It was funny that I felt the need to complain about smell, when I likely smelled just as bad. I should be grateful if one of these men took pity on me.

When one man grabbed at my hand and yelled in my ear, "Part of the entertainment?" I shook my head in panic, snatched my arm away, and dashed away, back to my corner.

Mentally scolding myself, I regrouped. He would've been a good candidate. Sure, he was old and fat and balding, but he wore nice rings and likely had a full wallet. Closing my eyes, I sighed.

What am I doing?

I scoffed, shaking my head before I stood. I couldn't sleep with any of these men; it didn't matter how hungry I was. And I was stupid to think I would be able to go through with my ridiculous plan.

Straightening, I moved to leave the club. Just as I was walking past a group of rowdy men, an attractive middle-aged man leaned over the bar to speak to one of the gorgeous bartenders.

I stilled, and everything else melted away.

The man's wallet hung out of his back pocket half an inch.

It wasn't a lot, but it was enough.

My feet took me over to him before I'd even mentally decided on what to do. I really didn't want to steal this guy's wallet. I just wanted to live another day. It wasn't personal. It was life.

A foot away from the man, I stood with my back to him, and with quick fingers, I lifted the wallet out, whisper soft. I shoved it into my coat and, heart racing, looked around until I saw the neon light for the ladies room.

I didn't stop to think. I ran.

Making my way down the narrow hall, I shoved the heavy door open. It was empty. I looked around with wide eyes before rushing into one of the many vacant stalls, seating myself on the closed toilet seat to see how I'd done.

The wallet was heavy. I opened it with shaking fingers. My curse hung in the air then I laughed to myself as I pulled out the stack of hundred dollar bills. I didn't count them all, but I was sure there was close to seven hundred dollars there. Dropping the wallet on the floor, I shoved the money into my pocket and moved to unlock the stall. Just as my fingers touched the cool metal, my conscience glared at me.

Why was the man carrying so much money? I wondered. Perhaps that withdrawal, that specific amount, was for something important. And I was taking it from him. He likely worked hard for that money, and here I was, stealing it.

I pulled the money out of my pocket, a frown marring my brow. I didn't need *all* this money. I only needed enough to get by for a little while.

Removing two of the hundred dollar bills, I placed the others back into the wallet. But my conscience still wasn't happy. Sighing, I took another hundred and put it back into the wallet, leaving me with only one.

A hundred dollars was nothing to sneeze at. I could make that hundred go a long way. It would feed me for two weeks, three at most. I'd come by something else by then.

Satisfied with my haul, I held onto the wallet, opened the stall door, and froze.

I hadn't heard the door open, but the tall man leaning against the wall had clearly been there a while. His light brown eyes on me, arms crossed over his chest, he looked down at the evidence in my hand and said one word.

"Explain."

CHAPTER FOUR

LEV

Although I didn't understand other people's emotions, I understood my own quite well. And right now, I was disappointed.

"Explain," I ordered.

Her hair still covered most of her face, but I could see one wide green eye peeping out at me. She looked frightened.

No. From the way her hands shook and her chest heaved, it hit me that she wasn't frightened. She was terrified.

Nodding toward the wallet in her hand, I spoke softer this time. "That belongs to my brother."

Her shoulders slumped. She uttered a quiet but remorseful, "I'm sorry."

Taking a step forward, I took the wallet from her hand and held out the other. She reluctantly placed a hundred dollar bill into it and stepped away from me. I opened Sasha's wallet and stilled.

I looked up at the girl. She had dipped her chin to avoid looking at me. "There's a lot of money in here." She nodded. I asked, "Why didn't you take it all?"

When she looked up at me, she blinked away tears and whispered a trembling, "I just wanted something to eat."

A wave of emotion ran through me. First, anger, then sadness, then something I couldn't quite explain. Protectiveness, perhaps. "You're hungry." A statement, not a question.

She nodded once more and it was done.

The girl had unexpectedly become my responsibility.

Mina

Gentle fingers under my chin lifted my face until I couldn't avoid him anymore.

He spoke in perfect calm. "You have a choice." I stared, confused. I hadn't realized I'd be given a selection. "I can call the cops and have you arrested." I almost bunched my nose, but stopped myself in the nick of time. I didn't like that choice. "Or you can work for the club, make good money, set yourself up." He added, "Never go without a meal again."

Was this guy nuts? My mind gaped. Like I even had to think about which option I preferred.

Then he added a third option, taking the hundred-dollar note I'd nabbed and he held it up high. "Or I can give you this. You can leave and disappear into the night." His eyes trained on me, he theorized, "A hundred dollars will get you more than one hot meal."

My head swam. I was sure this was a trick.

A hundred dollars was enough to get me by for a little while but a job, a place to stay and food. How could I pass that up?

Oh, God, food was important to me.

I swallowed hard. "Option-B sounds good."

He seemed pleased. "I thought so." He extended a hand. "Come along."

Pulling my sleeves down over my hands, I leaned away from him. "Wait. What kind of work? I—" My train of thought went elsewhere and I blushed. "Dancing? Like those girls out there?"

A single brow rose. "You think I want you to strip?"

My blush turned into a full-blown flush and I felt my neck heat.

Of course he doesn't want you to strip. You're not exactly Jennifer Lopez.

"I don't want you to strip. I want you to stay clothed." He looked disgusted that I would even make the suggestion. "*Fully* clothed," he added testily, and mortification turned my stomach. "You'll tend the bar with the others."

"I don't know how."

His stare was blunt. "You'll learn."

That didn't sound bad. In fact, it sounded great. He held out his hand once more and, keeping my hand covered with my sleeve, I placed it into his. When his warm hand cocooned mine, I realized how large it was. It didn't take long for me to take in the rest of him. He was tall, around 6'1" or 6'2", had broad shoulders, narrow hips, long legs, and a stern face. He was dressed in a perfectly tailored black suit. It had to be. It didn't look like this guy could buy off the rack. I glanced up at his face, and his light brown eyes stared right back at me.

A shiver went through me. His face came across harsh. His cheekbones were high, his chin was strong, his nose slightly crooked, and he had generous lips. His skin was lightly tanned and flawless; he didn't have any laugh lines. It was almost as if he didn't smile at all.

It suddenly hit me. Why would a man who wore suits and spoke in such a classy manner help a homeless girl who he caught stealing?

I pulled my hand out of his. "If this is a trick..." My hair covered half of my face, but I could see the sudden tilt of his head and narrow of his brow. I told him honestly, "If you want to call the police, call them. I promise I'll stay and tell them I stole the wallet." I lowered my face and added thoughtfully, "They might even feed me." I peeked back up at him. "But getting a person's hopes up and joking about things like that to someone who has nothing...it's cruel."

He looked at me for a long moment before taking my hand again—without permission, I might add—and stating, "I don't lie."

He said this confidently, in a way that left me inclined to believe it. I was led out of the bathroom and down the hall before I asked quietly, "Why are you helping me?"

Without looking at me, he led me on and responded, "You look like you need the help."

⚓

LEV

The later it got, the quieter the bar became. Paolo's memory had been celebrated long into the night, and while patrons were calling it a day, the club would be open until three a.m., regardless of if it were empty.

I led the girl back out to the floor, and I couldn't help but notice how tiny her hands were. I liked the way they felt in mine. I did not like how cold her skin was. I'd have to buy her warmer coat.

I gazed down at her. Scratch that. I'd have to buy her a coat—*any* damn coat—in her size.

At the lip of the foyer, I leaned down to the girl's ear and ordered, "Stay here," and then walk over to spot Anika behind the bar. Her face brightened at the sight of me.

My lip quirked. I liked Anika. She'd always been kind to me. We'd known each other since we were children, and her brother, Viktor, was somewhat of an honorary family member and could be found at our house, eating our food.

"Hey, Lev," she said as she gently tossed her long, red wavy hair over her shoulder. She puffed out a breath, blowing part of her fringe off her forehead. "What a night, huh?"

I liked the way Anika spoke. It always calmed me. She had such a soft lilt to her voice that at one point I thought her an angel. "Hey, Ani." I handed her Sasha's wallet. "Can you make sure my brother gets that?"

She smiled sweetly. "Of course. You off for the night?"

I nodded. "Have a good one."

Her smile dissipated at my hurried goodbye. She spoke quietly, "You too, handsome."

Walking back to the girl, I was almost surprised to see her still standing there, chewing nervously on her thumbnail. Part of me figured she'd disappear while my back was turned. But at the sorry state of her, I knew she likely had nowhere to go.

I held out my hand, and she placed her small one into mine without question. And goddamn it, that satisfied me. Immensely. We walked hand-in-hand through to the parking lot, where my black Chevrolet Camaro sat waiting. I pressed the button on my keys and it chirped twice, then I opened the passenger door for the girl, helping her inside. "Buckle up."

Perhaps it should have worried me that she didn't even hesitate to get into a car with a complete stranger. But it was obvious that anywhere was better than here.

Once seated, I started the car and drove out of the parking lot. Without asking, I drove down the street to the twenty-four-hour burger joint and headed down the drive-thru. When I stopped at the speaker, I turned to the girl. "Anything in particular?"

She eyed the menu, but shook her head. She licked her lips. "I'm not fussy."

I ordered her the biggest burger meal, supersized, and an extra cheeseburger, just in case she could down it. I doubted it though. She was positively tiny. Once the food came, I handed it to her, and she held the paper bag close to her chest as if she was worried someone would take it from her.

I waited. And waited. And waited.

My brow furrowed as I parked the car. "Aren't you going to eat?"

Her eyes darted here and there. She held her tongue for a moment before she uttered an uneasy, "I don't want to mess up your car."

The loud growl of her stomach was an objection if I ever heard one.

I reached over, opened the bag, took out the burger, unwrapped it carefully, and handed it back to her. She took it with shaky hands, closed her eyes, and took a big bite, chewing slowly.

She ate soundlessly. I opened my window, turned up the radio, and waited patiently. I couldn't help but look over at her every now and again. She was so quiet. A few minutes passed, and I turned back to see how she was doing, working on her food, and my chest seized.

Her shoulders jerked daintily as she cried in complete silence, eating all the while. She must have felt my eyes on her, because she turned toward the passenger door, her back to me, as her breath hitched quietly while she wept.

This was one of those moments that did it to me. I was officially overwhelmed. I didn't know what to do. I was clueless, and that caused irritation to well up inside of me.

I took the decorative handkerchief out of my breast pocket and held it between my fingers, nudging her gently. She took it, muttering a low,

"Thank you," then I stepped out of the car to give her some time to recover from her emotions.

Ten minutes passed, and I looked in through the car window to see the girl sitting in silence, her hands clutching the paper bag tight. Sitting inside the car, I reached for the bag, but she snatched it out of my reach.

My brows rose.

Her hair was becoming a problem for me. Her visible cheek flushed as she explained, "I didn't finish. It was a lot of food." She added hesitantly, "I'd like to take it with me if that's okay."

Who was I to object? I bought the food for her, after all. "Not a problem. Where can I drive you? Do you have anywhere to stay?"

She paused. "Yeah, um, I'm actually only a few blocks away, so I can walk from here."

I was already shaking my head. "I'll drive you." She tried to object a second time, but I added inflexibly, "I insist."

She stared at me a long while then nodded. "Okay. Turn left and drive until you see Café Alonzo."

I knew where that was. I wasn't aware of any housing in that area, but I drove anyway. Slowing to a stop, I looked out the window, unconvinced this was where she lived. "Are you sure this is where you live?"

She smiled faintly. "Positive." At my frown, she quickly added, "It's not much, but it's home." She turned to me then and did something I'd been longing for her to do from the moment I saw her.

Placing her fingertips to her cheek, she moved the hair away from her face, tucking it gently behind her ear.

I was mesmerized.

She was gorgeous. Absolutely stunning.

Her heart-shaped face looked too thin, but her mouth was small, full and pink. Her green eyes were large and expressive, framed prettily with long, dark lashes. She was pale, her skin unblemished. She had black makeup smudged under her eyes, but I could see the beauty she tried to hide from the world. And what a rare beauty she was.

Her expression soft, she avoided eye contact and dipped her chin as she spoke. "I want to thank you for your kindness tonight. Not many people would have done what you did." Her rosebud mouth quirked into an awkward smile. "I owe you. More than you'll ever know."

Feeling mildly uncomfortable of her thanks, I turned off the car, ignoring her suddenly anxious expression. "Are you able to get yourself to the club tomorrow by seven? If you can't, I'll have someone pick you up."

I would pick her up.

Her brow bunched and she bit the inside of her bottom lip, thinking. "I think so. I don't have a watch, but I'll make sure I'm there, even if I'm early."

I pulled up my shirtsleeve, undid the latch on my Tag Heuer watch, and handed it to her. She frowned at me. "What...?" When I did not retrieve the watch, her eyes widened. "I can't take that."

I fought to control my anger. Gritting my teeth, I spoke calmly. "You can give it back to me tomorrow."

Her expression turned panicked. "Do you know what would happen if someone saw me with that? I'd get mugged!"

I scowled. *Just let them try. I fucking dare them.* "Then I'll buy another."

The change in her expression was so sudden that I blinked. She took the watch carefully and muttered, "Must be nice to have that much money."

Shame caused me to flush, and my anger showed itself. I snapped, "Do you need a ride or not?"

"No."

She held the fast food bag tightly and peeked over at me before evading my inscrutable gaze. "I'm Mina."

"Mina," I tested it out. It felt good on my tongue. "I'm Lev."

She opened the door and stepped out, leaning down into the open space. "Thank you, Lev. For everything. I'll work hard." She smiled tiredly. "You won't regret it."

My stomach flipped at her sweet smile. "Goodnight, Mina."

She lowered her lashes. "Goodnight."

LEV

I watched her walk down an alley connecting to the street behind, waited until she was out of sight then started the car and drove two blocks down.

With a light sigh, I parked my car, turned the lights off, and waited.

CHAPTER FIVE

Mina

My *God*, but was Lev intense or *what*?

The car drove away and I waited a full two minutes before I walked out of the alley and started the three-block walk down to *my* alley.

I fanned my face thinking about *him*. Gods above, he was simply divine.

I looked down at myself, my face heating. Here I was, thinking about my handsome guardian angel, and I looked like an extra from the movie *Swamp Thing*.

I hugged myself tightly with my free arm. Clutching the watch in my hand, I decided not to risk losing it and put it on. Unfortunately, as I struggled with the latch, I realized a little too late that even in the smallest position, it was too loose. Still, I pushed it up my forearm.

I would return this watch, dammit. Even if it was the last thing I ever did.

The bag of food by my side, I walked hastily. I didn't want to risk any unwanted attention tonight. I needed to get home quickly.

Finally, I reached my destination and, moving behind the dumpster, I fished out my bag of miscellaneous crap.

Great. All my clothes were dirty. Not that I had much, but at least I could wear my too-big black jeans and my white tee. I held up the garments, immediately spotting the brown stain on the once-white shirt.

I'd have to do laundry tomorrow. But, *shit*, I still had no money.

How embarrassing. I would not be starting work in dirty freaking clothes. I would just have to beg tomorrow morning, praying someone would gift me the quarters I needed for a single load.

The voice behind me startled me, so much that I jumped, squeaked, and fell flat on my ass into a puddle of piss-smelling mud.

"It's not much, but it's home, huh?"

Panting, I turned to Lev, my voice cutting. "What the heck are you doing here?"

My derision didn't deter him. I wasn't really angry at him, just mortified. I couldn't exactly greet him with a 'Welcome to my humble abode. Mineral water? Whiskey?'

All I could offer was the smell of trash and questionable puddles.

He stepped closer, his eyes flashing dangerously. "I had a feeling you weren't being completely honest with me. So I followed you."

Yeah. No shit, Sherlock.

Ass in puddle, I held my arms wide and smiled mockingly. "Do you like it? I just had the walls done. I think the color is called shit brown." I sniffed noticeably. "Oh no, wait." Sarcasm dripped from my every word. "That *is* shit."

That brow rose, and I wanted to take a handful of my piss puddle and fling it at him. Instead, I stood, the cold puddle liquid dripping down my legs. My cheeks colored as I toned down the sass. "I think, after seeing the place, you can understand why I didn't want company."

He ignored me. "Do you have a family somewhere?"

Shoving my clothes back into my bag of crap, I shook my head.

"I'm sure there are shelters around these parts. Why aren't you staying at one?"

I zipped the bag harder than I should have. He wouldn't understand, even if I spelled it out letter-by-letter. "Trust me when I tell you that they aren't all they're cracked up to be." I threw the bag over my shoulder. "If you'll excuse me, I need to find a Laundromat to beg in front of tomorrow morning so I can *not* smell like a pool of urine."

He straightened, keys in hand, and turned, jerking his chin at me. "Come along, mouse."

I sighed. Why was he being so kind? "I don't need a ride. I can find one myself."

He paused at the beginning of the alley. "Not taking you to the damn Laundromat. I'm taking you home." He cocked his head slightly. "That is, unless you don't want a warm bed to sleep in and somewhere to wash those rags."

I ignored the jibe and watched him walk back out onto the street.

Time passed. I didn't even know this guy. I shouldn't have even considered it. But anything was better than the street. I hauled my bag up higher onto my shoulder.

And like the lost puppy I was, I followed Lev home.

⚓

"*This* is home?" I asked in astonishment as he pressed the button on the remote attached to the sun visor above his head.

The huge iron gates opened and he grunted his affirmative response.

Still in awe, I asked, "Do you get lost in here?"

He snuffled, and it sounded awful close to a laugh, but I seriously doubted it. "Don't be fooled. It's actually three houses in one complex. My brother and sister live here also."

That drew me out of my admiration instantly. A shiver went down my spine as dread took me by surprise. "Wait, what? Your brother? The same brother whose wallet I stole?" He nodded silently and, eyes wide in alarm, I squawked, "I can't stay here!"

"Relax." He said this in such a bored tone that it sounded as if it took him all the effort in the world to say it. "It's fine. He's not home yet, and my sister is out of town at the moment. We have the entire complex to ourselves. For now."

My stomach tightened in a bundle of nerves, but I stayed quiet for fear of losing the food I'd just eaten. He drove farther down the long drive until it split into a T-junction. He turned left, and I saw one of the three houses.

It was still massive compared to the regular homes and apartments I was used to seeing. The two-story home was beautifully designed from the outside, and held a romantic style with quaint terraces in off-whites and light sandy yellows. The lights were on, and I suddenly wondered if anyone else lived with him. The thick silver ring on his wedding ring finger would suggest so.

"Are you married?"

"No."

My tense shoulders lowered a little. Well, that was good. I didn't need a woman around accusing me of all kinds of nastiness. Women could be brutal.

He parked outside the property, walked around, and helped me out of the car, taking my bag of crap from me with one hand and holding out his elbow graciously. I took it almost immediately, and he led me up the front steps, unlocking the door. The giant glass door was pushed lightly, and the house revealed itself.

My gut rolled aggressively. I *so* did not belong here.

The inside of the house was pristine, with white, sparkling marble and wooden masculine furniture. The very first thing that caught my eye in the giant foyer was the staircases on the left and right, leading up to the second floor and meeting in the middle.

What was it called when stairs did that?

"It's an imperial staircase. Many royal houses in Russia have it."

I turned to him, not realizing I had asked the question out loud. Then I turned back to the stairs. "That's a little arrogant, don't you think?" I side-eyed him. "Comparing yourself to royalty and all."

His lip lifted so slightly that I might've imagined it. "That's a little presumptuous, isn't it?" He side-eyed me right back. "To assume I don't stem from royalty."

My eyes widened as I whispered, "Do you?"

He turned to me and, I *swear*, his eyes smiled. "No."

Rolling my eyes, I shook my head as he walked to the left side of the stairs and began to walk up. "Follow me, mouse."

Mouse? Why mouse? *Why not just call me what I am?*

A street rat.

At the top of the stairs, we came across two halls, one leading left, and the other leading to the right. He seemed to hesitate a moment before he turned left, and took me to the door at the very end of the hall. He placed his hand on the fancy brass lever and threw the door open, lifting a hand to turn on the lights.

It was a bedroom. Definitely a man's bedroom. A woman would be too conservative to furnish a room in such garish furniture and strong, royal colors.

It looked more like an apartment, really, at least four times the size of a normal bedroom. I definitely couldn't complain about the room, if this was to be where I was going to sleep. There were three floor-to-ceiling windows in this one room. The drapes were the fancy, ruched kind in a dark burgundy with gold trim. In the right corner of the room was a large, maroon, suede sectional sofa, which took on an L-shape to fit into the angle perfectly. The bed was placed opposite the couch, a king-sized mahogany sleigh bed with heavy dark red covers and more pillows than was necessary. There was no TV, or any sort of entertainment other than the full wall-to-wall bookshelf on the left.

I stood there, mouth gaping. "Wow. This is so fancy."

His next sentence had me confused. "This is my room."

"Then why—" Realization had me taking a step back and away from him. My voice deceptively calm, I stated, "I am not sleeping with you."

He looked me up and down then scoffed. "I don't want to have sex with you."

Oh, Mina...again with the assumptions!

I turned my head to hide the fact that my face was now beet red. I was making a goddamn fool out of myself. Of course he didn't want to sleep with me, not when he had an endless stream of gorgeous women likely panting for him down at Bleeding Hearts. I was such a jerk. "I don't understand."

Lev stepped farther into the room before turning left and disappearing into what must have been a hidden closet. When he came back to me, he was minus his suit jacket and his sleeves were rolled up. He stopped a foot away from me, held up his phone, and before I could say a word, the flash went off.

"Hey," I complained, scrunching my nose.

He shrugged, placing the cell into his pocket. "Just a little insurance policy, in case you decide to leave in the middle of the night with some of my things." He looked at me. "It's nothing personal. I don't know you. I'm positive you're not sure about me either. You don't know me. But as long as you're in my home, you and I will be sleeping in the same room."

I opened my mouth to protest, but he held up a hand and kept talking. "The sofa folds out into a bed. That's where I'll sleep. You can take the bed. You'll forgive me for not putting my trust into someone who I've known for less than three hours. Especially under the circumstances we met."

Well...when he put it like that, maybe I was being a bit of a brat by protesting.

Okay. I was just going to have to pull up my big-girl panties and deal.

Speaking of panties... "I don't have any clean clothes." I held up my bag. "Is there somewhere I can wash these?"

He took the bag from me and I blanched. "No, wait, I can do it!" I jumped for it, but he held it out of my reach. "Give it back!"

"I just want to be sure you don't have anything dangerous in here." He eyed me good. "My safety will always come before your pride. Got that?"

Well, shit.

It took me a whole five seconds to give in. "Okay, but can I please be the one to empty it?" He hesitated. I plead gently, "Please."

He waited a moment before he handed me the bag. "Okay, but you'll do it right here. Right in front of me."

Damn it. I would just have to try and conceal what I needed to as inconspicuously as I could. One by one, I took things out of my pack. Two t-shirts, a ratty men's sweater, which served me well in the colder weather, a pair of black jeans with holes at the bottom, a pair of grey socks, and…

Wrapping them quickly, I tried to slip them into my pocket, but a hand gripping my wrist stopped me. He squeezed tight and I went rigid.

"Show me."

Pride held me captive. My cheeks burned.

He squeezed hard enough to bruise and I winced. "*Show me.*"

I pulled them out of my pocket and tossed them onto the bed. Distressed, I whispered, "Panties. Just panties."

He glanced at the black balls of material on the bed before turning my bag upside down and shaking it. The small Swiss army knife I'd found on the street fell out of the side pocket. I immediately defended the concealment. "It's blunt."

With analyzing eyes, he held it up to examine it. "You could still stick it through someone if you needed to." He put it into his pocket. "You won't need this anymore."

Of course I wouldn't. How about my soul? Want that, too? It's not like I need it.

I was grateful, of course, but I still didn't understand this guy's motive.

Taking my bag, he shoved the clothes back into them and threw it high onto his shoulder. "Come," he ordered, and dutiful as I was, I followed. A door on the left side of the room, next to the wall-to-wall bookshelf, was opened, and at the sight of the bath, shower, shampoo, and soaps, a tremor of delight coursed through me.

"You can wash up in here. Take your time." He stepped back and added, "I only ask that you don't lock the door. I won't come in unless I need to. When I call out, please respond, or else I'll believe you're in need of assistance."

That sounded reasonable. But still, I asked, "You promise you won't come in?"

His cold eyes pierced me. "I'm not looking for a cheap thrill." At my blunt stare, he uttered, "I won't enter. Not unless you ask me to."

"Trust me, I won't be asking you to." I stepped inside and moved to close the door, but it stopped an inch short.

A light whiskey eye peered in at me. "Remove your clothes and hand them to me through the door." Just as I was about to ask 'what for?' in the snarkiest tone possible, he went on, "I'll put them in to wash with the others."

The door closed and I removed my clothes, and wrapping a fluffy burgundy towel around me, I turned the knob, threw the clothes, and called out, "Thank you."

A moment of silence, then, "You're welcome."

Lev left me in peace and quiet while I filled the tub with hot water and men's scented body wash. I glanced down at that tub before looking back at myself in the mirror.

I was dirty. *Grimy*.

As much as I wanted to slide down into that bath, I decided to shower first, and from the moment I too warm water hit me, sluicing down my bare body, warming the chill from me, something crossed between a laugh and a sob escaped me. Lifting my face up into the spray, I let myself be consumed by the feeling of ecstasy as I reached up and massaged shampoo through my hair. And I did this smiling, although it was wobbly.

I resumed washing away four months of filth. To say it felt good would have been understatement of the century.

It felt divine.

Showering as quickly as I could, I made my way out and moved to the tub, carefully stepping into the near-scorching water and bathed away lonely nights in a cold alleyway.

And true to his word, Lev didn't intrude.

CHAPTER SIX

Mina

Mirrors did not lie. They could boost an ego, but they could just as easily be cruel and punishing.

Lev's bathroom mirror was a heinous bitch.

It showed every bruise, every line, and every protruding bone in a way that left even me shocked. But my hair was clean, and I might've smelled like a man, but I no longer smelled offensive. I scrubbed my face clean, and although my face was a nice shade of pink, I didn't have three-day-old makeup congealed and stuck to my lashes, which was great.

It came time to leave the bathroom, and I quickly realized I had no clothes. I opened the door an inch and peeked out, letting steam waft out around me. "Lev?"

He stepped back inside the room and, uncomfortable at my nude state, I slammed the door shut. He knocked lightly. "Mina?"

"Hey," I started. I looked at the door, wringing my fingers. "Hi." I rolled my eyes at my muddled mind and took a deep breath. "I just realized I have no clothes and I…" I swallowed hard, passed the apprehensive lump in my throat, and finished softly, "I need clothes."

He didn't respond for a long while then he knocked again. "I don't have any women's clothing, but this should do for the night."

I opened the door, hiding behind it, and his large hand popped inside. It was gripping a white shirt. Thanking him, I took it. I threw it on and did the buttons up. It saddened me the way I swam in it. Once upon a time, I had curves that would've filled this shirt out nicely. It looked more like a freaking sheet on me. I glanced down at my legs and wondered what I ever thought wrong with the extra weight I used to wear. It was so disappointing to see large knobby knees through the thin pale skin there.

I felt ugly.

When I let out a long sigh and straightened, I nearly swallowed my tongue. My small breasts stood pert and my nipples were visible through the thin material of the shirt.

Oh, hell no.

I looked down to see the dark patch between my thighs also making itself apparent.

Um...double hell no.

I tiptoed to the door and called out softly. "Excuse me, Lev?"

He was there in a second flat. "Problem?"

"I was wondering if you have a darker shirt I can wear?"

He paused a moment then asked in disbelief, "You have a color preference?"

Tonight I did, dammit.

I realized I sounded needy, but I didn't want him to see me like this. "I'm sorry. It's okay. I'll make it work." I added a contrite, "Sorry."

Holding my head in my hands, I gave myself a mental pep talk.

This man has been extremely kind to you tonight, Mina. In a few measly hours, he's given you things you could've only dreamed of. Don't be ungrateful.

A light knock at the door then it opened a few inches. His hand came through holding something dark. I took it and the door closed. I held it up.

It was a black shirt.

Tension I hadn't known was there unfurled from my gut as relief had me laughing softly. I called out, "Thank you."

He replied softly, "You're welcome, mouse."

I redressed, holding the white shirt in my hand as I walked out of the bathroom. The lights were off, but Lev had switched on two tall lamps, one beside the sofa, which was now folded out to make a bed, and one beside the nightstand, next to the bed.

My eyes widened as I saw Lev's back to me.

His bare back.

Oh, dear me. His *muscled* bare back.

He turned at my light gasp. Even though he still wore his dress pants, he'd removed his shoes and socks, leaving his large feet free. Lowering my flaming face, I rushed over to the bed and threw myself into it, covering myself up to the chest with the heavy covers.

He looked closely at me, searching my face. His eyes took me apart bit by bit and it was unnerving. Discomfort forced me to avoid his eyes. Quiet surrounded us then he stated quietly, "You don't like people seeing you."

My eyes met him then. "I beg your pardon?"

His eyes roamed my fresh face. "You can't hide behind makeup. You can try, but you won't succeed. Not with me." He paused then said, "I see you."

It was not something a normal person would have said. It was relentless and calculated and very much to the point, almost as if he didn't know of the discomfort his words stirred within me. Almost as if he didn't care.

But I saw he did care. He said the words in a gentle manner so as not to frighten me. He stated what he saw, and that was all.

My words chosen carefully, I spoke slowly, "Any mask on the street is a good mask."

He sat on the sofa bed, moving himself back until his legs were stretched out in front of him. He crossed his arms over his broad chest. "Masks don't suit a person with your face."

"My face?" I asked with a narrowed glare. I knew I wasn't gorgeous, but I didn't think I was unattractive.

He clarified, and my heart skipped a beat. "A face like yours makes men stumble over themselves." He tilted his head to look at me through a new angle. "Faces like yours are carved into statues, immortalized in stone for the world to see over the ages." He let in a deep breath then exhaled slowly. "You…are art."

My skin broke out in gooseflesh as a flush stole up my neck. My lips parted and my ears burned.

What the hell did he just say?

"I'd like to know more about you, Mina, but the hour is late and I have an appointment in the morning."

I wondered whether he would leave me alone in the house or if he would take me with him.

He got under the covers then turned off his lamp. I heard rustling and realized he waited until he was covered before he removed his pants, which landed on the floor with a soft thud. I was sure that was for my benefit rather than his own. After all, he had no issues removing his shirt in front of me.

The small gesture turned my manner. Some of the standing tension slid out of me. He really seemed like a nice guy. But still, I didn't know this man, and after all he'd done for me, my mind warned me to be weary of him. After all, no one was *that* selfless.

Finding the switch, I turned off the lamp by the bed and snuggled into the covers. It was so warm and cozy that I could've cried. I hadn't had a bed in months.

My eyes became heavy and I blinked slowly. It was then that words escaped me without permission. "Lev?" He grunted sleepily in reply. "If you try to sneak into this bed tonight, I will scream bloody murder, and I scream loud."

He sounded amused when he responded, "Ah, but Mina..." he paused for effect, "Who would be around to hear you?"

⚓

Morning broke and, like most days, I woke with the sun.

I hadn't slept so well since...well...ever. I felt rested and refreshed. I couldn't seem to find the strength to leave the warm covers of the bed, but the bathroom called my name in a semi-urgent way. I thought about waking Lev to ask him where the toilet was since there hadn't been one in the en suite but decided against it. I didn't want to be a pain.

Removing the covers without a sound, I slipped out of bed and made my way on my tiptoes to the door. I pressed on the lever, but it stuck. Frowning, I looked down to see a key inside the lock.

Why was this door locked from the inside?

I didn't have time to think about it. I gently turned it, heard the latch click over, and thankfully the door opened without a squeak. I slipped through undetected.

I walked delicately down the hall, attempting to open doors as I went. The first two were locked. I got lucky on the third. It was exactly what I needed and I took my time, grateful for a moment to myself.

My time on the streets meant I was used to my own company. It felt weird to be around people. I supposed that was something I would have to get comfortable with quickly, seeing as I was going to be working serving drinks to people. Bartenders were expected to be social, and I mentally vowed to do my best to not come across awkward.

I flushed the toilet, washed my hands, and then opened the door and shrieked. Loudly.

Lev stood there, dressed only in a pair of grey boxers, leaning against the wall, blinking his eyes sleepily.

Clutching my heaving chest, I panted, "I needed to use the bathroom."

His voice heavy with sleep, he muttered, "I can see that."

My cheeks began to burn. "You didn't show me where the toilet was last night."

He blinked again. "I realize that."

My palms began to sweat. Eyes wide, I blurted out an anxious, "I wasn't stealing anything."

His eyes roamed my shirt-clad body. "No, it doesn't look like you were."

I then felt the need to remind him, "I left your watch on the bathroom counter."

He gestured with a jerk of his chin down to his wrist...where the watch was, secured tightly.

"Okay," I whispered in relief. I swallowed hard then nodded once. "Okay then."

Pushing himself off the wall, he stretched languidly in a feline manner. I spied the muscles of his abdomen tighten in a most delicious way. My eyes were drawn to the small smatter of hair leading from his bellybutton down lower still.

It was then I noticed I was looking directly at his material-covered crotch. With a light gasp, I turned my face to look straight up and stared at his chest.

He scratched lightly at the stubble on his steely jaw. "We should dress for breakfast."

Yes! my mind yelled. *Clothes are good!*

I followed him back into the bedroom and saw my clothes neatly folded on the nightstand. He must have taken them out of the dryer in the middle of the night.

The pile was small. I went through it, my brow bunching in confusion. "Where are the rest of my clothes?"

Walking into the closet, he replied coolly, "Where they belong. The trash."

Anger ignited, but I spoke calmly. "They were all I had."

"I know."

Irritation clear, I pulled on my one clean pair of panties underneath the long shirt. My black jeans followed, and with my back to the closet, I slipped off the black shirt to replace it with my white tee. I looked down and cussed softly.

My nipples had come out to say hello. "Where's my bra?"

He walked out of the closet, still in boxers, and going about his business without looking at me, he uttered, "I told you. The trash."

Lifting the black shirt to hide my lady lumps, I gaped in shock before sputtering, "It was the only one I had!"

"It was threadbare."

"It did the job," I returned, falling into hysteria.

Hearing my prickliness, he turned his face up to look at me then eyed my chest before raising a brow. "You don't need a bra."

My face flamed. I hugged my arms around myself as tight as I could without folding into myself.

Well, that was rude. He should've just told me my tits were tiny and one needed to pull down my pants to make sure that I was, in fact, female.

Man, this guy was doing wonders for my self-esteem.

"I need to shower," he stated. "And you will wait right here."

My surly response of 'Sir, yes, sir' was cut off as the bathroom door closed behind him.

Great. Just great.

LEV

I waited obediently on the edge of the bed and silently wondered whether putting my faith in a man I didn't know was a terribly good idea.

CHAPTER SEVEN

Mina

Lev, freshly showered and dressed in a gunmetal grey three-piece suit over a crisp white shirt, led me out the back door of his house, down a scenic path to an even larger house.

We walked in complete silence, but as we approached the front door, he ordered quietly, "Don't talk."

Repositioning the giant cashmere sweater he lent me, I nodded, allowing him to take me by the hand and lead me down a near identical foyer to his own and to the right, into a large dining room. A tray of fruit sat in the center of the table with two vases full of decorative greenery on either ends. A man sat at the long table in the well-lit room, reading the newspaper, his ankle resting across his knee. He was also dressed in a suit, but, unlike Lev, he was kind of scary-looking.

I recognized him instantly. It was the man I'd stolen the wallet from the night before. This was Lev's brother.

"Sasha," Lev said in way of greeting as we stepped into the room. I tried to pry my hand from his, but he held it tightly. I pulled a few more times and finally, compromising, he placed my hand into the crook of his elbow.

The man, Sasha, did not look up from the newspaper. "Morning." He picked up his cup of coffee and sipped at it. Still reading the paper, his brow furrowed. "Where did you go off to last night? And where did you find my wallet? I didn't realize I dropped it until Anika gave it back to me."

"You didn't drop it," Lev responded. "Mina stole it."

And my heart stopped.

What the fuck, Lev?

Oh, God. I was in trouble.

"Who the fuck is Mina?" Sasha uttered as he lifted his face. Spotting me, he looked me up and down before turning to Lev. "Any reason we're discussing this in front of...whoever that is?"

Lev clarified, "Yes, and this is Mina."

My palms began to sweat. I almost fainted dead away, but dug my nails into Lev's arm to anchor myself.

"Ah. I see." Sasha sipped at his coffee again before sneering at me. "Sit. Please."

His please did not sound like a request, more of a command, and yet, he spoke softly.

My brow felt suddenly clammy. I looked up at Lev with wide eyes and whispered, "Is this a set-up?"

Looking down at me, he patted the hand at his elbow, pulled out a chair, and helped me sit. "Relax. We're just talking."

Sasha folded the newspaper and set it down in front of him. "So, Mina, is stealing wallets a habit of yours?"

"No," I answered quietly through the thickness in my throat.

Lev spoke then. "You had seven hundred dollars in your wallet."

Sasha glared at his brother. "I'm well aware of that fact."

Lev reached over to the fruit platter in the center of the table, carefully took a handful of grapes, and threw one into his mouth. Chewing, he nodded toward me. "She took a single hundred." He threw another grape into his mouth. "Left the rest behind."

Sasha's brow rose in a similar fashion to times I had seen his brother do it. He eyed me harshly. "Not a very good thief."

Lev tilted his head to look over me. "Not a thief at all."

"I see," Sasha muttered as he absently scratched at his chin. "Okay, so why is she here?"

My brow furrowed. I didn't like being spoken about as if I wasn't even there.

"She's staying with me until she gets back on her feet. I hired her. She's the new bargirl. And what with her background, I'm hoping she'll be able to spot trouble before it starts. She'd be assisting me." Lev looked to his brother and laid it out there. "Mina's homeless. She took the money because she was hungry."

"I see." But Sasha looked as though he didn't. On top of that, he looked at me like I was a cockroach that needed to be squashed. He spoke directly to Lev, "You take responsibility for her. She fucks up, it's your ass, *moy brat*."

Lev looked to me. "She won't fuck up. She has too much to lose."

I wanted to protest. I wanted to explain that a person with nothing had nothing left to lose. But I kept quiet. This conversation was *about* me, not *including* me. Clearly.

It was then Sasha spoke directly to me. "I think you've already gathered that my name is Sasha. And although Lev is in charge of the floor at Bleeding Hearts, *I'm* the boss." Picking up a fork, he pointed it at me. "There is no 'three strikes and you're gone' bullshit, little one. One fuck up, and you're gone. No second chances."

I didn't respond, simply because I didn't want to tell him to take that fork and shove it up his ass.

But at the continued silence, I realized a response was necessary. "I understand."

Sasha smiled then, and I got a glimpse of how handsome he was. "I'm glad. Welcome to the team."

He and Lev looked similar, only Lev was slightly taller, but Sasha was more muscular. Both had dark brown hair, styled neatly. Both had hard eyes the color of cognac. Both had generous lips, and both wore a suit rather well.

Sasha ignored me from then out. He did, however, speak to Lev. "I need you today. Can you spare some time after lunch?"

Lev ate another grape and my mouth watered. "Yes. Have you given any more thought to the first aid course I put forward?"

I hadn't eaten fresh fruit in a long while. I wanted to sample the sweet juice to see if it tasted as I remembered.

Sasha responded, "Yeah. We'll go ahead with it. All the security and bar staff will take it. As the roster rotates, they can pick a day off of their choosing to attend, and they'll be reimbursed for their time." He paused. "And Lev? Feed your fucking pet before she expires."

Glaring at Sasha, I ran to Lev's defense. "I'm not even hungry."

Just as I finished saying this, my stomach gave an excruciatingly whale-like growl. And it went on for what seemed like days.

I turned to Lev, cheeks heating in embarrassment. "I'm okay, really."

But he was frowning down at me, looking mildly ashamed of himself. He leaned toward me and spoke for my ears only. "I'm sorry."

I whispered back, "Don't apologize. You've been so generous, Lev." I reached over to squeeze his arm. "I can't thank you enough."

His brow low, he muttered quietly, "I wish you would've told me you were hungry. I'm not very good at reading people, Mina."

How had the situation reversed so quickly? Why was I the one left feeling like I'd done something wrong?

At the sorry state of him, I apologized. He was obviously embarrassed. "I'm sorry. It's just that you've been so nice to me and I didn't want to seem like I was being ungrateful. The next time I'm hungry, I'll tell you. I promise."

He nodded as a plump, grey-haired older woman with glasses dressed all in black walked into the room holding a plate of eggs and bacon with sautéed mushrooms. It smelled incredible. She set it down in front of Sasha then smiled up at Lev. "Morning, Mr. Leokov. What's this morning's fare?"

Lev's lip tilted up at one side. "Good morning, Ada. I'll have oatmeal, please. And Mina will have..." All three of them looked at me. Lev waited patiently while Ada smiled encouragingly. Sasha watched me with a hawk's eye.

"Oh," I started, uncomfortable with the attention. "I'm not fussy. Anything will do, really."

Ada clucked. "*Anything* is not a food, honey." She smiled. "I can do eggs and bacon, pancakes, toast, waffles, oatmeal or cereal, or I have some freshly baked blueberry muffins. What's your poison?"

I smiled at the kind woman. "Eggs and bacon sounds great." I was already salivating at the look of Sasha's plate.

"Scrambled?"

I nodded. "Sure."

She winked. "Be back in a jiffy."

I was not shocked easily, but what happened next stunned the speech out of me. Sasha stood with his plate, walked around the table, and placed it in front of me. He walked back to his seat, sat back down, and he did this all without a spoken word.

I blinked down at the plate for a moment before I looked up at him. He stared, his gaze cutting, and I wondered if this man was as hard as he wanted people to believe he was.

"Thank you," I said softly, sincerely.

He broke eye contact, lifted his paper high enough to block me from his view, and continued reading. "You're welcome."

I ate slowly, savoring every bite of the fluffy scrambled eggs, the tender, garlic-garnished mushrooms, and crispy bacon. It was perfect, and I secretly wanted to leave my seat, walk into the kitchen, and hug Ada half to death.

Lev watched me eat. He did it so obviously that without even turning my head to catch him in the act, I felt it.

LEV

I lifted another forkful of eggs to my mouth before I heard a door open. A woman called out, "I'm home!"

The food suddenly felt heavy in my stomach. Women did not like me. They found whatever issue they could with me, and I never really understood it. I always tried to be nice to everyone.

A tall, stunning brunette with long wavy hair, a wide mouth, and gleaming white teeth stepped inside the dining room pushing a stroller with an adorable little girl in it. She was dressed in jeans, heels, and a caramel-colored sweater. Her light brown eyes immediately lit on me. Her smile fell. "Sorry. I didn't realize we'd be having company."

Stepping forward, she leaned down to kiss Lev's cheek and uttered, "Brother mine." She turned and did the same to Sasha. They accepted her kisses graciously. She didn't need to mention the fact that Lev and Sasha were her brothers. Anyone could see they were closely related.

She walked to the farthest seat, pulling the stroller up close to her, unbuckling the young girl, and lifting her out. "I'm Nastasia," she uttered distractedly.

Lev responded for me as I chewed. "This is Mina, the new bargirl." Then he did something unbelievable.

He smiled.

It was wide, and shining, and perfect. His teeth were white and perfectly straight. He had a single perfect dimple cut into his cheek, and his face was perfectly transformed with it.

My God.

My heart stuttered as I realized just how handsome Lev was. I mean, he was attractive before, but now he was incredible. Delicious.

The woman, spying Lev's smile, handed the little girl to him, and again, I was surprised when he took her without complaint, sitting her onto his lap and hugging her gently before kissing the top of her head.

Nastasia looked back at me, her smile fading rapidly. She regarded me much as Sasha had. She was unsure of me. And I didn't blame her one bit.

Her little girl was gorgeous though. She had the family's light brown eyes and dark hair, but unlike the rest of the people sitting at the table, her hair curled into sweet, bouncy ringlets and was currently styled into high pigtails. It was hard to watch her and not smile. She was adorably chubby, and her lashes were so long that she looked like a porcelain doll.

Nastasia's stare became borderline painful. I needed to do something and quick.

Standing, I walked over and stopped a foot away from her. She looked up at me, and a single brow rose. I stuck my hand out. "Sorry, I had a mouthful of eggs. I wasn't trying to be rude. I'm Mina."

Her eyes narrowed at my hand and, eventually, she took it, shaking it slowly. "Call me Nas. Everyone does."

She released my hand and I took my seat, picking up my fork. I glanced at Nas, who watched her brother and daughter with a tender look on her face. I couldn't help but smile at the woman. "She's beautiful."

"I know." Nas smiled softly. "So does she."

Sasha stood, walking over to Lev. "Give me my girl."

Lev handed her over, and Sasha kissed her cheek lovingly, speaking softly into her little ear as she snatched up his decorative handkerchief and shoved it into her mouth. I sat there, suddenly confused.

Whose child was this?

Ada brought out another plate of eggs and, spotting the plate in front of me, she smiled at Sasha, replacing the plate he'd given me. As she passed Nas, she leaned down and kissed her head before placing the oatmeal in front of Lev. She was walking out the door before she asked Nas, "You want something, honey?"

Nas suddenly looked tired. "No, I ate on the plane. Thanks anyway, Ada."

Lev stated, "I'd like to ask why you're home early, but I have a feeling I already know the answer to that question. How was the flight? Did Lidiya fuss much?"

It was then the little girl started babbling. "Eeya. Eeya. Eeeeeeya." She looked at Sasha and said, "Asha. Ma Deeya. Deeya." She looked at Lev and stuck a hand into Sasha's mouth. I was stunned that he offered no complaint and that he simply smiled around the tiny fingers. "Otet. Papa. Papa. Otet." Nas came next. "Azeeya. Azeeya. Ma tetu. Tetu." Then she glanced at me, blinking before turning to Sasha and uttering an unsure, "Zzzzhena."

Sasha huffed out a soft laugh around the fingers, and little Lidiya smiled a toothy grin, her eyes smiling just as Lev's had.

I turned to Lev and smiled. "She kind of looks like you."

He turned to me, his eyes full of amusement. "That would make sense." He paused a moment before adding, "After all, she is my daughter."

CHAPTER EIGHT

Mina

Nastasia drove in silence, and I was thankful for the song on the radio for making a ridiculously awkward situation a little less awkward.

After Lev told me that Lidiya was his daughter, leaving me officially shocked, the conversation took a quick turn as Lev stood with the little girl, walked over to his sister, kissed her on the cheek, and thanked her for bringing Lidiya home. The next words out of Nas' mouth were in another language. Although she spoke softly, the words sounded harsh. Sasha added to the conversation, and Lev responded easily. I couldn't be sure, but I thought they might be talking about me. When the three of them turned to look at me, it became clear I was right.

Rude much, guys?

Lev kissed his daughter's head but spoke to me. "You need something to wear tonight, and I'm afraid the clothes you have aren't appropriate. Nastasia will take you shopping. Buy whatever you need."

Buy clothes? With what? Love? "In case you hadn't noticed, I don't have any money."

His brow rose. "I know you don't. Nastasia has my credit card. You'll buy whatever my sister thinks you need."

The protest began before he even finished. "I can't accept that. You've already done too much."

Sasha eyed me closely, searching my face for a sign of deception, but I meant it. Nastasia's hard eyes softened, but only slightly. Lev glowered at me. "I threw away your clothes with the intention of replacing them. At the very least, you'll need a pair of jeans and a coat that fits." He sighed, irritated. "You don't even have any undergarments."

Thanks for bringing that up in front of your whole family, asshole.

That was true though. He did throw out my clothes, leaving me with little to work with. My shoulders slumped. "Okay, well, how about we call it a loan? You can dock my pay until I've reimbursed you."

All three of their faces took on a look of disbelief.

No one spoke until Lev let out a firm, "No."

I stood taller, crossing my arms across my chest. "I'll be paying you back, Lev, whether you like it or not." After a short pause, I admitted quietly, "I don't like owing people."

Nastasia rolled her eyes and groaned, taking my wrist and dragging me toward the door. "Don't bother, little girl. He won't give in."

Now, as we drove in silence, I slid down farther in my seat and sighed. "Any chance you'll let me borrow some clothes and tell your brother we bought them?"

She looked at me then, and with her eyes covered with sunglasses that made her look like a model, she peeked over the top of them. I didn't miss the slight curl of her lip. "I'm a whole foot taller than you, and you weigh less than me. Besides, I don't lie to my brothers."

"Great," I muttered.

Another few minutes of silence then she started, "Listen, I don't know you, so no offense and all, but if you fuck over my brother—"

I didn't let her finish. My shoulders rigid, I cut in, "I haven't known your brother for more than twelve hours, but in that time, he has been extremely kind to me, and I would rather eat my own tongue than do something to hurt him."

Silence.

"Not many women would have the lady balls to speak to me so boldly, let alone cut me off." Her lips pursed in surprise.

Perhaps it was a compliment, but I was still pissed at her assumption. "Your brother seems like a smart man. And he's always a step ahead of me. I'd like to think he knows what he's doing, even if I don't know why he's doing it." I kept it real. "Your brother doesn't know it, but he saved my life."

She turned back to the road, indicated left, and turned into a mall parking lot. "I will beat you bloody if you do anything to make him regret that."

Placing my chin on my knuckles, I looked out of the passenger window and grumbled, "Got it."

⚓

The clothing store Nas took me to was unlike anything I'd ever seen before. Upon entering, we were served champagne, which I sipped once before putting it down, because it tasted like a thousand smarmy assholes. The clerk stood by, assessing me as Nas told her what I needed.

I was shoved into a dressing room that smelled of wildflowers and was the size of a single bedroom, with three outfits in hand. As soon as I undressed, Nas pulled the door open and stepped inside.

Squeaking, I used my arm to cover my boobs and hissed, *"What the fuck are you doing?"*

She snorted. "You got nothing I haven't seen before, *kukla*." At my clear panic, she rolled her eyes. "Relax, Max. I just wanted to see how the clothes fit."

"Turn around," I ordered.

She watched me closely. "Jesus." She finally turned. "Prude much?"

Reaching for the closest dress, I threw it over my head. "You can turn around now." I looked at myself in the mirror. The dress was black, tight, and undeniably sexy, but… "This isn't me."

Nas stepped closer, pulling at the garment, her brow furrowed. "I think that's kind of the point, right?" She stepped back, assessing the dress on me. She shook her head. "No, no. Not good. Try another."

She turned before I could ask her to and I was grateful. I took off the black dress and tried on the white one. In very much the same style, tight and tailored, but this one had a pencil styled bottom. I liked it.

From the way Nas smiled, she liked it too. "Yes. Put it in the yes pile." After trying on all the other clothes, it was clear that nothing else looked good on me. Nas cracked under the pressure, growling, "You're so fucking thin. You look sick."

It was said in anger, and I knew I shouldn't have taken it to heart, but I did. Turning my back to her, I hid my shining eyes, blinking away tears of shame. I knew what I looked like. I didn't need reminders. The way I looked made me sick. I know I looked ill. I felt ill. Did she think I had a choice?

"Hey," she uttered softly then awkwardly added, "sorry." I nodded, still facing away from her. She sighed. "I'll have this wrung up and we'll try somewhere else, okay?"

The latch of the door closed gently behind her, and I quickly changed into my too-big jeans, scruffy white tee, and Lev's oversized sweater, slipping on my flip-flops. From outside the door, I heard Nas talk to the clerk. "We'll take this one. The rest we'll think about."

"Very good," the clerk stated. "That will be $849.00. How will you be paying today, miss?"

Before Nas could respond, I flew out of the changing room in a rage. "Are you out of your goddamn mind?"

The clerk sniffed with derision while Nas glared openly at me. "The hell is your problem?"

"*No!*" I shouted. Looking directly at the clerk, I spat, "That dress is not worth that much money. Do you know how many starving kids you could feed with $800.00? *Do you?*" My voice shaking, I muttered, "Shame on you."

Without waiting for a response, I made my way out of the uptight boutique, my feet rushing to get somewhere—anywhere away from there. I made it a short distance away before Nas came running after me.

"Yo! Wait up, you little fucktard."

"Piss off," I turned my head, hissing.

She caught up to me thanks to her ridiculously long legs. "So the kitten has claws." She grinned. "We might get along after all."

We walked side-by-side, and patiently, she let me walk off the anger. She chuckled and I side-eyed her. "What?"

Stopping, she laughed harder, clutching her stomach and wiping away tears of mirth. When she got herself under control, she snickered, "You should've seen the face on that stuck-up bitch after you walked out." She straightened herself, placing a hand to her chest, and imitated the store clerk, "'Well, I never!'"

I couldn't help it. I snorted. I laughed softly, then harder, until I was hooting in hilarity. "At least I gave her something to talk about with her stuck-up friends."

We came across a bench and I sat, Nas taking the place beside me. "So," she began, "what are we going to do about the clothes situation?" I opened my mouth, but she held her palm up to stop me. "Before you come out swinging, we're going to have to compromise."

I bit the inside of my lip, chewing on it while I thought up a suitable solution. With a sigh, I swung my arm out in the direction of the boutique. "I don't need stuff like that. I wouldn't spend that much on principle alone. You know how long I could've lived on the streets with $800.00?"

Her face softened, as did her tone. "How long have you lived on the streets?"

"Since I was seventeen." I quickly calculated. "I'm twenty-four now, so around seven years."

She nodded slowly. "You never applied for help or housing?"

I shook my head.

"Why?" she enquired.

I glanced at her. "Honest answer?"

"Nothing but."

"Takes about eighteen months to two years to get placement. It got real bad for me." A small shrug then I took it deep. "I guess I never expected to live that long."

Nas turned away from me then, keeping her eyes on the ground, contemplating something I couldn't quite put my finger on. We remained in a comfortable silence, enjoying it immensely, when she spoke. "Okay, so where are we going next? We need to get you something to wear tonight."

I huffed out a long breath then smiled. "Any thrift shops around here?"

Her brow rose. "I wouldn't be caught dead in one of those, let alone wearing clothes that someone else owned." She quickly added, "No offense."

"None taken." My smile turned into a grin. "Give me an hour. I'll bet I can even find something for you."

She scoffed. "Not bloody likely."

My smile was cat-like. "Want to make a bet?"

⚓

Our trip to the thrift shop lasted almost two hours, and by the end of it, Nas was a convert. As promised, I found something even she couldn't deny was amazing. She snatched up the Italian leather cropped jacket, and when I took it to the counter, I managed to talk the price down to thirty dollars. Nas watched with wide eyes, clearly impressed. She later told me that retail on a jacket like that would've cost a minimum of $400.00.

I had to admit I did well under the circumstances. Some of the clothing I chose were slightly big on me, but I planned to put on a few pounds and fill out the weight I had lost over the past year. I settled on a few retro t-shirts, a pair of blue jeans, a pair of black jeans, a pinstriped black pencil skirt, a white blouse that smelled a little like a grandma's closet but looked classy and feminine, a black shirt, an off-white sweater (also too big), and a pair of bright yellow pajamas, which still had tags on them.

After we left with bags in hand and Nastasia in a considerably better mood, I asked her to take me to a local superstore where I could get underwear, socks, a few cheap pairs of heels, flip-flops and sneakers, and a toothbrush. Nas helped me pick bras in my size, and after looking at the sorry state of my body, she vowed to put some meat on my bones, assigning Ada to keep me fed. As we were leaving, we passed the cosmetics counter, and Nas told me to choose the basics, asking me if I knew how to do my own makeup.

I smiled to myself. "There was a mall a few blocks away from my alley. Every now and again I'd go down there. There was a sweet lady working cosmetics, and she must've known I didn't have the money to spend, because she would sit me down and teach me how to apply my own makeup, telling me I could come in anytime to use the testers. So eventually, I learned."

Choosing the appropriate shade of foundation proved difficult, as I was so pale, but Nas helped, picking out a light blush, black eyeliner and mascara, a palette of eye shadows, and assorted colors of lip gloss.

I was done.

As we walked to the car, I asked, careful not to gloat, "How much did we spend all together?"

Nas attempted to glare at me, but her eyes were amused. "Just over a hundred eighty dollars, smart ass."

A hundred and eighty dollars.

I would pay it all back. It didn't matter how long it took me.

As we drove, Nas caught me yawning. She nudged my shoulder. "Hey. Don't you dare fall asleep. There's one more stop we need to make."

Mid-yawn, I croaked out, "I'm so tired."

"You can have a nap when you get back to the house. You'll probably need it. Your shift will likely finish around two a.m."

I *would* need a nap. I wouldn't make it until two a.m. without sleep.

"Where are we going?"

She smiled slyly. "You'll see."

CHAPTER NINE

LEV

What was taking them so long?

I checked my clock. It read three thirty-six in the afternoon. Not surprisingly, only five minutes had passed since the last time I checked.

Pulling out my cell, I punched in Nastasia's phone number and hit dial just as I saw her silver Mercedes-Benz E400 Cabriolet pull into the driveway. The car was a recent gift from me for her thirtieth birthday. From the way she drove it, you would've thought she hated it.

My hand was on the door handle before either of the girls had opened theirs. I hesitated, not wanting to come across as hovering. Nastasia opened her door first, and my brows rose at the sound of her laughter. My sister only had one female friend in Anika. Nastasia did not like women. To see her openly laughing with another female confused me.

Out stepped Mina, and my breath left me in a fast whoosh. She looked beautiful. Dressed in skintight blue jeans and a loose white blouse, unbuttoned one button too many, her tiny feet parading around in black pumps, caused my mind to act erratic.

Her long wavy hair had been freshly trimmed and straightened, the shiny locks cascading down her back. Mascara had been lightly applied to her lashes, framing her big green eyes. Her lips glittered in the sunshine and were heavily glossed.

She was still far too thin, but as I told her the night before, she couldn't hide from me.

I stepped back as the door flew open. Nastasia grinned. "Hey, bro." She moved aside, her arms out toward Mina. *"Ta-da!"* She waited. And waited. But all I could do was stare.

Finally, my sister gave in to irritation. "Well? You just gonna stand there?" She huffed out a breath. "How does she look, Lev?"

Mina looked up at me through lowered lashes, biting the inside of her lip. She wrung her fingers together, and I wondered how it would feel to have those fingers run through my hair.

How did she look?

"Like art," I responded sincerely.

Mina blinked, releasing the inside of her lip. Her mouth gaped slightly. Those full lips calling me to taste them.

She blurted out, "Nas took me to a fancy beauty salon. They did my hair and makeup." She threw out her hands to show me her polished nails. "I had a manicure and pedicure too. Then I got my brows shaped and they waxed my le—" Realizing she was rambling, her cheeks turned pink and she finished quietly with, "But you don't want to know about that."

And still, I stared.

Taking a handful of bags, she slid past me, her upper arm brushing my chest. "I'll take these upstairs." I watched her make her way up the stairs in her heels.

She walked like a newborn calf.

Nastasia whispered, "We're working on that. Give her time. This is all so new to her."

"I didn't say anything."

My sister laughed. "You didn't need to, Lev. You never need to." She waved a hand over my face. "It's all written there, plain and simple, for the world to see."

I followed her into the family room, where Lidiya played with her dolls. "I gather today went well."

"Not at first, but," she smiled, "I had fun. It was fun. We went shopping, did girlie things, stopped for something to eat, and then..." She paused. "Okay, so we finished what we were doing, and I asked Mina if she'd show me where she lived." Her face darkened. "I don't know how anyone could've lived like that for seven years."

Seven years? She lived like that for seven *fucking years?*

I fumed in silence, wanting to beat to death the person who put her in this position, and I *would* find out who.

"We're passing through the area, and suddenly she yells out '*Stop!*' so, of course, I freak the fuck out and pull over. She jumps out the car with her lunch and chases down this little teenage thug. He was just a kid, Lev." She shook her head. "So I'm watching in the rearview and, finally, the kid stops. Looks about ready to smash heads. But then, he recognizes her. They talk. She hands him her sandwich. He smiles at her. She waves, walks back to the car, gets in, and acts like the whole thing never happened."

"I see." I saw from the very beginning. This girl was no thief. I was right about her.

Nastasia looked me dead in the eye and uttered, "I like her, Lev. She's good people, you know?"

"No. I don't know. Not yet."

But I intended to find out.

CHAPTER TEN

Mina

"Mina?" I heard vaguely.

I wasn't interested. Instead, I burrowed farther into the covers, desperately wanting them to merge with me so I'd never have to leave.

"It's time to wake up, mouse."

Pulling my chin under the quilt, I groaned long and pained. "Five more minutes."

"You might recall that you said the same thing the last three times I've tried to wake you."

Oh. That's right.

It all came back to me.

Lev had been trying to wake me for the good part of twenty minutes, but every time I swore I was awake and fine to be left to get ready, I fell back asleep.

I peered up at him. He stood by the bed, looking and smelling freshly showered. His jaw was dark with stubble, and his light cologne smelled edible. My reply was muffled by bedding. "Okay, I'm up. Give me five minutes."

"I'd leave you to it, but you've proven to be quite the fibber on that front," he accused lightly.

I tried to scowl, but my sleepy eyes kept blinking, ruining the effect. His eyes, the color of warm honey, crinkled in the corners as he looked down at me.

I knew there was only one thing to do. In one fell swoop, the covers flew off me and I sat up, shaking my head to clear it of sleep. "Okay," I chirped. "Yep. That did it. I'm awake." But as my eyes began to droop again, I mumbled, "I'm sort of awake."

"What are you wearing?" he asked, his disgust clear.

"My new pajamas," I looked down at the canary yellow jammies and returned a little defensively.

He looked me up and down, and not in a good way. "They're hideous."

My nose bunched. "I didn't choose them for the way they looked. They're comfortable."

I did not dare tell him that they were the bargain price of $4—new in pack, I might add.

My eyes had closed on me again, gosh darn it.

Lev had obviously never had an issue getting up in his life, because his large, warm hand was suddenly on my forehead. "Are you sure you're all right? You seem lethargic."

Lifting my hand, I pushed his away gently, and snorted. "I'm fine. It's this bed. It's magical. I never want to leave it. If I could, I would have all my meals served in this bed. This magical bed."

I smiled sleepily up at him, but all I could focus on was his hard frown. He shook his head. "No, I don't think you're okay to work tonight. Perhaps next week."

I stilled. "Wait, what?" Well, that had the desired effect. I shot out of bed. "I'm good. I'm fine. I just need…" My brain had yet to awaken with my body. "I don't know. I need something."

"Coffee," he supplied.

I could have kissed him. "*Yes*." This came out in a long whisper.

"Already have a pot brewing. Maybe a shower would help."

He was right, of course.

Opening my eyes as wide as I could, I dragged my feet toward the bathroom. He called after me, "I'll be downstairs." As I shut the door, he reminded, "Don't lock the door, mouse. I'd hate for you to fall asleep and drown in there."

I scoffed, but didn't bother bringing the sass. Rather, I rolled my eyes, clipped my newly straightened hair up, and jumped under the warm spray, careful not to wet my face. Once I was awake, I soaped up, rinsed off, and stepped out.

This house was like one giant, warm hug.

The bed was snug. The shower was toasty. The bathroom lights heated my naked body, drying me as a stood there, soaking it up like sunlight. It was like a five-star hotel. Or so I imagined one would be like. I'd never actually stayed at a hotel before, let alone one that was five stars.

As I stood there naked, I thought about Lev and why he brought me here. I had yet to figure him out. He seemed genuine in his gesture, but my history had told me that you never got something for nothing.

I was mentally ready for the ball to drop.

Having placed my clothes in the bathroom that afternoon before my nap, I dressed in what I had on when I returned from my shopping expedition with Nas. Taking the clip out of my hair, I brushed it gently, as per the instructions of the hairdresser; otherwise, I was destined for frizz. Apparently. Whatever the heck that meant.

My makeup still looked good. I was surprised by how much makeup was applied to my face to get the 'natural' look. I laughed to myself. It really was silly.

As we'd left the beauty salon and made it back to the car, Nas had handed me a small bag. With my brow furrowed, I peeked inside.

All the expensive makeup that had been used on my face by the beautician was neatly stacked at the bottom.

"Wha—" I gaped at her. "Why?"

She shrugged. "It looks good on you, and you're not going to be able to get the same effect with the cheap stuff we bought earlier." She spotted my obvious discomfort and tried to ease it. "You don't have to use it, but I can't return it. I'd like for you to use it."

I was still unsure.

She tried another route and attempted to look bored. "Besides, the club has a reputation for some of the most beautiful faces in the country." She side-eyed me. "You'll pull down that standard with your shitty makeup."

I smiled then. "Thank you, Nastasia."

She returned it. "You're welcome, Mina."

Holding my heels in my hand, I came down the stairs and found Lev holding Lidiya on his hip as he poured two cups of coffee. She babbled, gripping his lapel in her tiny fist, and he kissed the top of her head.

I cleared my throat at the door, not wanting to interrupt. "Sorry."

"Don't be sorry. Mirella will be here in a few minutes." He answered my unasked question, "Lidiya's nanny. You'll be seeing a lot of her." He handed me one of the coffee cups. "I'm sorry, I didn't know how you took it."

"Straight up black," I uttered, taking the cup with a smile of thanks. I sipped at it slowly and it was wonderful. I couldn't help watching the chubby, long-lashed little girl. My chest tightened in awe. "She's adorable, Lev."

He pulled back to look down at his daughter. His soft response nearly had me swooning in a dead faint. "She is my life."

Warmth flooded me, leaving me in a haze of wonder. What had I done so well in my life that I'd come across Lev Leokov? Whatever it was, I was thankful for it.

The little girl turned and, finally spotting me, gabbed. "Zhena. Zhena. Zhena."

My nose bunched with my smile. "What is she saying?"

Lev watched me closely. "She doesn't know your name. She's calling you her version of 'lady' in Russian."

"Oh, so you're Russian then?" I asked stupidly.

Patiently, Lev responded, and I commended him on not calling me a dumbass. "Yes, from both my father and mother's sides."

"Oh, cool," I said. And what followed was a long, awkward silence.

Finally, after what seemed like hours, Lev asked, "Where is your family, Mina?"

My response was curt. "Dead. I'm an orphan. I didn't know my father. My mother died when I was twelve. My grandmother didn't want me, and so I went into foster care. I ran away when I was seventeen."

Affected by my sudden change of manner, Lev whispered, "Okay," and it sounded off. Almost childlike.

The door opened suddenly, and a gaggle of people came through it, conversing loudly and openly.

Nastasia came in first, face red, lips tight, arguing with the man behind her. "I don't give a shit who she was, Vik."

The man, who I easily guessed was Viktor, came in behind her, grinning like a Cheshire cat. "Sure you do, baby."

Nas turned and her lip curled. "She was kind of pretty in that 'I hope you don't mind STDs' kind of way."

Viktor was tall, brawny, and wore a pair of dress pants, a white shirt rolled up at the sleeves to reveal a bunch of colorful tattoos, and had a toothpick sticking out the side of his mouth. His blue eyes popped in a way that made you want to stare into them for days, and he wasn't at all fazed by Nastasia's wrath. "You know me. No jimmy, no hanky."

A beautiful redhead came in behind Viktor. I immediately noticed she had the same eyes that Viktor did. From the way she smiled, she only had eyes for Lev, and when she looked to me, her smile fell fast.

Lev winked at her, a tender look in his eye. "Anika."

My stomach churned violently at the way Lev looked at her. I didn't understand it.

I mean, I *understood* it. She was pretty in a way that I just couldn't compete with.

"Well, hey there, princess." Anika held out her hands, smiling once more, and Lev handed over Lidiya as if this were a regular occurrence.

My gut rolled. Again.

What the hell was going on here? Stop it, stomach!

She bounced Lidiya on her hip, kissing her cheek. Lidiya showed no signs of discomfort with the woman. She looked to me and spoke softly, her voice melodic. "Hi. I'm Anika."

I opened my mouth to respond, already reaching out with my hand when Lev straightened. "This is Mina. The new bargirl."

I smiled at her. "Yeah, what he said."

At his explanation, Anika's tension visibly faded and she warmed up toward me. She shook my hand lightly. "Oh. That's great. We'll be working together."

Viktor looked at me then, and seemed surprised, as if he'd just noticed another person in the room.

"What's up? I'm Viktor." He looked me up and down appreciatively before turning to Lev and smiling slyly. "Where'd you find this one?"

His eyes on me, Lev responded without emotion, "Stealing Sasha's wallet."

My heart stuttered before it started to race. Everyone had gone silent apart from Viktor, who blinked at me a solid ten seconds before erupting in laughter.

My cheeks heated, but my body turned cold. I felt the stares of everyone in the room and the tension became too much.

I got it. I stole his brother's wallet. It was a shitty move. If I weren't desperate, I wouldn't have done it. Was I going to be punished for it forever?

Under my breath, I muttered, "Asshole," before slipping on my heels and clomping out the kitchen door. I almost fell ass-over-tit in those damn heels, but Nas told me I needed to get used to walking in them.

Ten minutes passed, and down the path, I spied a mature woman with dark curly hair and kind eyes coming up toward the house. She slowed when she saw me, so I smiled. "You must be Mirella."

"I am," she stated carefully.

I took a step forward. "I'm Mina." I pointed back to the house with my thumb. "I'm living here temporarily. Lev told me that I'd be seeing a lot of you."

Her eyes widened and her jaw nearly dropped. "You're staying...here? In the house...with Mister Lev?"

My nod was slow. She seemed beyond surprised. More like astonished. What was with that reaction?

Catching herself, she attempted a smile, but it was uncomfortable. "Nice to meet you, Mina," she said, moving toward the kitchen door.

"You too," I returned just as she closed the door behind her.

I waited out in the cool breeze for another few minutes before the door opened and everyone, sans Mirella and Lidiya, came outside. I felt Lev's eyes on me, but I didn't give him the satisfaction of looking up.

Nas smiled sympathetically as she watched me avoid everyone else's scrutinizing eyes. "Ready to get that blood pumping?"

"Sure," I sighed.

I mean, really. How bad could it be?

⚓

LEV

"How's she doing?"

Nastasia smiled too widely, and it came across more like a grimace. "She's only broken four glasses so far, so—" The sound of glass smashing followed by Mina's "Ah, crap. *Sorry!*" sounded. My sister shook her head. "Five glasses in two hours. Is she trying to set some kind of record or some shit?"

"She'll get the hang of it." I didn't sound as confident as I hoped.

I watched Mina closely as she listened to Anika. She was concentrating hard, nodding on occasion. I couldn't understand why this was so hard for her. Her shoulders looked tight with tension.

"Listen," Nas broke into my thoughts. "I gotta tell you, Lev, telling Vik and Ani that you met Mina when she was stealing Sasha's wallet..." She winced. "Ouch."

I was suddenly confused. "What?"

My sister had always been patient with me, but tonight, she sighed. "It's not cool, bro. You only get one chance to make a good impression, and before Mina had the chance to do that, you tore it out from under her feet."

"I don't understand." I really didn't.

Nastasia leveled me with a hard stare. "You introduced her to our closest friends as a thief."

Oh.

I was beginning to comprehend what I'd done. "I see."

"No, you don't." Nastasia took my hand in her own and squeezed. "You're a wonderful person, Lev. But you don't see."

Panic welled up inside of me. I lowered my gaze, training my eyes on my feet. What was I to do now? I didn't know how to react. I felt *wrong*.

Releasing my hand, Nas assisted me in my unspoken query. "When you get the chance, apologize to Mina."

My stomach ached. I hated this, unintentionally hurting people. I nodded.

My sister kissed my cheek and assured, "You're a good man, Lev. You just need a little help sometimes. No biggie."

But it was a big deal, to me more than most.

⚓

Mina

"Mina."

It was childish, but I ignored him. "Mina, please look at me."

I took a moment from reading my handy little guide to mixers and turned my face toward him, but my eyes strayed, focusing on his chin. He spoke softly. "Nastasia informed me that what I said in front of Anika and Viktor was inappropriate and I likely embarrassed you." My brow furrowed in confusion. He spoke about it as if he didn't know why I would be embarrassed about it. He went on, "It wasn't my intention to cause you distress, and I now understand why you called me an asshole. I apologize."

Saying sorry was one of the hardest things to say to a person, and Lev had done it in such a sincere manner that my anger ebbed away. Mostly. "I suppose you're going to go around telling everyone that I'm a homeless thief?"

He tilted his head in that way of his and concentrated hard, searching my face. "You're ashamed of your past."

My eyes went down to the book in front of me and I uttered quietly, "There's a stigma behind vagrants. Everyone looks down on the homeless. Of course I'm ashamed of my past."

"I'm not ashamed of who you are. And the only time I would look down on you is if I were helping you back up."

He had a way with words. I'd give him that. I wondered how he could say something, essentially stealing the breath from me. He seemed to enjoy doing it. He had to, otherwise he wouldn't do it so often.

"Stop doing that," I whispered.

His honeyed eyes narrowed in confusion. "Doing what?"

"Being so nice to me." I'd had enough. Slapping the book down on the bar, I gave in to myself and said what I'd been thinking. "Why am I here, Lev? Why have you brought me here? Here specifically? Why am I staying in your house, in you *bed*?" I paused. "Am I..." I swallowed hard. "You work in a gentleman's club, surrounded by gorgeous women, I..." My voice hushed, I asked hesitantly, "Am I being groomed into prostitution?"

A heavy silence followed. Then, "No."

My heart heavy, I turned up my face to look into his gorgeous eyes. "Tell me I can leave at any time, Lev."

His eyes on me, I watched as they flashed. Finally, he lowered his face and muttered, "You can leave at any time, Mina." He stepped back and away from me. "Although I hope you choose to stay." His face became impassive. "You deserve better than the unfortunate life you were dealt."

I watched him walk away from me and I was suddenly overwhelmed. My nose itched as my eyes filled with tears. I blinked them back, sniffling to myself in the dark corner of the bar, thankful for the solitude.

CHAPTER ELEVEN

Mina

I wasn't sure of the time when I first opened my eyes the next morning, nor the second, but each time I opened my eyes, I lifted my head to check the sofa bed. The first two times, the outline of Lev was apparent. The third time I checked, the sheets had been folded and rested on the edge of the mattress.

I blinked drowsily at the made bed, and regardless of how many times I tried to get back to sleep after that, slumber wouldn't take me.

Yawning, I slipped out of bed, straightening the covers, and shuffled tiredly into the en suite to wash my face and brush my teeth with my snazzy new hot pink toothbrush. I brushed my hair and pulled it into a low ponytail. When I deemed myself presentable, I made my way downstairs, calling out, "Hello? Anyone home?"

From the room to the left came, "In here, Miss Mina."

As soon as I stepped into the kitchen, I smiled. Lidiya, dressed in a light pink dress with frilly sleeves, her hair in a perfectly curly ponytail at the top of her head, sat in a high chair, spooning up what looked to be pasta straight into her mouth.

Mirella, sitting by her side, smiled over at me. "Good afternoon, Miss Mina."

My voice still croaky from sleep, I groaned. "Oh, God. Please. You don't have to be formal with me. Mina will do nicely, since I intend to call you Mirella."

The older woman grinned. "I can do that." She mock-glared at Lidiya. "Now, you, missy. You need to eat up. Mirella needs to use the bathroom."

I looked to Lidiya, who was the picture of calm as she fed herself. "You can go ahead. I'll watch her."

She looked uncertain. "Have you ever looked after a two-year-old before? They can be quite a handful."

I blinked. "You're planning on spending the entire day in the bathroom?"

The woman chuckled. "No, only a few minutes."

I walked over to the coffee machine and filled a mug. "Well, okay then." Taking the seat she'd just vacated, I assured her, "We'll be fine." I smiled at the little girl with the lashes that would make a grown woman weep in a fit of jealousy. "All right, kiddo. Take it easy on me. I'm new at this."

Lidiya responded by scooping up some food onto her little spoon and holding it out to me while jabbering away.

I was touched by her offer. My smile softened. "No, sweetie, that's your lunch." I lifted my coffee. "This is Mina's breakfast."

But she insisted, holding the spoon out with more force than previously. I shook my head once more. "I'm sure it's delectable, but really, I can't."

She babbled harder and said something like, "*Yest*, Eena. *Yest*."

I pulled back, surprised. "Did you just say Mina?"

She uttered, "Eena. *Zhena*. Eena. Eeeena. *Yest*."

I broke out into huge grin. "You *did* say my name, didn't you? Smarty pants."

From behind me came. "She wants you to eat with her."

Gasping in shock, my entire body jerked in fright and, lifting a hand to my chest, I spun around to see Lev leaning against the doorway that lead to the laundry, watching the two of us.

"You scared the poop out of me. How long have been standing there?"

He walked farther inside the room and I nearly swallowed my tongue. Lev in a suit was delicious, but Lev wearing loose grey sweatpants hanging low on his hips, his tight black tee sticking to his broad chest with sweat, and his dark brown hair delightfully mussed was *incredible*.

"Long enough to know that children scare you."

I was just about to deny that fact when Nas came in through the back door wearing a teeny see-through white t-shirt that showed her navel, her black bra visible to anyone with a pair of eyes, her blue jeans and flat strappy sandals the color of sand. Taking off her oversized sunglasses, she pointed at me. "You. Get your ass up, shower, and dress. We've got shit to do."

I looked from her to Lev then back. "We do?"

She nodded. "You and me, down at the club, mixing drinks. We may end up too drunk to work tonight, but hey,"—she threw a light shrug of her shoulder then grinned wickedly—"it's a risk I'm willing to take."

I bit the inside of my lip. "I actually wanted to talk to you guys about that." I cleared my throat and began, "I'm sure you saw me last night. I tried to do a good job. I really did, but I don't think I'm cut out for it." I paused a moment then added, "I smashed so many glasses that Anika took the blame for the last one. Then I was sent to the end of the bar to 'study' the drinks guide." I huffed out a humorless laugh. "I'm not stupid. I know they were trying to get me out of the bar so they could do some real work. Babysitting isn't part of the job."

Silence, then Nas spoke. "Oh, wah wah *wah*. Poor Mina's having a hard time serving drinks. Someone get out the violin already."

"*Hey*," I returned testily.

Lev frowned. "You don't like the job?"

"I can't do the job if I'm dropping glasses left, right, and center," I explained, my voice pleading for him to understand.

Nas shook her head, looking mildly disappointed. "I never took you for one of those girls who mopes around feeling sorry for themselves."

"I'm not!" I shot back.

"Then buck the fuck up, precious." She uttered in complete calm, "You gonna fall off the horse and let it trample you? Or are you gonna get back up and show the horse who's boss?" I fumed in silence, and from Nastasia's smug expression, she loved every moment of it. She smirked. "Make that horse your bitch, Mina. Do it."

I stood and stomped out of the kitchen, nearly bowling Mirella over on the way.

⚓

Mina

The club had a different feel about it during the day. With the music off and a stream of people restocking the bars, waxing the floors, and wiping down the tables and chairs, the pressure was off. My shoulders were loose and the tension I had felt the night before was gone.

After Nas had yelled at me, which I noticed was kind of a theme with her, I went upstairs, let my hair down, dressed in a pair of black jeans, a white pair of strappy flip-flops, a white tank, and my caramel-toned sweater that hung off my shoulder. After seeing what Nas was wearing, I figured casual was acceptable for during the day.

As we walked inside, I met two of the security crew, Brick and Tommy. Brick had been the one on door duty when I'd come in that very first night. He was pleasant but stern, and I was thankful he didn't recognize me. I was going to ask why they called him Brick, but it was obvious. He was built like a brick house.

Tommy, on the other hand, went from fierce to funny in a split second. He was tall and not quite as built as Brick, but when he scowled, he could scare the pants off anyone. He took my hand and kissed the back of it, lingering far too long. It had been a while since I had been shown any male attention. It felt nice and I giggled like a schoolgirl, my cheeks flaming around my smile.

Nas laughed at me as I fanned my face, making our way to the bar. She nudged me. "You better get used to guys falling over themselves like that. Especially with a face like yours."

I was confused. "What do you mean?"

She raised a brow. "Fishing for compliments?" But as I lowered my face, my brow furrowed in confusion, she muttered to herself, "Dear God, she doesn't know." Before I could say another word, she pulled me into the mirrored foyer. Thankfully, it was deserted when she placed me right in front of it and stood behind me. "What do you see when you look in the mirror?"

I hated my reflection. It was cruel to look so much like the person I missed most in the world, my mother. I loved her until the very last moment of her illness, and when she died, my love turned to feigned indifference. I pretended it didn't hurt to lose her, my mom, my best friend, although it was agony. Every breath I took over the next year proved difficult. My life would never be the same. She was pure sunshine. The person who took care of me when I was sick and made me laugh when I was sad. I depended on her. She was everything to me. And then she was gone.

My eyes trained on my chin, I shrugged. "I don't know."

"Look at yourself. I mean *really* look at yourself." My eyes met my reflection as she asked, "Don't you see it? Can you even comprehend how attractive you are?"

"I look like my mother," I whispered.

Nas smiled gently. "I'll bet she was beautiful."

She was. "She was lovely."

"Can you see it?" Nas probed softly. I shook my head. She reached around me to place her fingers under my chin, lifting it, and my reflection was forced into my line of sight. "Look harder." She moved to stand by my side. "You have elegant cheekbones. Your skin is impeccable and creamy, like porcelain. You have a small, full mouth, which I'll bet gives men all sorts of naughty ideas." My blush was intense. "Your hair is smooth and shiny, and dark without being black. Your big green eyes and long lashes make you look exotic and mysterious. And I'm guessing that when you get some weight back on that tiny tight body, you're going to have curves in all the right places." She placed her hands on my shoulders and squeezed hard enough to make a point. "You're lethal, Mina. And you don't even know it."

Her speech had me really looking at myself. I never viewed myself as beautiful. I'd always viewed myself as passable, but only just. But as she pointed everything out, bit-by-bit, I supposed it was there. For the first time, I could see it.

"I'm pretty?" I asked carefully, inspecting my reflection.

"*Now* you're fishing for compliments." She groaned as she pushed me to the side, causing me to stumble and laugh. "You little shit." She chuckled as we went into the bar area.

I winced as soon as my eyes hit the rows of glasses on the counter. "Are you sure you want to do this? Chances are I'm going to drop a glass, accidentally slit my wrist, and die on you."

Nas tilted her head up in thought. "Hmmm. Yes. That could be a problem." She shrugged. "Again, a risk I'm willing to take."

She gathered a bunch of different glasses and pointed to each one as she named them. "Highball. Tumbler. Sifter. Shot. Cocktail. Martini. Wine. Flute."

"No beer glasses?"

She seemed pleased that I'd noticed. "We are a high class establishment. We do serve imported beers, but you'll find that majority of our patrons will ask for mixers. Otherwise,"—she reached under the bar to pull out another tall glass from inside the refrigerator—"beer glasses are kept chilled and served with a wedge of lemon, strictly no ice."

"Chilled. Lemon. No ice." I nodded. "Got it."

For the better part of two hours, Nas taught me how to make several of the standard order drinks. She told me it was okay if I forgot what went in which drink then showed me recipe cards for all the drinks she'd taught me to make and more. With each additional drink, my confidence was boosted, and soon enough, I was mixing, muddling and shaking drinks like I was born to do it.

As I finished mixing my last drink of the day, Nas leaned her hip on the bar, looking extremely pleased with herself, and I bowed happily. "Thank you. Thank you. I'll be here all week."

An accented voice sounded from behind me. "And with a view like this, who could resist." When he said 'this,' it came out as *zis*.

I turned to face the man, who was smiling widely over the top of my head to Nastasia. She gasped, ran, and then threw herself into his waiting arms. Laughing, she pulled back and kissed him, smack on the mouth. Cupping his stubbled cheeks, she all but yelled, "Philippe Neige, you son of a gun! And looking hot as always, I see."

He was hot. Like, *smoking*.

The man smiled, and the lines around his eyes deepened. He looked to be in his forties, was as tall as Sasha, had dark blond hair, and smiling green eyes. I gathered he was French, not only from his accent, but also from the way Nas said his name. He wore a pair of dark blue jeans. His white shirt was left untucked, and he finished of his polished look with a pair of dark brown loafers.

He kissed Nastasia's cheek for a second too long. "I missed you, my dove."

All of a sudden, Nas pulled away, her expression turning arctic. "Heard you're working for Laredo." It sounded like an accusation.

His smile fell and his face turned stern. He didn't deny it. "*Oui*."

She stepped away from him, her face as pained as her voice. "How could you, Philippe? After what he did..." It became too much to speak about it, and I was stunned by the emotion she was showing. Nastasia seemed hard as nails. Whatever this Laredo guy did must've been pretty bad to warrant that kind of reaction.

Sasha walked in from the door behind the bar. He looked from an unrelenting Philippe to an emotional Nas, over to me, and then back to Philippe. "Back away, Nas." She looked over at him, her eyes a raging fire. Sasha spoke coolly as always. "Philippe came because I needed him. Don't disrespect him. You'll regret it." Although the words came out in threat form, the way his voice changed, softening slightly, suggested Nas didn't know all the facts.

She blinked away tears then turned her face down to stare at the ground by Philippe's feet. "I missed you, too," she whispered. And then she was gone, rushing out of the bar and down the hall to the ladies' room. We all watched her leave.

A long silence followed.

Sasha let out a sigh. "I told you to come straight to me, Neige."

Philippe responded miserably, "I never stopped loving her."

At my soft gasp, all eyes turned on me. I flushed and sputtered, "H-hi, I'm Mina."

Sasha glowered at me.

I glowered right back then followed Nas into the ladies' room. I sat on the bathroom vanity, looking at the closed door that separated us, waiting patiently for her to stop crying.

In Nas style, she flung open the door, her face blotchy and her eyes a nice shade of red, and uttered angrily, "Makes sense for men to have cocks since they're all dicks."

CHAPTER TWELVE

Mina

Our bartending lesson had concluded with the arrival of Philippe Neige. I was curious about the man who could bring a woman like Nas to tears. On the way home, I asked carefully, "So, I'm guessing Philippe is an ex-boyfriend?"

Nas tried to ignore me, but the silence was too thick to overlook. "We were engaged for a short time. It was a whirlwind romance. It was over before it even began."

"What happened?" I queried in my most sympathetic tone.

She sighed, aggravated. "He did what all men do eventually." She paused to add quietly, "He disappointed me."

"Did you love him?"

Nas went quiet. She breathed in slowly and replied on an exhale, "I've only ever loved one man. And Philippe wasn't him." Quickly changing the subject, she asked, "What about you, Mina? Have you ever been in love?"

"Yes," I responded easily. I side-eyed her, itching to spot her reaction. "I fell in love with my brother."

She did not disappoint.

"*Ewwwww*," was out of her mouth before I'd even finished. "Please tell me you're joking. If you're not, I'm going to pull over and ralph, because that's fucking nasty."

I leaned back in my seat, laughing. "He was my *foster* brother. No relation." I grinned. "God, you're good value."

She smiled then, reluctantly. "Bitch." She shook her head. "Tell me about mister brother man, then."

"I was twelve when I first got put into foster care. I was one of the lucky ones. The first family I was placed with was the one I stayed with till I took to the streets." My brow furrowed. I hadn't thought about Maggie and John Peterson for a long time. "Maggie was everything I needed at a time I'd lost it all. She was wonderful. John, her husband, was just as good. He included me in everything, made it like we were a real family. They had a pair of twins, five-year-olds, who adored me. Ben and Chris." I smiled. "I taught them how to ride a bike." I sighed.

"Uh oh," Nas began. "Something big is coming. I can feel it."

"When I was sixteen, Maggie came into my room. She looked kind of worried. That was when she explained that her son from her first marriage was going to come live with us after his father had a run-in with the law. I didn't know what the big deal was. This was her child. I mean, why was she even explaining this to me? I told her it was okay. I even told her he could have my room if he needed it, that I'd sleep on the couch." My voice turned soft. "His name was James. He was almost eighteen, a star football player and absolutely gorgeous."

"*Boom*. And there's the kicker."

I grinned. "He was sweet, and funny, and a total flirt. He was also the first guy to have the guts to kiss me, right in the backyard, under the noses of Maggie and John. I fell in love with him so effortlessly." I chuckled at the memory. "Before long, we were sneaking kisses all over the place, and he would slip into my room at night after everyone else had fallen asleep." I sighed dreamily. "We'd talk all night long until talk got in the way of kissing. And then I turned seventeen. One thing lead to another, and soon we were doing a lot more than talking and kissing, if you know what I mean."

Nas grinned. "I do. I really do."

"The story ends with us being careless and getting caught, Maggie blaming me for leading on her son and calling me a little tramp. Me realizing that no matter how much I loved Maggie, she was *not* my mother. And I was gone the next day."

"She called you a tramp?" Nas uttered, appalled.

I nodded. "A *little* tramp."

"And then you disappeared on 'em." Nas paused and added thoughtfully, "I'll bet she's thought about you every day since you've been gone."

Her statement made my heart stutter. "You think?"

"Um, yeah. She called a seventeen-year-old girl a nasty name in anger and that girl took off, never to be seen again." She snorted. "I'd say she's paying every single day for what she did, just by the memory of you. Serves her right, stupid bitch."

I didn't want to believe Maggie could have been suffering from guilt this entire time. Sure, she'd called me a bad name, but it didn't compare to the fact she'd taken me into her home and made me part of a family for close to five years. She deserved more than to live like that.

As soon as Nas dropped me off at home, I searched the house for Lev, finding him downstairs, sitting in a rocking chair, cradling a sleeping Lidiya, and speaking soft words into her curly hair.

I stood in the doorway unnoticed for a long while, watching this man be a father to his daughter. My throat thickened with emotion. Lev was proving to be more than I originally thought him to be.

With a soft clearing of my throat, Lev turned and caught my eye. I lifted my hand in a gentle wave and he lifted the little girl, carrying her across the room and tucking her into her toddler bed. He picked up the baby monitor, stepped out the room, and turned the device on. I backed away from the door as he closed it carefully.

My expression was tender when he approached. I'd forgotten my purpose momentarily. Placing a hand on his forearm, I squeezed gently and whispered, "You're a good daddy, Lev."

Looking mildly embarrassed, he ignored my compliment, but didn't step away from my closeness. "How did you do today? When Nastasia is determined to see something happen, she can be overassertive."

Linking my arm through his, we walked down the hall together. "You know, your sister might be a badass, but she knows how to motivate a person." I smiled up at him. "I didn't drop a single glass. Not one. And I now know how to make about ten different mixers. So I'm ready for tonight. Bring it on."

He stilled, pulling me to a stop, searching my face. "You look to be in better spirits today. I'm glad."

My face became void of expression. "Four days ago, you took me off the streets, fed me, gave me a place to sleep, and offered me a job." Slowly, so there was no mistaking my intentions, I stepped forward, slid my arms around his waist, and pressed myself into him, squeezing gently, resting my head between his pecks. "Thank you is not enough of a phrase to express how grateful I am that I met you, Lev Leokov." I breathed in the sandalwood cologne he wore. "You saved my life."

He didn't hug me back, but he reached up and stroked my hair kindly. "I would do it all over again, mouse."

I pulled away an inch, my arms still around him, to look up into his face. "It can only get better from here, right?"

His expression glum, he cupped my cheek with a warm palm. "Of course."

It was then I remembered my initial reason for interrupting him. Stepping back, I linked my arm through his once more. "I need your help."

He didn't ask what for; he simply responded a determined, "Anything."

And I knew—I just *knew*—he wouldn't let me down.

⚓

Mina

From the moment I stepped inside Bleeding Hearts, I knew my anxiety had returned with a vengeance. I wasn't sure what had brought it on, but I was definitely feeling the pressure after the fourth glass had slipped from my hand and shattered as it hit the floor.

Nastasia pulled me aside. "What gives, dude? You were doing so well today!"

I sputtered angrily, "I don't know! *Jesus*."

Anika came over, looking somewhat sympathetic. "I hate to be the bearer of bad news, but we've got a bachelor party coming in. They'll be here in ten and I'm their server." She looked at Nas, her striking blue eyes concerned. "What are we going to do? I don't think I can leave Mina behind the bar tonight, not without someone to help."

I slapped my hands over my face. "Oh, God. I'm so sorry, Nas. I don't know what's going on with me."

Anika spotted something by the door and straightened. "*Dammit*," she smiled widely as she muttered through gritted teeth. "They're early. I have to go play hostess. Nas, stay with her, please."

The second Anika had left, my stomach eased.

Nas sighed. "Come on." She took me by the shoulders and shook me once. "You can do this. I know you can. I told Lev I had you. Don't make a liar out of me, short stuff."

Nas' pep talks were mildly threatening, but they did the job. Tilting my head from side-to-side, I cricked my neck. "I got this."

"You got this," she repeated.

"I'm gonna make this horse my bitch," I grumbled.

She grinned. "Fuck yes, you are." She pushed me along, slapping my ass in encouragement. "Get out there and serve drinks, and don't freaking drop anything." I glowered at her. Using her fingers, she drew a big smile onto her face. "Service with a smile!"

I looked around and when I was sure no one was watching, I flipped her the bird.

She laughed and I felt eyes on me. Turning toward the far end of the club, by the stage, I found Lev looking right at me, unblinking. And his eyes...they were full of mirth.

He'd seen what I'd done. I was caught.

My face heated. I could hardly ignore him. He'd seen me look right at him. I lifted my hand in a two finger wave. He jerked his chin in response. I smiled and mouthed, "Sorry." I wasn't sure, but it looked like he mouthed back, "Get to work."

I settled behind the bar, took orders, and served drinks. I did this without further incident, and over the course of the next hour, made a hundred dollars in tips.

A man named Jeremiah came to take over for me while I took a fifteen-minute break. He wasn't as tall as the other men who worked here, but he definitely made up for it with his good looks. He had longish brown hair, slicked back, a beard, and tattoos running up his arms. He wore tight black jeans, a tight black tee, and had an easy smile. I took the hand he extended and was surprised when he lifted it to his mouth to press a kiss on my knuckles.

It seemed to happen a lot around here. My reaction was the same as when Tommy had done it. I giggled and covered my flaming cheeks with a hand. Jeremiah sent me off for my break, but I was intercepted. Lev stood in front of me, but his eyes were trained on Jeremiah. And he looked angry.

No. Not angry.

Pissed. With a capital P.

"Hey," I called over the music, tugging on his sleeve.

When he looked down at me, his face softened dramatically. He leaned down and stated, "Jeremiah sleeps around."

"Oh," I uttered, unsure of why I needed to know this.

Lev nodded, a piece of his hair coming loose and draping itself down across his forehead. "He likes to flirt."

Reaching up, I pulled on his jacket until his face was low enough for me to fix his hair. I checked him over, fixing his bent lapel then smoothing his vest before pulling his jacket closed. "Is that your way of warning me about unsavory men?" I looked back at Jeremiah. "He's quite handsome though, isn't he?"

Lev spoke through gritted teeth. "I didn't realize he was your type."

He moved to walk away, but I stopped him by grasping his wrist. My brow furrowed at his arctic tone. "I don't really have a type, Lev. I haven't had a man show interest in me since I was sixteen-years-old." I shrugged. "It's a nice feeling, to be wanted." I reached out with my free hand and touched his forearm, above the wrist I was gripping. "But thank you for warning me. Consider me cautioned."

His golden eyes roamed my face, relaxing immensely. "I don't want you to get hurt."

My body warmed tenderly. *God*, he was sweet. I grinned. "Then we have a common interest."

He took the hand at his forearm and squeezed it. "Men are dogs. They'll say and do anything to get a woman to sleep with them."

I couldn't see him being one of those men. I uttered quietly, "But not you. Right?"

His eyes closed and he shut them tight as he nodded. Releasing my hand, he urged, "Be careful, Mina. Your innocence is more appealing than you know."

And then he was gone.

Doom and gloom, I thought. Then a small smile tilted my lips.

How very Lev.

CHAPTER THIRTEEN

Mina

It was Friday, and I'd officially been employed by Bleeding Hearts a week and a half. You couldn't get the smile off my dial even if you tried. Over the past five days, I'd met every single employee, taking the time to find out a little about them without giving away too much about myself. When asked where I hailed from, I told the majority of the dancing girls that I moved around a lot as a kid, unknowingly earning myself the nickname Gypsy.

I understood that strippers didn't have the best reputations, but the girls I met were lovely. All but one, of course.

A small Hispanic woman with big brown eyes, smooth skin the color of coffee, strong on the milk, and curves that made men lose their ever-loving minds sneered at me. They called her ChaCha. It was hard to be nice to ChaCha when she looked at you like you smelled of shit.

People heard the girls calling me by my new nickname, and then soon enough, the technical and security staff, bartenders, and even some patrons were calling me Gypsy.

I didn't mind. It kind of gave me a sense of belonging. I mean, friends normally gave you nicknames, didn't they?

It made my heart smile.

That is, until Anika told me that Russians did not think highly of gypsies, and looking down at me, eyes lowered sympathetically, stated that she'd tell everyone to stop calling me that.

Putting on my biggest, flashiest smile, I thanked her but told her not to bother, because I liked it.

Take that, Miss Prim and Proper.

As my mind eased into the job, so did my tension, and I was becoming a crowd favorite. People wanted the gypsy to host their bachelor parties and paid ridiculous amounts to have me wait on them exclusively.

I didn't understand it, but I was sure it had something to do with what Nas taught me when she took me out for lunch yesterday.

The moment we sat down, she sat up straight and laid it out on the line. "We have to talk."

"Yeah, about what?" My heart started to beat faster.

Part of me thought I was being fired and Lev didn't have the balls to tell me himself. But what she said next just baffled me. "Don't take this personally or nothing, okay? But I thought when you settled a little it would come out naturally, and now that I can see it's not going to happen, I'm going to have to teach you."

I sipped at my lemon water, running my fingers over the condensation on the outside of the glass. "Teach me what?"

She took off her glasses and grinned. "How to flirt."

I blinked at her then snorted. "What for? It's not like I'm looking for a boyfriend or anything."

She sighed, and reaching up, she rubbed at her temples as if I were trying her patience. "Mina, you're a bar bitch at a gentleman's club." She paused a moment. "I didn't want to have to put the pressure on, but you've been booked to host a bachelor party on Saturday night."

Momentarily stunned, I gaped. Then I sputtered, "W-what? Why me? Can't Anika do it? *Make Anika do it*!"

Nas glared, speaking slowly through gritted teeth. "They don't want Anika. They want the gypsy." She leaned across the small café table to get into my face. "And they're going to get the gypsy, or I'm going to kick the gypsy's ass. You feel me?"

Sliding down in my chair, I whined, "I don't want to. I'll spill their drinks all over them. They'll complain to Sasha, and then I'll get fired."

"You haven't dropped a glass since your second day. You can balance a tray. You're getting more orders filled than any of us expected of you. And you have the men captivated." She pinned me with a sincere stare. "You're doing great. Even Lev thinks so."

Whining Mina vanishes as intrigued Mina appeared. "Really? He said that?"

"Yes, he said that, just this morning." Her brow furrowed. "You two are living in the same house. What the heck do you guys talk about?"

I shrugged. "Not much." I tilted my head in thought. "It's almost like every time I try to start a conversation, he gets all weird on me."

Nas' expression shifted. She spoke quietly but defensively, "It's not his fault, Mina. It's just the way he is. I don't expect you to understand, but trust me—he can't help it." She followed this with, "Don't judge him. He's not being rude; he just doesn't know how to be social."

I blinked at her protective tone. "I'm not judging him, Nas. I just have questions. Like, why won't he talk to me about himself, and why the hell does he lock us into his bedroom at night?"

Nas sat back, her mouth agape. "You're sleeping with him?"

"What?" I flushed and almost shouted, "No!" I huffed out an unimpressed laugh. "He doesn't trust me not to steal from him, so he told me as long as I'm staying with him that we'll be sleeping in the same room. I sleep in the bed, and he sleeps on the pullout." She didn't look convinced. I sipped at my water, my mouth suddenly dry. "I swear we're not bumping uglies, Nas. I *swear*."

A small smile graced her pretty face. "I honestly wouldn't care if you were; it's just that he doesn't let anyone..." She faded out, shaking her head, suddenly smiling like a loon. "You have no idea how much of a big deal that is, Mina. But we don't have time for that, so never mind." She cleared her throat, sitting up straight. "Right, so, flirting one-oh-one with Nas has officially commenced." She winked. "Take note, little Mina. Women would kill for the information I'm about to give you."

Whining Mina was back. "I still don't understand why I need to know this stuff."

Then Nas said the magic words. "I guarantee your tips will triple."

Well, that caught my attention. I listened intently.

She began. "Rule one: Lean in. Close the gap. You're going to want to get close to the men you're flirting with. Smile and give them your undivided attention. Don't forget to make eye contact." She leaned over the table and, smiling shyly, batted her lashes, touching my arm. "Slight touches are okay, just make it look like you couldn't hear their order over the music. If they compliment you, lower your lashes and smile shyly. Men love the innocent types."

That seemed straightforward. "Okay. That doesn't sound too hard to remember."

"Never—and I mean *never*—give your name on the first drink. It'll keep them coming back for more and they'll order again and again just to have a minute of your attention." She went on, "I'd advise you to start calling yourself Gypsy from now on, sort of like a stage name. It has men thinking you're all wild and free-spirited and shit." I rolled my eyes and she scolded me. "Hey, these men are helping pay your wages."

Oh, she didn't need to tell me. I knew it, and I was beyond appreciative, but it kind of seemed like we were treating these men like they were stupid.

"If a guy gives you a solid tip, thank him, fold up the money, and put it in your bra right in front of him. It's like putting on a little show for him. If he's feeling generous and leaves a ridiculous tip, lean over the bar, grab his shirtfront into a tight fist, pull him close, and kiss his cheek real slow. Men go bananas for that crap." I wasn't sure I'd ever do that, but it was good to know. I listened intently as she explained the art of flirting. "Words of caution though: Don't offer anything you're not willing to give. You give them an inch, and they'll take a mile. Don't ever kiss a patron on the lips. He'll take it as an invitation and possibly get grabby." Her brows rose. "It won't end well."

I nodded. Yeah, I could see that ending badly.

Nas finished up just as our meals arrived. "And that concludes our lessons for the day." She grinned, watching me eye my fettuccini Alfredo with avocado hungrily. "Eat up."

I ate with gusto, and she chuckled as I moaned throughout my meal. When we were done, I groaned and clutched my belly. "Oh, God, I'm so full." Then I laughed. "I never thought I'd hear myself say that."

She smiled, jerking her chin toward me. "You're looking a lot better."

I rubbed my belly proudly. "Already gained four pounds this week." Her lips pursed as if she were impressed. "Eighteen more to go to get to my regular weight."

Her fond smile warmed me. "We'll get there, Mina."

She said it as if we were a team. As if she would see me through. Like we were more than associates. Like we were friends.

It rippled like a bang right in the center of my chest. I valued friendship, especially as I hadn't had it in such a long time. I realized I was no longer alone, and no one would ever understand how humbling a feeling that was. Most would take it for granted.

I never would. From the bottom of my heart, I vowed it.

Saturday arrived and, aware I would be attending to eight rowdy men, I dressed accordingly.

I wore my tight blue jeans, a white gypsy blouse that showed a tiny amount of my belly flesh, and strappy, white, leather flat sandals. The blouse was thin cotton, long-sleeved, and decorated in navy blue embroider flowers. Nas had given me a headband she had bought but had never worn that she informed me was boho chic.

I didn't know what boho chic was, but Nas swore it would finish my gypsy look.

The headband went across the center of my forehead and over the crown of my skull, was made of a thin silver chain, had another strand of chain trailing down the middle of my part, holding it up, and had small coins attached to the sides by my brows. The coins jangled lightly, and it was a little distracting, but when I looked at myself in the mirror, it didn't look as ridiculous as I thought it might.

Nas instructed me to apply three coats of mascara to lengthen my long lashes and finish off with the bright red lipstick she'd given me.

It took a lot of correcting to get the lipstick right, and I felt the need to run my tongue over my teeth a bit. The thought of smiling brightly with red-stained teeth was downright mortifying. I checked my teeth ten times before I made my way downstairs, coat in hand.

LEV

As predicted, Lev was downstairs in the kitchen, holding Lidiya. Only this time, when I stepped inside and she held her little hands out to me, I moved closer, took her from Lev, and cuddled her tightly. "Hey there, sweetie pie," I cooed, pressing my cheek to the top of her head, breathing in her sweet scent. I closed my eyes, taking in her warmth. "My goodness, you're a big girl."

Lev, who stood by, not an inch of concern from him watching me with his daughter, took a step closer. "Here, I'll take her. I know she's a little heavy."

But I held her close. "Heavy? She's adorably chubby, is what she is." Lidiya sucked her thumb, leaning her head on my shoulder. A wave of mushiness took over. "Oh, you are winning major points with me, little miss. You've got me wrapped around your little finger."

Every morning, when Lev disappeared to work out, I rose and spent some time with Mirella and Lidiya. We'd gone on walks around the complex together, played blocks and dolls together, had exclusive tea parties, and on the rare occasion, I even let Lidiya feed me.

A smiling Mirella told me I'd spoil her if I kept treating her like a princess. I responded that little girls shouldn't be treated as anything *but* princesses. Something told me I'd officially won over the older woman with that remark, but it didn't matter to me. It was how I truly felt.

The back door opened and Viktor came inside, followed by Anika and Nas. I was likely the only person who saw the flash of Anika's eyes. We greeted each other, and the newcomers all doted on Lidiya, as per usual.

When Anika came forward and extended her arms to Lidiya, the little girl turned her head into my neck and held onto me. I saw the disappointment in the beautiful redhead's eyes, and giddiness rushed through me. But shame followed.

She was visibly upset, after all.

I tried to make a joke of it. "She probably thinks we're around the same age, being I'm the closest in height to her."

Anika blinked, smiling at me. But there was no warmth in that smile. I got the feeling that she thought I was overstepping in a big way.

Mirella came down after her shower and pried Lidiya from me, but the little girl didn't want to let go. After she started to fuss, I offered to put her to bed for the second time that week. Mirella was evidently grateful. She clearly didn't want to put Lidiya to bed in a state of distress. I didn't blame her.

I made it up the stairs as Lidiya started to doze. Mirella silently reached for her and I handed the chubby princess over. I waved silently, and Mirella returned it. I headed downstairs and entered the kitchen just as Anika commented, "So Mina's here a lot."

Neither Lev nor Nas felt the need to explain, and neither did I, quite frankly. Rather than telling her she was being obvious in a hideous way, I smiled. "Who's ready to make tonight their bitch? I am. Let's go."

Playing host was interesting.

Nas was right about the flirting. The bachelor boys couldn't have been more generous. I'd screwed up a couple of times, but had the grace to laugh at myself. My excuse for the order mix-ups being, "Well, if you guys weren't so handsome, a girl could work without distraction, you know?"

With common excuses like that, my charming party upped the tips at an alarming rate, leaving more for me than what they'd actually spent on drinks.

My cheeks hurt from smiling so much, but it was worth it when I learned that I'd earned a little more than $400 in tips.

Lev kept a close eye on me, getting up to check on me every now and again. I wondered what he actually did here at the club. From the looks of things, all he did was watch the show every night.

After one of the boys had grabbed my wrist and pulled me close, I panicked. But when I reminded myself that they'd had a lot to drink and getting grabby came with the territory, I pasted another wide smile on my face, leaned in close, and listened to the array of compliments the man wanted me to hear. After he was heard, he let go of me and relief went through me. I blinked up at him through lowered lashes, walked backward, and blew the man a kiss.

LEV

I don't know why I was so against this. This flirting stuff was easy. I had it *down*.

Walking backward, I walked straight into a wall. I looked up to see that wall glaring at the man who wanted to tell me how beautiful I was. I turned and smiled up at him. "I'm killing it!"

But Lev, looking dangerously handsome in his gunmetal grey three-piece suit, kept his glare level on the man. "He put his hands on you."

Warning bells went off in my head. My smile faded as I placed a hand on his chest. "Hey, it's okay. They're just having a bit of fun."

His glare faded as he looked down at me. "You looked frightened."

Oh. Had I?

That meant he had been watching me. I couldn't even think about that right now. I had to calm a murderous looking Lev.

His eyes fell to the ground as he asked a hesitant, "Were you frightened?"

My shoulder jumped in a small shrug. "I'm not used to people touching me, is all. It freaked me out for about a whole second, but I thought about it and I'm okay with it." I felt the need to defend the grabby man. "He didn't hurt me, Lev."

"I don't like them touching you."

That was a bold statement if I ever heard one. His eyes, blazing, went over my head, back toward the man. My hand still on his chest, I turned to see the group of men watching Lev, all looking tense and uneasy.

Lev fisted his hands and went to step forward, toward the men.

I couldn't believe what I was seeing. Sweet Lev getting all riled up over some random guys? I didn't get it. This wasn't the man I'd seen over the past week. This was someone else. Someone scary.

"Hey!" I shouted over the music, pushing my hand against his chest to stop him from going over there. He looked down at me, his eyes softening, and he stilled. I smiled reassuringly, patting the breast of his jacket. "I'm okay." I laughed softly. "It's okay, Lev. I can handle them."

He didn't look convinced. "I'm going to keep an eye on you."

I didn't want to test him. Not now. He looked like a bomb set to go off at the slightest touch.

"Okay," I said and headed back to the bar, confused about the reaction these men had spiked in Lev.

The rest of the night went splendidly, and my bra was full to the brim with tip money. My party left around two a.m. with wide smiles, but I wouldn't let them leave without calling taxis for them first. The husband-to-be kissed my hand and thanked me for a great night. It felt nice to be appreciated.

When the cleaners had come in and everyone was getting ready to leave, Sasha came out from the door behind the bar and advised that he'd be staying behind a while. I hooked my arm through Lev's and waved goodbye to Anika and Viktor.

Anika, looking down at my arm hooked around Lev's, smiled and offered, "Hey, Mina, I can drive you home."

Oh my.

Yep. It was obvious. She had set her cap for Lev. What was funny was that she thought me competition. She was gorgeous. I couldn't compete with that.

Lev, looking confused, uttered, "That would make no sense, Anika, since Mina is living with me."

The poor dove paled a few shades. She swallowed hard before turning to Nas and accusing, "Oh. Sorry. No one told me."

Nas eyed her friend hard. I was proud of her response. "Well, Ani, that would be because it's none of your goddamn business."

A shiver of satisfaction went through me as I was led to the car by Lev in complete silence.

CHAPTER FOURTEEN

Mina

The next morning when Lev awoke, I found myself waking at the same time. I was sick of spending my days in bed. There had to be better things to do than sleeping the day away. But if there was, I was yet to find an activity so enjoyable that it surpassed sleep.

With the bedroom door wide open, I assumed Lev had already left the room. I yawned, sliding out of bed and walking over to the en suite to wash my face and brush my teeth. Just as I opened the door, the shower was turned on and I went rigid at the sight of Lev's bare behind.

His *tight*, *muscled* behind and *long*, *thick* legs.

Oh, Jesus.

My small breasts tightened and my stomach dipped violently. Suddenly wide-awake, I gripped the door handle till my knuckles went white, and blinked at the heavenly sight.

He must have felt my eyes on him, because with his back to me, he turned his head, catching my eyes below his belt.

Shit. I was caught, eyes as wide as saucers and mouth agape. I lifted my face to look into his.

I remembered James. I remembered being intimate with James. I could describe to you every aspect of his body in detail. But the sight of Lev's naked body had me forgetting what's-his-name in a second flat.

James was a boy.

Lev was *all* man.

His broad back rippled, and I wanted to rub those bare, bulky shoulders. I wanted to run my hands all over him, to have the privilege of touching anywhere he would let me.

The sensitive spot between my legs pulsed lightly.

He watched me watching him, and his brow rose slowly in question.

I swallowed hard and my tongue felt like it was made of sand. My body was hot all over. I whispered, "I just wanted to brush my teeth."

His eyes on me, he stayed silent a moment. "Okay," he drawled as he stepped into the shower, steam billowing around us. The frosted glass surrounding the shower did nothing to keep my imagination tame.

Lev was a blur, but in my mind, I could see every strong, powerful edge of his body as though the glass wasn't even there. And what a sight it was. Impressive, fantasy as it was.

Part of me wanted to throw open the shower door and peer inside to look my fill.

I wondered what Lev's reaction would be to that. Would he be offended, or would he be flattered? Would his body respond to blatant looks of appreciation? Putting my hand where I needed it most, I squeezed my legs together, desperate to find relief from the dull throbbing. All I really managed to do was make my nipples bead. I closed my eyes, biting the inside of my lip, savoring the warm flow taking over my body. Perhaps he'd pull me under the spray, take my mouth in a deep, feral kiss, and take me against the cool wall of the shower.

Yeah, right.

I removed my hand from between my legs, making my way over to the bathroom mirror. Rolling my eyes at the crazy thought, I wiped the foggy glass and stared at my flushed reflection. It was obvious I would never find out what Lev's reaction would have been. I wasn't *that* adventurous. He'd probably ask me to leave in that bored polite way that only Lev could pull off, leaving me humiliated.

I'd already had enough humiliation to last a lifetime. This was my time to shine, and if I wanted male companionship, I would have to look elsewhere.

My heart panged sorely. It was becoming clear I felt something for Lev. I spent the last few days trying to deny that fact, but I could no longer lie to myself. Why else would jealousy have my belly twisting in knots when Anika was around, touching Lev and pressing herself up against him?

I ran through it in my mind. I told myself that perhaps I had a deep regard for Lev, because he happened to be the person who saved me. Maybe if Sasha were the person to have helped me, I'd feel the same way for him that I do Lev.

My nose bunched. I understood that our circumstances were way out there, but somehow, I seriously doubted I'd ever feel for Sasha the way I felt about Lev.

It was more than an alliance, not quite a friendship. Not yet, anyway.

After speaking with Nas the previous week, I quickly came to realize that unless I was the person to make the effort, Lev and I would remain in this casual acquaintance. And I wanted more than that. I wanted to talk to Lev without feeling like I was intruding or prying. I wanted Lev to feel comfortable with me. I wanted a friendship.

And more than anything, I wanted to make him smile. Currently, Lidiya was the only person who could force a happy response from him. I wanted to change that.

Damn it. I *was* overstepping. I knew this. But it was now my mission. I would give anything to hear him laugh. I had a feeling it would be groundbreaking.

With a soft sigh, I flossed, picked up my toothbrush, brushed my teeth, rinsed with mouthwash, and then left the bathroom to sit on the bed and await Lev's return.

I had a proposition for him.

Lying back on the bed, I didn't have to wait long for the door to open and see Lev come out of the bathroom, dressed in black sweat pants and a tight white tee. The condensation on his body caused the shirt to stick, and I could easily make out his flat, dark nipples through the thin material.

"Working out?" I all but croaked out as I moved to sit up.

He let out an affirmative grunt, sitting on the edge of the sofa to put on his socks and sneakers. Then he looked up at me, his honeyed eyes narrowed in suspicion. "You're up early."

My lip twitched. "You say that like I have a motive." I smiled and uttered an amused, "Okay, well, I sort of do."

That statement caught his attention. His elbows on his knees, his arms hanging down between his open legs, he asked cautiously, "What do you need?"

I needed a lot more than he had up for offer, preferably those full lips on mine.

"I *need*," I paused, pinning his eyes with my stare, "time to get to know you."

Puzzlement crossed his face. "I don't understand."

That, I was coming to learn, was one of his favorite phrases. The other one being 'I see'.

"I've lived here almost two weeks now. We've been under each other's noses working together, eating together, living together, and still, I don't know a thing about you, Lev. And I'd like to."

His brows pulled low. "I see."

And with that, I almost burst into a fit of laughter. But instead, I wove it into a bright smile. "Will you have lunch with me today? We'll talk. Get to know each other a little better. Dig deeper than the surface."

His face lost all expression and, for some reason, anxiety radiated from him.

I couldn't handle it. I made my way over to him, taking his hand and sitting by his side. I spoke gently, "Why do you shut down when I ask you about yourself?"

His throat worked, and his response will stay with me forever. His voice equally as soft, he muttered, "I don't know how to talk to people, Mina." He squeezed my hand lightly. "I'm worried I'll screw up, disappoint you."

My reply was quiet but fierce. "You can talk to me about anything. I don't think you could disappoint me, even if you tried. I just want honest conversation."

Looking down at our hands, he ran his thumb over mine, straightened, and conceded, "Okay. Yes." He paused then added, "I would like to have lunch with you, Mina."

My shoulders bunched in time with my nose and, lifting my arms high in the air, I cheered, "Yay!"

He looked up at me, and when he looked at me like I was crazy, I tipped my head back and laughed, just happy to be sharing this moment with him. I stood, gathering some clothes and walking over to the bathroom. "One o'clock?"

He inclined his head. "One o'clock."

Feeling equal amounts of relief and joy, I closed the door behind me and washed away my long night.

⚓

Mina

The morning dragged on, mainly because Mirella had taken Lidiya on a day excursion and I didn't get to see the little sweetheart before they left. Nas came by around eleven, and without uttering a single syllable, she sat at Lev's kitchen table, her humungous sunglasses covering her eyes, and threw a paper bag onto the table.

I huffed out a laugh and asked on a whisper, "Didn't sleep well?"

She pulled off her glasses, wincing as sunlight touched her red eyes, but she smiled cunningly, "I didn't sleep at *all*."

It took me a second to get it. And when I did, I leaned over the table and shoved her. "You little skank. Was it anyone I know?"

She shrugged. "Probably."

I stared at her. "And you're not telling?" She shook her head, a Mona Lisa smile appearing on her lips. "Fine," I said. "At least tell me if he was any good."

"*Mmmm*," she hummed, her eyes closing slowly. "It was exactly what I needed. He was incredible. A god."

My lips pursed into a pout. "I want someone incredible. I want a god." I blinked at her. "What is wrong with me?"

Nas chuckled. "By the look of it, you're thirsty, *kukla*."

"Huh?"

"You need a tall glass of water."

I was starting to get a headache. I rubbed at my temples. "English, Nas. Please."

She huffed out an annoyed sigh and shot me the stank eye. "You're horny."

"No, I'm not," I objected a little too quickly.

"It's totally natural to want the *D*, Mina. Nothing to be ashamed of. It's been a long time. You've just got your life back." She assured, "You're twenty-four years old. It's okay to want sex."

I blinked down at the table, thinking hard. "You know, you're probably right. But I think it's not what I want at all. It's just the *idea* of it is mighty appealing." I snickered. "Knowing my luck, I'd hook up with the one guy who doesn't know how to take a woman there. Then, of course, I'd fake it so he didn't feel bad, and end up feeling twice as horny, going home and flicking the bean." I grimaced. "Not ideal."

Nas gawked at me, her eyes narrowed and her lip curled. Finally, she theorized, "You're fucking crazy."

"I know," I sighed.

I opened the bag on the table to find Ada had made a batch of her blueberry muffins. Even though I wanted to keep them all for myself, I reluctantly offered one to Nas, who snickered at my obviously forced offer. She took one anyway. We talked over a cup of coffee and I realized time flew as the back door opened.

Both Nas and I turned to watch Lev walk inside. He looked down at his sister and his hard eyes turned warm. "Good morning, Nastasia. Are you joining us for lunch?"

"Lunch?" She perked up. I spun around and scowled at her. Her brows rose in surprise. "I guess not."

"Next time," he muttered before turning to me. "I need to shower. We'll leave in ten minutes."

"Okay," I breathed, staring directly at his t-shirt-covered broad chest.

When he left to walk up the stairs, Nas pinched me and whisper-hissed, "You have a thing for Lev!"

"*Ow*, that hurt!" I howled, rubbing at my arm. "I finally got the guts to ask him to lunch. We're going to get to know each other." I vowed, "I'm not letting him avoid me anymore. We're going to be friends."

Nas warned, "Lev doesn't do friendship."

I looked toward the doorway he walked out of. I declared resolutely, "Well, I'm going to change that."

⚓

Nas left before Lev had finished showering, giving me a moment to apply a tinted moisturizer, mascara, and clear lip-gloss. I brushed my hair and left it down. It was no longer straight, rather cascading down my back in loose waves.

I changed into the navy blue sundress I'd bought two days prior after talking Nas into taking me to another thrift shop, throwing an eighties-style white blazer over the top and slipping on my white, low-heeled mary janes. Nas acted annoyed that I made her come, but she left with a stunning vintage *Glomesh* clutch circa the seventies.

I grinned at her. She spat oversensitively, "Hey, these are back in fashion!"

As we were leaving, Mirella pulled up into the driveway. She brought Lidiya out, and the moment she spotted her daddy, her arms went out toward him and she started babbling, "Otet! Otet! *Otet!*"

He looked to me then back to her, and I knew I was losing him. There was no competition when it came to Lidiya. I understood that. And to be honest, I respected that.

Rather than losing my lunch date, I placed my hand on his arm and hinted, "Maybe Mirella could do with an afternoon off." At his confused look, I suggested, "Let's take Lidiya with us. We'll bring a picnic blanket, some of her toys, get some lunch, and eat it in the park."

He looked from me to Lidiya then back to me. "Are you sure? She's demanding when it comes to my attention."

I didn't blame her. He was pretty wonderful. Smiling, I assured him, "I want Lidiya to come. I love her to bits."

"Okay," he stated with a firm nod. And when he went over to his daughter, he beamed, taking her chubby self into his arms, and I knew I had done the right thing.

CHAPTER FIFTEEN

Mina

Lev drove past three parks before he found one he deemed suitable. When I pointed out the first two, he lowered his sunglasses, peered out my window, shook his head, and muttered, "Too crowded."

When he did things like this, I reminded myself that although it seemed strange to me, I didn't know this man—hence the purpose of today. I would sit by and let him do things his way. I had all the time in the world for Lev and his eccentricities.

I helped Lidiya out of the car, took her little hand, and waited for Lev to retrieve the blanket and picnic basket and lead the way. He walked us a short way from the car to a small copse of trees on the outskirt of the greenery. As Lidiya pulled on my hand, I picked her up and hugged her tight, allowing Lev time to stretch out the thick, wooly blanket and set down the basket.

Lidiya squirmed to be released and, reluctantly, I let her go. The moment she escaped my hand, her chubby little legs took her away from us at a surprising speed for one with such tiny feet. A gasp escaped me, and I went to chase after her, but Lev stopped me with a hand on my arm. "She's okay. She never goes far."

He was her father. He knew her better than I did, but still, I worried. "Are you sure?" I asked hesitantly as I kept a keen eye on her. She had found a leaf that was to her liking. I knew this because she stood there enraptured, smiling down at it as if it were a ruby glittering in the sun. She held it delicately in her clumsy hand and turned, running back to us with her hand raised above her head to show us her spoils.

My racing heart slowed. I looked up at Lev, who smiled down at the little girl. "Thank you, Lidi. It's lovely."

She ran off a second time, but I saw that she stopped at the same distance as she had before, as if she consciously knew that going any farther was going *too* far.

A warm hand closed around mine and I spun around. Lev motioned to the blanket. "Sit."

I was about to tell him I didn't need help sitting, but when I realized I was wearing a dress, I decided against it. I didn't want to show Lev my no brand white panties. Not today, anyway.

With his help, I sat as gracefully as possible without showing my undies, and he sat as close to me as he could without actually touching me. It was a gorgeous day, and with the trees acting as shade, it was positively delightful. We both turned our heads to watch Lidi as she played a safe and close distance. Lev opened the picnic basket, started to remove items, and handed them to me.

When Lev told Mirella that we planned to steal away her ward for the afternoon, she insisted on putting together a picnic basket for us rather than having us buy something to eat. I was okay with that. I mean, Mirella had made toast for me on occasion, and she was pretty good at that. I was positive she could make sandwiches with ease. Within ten minutes, we had a relatively full picnic basket, a doll and ball for Lidiya to play with if she got bored, her blankie in case she felt sleepy, and bottles of water to sip on.

As Lev handed me items, I placed them down in front of us. Mirella had done well packing potato chips, zip-locked bags full of sliced apples, strawberries, carrot sticks, spears of cucumber, squares of cheese, and wafer-thin crackers, sandwiches, some of Ada's ridiculous blueberry muffins, and lastly, bite-sized brownie pieces. He took out bottles of water and handed me one. I opened it, sipping slowly, watching him from the corner of my eye.

He removed his jacket, placing it over the basket so it wouldn't touch the ground, then removed his cufflinks and rolled up the sleeves of his shirt to his elbows.

"I have my first question." I smiled to myself. "Do you always wear a suit?"

He inclined his head. "Yes, mostly."

I waited for more of an explanation.

I got nothing.

My eyes narrowed, I motioned with my hands for him to tell me more.

His brows rose. "That's it. There is no more."

I scoffed. "Oh, we are going to have to do better than that. Why do you wear suits all the time? Do you own anything other than business-wear? How about a pair of jeans?"

He looked out at his daughter, who had collected a bunch of leaves, and responded, "I don't know why I wear suits all of the time. It's habit, I suppose. And yes, I own other items of clothing, including a pair of jeans."

Oh my.

What I would give to see that ass in a pair of well-fitting jeans. *Gah*!

"Okay." I was satisfied with those answers. I opened a bag, picked up a piece of cheese, and threw it into my mouth. "Now you ask me a question."

He didn't respond for a long while, and for a moment, I didn't think he would, but then he opened his mouth and spoke, clinically. "Did you love your mother?"

My brow furrowed.

What kind of question is that?

I answered with ease, "Of course I loved my mother. She was the best. Her name was Clara, and I look just like her."

"She was beautiful then," Lev uttered, almost to himself, and I reverted to the old me, turning my head to hide behind my hair.

"She was beautiful, but you know what made her stunning?"

"What?"

I turned to face him. "Her smile." I grinned. "It was contagious. And when she laughed, her whole body shook in one joyous, choreographed movement. It was as if she danced with her laughter. She smiled all the time, even when it was hard to muster, and she laughed a lot too." My throat thickened the more I spoke of her. I finished on a whisper, "She was pure sunshine."

"And then she died." It was so morbid, so morose that I winced.

"And then she died," I confirmed with a nod. "It all happened so quickly. She went to the doctors with stomach pains and bloating, and was misdiagnosed at first. We found out that she had bowel cancer, and it was too late. They told us she had three months." I frowned at the memory. "She barely made it to two."

"I'm sorry."

I shrugged just as Lidiya returned with another handful of leaves to add to the small collection she'd gathered. This time, she sat down, right on my lap, and reached for the bag of apple slices. I opened it for her and handed her a slice, hugging an arm around her belly and resting my cheek on her head. "What about your parents, Lev? You haven't mentioned them."

"They're dead," he stated without emotion.

I turned his question back on him. "Did you love them?"

He picked up a blade of grass, his brow bunching. "I don't understand love," he started. "Love is just a word."

My brows rose in surprise. I could see he loved Lidiya, loved her with all he had inside of him. I could see he loved Nas, and even Sasha in his own way. I did *not* understand how a person surrounded by people who loved him did not understand love. "But you love Lidiya. You love Nas and Sasha."

"Do I?" he questioned. "I would put myself in harms way to see them happy. I would give my life to see them safe. I would. Is that love? Perhaps." His head tilted to the side. "Perhaps it is more."

Lidiya ate, babbling quietly, handing me things she found fascinating, like the lid to my water bottle. I pondered his words in silence, and when I thought I understood, I spoke gently. "You believe in love the verb. Not love the word." His face spun and he looked at me as if he was shocked I understood. I added, "Love, the action. Not love, the watery emotion."

"Yes," he uttered, awestruck.

I could love you, Lev Leokov.

The thought took me by surprise. It both excited and terrified me at the very same time.

I bit the inside of my lip. "I get it."

My focus was drawn to the little girl, eating her weight in apple slices, but I felt his eyes on me.

LEV

Twirling my fingers through Lidiya's sweet curls, I held her close, using her as a too-cute distraction.

Her father's intensity was killing me.

"Before, when you had a home, did you plan on college?" His question surprised me.

"Yeah," I beamed. "I was going to be a photographer. Spend all my money on a camera and take off, snapping pictures of this and that." I grinned. "Selling my photographs for thousands of dollars and being the go-to person when the people at *Vogue* needed inspiration." I chuckled to myself. "That was the dream, anyway."

"What would you take pictures of?"

Lidiya had put her thumb into her mouth, snatched up her blankie, and settled on my chest, resting her head on my shoulder. I kissed her forehead. "I wanted to take edgy photos. Pictures of people and situations that made people do a double-take. I wanted to be rash and reckless, and bring awareness to subjects that were often forgotten." I shrugged, accidentally jolting Lidiya. "Oh, sorry, honey," I whispered. "I wanted to make a difference."

Lidiya, getting sick of my chatter and movement, picked herself up and crawled over to her daddy, who already had his arms open for her. He folded them around her, holding her close, and the moment she tucked her nose into the side of his neck, she closed her eyes and sighed, dozing almost immediately.

I smiled at the pair. But the sight triggered my next question. "Where is Lidiya's mom?" I asked cautiously. "I know she lives with her but no one mentions her."

Without thinking, he answered through a growl, "Lidiya's mother is a poor excuse for a human being, and as soon as the opportunity presents itself, Lidi will live with me permanently."

I was momentarily stunned. It was the most emotion I'd ever seen pulled from him. I couldn't understand what the woman had done to him that he'd hate her so much. I had to ask, "What did she do?"

His lips thinned and his nostrils worked, as if he was having a hard time controlling himself. "Irina thought she could extort money from me by getting pregnant. She'd tampered with condoms, and I never thought to question her. I never had to question a woman before. She taught me how cunning a woman could be." He shook his head. "The look of shock on her face when I told her I wanted the baby was amusing. After that, she demanded money to not terminate the pregnancy." He kissed a sleeping Lidiya's head. "She never wanted Lidiya. She despises her. Mirella isn't just Lidiya's nanny." He sent me a fierce look. "She's her bodyguard."

"Oh, my God," I whispered, my face pale. "Does she hurt her?"

"No, she wouldn't dare. Not with Mirella around." He readjusted the little girl, holding her close. "It's the reason I hired her. Mirella is a retired Marine. I explained our need for someone who could act under pressure. She doesn't let Lidiya out of her sight. Not ever."

My shoulders slumped in relief. "I hope I never meet this woman. I would love to give her a piece of my mind."

"You'll have to get in line," he uttered, and confusion swept through me, because it sounded as if he made a joke.

He *never* joked.

I worked on unwrapping a sandwich and handed half to him. He took it without a word and we ate in silence a while before I thought of another question. "I hope this doesn't sound rude, but I've been wondering." I smiled through a grimace, knowing it would sound rude. "What exactly do you do at the club?"

His eyes locked onto mine, and they smiled. "At night, I keep an eye on the patrons. Look out for trouble. Make sure people are having a good time. During the day, I look after the books, transactions and such."

"Bookkeeper." I snorted lightly. "Who would've thought? When I think about bookkeeper, I see a balding middle-aged man with a bulging midsection, not someone like you."

"Like me?" he asked, his puzzlement evident.

I rolled my eyes at his attempt at modesty. "Come on, Lev. You must know you're gorgeous. If your eyes couldn't hypnotize women, the rest of you would for sure."

His brows rose. "You think I'm handsome?"

LEV

I would've decked him if it weren't for the sweet little girl currently using him as a mattress. Instead, I picked up my bottle of water and sipped, keeping my eye on him. He seemed sincere in his disbelief that I would find him attractive.

Life had this way of sneaking up on you. You'd just be sitting there, lost in a moment, when all of a sudden, a cold feeling swept across your belly and you asked yourself if you ever lived a day in your life.

Being alive was easy. Living, on the other hand…well, that was a little harder. Courage rose from deep within me, and my heart pounded. I didn't have a thing to lose, so I went for it. "You're the most handsome man I've ever seen, Lev. Hands down."

He blinked at me for a long moment, and then turned his head, looking out into the open greenery. His face was stuck on a frown. Then he muttered, "Okay."

It came out in a way that nearly sounded as if he was reassuring himself, and it hurt my heart. I waited a while, but it seemed he was done questioning me. I took advantage. "Tell me about your family."

He took in a long breath and started to speak as he exhaled. "Sasha is an asshole. That's all he wants people to know about him. He was twenty-one when my father died, and took over raising us. He lost much of his youth so suddenly that I don't think he ever recovered from the loss. My mother ran off when I was eight. We never saw her again. That hit Nastasia relatively hard. She was Mom's favorite." A dull throb worked in my chest. I ached for this family. "Nastasia may come off as rough, but she is one of the most generous people I know. When she loves, she loves so much it hurts. And I'm grateful for that."

I smiled at hearing him speak about his sister. "Why doesn't she have a boyfriend?"

"Like I said, she loves so much it hurts. And Nastasia has loved Viktor from the time we were children."

I sat up at that point, mouth gaping. "*What*? *Vik* Viktor? *That* Viktor?"

"The very one." He was enjoying my astonishment. I could tell.

I was stunned by this information. I sputtered, "But they don't even like each other!"

"On the contrary," Lev revealed. "Viktor loves Nastasia very much. In fact, he spends every night in her bed."

I wheezed out in disbelief. "No *way!*"

He shrugged, his eyes alight with mirth. "She thinks no one knows, but often, when I can't sleep, I walk around the complex and his car is parked in front of her house. Every single night."

Oh, my God. That was who she was with the night before. The *god* who kept her awake with his tongue skills was Vik. But then...

"But Nas makes out like he's a womanizer." I was baffled.

Lev nodded. "He is."

My head was starting to hurt. "I don't understand. Why would she put up with that? I wouldn't. He'd be out on his ass."

"Love," he advised gently, "is a doing word. And sometimes the people who least deserve it are the ones who need it most."

He was right, of course. This conversation we were having was easy. Almost *too* easy. I was coming to recognize that Lev Leokov was an open book. I only needed to discover the language in which his pages were written.

CHAPTER SIXTEEN

Mina

The impromptu picnic Lev and I had been on came to an end soon after Lidiya had fallen asleep. The poor thing started to sweat in the mild heat, so we took her home to finish her nap in the comfort of her own bed.

I left Lev to do whatever it was he did in the afternoons, and went upstairs to shower and change for work. I decided on comfort over class and wore a plain black tee over my blue jeans, finishing off with the black pumps that were clearly going to be the death of me—that is, if I couldn't learn to walk in them.

It was like walking on stilts, for crying out loud!

I zhuzhed my long, wavy hair, taking it into my hands and scrunching it as I lightly sprayed it with hairspray, and then I washed my face and reapplied my makeup, thickening the eyeliner a little for that dramatic cat's eye effect. I lightly glossed with something that was pink and smelled of cake, and the scent was so delicious that I wanted to eat it.

Don't worry. I didn't. Licking your lips didn't count.

My feet bare, I took the stairs two at a time, being as quiet as I could as I made my way to the kitchen. I was hungry and remembered there being leftover brownie bites from our lunch. I opened the fridge, held onto the door, and peered inside, leaning in to get a closer look.

The brownies had disappeared.

Hmmm.

I looked harder.

So had the apple slices, the cheese, and Ada's muffins.

My brow bunched. I wasn't going crazy. I know I put them in there when we got back to the house. I even hid the brownies behind the juice so no one would touch them.

I checked again, looking deeper into the fridge than was necessary.

Nope. They were gone.

The fruit bowl sat on the kitchen counter, and although it had ripe bananas, shiny apples, and bright green pears in it, I wanted those damn brownies. So I started to search for them.

While I was downstairs, I went to check on Lidiya, and smiled when I saw Mirella sitting on the chair by her bed, reading. She spotted me and lifted her hand in a wave. I returned it, my eyes sweeping over the little princess sleeping soundly in her toddler bed.

That only left one place.

I made my way back up the stairs, but turned right and walked the length of the hall toward Lev's office. He told me he went up there to work, but I had the sneaking suspicion he might also have another reason to go up there.

The door was open a crack, less than an inch, and I peeked inside.

I knew it!

I swung open the door and uttered a victorious, "Gotcha."

Lev paused, a brownie bite halfway to his mouth.

My feet carried me over to his desk, where his laptop sat open. I took the brownie out of his hand, threw it into my mouth, groaned with pleasure as the bitter sweetness hit my tongue, and then straightened and garbled, "Oh, I'm sorry. Were you going to eat that strategically hidden brownie?"

His lips thinned and he glared at me. "Yes, I was."

I had to cover my mouth and laugh by how put out he sounded. "I'm sorry. I know better than to take food from someone. On the streets, that kind of thing could get a person killed."

His expression grew somber at the mention of my time without a home. "It's okay."

Without waiting for an invitation, mostly because I didn't think I'd get one, I pulled out the guest chair and sat opposite him. I know it had only been a few days since I asked him, but I wanted to know if any progress had been made. "Any luck finding the Petersons yet?"

His jaw set, he pulled his laptop close and began typing. "No."

I nodded slowly. "Okay."

Suddenly, he shut the lid of the laptop and asked, "Why do you want to find them? Nastasia told me what they did, that they're the reason you were homeless." He paused. "They aren't good people, Mina."

Well, someone was a little judgey today. "You don't even know them, Lev. They took me in when I was twelve years old, hating on the world, and they gave me a home." I stressed, "One mistake doesn't undo all the good they did. And, by the way, they didn't force me into the street. I did that on my own."

He leaned over the desk, his golden eyes hard. "Because they made you feel unsafe."

True enough, but I wasn't about to admit that. I shrugged, feeling helpless. "If you don't want to help me find them, that's fine. I'll find someone else to help." I stood, turning toward the door.

His voice had me stopping mid-step. "I can't control the report, Mina. It might not be all good news. Do you understand that?"

Holding the doorframe, I kept my back to him and reiterated, "I just want them to know I'm okay."

I didn't listen for a response. My feet took me back to our room, where I spent the remainder of the afternoon lying on my back in the giant bed I had fallen in love with.

⚓

Mina

The night started off well. Learning that my shift behind the bar would be shared with the tall, African-American beauty with the crazy-beautiful afro, Birdie, rather than Anika, made me mentally cheer and do cartwheels.

I didn't mind Anika, but we didn't have a common interest…apart from Lev, of course. And I had a feeling we wouldn't be seeing eye-to-eye on that matter.

Men flocked to the bar to be served, and although it was busy, Birdie and I kept it under control. During the night, I'd seen Birdie clink shot glasses with men and down them. She'd done this multiple times, and I wondered how she wasn't stumbling over her feet. The girl could hold her drinks.

So when a group of men bought a round of shots and added an extra for me, I looked to Birdie. She smiled and nodded. So I went for it.

I picked up the glass, lifted it to my mouth, and tipped it back, listening to the men hoot and cheer as I sputtered and coughed.

Holy shit, that burned.

Coughing up a lung, I raised my hands and grimaced through a smile, showing them all I was okay. They shouted and applauded some more and, thankfully, stayed close to my side of the bar.

I knew the tips would be off the charts tonight. The men had money to burn, and with every round, I was left a nice, neat sum for myself.

My body started to feel warm all over and my head spun lightly. And this was only after the first shot.

After the fifth, I could barely stand without swaying from side-to-side.

The sixth shot had done it.

Laughing to myself, I held onto the bar, because the ground was spinning in circles. It was sucking me in.

I should tell Lev about that. That's an occupational health and safety issue, if I ever saw one.

Birdie was by my side before I knew I was lying on the floor behind the bar. "Mina, baby, what's wrong?"

I laughed out loud. "Oh, God, Birdie. The floor won't stop moving. Make it stop. My stomach hurts."

"Shit," Birdie uttered as she moved away from me.

A minute, or it could've been an hour later, she returned with Nas who knelt by my side, taking my arm and helping me stand. She took me out the door behind the bar and into the backroom. She helped me sit and sighed, "Jesus, Mina, what the fuck? You're not supposed to drink when you're on shift. You're in a ton of trouble if Sasha finds out."

What?

I blinked away the rogue white lights attacking my vision. "But, I saw Birdie do shots. When I looked at her for the go-ahead, she nodded. I thought it was okay."

"Wait, what?" Then she chuckled. "Oh, my God." Her laughter intensified. "Please tell me that Anika told you about the marked bottles we keep behind the bar?"

At that point, Anika strolled into the backroom. "Hey, is Mina okay? I thought I saw her faint."

Nas stood, holding down her laughter. "Did you tell Mina about our special blend?"

Anika frowned. "No, I thought you did when you brought her for your lesson."

Nastasia couldn't hold it in. She tipped her head back and burst into laughter.

While I burst into tears. "Am I fired?"

Anika spoke quietly to herself. "Oh, God, she didn't know." Then she covered her mouth with her hand and giggled. "She didn't know!"

They laughed loudly, whooping and doubling over. And there I was, howling as tears trailed down my cheeks. "*Am I fired?*"

"No," Nas uttered through a chuckle. "No, Mina. It was my mistake. I'll take the rap for it. You're not fired, I promise."

I didn't believe her. I threw my head back and wailed, "But Sasha won't care." I took in a deep stuttering breath and blurted out, "Because he's an asshole!"

From behind me came a calm, "Please, Mina. Don't hold back. Tell me how you really feel."

I turned to see Sasha scowling at me from the door and did the only thing I could do. I threw my drunken ass on the ground and cried some more.

Nastasia snorted. "I forgot to tell her about the special blend. This one's on me."

Sasha shook his head. "This is bad for business. She needs to go."

Nas' face turned dramatically. She sneered at her brother. "For one mistake? One that wasn't even her fault?"

"It's not my problem, Nas," he muttered, and I cried louder.

"Oh, God," Sitting up, I panted. "Please don't fire me. I'll do anything. *Please*."

Anika spoke then, and I was stunned by her support. "Sash. Don't do this. She needs this job." She paused a moment before she murmured, "Have a heart."

Sasha stared at Anika a long while before he turned to walk out. "This is the first and only chance she gets. No more. Next time, she's gone."

My blotchy face turned upward to land on Anika. I blinked a second before I whispered, "Thank you."

To my further surprise, she helped me off the ground and sat me down on the leather sofa. Nas brought me a glass of water and a couple of aspirin. "We've still got a full night ahead of us. You may as well lay down and sleep it off, boozerella."

My head was whirling, and I didn't need to be told a second time. I lay my head down just as my stomach gave a sharp pinch of disapproval at my night's choice of drinks. I groaned, "I am never drinking again."

"That's what they all say," she muttered as they both moved toward the door, turning the light off and leaving me to sleep off the night that never should have happened.

⚓

LEV

It didn't take long for me to notice that Mina was no longer working the bar. Nas had taken over for her.

I waited. And waited. And the longer I did, a cold feeling passed along my spine.

An irrational protectiveness passed through me.

Standing, I strode across the floor, moving around tables and patrons to get to the bar. Nas saw me just as I leaned over the bar. I hadn't meant to, but I growled, "Where is she?"

She put her hands up in a placating gesture. "Don't you go off on her too. It wasn't her fault, okay? I forgot to tell her about the house blend." She sniffed a laugh. "She's had a couple of aspirin and is sleeping off the liquor."

It had been close to half an hour since I noticed her missing. My eyes immediately went to the side of the stage.

"*Shit*," I barked. Eyeing Nas, I asked accusingly, "How long has Jeremiah been away from his station?"

Her face paled.

I shook my head in disappointment, moved behind the bar, through the door, and made my way down the long hall, finding myself behind the closed door to the backroom. Lifting my hand, I tried to turn the knob, but felt resistance.

"Open the door," I sneered.

"Occupied," he called back in annoyance.

My chest began to heave. I breathed heavily through my nostrils, my anger burning, bubbling like a river of molten lava in my gut. "Open the door," I uttered through gritted teeth.

"Fuck! *Piss off*!" Jeremiah called back.

That's when it happened.

Everything shut down. My pulse slowed. The lights dimmed around me. The sounds turned dull in my ears until there was nothing.

The silence took over.

I had always feared it would arise again. I controlled it so well. It hadn't struck me in years. Not like this.

But I wasn't scared this time. I embraced it and let it empower me.

My hands balled into fists, and I took a single step back before rushing the door with my shoulder.

I felt it crack under my weight, but it did not break.

My legs walked me back and I threw my shoulder at the door again.

Another whining creak, and the wood prepared to give way under the slightest amount of pressure.

Nas yelled from behind me. "Lev, what are you doing?"

Jeremiah called out in disbelief, "You're fucking crazy!"

I pulled back, lifted my leg, and kicked as hard as I could.

The door came apart from its lock and flung inwards. My eyes swept the room and I found him standing by the leather sofa, tucking his tee into his pants.

I saw red.

Nothing could have stopped me from getting to him then.

Nothing.

Mina groaned quietly and squirmed weakly on the couch, passed out, and Nas ran to kneel by her side.

"What did you do?" I asked the startled man, gripping his shirt in my hand.

Jeremiah stood his ground. "Nothing," he said behind his beard. "We didn't do anything."

"Lev," Nas spoke quietly. I turned to her, watching her run her fingers over the side of Mina's neck. "She's got a hickey."

Just as I reared my arm back to beat the life out of Jeremiah, arms came across my stomach and my chest. I turned to glower at the person, but found Viktor standing there, looking me in the eye. "Calm down, bro. It's okay."

My heart pounded. I needed relief from the rage. Without relief, it would only get worse, and then I would hurt someone I cared about.

Like last time.

"It's not okay," I panted. "It's *not* okay."

Sasha appeared by my side. "It'll be okay, Lev. I got you. We'll take care of this." Then he spoke to someone behind him. "Shut it down. Party's over. Get everyone out."

Anika frowned as she leaned over Mina. "This doesn't make sense. She wasn't this bad before." She looked up at Viktor. "I think he might have slipped her something."

A loud growl escaped me. I stepped back from the man, knowing full well I would kill him if I got my hands on him. My fisted hands came up to my head and slammed into my forehead.

Sasha took my hands, lowering them, stopping me from hurting myself.

Seeing red, my nostrils flared as I tried to get my breathing under control. Jeremiah didn't look so confident now. He looked terrified.

I was glad. He should be.

Sasha cussed under his breath. "Nas, take Mina back to Lev's. Call Pox; get him there to look her over." He turned to Jeremiah, but spoke calmly. "What did you give her?"

"Nothing," he said defensively. "She's drunk."

Sasha left my side and walked over to the sofa. He lifted Mina's hand high and dropped it. She didn't move an inch. He placed a gentle hand on her brow and frowned before moving toward Jeremiah. "I'm going to ask you one last time, J. What did you give her?" He opened his mouth to answer, but Sasha cut in, "I have a medic on standby. He can take care of her in a discreet way. If we take her to the hospital—and we could—and they find something inside of her that shouldn't be there, you're going to jail for assault at the very least. Even worse if they charge you with drink spiking. If you tell me what you gave her, you'll leave here a free man…after you've had your ass handed to you, of course." He eyed Jeremiah. "A pretty boy like you in jail…" He titled his head. "You'd be mighty popular."

Jeremiah flushed; his pupils were dilated. He was high. He was sweating. "*GHB.*" He swallowed hard. "I gave her *GHB.*"

Vik's arms loosened on me. I could hear the growl coming from low in his throat. Sasha sneered at him, his eyes low in disgust. "Nas, get her home. Ani, she'll need your help."

Blood roared through my ears as I bit out, "He's not to remove her clothing, Nas."

It was a warning and knowing Pox, he wouldn't dare go against me.

The women helped Mina up with ease, due to the fact that she was so tiny. I watched helplessly as her head lolled to the side, her eyes partially open but clearly not seeing a thing. A sheen of sweat had beaded across her forehead, and she had a large hickey on the side of her neck.

My blood boiled.

This man thought he had the right to touch my mouse?

No one had the right to touch *my* mouse.

I found her, and I was keeping her.

The thought stunned me. I didn't know it until this very moment, until I thought she was in real danger.

I wanted Mina.

I wanted her more than anything, but she was so fragile right now. I would wait until the time was right.

She would be mine.

I would show her that life with me could be good. I would make her see past the damaged part of me to the little good I had inside. I couldn't give her romance, or offer her marriage. I couldn't give her more than I had to give. But I would provide for her, give her whatever she needed. She would laugh and smile like the mother she loved, and she would be happy with me. I vowed it right there and then.

The three of us alone with Jeremiah, I flexed my hands, cracking my knuckles.

Vik pulled something out of his pocket and handed it to me. "Have fun, you two."

He motioned to Sasha and, reluctantly, he followed behind Viktor, leaving Jeremiah's fate in my hands.

Jeremiah looked up at me from his place against the wall, his eyes wide. "I'm sorry."

"No, you're not," I responded as I slipped the brass knuckle-dusters over the fingers of my right hand. "When I'm done with you, you will be."

It took a solid hour to relieve myself of the fury. With every yelp and groan pulled from the disgusting excuse of a man, my rage ebbed.

As my calm was unearthed, Jeremiah found fear.

And with every punch, kick, and head-butt, Jeremiah discovered what sorry felt like.

CHAPTER SEVENTEEN

LEV

I drove home without feeling my hands. Overexertion did that sometimes. I was numb, and as I pulled up to my house, I looked out from my car window, unsure of whether or not I wanted to enter my own home.

I was anxious. I didn't like that.

Licking my dry lips, I stepped out of my car and made my way up to the front door. I opened it, listening out for any signs of life.

I heard nothing.

My heart skipped a beat.

The lights were turned off. The only room that had illumination was the kitchen. I headed straight for it, and found Nas sitting at the kitchen table, a mug of coffee in her hands. She sat there, eyes closed, a frown etched on her pretty face, obviously not hearing my entrance. I cleared my throat.

Her eyes snapped open and she spun around.

She smiled sadly. "How did it go? Is he still alive?"

I sighed, flexing my sore fingers. "Alive enough to feel my hands on him for a long time to come."

Her brows rose. "You stopped?" She huffed out a breath. "I didn't think you'd be able to."

"I almost didn't," I confessed quietly.

Her brow furrowed. "Why did you?"

"Mina."

My sisters brow softened, a warm look taking over. "She's something, huh?"

"She's a disaster," I told her. "Trouble follows her everywhere. She corners me when I don't wish to speak. She smiles and laughs at things that aren't funny. She steals food right out of my hand." I shook my head. "All of which makes her perfect."

Nastasia looked as if she wanted to cry. I cleared my throat and asked, "Is Pox still here?"

She blinked rapidly, swallowing hard. "Uh, no. He says it looks like Jeremiah didn't use much of whatever he gave her, probably because she was so drunk. He said she'd sleep through the night and maybe some of tomorrow. You'll need to wake up every hour and check on her." She lowered her eyes. "Make sure she's breathing."

"What?" I didn't think it would be that serious.

Nas shrugged and cleared her throat, her voice cracking. "Pox wasn't sure if Jeremiah gave her what he said he did. Without knowing exactly what he gave her, it's hard to tell what the side effects could be. Because she's so tiny, you know? We're lucky that all she's got are hickeys." Her face crumbled and she dipped her chin to hide her tears. "It's my fault," she whispered, and her shoulders shook. "I should've been keeping an eye on her."

It had been years since I saw my sister cry, and it hurt to watch as much today as it had back then.

I made my way over to her, grabbed her by the upper arm, and pulled her out of her chair. She didn't need coaxing. She fell into me, pushing her head into my chest and sobbing quietly. I wrapped an arm around her shoulders and used the other to stroke her hair. "It's okay."

She shook her head.

I kissed her head. "She'll be okay. She's survived for so long without us. Mina is strong."

Nas nodded in agreement then lifted her tear-streaked face and muttered, "I just feel responsible."

"No," I uttered, and squeezed her to reiterate my point. "You didn't do this. This was not your fault."

She rolled her eyes but smiled. "Don't lie to me, Lev."

"I don't lie," I vowed.

She nodded and responded quietly, "I know." We separated and she picked up her bag. "She's sleeping on the sofa in the living room." When I raised a brow, she gave me a look of boldness. "Hey, I'm strong and all, but not strong enough to lug her up those stairs without breaking both our necks."

I raised my hands and gave her a look that said *I didn't say a word*.

I walked her out, hugged her once more, and closed the door behind her. I made my way into the living room, stopping to turn on the hall light so I could see what I was doing. I stood in front of the sofa, looking down at the small woman.

Even in her unconscious state, she was beautiful.

Leaning down, I scooped her up without effort, and walked us both up the stairs, down the hall, and into my room. I switched the light on and stilled.

Anika was sitting on the edge of my bed, waiting for me.

She looked up at me then down at Mina. Her brow furrowed in confusion. She looked around the room, blinking, and started to notice Mina's things around the place. She stood. "I don't get it," she began.

"What don't you get, Ani?"

"She can stay in your room, a person you've known for a whole second, and me, a person you've known your whole life, is sent to sleep in the guestroom?" She sounded hurt.

I shifted Mina in my arms then moved around Anika to pull back the covers on the other side of the bed and laid her down gently. "I need to keep an eye on her," is all I said.

I didn't hear Anika leave. I was busy fussing over Mina, removing her clothes, leaving her in her top and underwear. I pulled the covers up to her chin. Her forehead was warm to the touch, but she was shivering.

Making my way over to the door, I locked it from the inside, jiggling the handle to make sure no one would enter, and then turned off the light. When I was satisfied, I took off my clothes, pulled out the sofa, and lay down, a sheet draped over me.

In the darkness, I heard her teeth chatter.

My jaw steeled.

It wasn't a good idea. I shouldn't have done it. But I did.

Pulling the sheet off, I walked over to the bed, pulled back the covers, and lay down, reaching for Mina. Once her small frame was in my arms, I pulled her close, holding her tight. Perhaps too tightly. But soon enough, her teeth stopped chattering and she settled into me, burying her nose into the crook between my neck and shoulder.

She slept in that position all night.

I slept too. Better than I had in years.

⚓

Mina

Oh, God.

My head was pounding like a mofo.

Hell in a hand basket.

Every time I moved to lift it off the pillow, curse words ensued.

Never again. Never *again.*

But then the pillow moved and flexed right underneath my head. Forcing my eyes open, I peeped out, blinking away sleep, a frown on my face, and met warm whiskey eyes.

I tried to speak, but all that came out was a long groan.

Arms tightened around me and pulled me close. I went willingly. My body was sore all over, and I suddenly had my very own hot water bottle in the shape of Lev.

Who was I to complain?

"How are you feeling?" he grumbled sleepily.

My nose in his throat, I muttered, "I'm never drinking again. I have a hangover."

"You probably do, but it's more than that, Mina," he explained gently. "We need to talk about what happened last night."

I pushed my nose deeper into him. "Will this explain why we're in bed together?"

"Yes."

I nodded slowly. "Okay. Talk. But do it softly."

His strong arm cinched around me, holding me tight, and I didn't want to think about how nice that felt. I should've been too distracted by my headache to notice. The other arm slid from my hip, slowly trailed my back, up to the base of my neck, where he cradled me.

"The club was busy. I took my eyes off you a while then noticed I hadn't seen you for a long time. I went to the bar, where Nas told me you'd been drinking and were sleeping it off." The hand at my neck grasped me lightly, as if he was worried about my reaction, worried about me fleeing. "That was when I also realized I hadn't seen Jeremiah for a long while."

I blinked.

Jeremiah? What did this have to do with him?

He turned his face and his lips went to my temple. "He drugged you, Mina." He added, "I'm sorry. I should've been watching you."

I pulled back to look up at him and whispered, "What did he do?"

Lev searched my face. "Nothing, I think. Nas noticed the hickey on your neck right away, but I'm sure we interrupted before he could do any real damage. Now that you're awake, maybe you can tell me if you're sore."

"I'm sore everywhere. My body aches."

He shook his head. "No, Mina. Can you tell me if you're sore anywhere you shouldn't be?" He gave me a pointed look. "Intimate areas."

I was too shocked to blush. I was still stuck on Jeremiah's attempt to use me as a real life sex doll.

Focusing on the area he'd mentioned, I shook my head. "No, I don't think so." Then I got angry. "Where is the asshole? Where is Jeremiah?"

He lifted his hand and brushed back the hair that had fallen over my forehead. "He's not going to hurt anyone anymore. Trust me."

I did trust him. I trusted him with every piece of my broken soul.

If there were anyone looking out for me, I'd want it to be Lev. I trusted him to protect me and keep me safe, and to be honest with me.

Then I looked down between us, and my brows rose. "Who undressed me?"

No hesitation. "I did."

"I see," I murmured, and quickly realized that perhaps I'd been hanging out with Lev too long when I gave answers like that. My eyes passed over his tented boxers and my brow rose higher. "Want to explain that?"

He frowned and squirmed. "I thought it was self-explanatory." Then I did flush. "You were pressed up against me all night. I was told to check on you every hour and I did. I only did what the doctor ordered."

My ego shrank ten whole sizes. "So you were only doing your duty."

His brow furrowed, and he sent me a curt nod. And the remainder of my ego popped like a balloon and went whizzing through the air before it flew out the window.

Then he sighed as if he needed to get something off his chest. "It's difficult to hold a beautiful woman all night and not be affected. I'm sorry if that offends you, but I don't always have control of my body and its reactions."

My ego flew backwards through the window and whizzed around the air before it came back to me, inflating six more sizes.

It was time to say something, preferably something clever. "I need to pee."

Lev seemed frustrated. "Mina, I just told you that you were assaulted by a man who probably would've raped you, and you have yet to react."

LEV

I looked Lev in the eye and told him honestly, "It wouldn't be the first time." I didn't wait for his reaction. I slipped out of bed, held my pounding head, and shuffled to the bathroom, closing the door behind me, making an effort to lock it as loudly as possible.

⚓

The tears got to me in the shower. It seemed like an appropriate place to let them fall.

Sure, I acted like it didn't bother me, but when I undressed and saw the hickeys covering my breasts, my pride fell fast and it hit me how serious the situation could have been.

I lifted my hands to run them over the deep red marks and hissed as my fingers brushed my tender nipples. His mouth had been there, and it had been harsh. I didn't like that. And what was worse was that I couldn't remember any of it.

It wasn't a blur. It wasn't a fuzzy memory. It just wasn't *there*. And that didn't feel good. It was confusing, and appalling, and it made me feel dirty, regardless of whether or not I was a willing participant.

I showered in silence and reasoned with myself. No one would see the other hickeys. I would enlist Nas to help me cover the one on my neck as best as we could. It would all be forgotten soon enough, an incident I would push aside and soldier on past. Just as I did with the other bad things in my life.

When I was done, I dressed in my yellow pajamas, as I intended on going back to bed, and walked back out into the bedroom. The curtains had been drawn open, sending sunlight flooding in. My eyes burned, but I was too busy focusing on the furious man, pacing by the bed.

I took a step closer. "Lev?"

He continued to pace.

Another single step closer. "Lev? What's wrong?"

He turned to face me, his eyes blazing. "Who hurt you?"

My brow bunched and I shrugged lightly, indicating that I didn't know what he was talking about.

He paraphrased, "'It wouldn't be the first time.'" His bare stomach clenched as he gritted his teeth and growled, "Who hurt you? Tell me. Tell me and I'll kill them."

Was it wrong to be turned on by this scene?

Something told me it was highly inappropriate. Somehow, that didn't stop the flow of warmth sailing through me, or the feeling akin to winning something big, like the lottery.

And Lev was a fine lottery to be won.

But then I looked closer, and that feeling receded. He was distressed. He also looked as though he didn't know how to deal with that. I could feel the anger and frustration pulsing off him.

Knowing that anger wasn't directed at me had me by his side in a second flat. I took his hand and led him to the sofa, sitting and pulling him down next to me. I placed his hand in my lap and covered it with mine. "I was on the street for a long time, Lev." I tilted my head and gave him a regretful look. "Shit happens."

"No," he uttered, shaking his head. "No, it doesn't. People cause those things to happen, and they need to be punished. They need to suffer the consequences." He declared, "There is always a price to pay."

"You want to search the streets to find a group of young thugs who tried to force sex on me *years* ago? Does that sound like a normal thing to do?"

Lev lowered his head and revealed, "I'm not normal."

I wasn't about to lie to him. "No, you're not." Then I admitted quietly, "But sometimes I think you're better than the normal person. Extraordinary. Unique. Elite. Gallant." He didn't look up at me. I didn't like when he tried to hide from me. I squeezed his hand. "Hey. They didn't succeed, you know. That knife you took from me when I first got here...it did its job."

When I ran my thumb over his fingers, he winced. My brow drew taut as I lifted his hand to examine it.

My heart stopped.

The middle finger on his left hand was swollen, purple, and very obviously bent in a direction that it shouldn't have been going in. "Lev, sweetie," I spoke calmly. "I think your finger is broken."

He nodded as if that wasn't news to him. "It'll be fine."

"Jeremiah?" I asked.

He grunted affirmatively.

I sighed. "I suppose you're going to tell me that it doesn't hurt."

"No." He shook his head lightly. "It hurts very much." He turned to me, looking me in the eye. "But the reason behind it was worth every ache."

I am falling in love with you, Lev Leokov.

This time, the sudden thought didn't surprise me. I think I'd known it a while now.

CHAPTER EIGHTEEN

Mina

Another week went by, and as I was forced to take a week off work (doctors orders), I spent every waking moment with Mirella and Lidiya, learning as much as I could about the little girl's likes and dislikes.

Turns out, Lidiya loved only one of her dolls. She was extremely attached to the Cabbage Patch Kid named Ivy Gail.

I didn't know this. I thought she liked Cabbage Patch Kids in every way, shape, or form. So, early in the week, when Nas and I went to the mall, I bought Lidiya a new Cabbage Patch Kid, called

Annabel Cherish, with some of my tip money. I got this one, because it looked a bit like the chubby little cherub. I also bought a tiny doll stroller so Lidi could walk her new friend around.

When we brought it home, I showed it to Mirella who, through a grimace, told me that although it was very sweet of me, Lidiya would likely not take to it and that she was very particular.

I was slightly devastated. And I moped.

Why would she not like my doll? I bought it just for her. She should like my damn doll! I spent fifty dollars on this freaking doll and stupid stroller.

But when Lidiya woke from her nap, I handed her the doll, and sulked all the way upstairs without waiting to see her negative reaction. I threw myself under the covers and was rudely interrupted from my pouting when Mirella called for me.

Flipping the covers down off my face, I called out, "Yes?"

I could hear her smiling. "Lidiya is asking for you."

My feet shuffled the entire way down, but when I entered the living room, my attitude changed.

Lidiya sat in the middle of the floor with Annabel Cherish, hugging her to her side and muttering, "Eena, pay. Mine." Then she spotted me and smiled. "*Eena*. Lookit."

She stood and rushed over to me on her little legs, showing me her new dolly. I beamed, "You like it?" She thrust the doll at me and I gave it a little squeeze. "Her name is Annabel Cherish."

Lidiya took the doll, hugging it around the neck. "Eena."

I shook my head. "No, angel pie," I corrected. "Annabel."

"Eena," she muttered as she walked the doll over to meet her kin, Ivy Gail.

Mirella chuckled. "I don't believe it. She's had other Cabbage Patch dolls. She never took to them. Only to Ivy."

I smiled at the woman. "Now she has Annabel."

Mirella shook her head lightly. "No," she observed. "Now she has *Mina*."

And that was how little Mina came to be.

Lev would come down on occasion and thoughtlessly interrupt *my* time with *his* daughter, often times sneaking in lunch or snacks with us.

A nice man with a pockmarked face and glasses who the guys called Pox came down every day that week to check on me. When I asked if he was a doctor, everyone seemed to avoid the question.

He told me it didn't look as if there would be any lasting effects from being drugged. I was glad to hear it, not that I was worried. I took Lev by the uninjured hand and sat him down, forcing Pox to look at his finger. Lev tried to argue, but I wasn't hearing it.

Everyone seemed stunned that Lev was allowing the man to look over him, including Sasha. But he sat in silence with my hand on his shoulder and let the doc splint and buddy tape his fingers, leaving me satisfied.

I asked for a moment of privacy with the doctor and, reluctantly, Lev watched me walk him to his car. As soon as we were out of hearing distance, I cleared my throat. "I want to thank you for checking me over that night."

He smiled lightly. "You're welcome. But I have a feeling you didn't call me out here to thank me."

"No." I chuckled nervously. "I guess I didn't."

He spotted my discomfort and tried to soothe it. "Mina, whatever you tell me will be kept in confidence. Lev could beat the shit out of me and I'd never tell."

I chuckled for real then. "Sounds like something he'd do."

His smile fell. "Mina, when Jeremiah..." He cut himself off and spoke quietly, "Did he hurt you?"

"No!" I gasped, placing a hand to my chest. "Not in that way, no. But that's sort of what this is about actually." I scratched at my arm, embarrassed. "I haven't had my period in months."

He leaned back against his car. "Any possibility that you could be pregnant?"

"No," I muttered. "But what if Jeremiah *did* hurt me? Could I have gotten pregnant?"

Pox made a *hmmm* sound. "Well, I'm guessing you stopped menstruating, because you were emaciated quite a while. But sometimes, on the rare occasion, women who haven't been spotting at all can get pregnant, so although I'm not inclined to give a definite yes, I wouldn't give a definite no either."

It was enough beating around the bush. "I'm not on birth control."

"Ah." He smiled. "That's what this is about." He stood. "There are a handful of options. However, if you're a little scatterbrained or work nights at a gentleman's club and would forget to take the pill," he winked at me, "I'd recommend an implant. There's one—a small bar—that's injected into the arm after it's been numbed, and it's good for around three years. It's extremely popular amongst young women." At my hopeful look, he shook his head. "I would not recommend getting that until you've had a chance to gain some more weight."

I immediately argued, "I've already gained ten pounds!"

Well, almost. Nine-point-three pounds, to be precise.

He smiled kindly. "I'd like to see you add another ten to that." At my glare, he caved, "Six more, at the very least."

He handed me his card and told me to call when I was ready. I took the business card eagerly, stuffing it into my bra.

⚓

Later that week, I was undressing for the shower when Lev walked in on me.

At the look of shock on his face, I doubted it was deliberate. I didn't judge the slack look on his face. I was shocked too. Being caught in nothing more than your plain white panties did that to you.

I opened my mouth to yell, "Get out!" but only a squeak came forth. When his cool brown eyes roamed my body, I lifted my arms to cover my bare breasts, having momentarily forgotten about the dark red hickeys all over them.

I was embarrassed. My cheeks flamed. My boobs were tiny. I looked like a young boy, rather than a young woman.

I would never—*not ever*—be one of those women who were comfortable in their bodies. I always had self-confidence issues. They had not improved with age.

He spoke then, and it was deathly quiet. "He *did* hurt you." It sounded like an accusation. Aimed at me.

Reached for the towel, I draped it over myself. "It's nothing." I didn't sound convincing.

He reached up with both hands, closed his eyes, and ran his hands over his face, slipping back up to massage his temples.

He looked ready to lose it.

"I'll kill him," he muttered. Then he threw his hands down, punched the door with his good hand, and snarled, "*I'll fucking kill him!*"

"Lev," I whispered fearfully. When he stormed out of the bathroom, holding the towel up, I took chase. "*Lev!*" My legs shook at the fear I'd felt then, but I made it down the upstairs hall and caught up with him. I stood in his way. "Lev, stop!"

He tried to move around me, but I held out the hand that wasn't holding the towel. "Please, stop it." He growled aloud and I shrank back, my quiet voice shaking as hard as my hand. "Lev, you're scaring me."

That seemed to hit home. His eyes regained focus and, panting, he looked down at my wide eyes and trembling body. His fists loosened and his face became pained. "I'm sorry."

He was back.

My Lev was back.

My heart raced and I rushed over to him, wrapping my arm around his middle, placing my head on his heaving chest. I squeezed my eyes shut and hugged him tight. "I don't need you to beat up every person who does something shitty to me, Lev." My hand, behind his back, gripped his shirt, pulling him even closer. "I just need you to be Lev, okay?" I spoke into his chest, "When people do shitty things to me, that helps." I looked up at him, my eyes shining. "*You* help. Just *you*."

He peered down at me, confusion marring his beautiful face. "I won't let anyone do shitty things to you, Mina."

"No." I shook my head. "You can't stop people from doing what they're going to do, sweetie." I swallowed hard. "But after, if you could hold my hand, that would be nice."

He did not delay.

Reaching down, he unhooked my arm from around him, led me back to the bedroom, lay on the bed facing me, and held my hand for the better part of an hour.

And something told me Lev needed it more than I did.

⚓

I was becoming bored at the house. It had been five days since I'd been at the club, and after hours of incessant begging, Lev granted me a boon, letting me come to work on the condition that I sat with him all night.

It was better than nothing. I didn't even have to think about it. I jumped at the chance to leave the house. I was getting stir crazy.

Dressing in black jeans and my white tee with the golden elephant printed on the front, I slipped on my flat strappy sandals, grabbed my coat and met him in the kitchen.

Anika and Vik were already there, waiting for Lev. Vik came around and wrapped me in a bear hug, his enormous frame cocooning me. From the look of him, you would never guess that Viktor seemed to be the needy guy of the bunch, with all his tattoos. His body was his very own canvas to decorate.

Anika, however, eyed me as if I were ready to break at any moment. "You're working tonight?" she asked anxiously then added in a cautious but patronizing tone, "Are you sure you're ready?"

I wanted to bitch slap her.

Instead, I smiled. "No, I'm not working tonight. I'm just getting crazy being locked up in the house. I'll just be observing tonight." I added for Anika's benefit, "Don't worry. Lev will look after me."

Vik grinned. "I'll look after you, Mina." He winked. "Hold your hand and everything."

I tilted my head to the side, pouted my lips, cupped his cheek, and cooed, "Aw, Vik. Now why would I want you to do that?" I winked. "Who knows where that hand has been?"

Nas happened to walk in the back door at that very moment. And for some reason, I felt caught. She made me feel caught. Like a naughty child doing something I wasn't meant to be doing. Especially when her eyes flashed at my hand on Vik.

She covered herself quickly, sneering at Vik in the way she normally would. "*Ewww*. Don't touch that, Mina. You don't know where it's been."

But Vik clearly wasn't in the mood for Nastasia. I knew this, because he grabbed me around the waist, pulling me back into him, making a show of his hand being low on my hip. He stared right at her then lowered his mouth to my ear and mock whispered, "Don't listen to her. We'll run away together, fuck on every beach in every country, and have beautiful children together."

Anika gagged in disgust. "*Jesus Christ*, Vik. Watch the shit you're talking. My mouth was open and everything."

Nas, however, looked hurt. I didn't understand why. She sort of had it coming, what with the way she talked to him.

But Nas was my friend, and that meant taking her side, even when she was wrong. I could cut a bitch without a crowd, but in front of people, I had her back.

Bumping my butt into his thighs, I scoffed. "I've gone through trash, Vik. I'm not picky when it comes to food." I turned to him and uttered, "And I still wouldn't eat your dick."

I heard Anika bark out a laugh and Nas snort at that, and Vik smiled proudly down at me. "*That's* what you call a burn."

The unfortunate thing was that as Vik bent down to kiss my forehead, Lev walked in. There was a tense moment of pressure building in the room as Lev's eyes flashed at Vik's hands on me. He had that look in his eye, the one that I'd met a few days prior, and I knew I'd have to intervene. Otherwise, Lev would rip his childhood friend a new asshole. He was protective of me. I got it. I understood it. That was what friends did.

Taking a moment to gather my thoughts, I removed myself from Vik and quietly made my way over to Lev, lifting my hand, palm out, and communicating with him in complete silence.

He looked down at my hand then up into my eyes. The sharp edges of his face softened and he took it without a word, holding it tightly. The gesture said so much more than words could have. I would be his rock when his reason floated away. And he would be the person I needed to remind me that I was no longer alone in the world. A perfectly imperfect friendship had somehow formed, and losing Lev was not an option.

He found me, and whether he knew it or not, I was his, in a way.

You know what they say...

Finders keepers.

⚓

The club was not very busy for a Friday night.

It was unusual since Fridays had been a major moneymaker in the past, according to Lev. Men who were finished with the work week came to Bleeding Hearts to unwind, drink in good company, and treat themselves to a private dance or four.

Lev and I sat in the far corner on the left side of the stage. It was the perfect place to watch the room with a view of everything and everyone.

I watched in curiosity as Lev pulled something out of his pocket and showed me an earpiece before he put it on. He spoke into it, "Cam, you ready?"

From the right-hand side of the stage, a young man in a suit raised his hand to show Lev he could hear him.

Lev sat back, turned to me, and stated, "Tonight will be a good night."

Was he trying to reassure me? I was convinced that the safest seat in the house was sitting next to the hot guy in the suit, giving orders over an earpiece. I didn't need reassurance.

The girls took to the stage. First, Lana, doing a pole routine, then ChaCha with her slow striptease, then Birdie came by with a glass of soda and a hug for me, telling me she'd been so worried about me.

A feeling of warmth bloomed inside of me. Yes, I was sitting in a gentleman's club, watching women take their clothes off for cash, knowing the man by my side would hurt anyone who looked at me funny, but I had never felt more at home in a place apart from my family home, when I lived with my mother.

Lev spotted a man sitting on his own, looking forlorn. He spoke into the earpiece. "Cam. Table twelve. Send him a whiskey neat on the house."

My brow rose. "He looks pretty down. You sure you want to liquor him up some more?"

Lev kept his eye on the floor, but tilted his head toward me. "Free *anything* makes people happy. Watch."

Sure enough, the man watched as Anika smiled seductively, placing the drink on his table and leaning down to whisper something in his ear. The lonely man smiled immediately.

Impressed, I asked, "What is she saying to him?"

"That we appreciate his business and loyalty."

I nodded. "Right. Okay. You clearly know your shit. I bow down to you, oh great one."

His eyes smiled in that way I loved, and I almost slid down the front of my chair, sighing dreamily.

I asked Lev if he wanted his drink topped off. He said no. I didn't think he realized I wanted to go visit Nas behind the bar. I kept hinting, saying how thirsty I was. He kept frowning, telling me to signal Anika.

There was no being inconspicuous with Lev. It was all or nothing. I finally blurted out, "I really want to talk to Nas."

His brow furrowed. "Why didn't you just say so?"

"Because I'm grounded," I muttered and slumped lower into my chair.

He snuffled, and I liked to believe it was Lev's version of a laugh. He nodded to the bar. "I can still see you from there. Stay in sight."

I perked up, leaning over my chair and showing my enthusiasm. "Really, Pop? No foolin'?"

"Go," he murmured in a bored manner, but his eyes were laughing.

"Neat-o!" I cheered as I rushed over to the bar. I wanted to fuck with Nas. I'd been planning it for days. Tonight's episode with Vik fit in perfectly with my devious plan.

Strolling up to the bar, I sat in the hidden corner and waited. When she approached, she mumbled, "What a shit night. Not even worth having full staff for this measly crowd."

"Yeah, I know." I got right into it. "So, what can you tell me about Vik?"

She turned to me, her eyes narrowed. "Why do you want to know about Vik?"

"I don't know." I purposefully acted aloof. "He's hot, no doubt." Then I planted the bomb. "And there was that thing tonight. I don't know, but I think we've got a bit of chemistry going on." I leaned forward and grinned. "I think he's into me."

I wanted to burst into laughter at the way Nas' face turned bright red. She gritted her teeth and spoke through them, "He's not all he's cracked up to be, Mina."

I shrugged. "Who am I to judge?" I pointed to myself. "Homeless girl...*hello*!"

Her nostrils flared. "He's not your type."

"Who's to say what's my type? Besides, we don't need to be each other's type to scratch an itch." I used my elbow to nudge her and finished off with a lewd wink. "Know what I mean?"

That was the straw that broke the camel's back.

Nas planted her palms on the bar, leaned forward, and snapped, *"You stay away from Viktor!"*

My mission complete, I quickly got out of character, threw my head back, and hooted with laughter. Nas stared at me, confused for a second before she caught on.

Looking mildly pissed off with herself, she shook her head slowly. "Who told you?"

I smiled victoriously. "It doesn't matter who told me. The question is, why didn't *you* tell me?"

Her face fell. She looked sad. "It's complicated, Mina."

"Complicated in the the-guy-I-love-sleeps-with-other-women way? Or complicated in the the-guy-I-love-has-issues-with-commitment way?"

"Neither," she hushed, her eyes shining. "In the the-guy-I-love-doesn't-love-me-back kind of way."

My smile fell. That sucked.

"That sucks," I told her, my heartbreak apparent.

She smiled sadly. "That's life, my dear."

CHAPTER NINETEEN

Mina

Saturday morning brought a shock to us all.

Lidiya was summoned back to her mother, Irina. What was surprising about it was that Lev let her go.

I didn't want her to leave. The thought of her staying with a horrible woman who didn't even want her drove me crazy. It quickly hit me that if this was the way I, an outsider, was feeling, Lev must have already crossed the border of Crazytown. He hid his sadness so well, but I didn't miss the way he snapped at Sasha when his brother suggested moving Irina close by so Lidiya would at least live in the same state.

The awful woman had already booked flights for Mirella and Lidiya leaving just after midday, and her warning had been that if the two of them weren't at arrivals at the designated time, she would be catching the next flight down and raising hell at the club.

Frankly, I thought the woman was full of shit, and I aired that view. Nas sent me a look advising me that her threat would likely be seen through. I was stunned. Who was this woman that she had the Leokov family becoming yes men?

As I sat cross-legged on the floor of the living room, Lidiya made a home in my lap, playing with little Mina, unaware that she was about to be thrust away from us in a most rude way. The arm I held her with tightened around her. I found myself mighty protective of this little peanut.

I watched in silence as Mirella's face fell a degree. She covered it quickly, standing and heading over to Lidiya's room to pack their things.

"No," I muttered angrily. I turned to Lev, hugging Lidiya with everything I had. "You're just going to sit down and let that bitch take her away from us?"

He looked as if he'd aged ten years in ten minutes. He looked haggard and worn. He spoke calmly, "What would you have me do, Mina?"

I blinked at him. This attitude was not going to get us anywhere. "*Fight for her*, Lev. Tell Irina she can't have her. Let her come here. What's she going to do? Show everyone how screwed up in the head she really is?"

"I'll lose the partial custody I have and be charged with kidnapping my own daughter." He looked at me, pinning me down with a single glance. "Does that sound like a good plan to you?"

Well, no. It didn't. But there had to be *something* we could do.

My heart began to race as I realized that no one would be fighting this. "Nas," I called.

She looked miserable. "Pick your battles, shorty. You aren't going to win this one."

My last resort. "Sasha," I whispered, frightfully close to tears. "Do something."

He was already shaking his head then he stood suddenly, glowering at me. "Life ain't fair, little girl." He stared at me. "You of all people should understand that."

I was out on a limb, on my own.

"Lev," I pleaded. "Please. Don't let her win. She's just a woman. How much pull can she have?"

I wasn't prepared for what happened next.

Lev stood. Then he yelled.

At me.

"What the fuck do you want me to say, Mina? That I fall over my feet to please the mother of my child?" He panted, "Yes! I *do*." He walked away. "I have my reasons, and I don't owe an explanation to anyone, certainly not *you*."

He said 'you' like I was something disgusting. Like I was a nuisance. Like I was not worthy of the explanation that even I knew I didn't deserve to hear.

It brought my back down to reality.

I was nothing to Lev Leokov.

And yet, he remained my everything.

⚓

LEV

Sometime after midday, after Lidiya and Mirella were gone, I made my way upstairs with my tail between my legs. I should have known this was a hard time for Lev, and I pushed him over the edge. I was sure it took a lot to do that, and I was feeling like crap about it.

Standing by the open door, I peered inside. Lev, dressed in his usual uniform of a three-piece-suit, lay on the left side of the bed, his forearm covering his eyes. It was heartbreaking to see him so lost.

I made my way over to him, kneeling next to him and speaking from the side of the bed. "Hey," I started, gently. Reaching up, I tugged on the hand covering his eyes. He allowed it to fall, turning his head to the side to look at me. His warm honeyed eyes were full of sadness. I squeezed his hand. "Oh, sweetie," I hushed. "I'm so sorry. I'm an idiot. I didn't think."

He blinked at me a moment. And when he spoke, I knew I was forgiven for my careless commentary in a situation that didn't call for it.

"Will you hold my hand?"

I didn't need to be told twice. Rather than moving to the other side of the bed, I stood and climbed over him, laying half draped over his right side, my right leg hooked over his hip, and taking his left hand in mine, entwined, palm-to-palm.

His right hand came around me, holding me close, and his hand stroked my back. A soft sigh escaped me as I rest my head on his shoulder, my eyes closing in satisfaction. I'd never been more comfortable in all my life. And that would be the reason I fell asleep tucked into Lev Leokov.

⚓

After my nap, I got up and showered, getting ready for the night ahead. When I returned, my makeup game strong and my hair newly straightened, flowing down my back, dressed to the nines and ready for the club, Lev shook his head. It seemed he didn't want me at the club tonight.

I didn't beg. I wouldn't beg. It wasn't the way I did things, not normally.

Instead, I tried honesty. Walking up to him, I hooked my fingers into his front pockets and looked up the whole foot to his face. "You've had a rough day. Let me be there for you tonight. If you feel like you want to crack heads, all you need to do is reach over and take my hand." I shook him a little. "You've been there for me. Will you let me be there for you?"

He thought about it.

His response was quiet. "Okay."

I liked that response. I showed him so by reaching up and cupping his cheeks, pulling his face down so I could kiss his forehead.

⚓

We got to the club a little after seven. The crowd always took a while to perk up. The later it got, the more crowded it got.

Tonight, however, the crowd dribbled in just as it had the night before.

Lev, spotting what I had, commented, "Something's up."

I frowned, nodding in complete agreement. Something was indeed up. I'd never seen the club so empty since I got here. Compared to the day I stole Sasha's wallet, this crowd was embarrassing.

That was when Birdie approached, looking mildly anxious. "Can I have a word?"

"Of course," Lev replied.

Her nervousness increased as she wrung her hands together. "I think you should call Sasha. Nas is on her way. I need you all to hear this."

Lev did as she asked, taking out his cell and calling his brother out from his office. Nas arrived and sat on the arm of my chair. When Sasha arrived, he spoke kindly to Birdie. "Little bird, why are you looking so worried?"

She reached into her jeans pocket, pulled out a piece of paper, and handed it to Sasha. "I found this on my car when I went out for my break. It was on all the windshields. I collected whatever I could, but…" She shrugged. "Some people were bound to get them before I could remove them."

Sasha unfolded the paper, read in silence, and then cussed softly.

His jaw tight, he handed the note to Lev. "I think we just found out where our customers have gone."

Nas and I both leaned over the seat to read with Lev.

Aphrodite's Kiss. New show. New girls. Completely refurbished. Faces that will stop your heart. Free drink with flyer.

"That's not all." Birdie winced. "One of Laredo's goons approached me just as I was coming in from my break." Her eyes apologetic, she looked directly at Sasha. "He's recruiting from right under your nose, baby."

"*Motherfucker*," Sasha whispered. "That would explain why ChaCha quit on Wednesday."

My jaw dropped. "He can't do that!"

Lev's lips thinned. "He can; he just shouldn't. It's an unwritten rule of sorts. It's considered bad form."

I sat back in my chair, feeling glum. I turned to look at Sasha. "Why does he hate you so much?"

For once, Sasha didn't glare at me. He spoke quietly, "I scarred up his son's face when he tried to off me. The pretty boy ain't so pretty anymore." He sighed. "Laredo didn't give a rat's ass that his boy brought that shit to *my* property. He sees those scars and he wants to end me."

"What happened?"

Nas explained in a short tone, "Sasha slept with Alessio's wife."

Sasha uttered a defensive, "She said they were done." He ran a hand through his dark hair. "How was I supposed to know she was using my cock as a weapon against him?" He smirked at the memory of her. "I'd like to say she wasn't worth the trouble, but she was a goddamn wildcat."

"Well, it's not Sasha's fault the lady is a tramp," I muttered.

Sasha seemed surprised by my support. But, still, his glare returned. "What new show? What's he got that we don't?" Frustration took over. "I can't even send anyone down there to see what's up. Not anyone I trust. He knows everyone who works for us. Knows our faces."

I looked around at them all, their thinking faces on.

Was I the only one who had the solution to this problem?

"He doesn't know me." I offered with a mild shrug, "I'll go."

Lev barked, "*No*," at the very same time Sasha grinned deviously and hissed, "*Yes.*"

They looked at each other.

Sasha spoke quietly, "You want this ship to sink, *moy brat*?"

"*Net*," Lev replied unenthusiastically.

"I don't mind. It's the least I can do," I uttered sincerely.

Sasha grinned at me while Lev frowned unhappily. Nas squeezed my shoulder in silent support.

And so, a plan was hatched.

⚓

Mina

"If I think for a second that you're in danger of being caught, I'm coming in there," Lev muttered as he drove. Vik remained silent in the back seat.

I smiled to myself at the protective tone in his voice. "Got it."

"Make sure you have your cell on you at all times," he insisted.

I patted a hand over my front jeans pocket for the sixth time since we began our journey. "Still there," I told him.

Lev surprised me this morning with a new cell phone. It was one of those fandangle ones with the big screen that you could use the Internet on, and download apps, and probably track when you were about to go to the bathroom.

It was fancy.

He spent the morning showing me how to use it. By the end of it, I knew most of the basics. I still didn't understand what the app things were, but he said we'd get to that another day.

Calling, answering, and texting was easy enough to remember. I practiced by sending Nas messages.

> **Me: What do you get when you cross a caterpillar with a parrot?**
> **Nas: Who is this?**
> **Me: A Walkie Talkie!!!!!**

Nas: Who is this?
Me: Hey, that was funny. You could at least courtesy laugh.
Nas: Who the fuck is this?

Lev also managed to get me a state ID card, which explained why Nas had me get some wallet-sized portrait photographs done the last time we were at the mall. I shouldn't have been surprised that it had all my accurate details on it, but I was. I smiled. "How'd you get this, you sneaky goose?"

He sat at the kitchen table, seeming pleased by the reaction. "I know people." That much was clear. He seemed to have connections in every industry. "I also have a copy of your birth certificate, your social security card, and your passport."

I glanced down at the ID card.

Mina Clarabelle Harris.

The address listed was…Lev's.

I didn't bother questioning why. I was sure he did that because he had to provide some address that was partly valid, and I'd been living here for the past four and a half weeks.

Parking a block away, Vik worked quickly, placing the surveillance camera disguised as a large button on the lapel of my black jacket, underneath my coat. The big black button appropriately read 'I'm silently judging you.'

Vik explained, "This isn't a live cam. I'm not going to be able to check the footage until you get out of there and we get back to the club. If you think anyone's onto you, don't think; just hightail it." At my nervous nod, he smiled. "Just sit down, order a drink, and watch the show, like you would with us. No biggie." He added, "It would probably help if you lost the I'm-out-of-my-depth expression."

"Shut up, Vik." I shoved his arm away and he chuckled.

I was ready to go. Leaning over the seat, I gripped Lev's shirt and pulled him to me. "Hey, don't worry. I'll be back in an hour, okay?" He grunted, not looking at me. So I forced his attention. Getting closer, I pressed my glossed lips to his cheek softly. "Be back before you know it."

Aphrodite's Kiss shocked me. The way the boys talked about it, I expected a hole of an establishment, but it was gorgeous.

The Greek theme meant strategically placed large white pillars with delicate flowers and greenery painted on them, big wooden booth tables intricately designed and trimmed with gold, the booth cushions decorated with the typical Greek meander pattern (in gold, of course), and the stage...wow. It looked as though it had been designed in a dramatic 1900s style, complete with heavy red velvet drapery.

I was impressed.

I did as Vik told me to. I ordered a drink, took a seat, and faced the stage. Half an hour later, the show started. The lights dimmed low and spotlights shone on the stage; the curtains opened and I gaped.

Four men, gorgeous and ripped, wearing white material draped over their upper thighs, showing the tops of their asses, holding up a woman draped seductively on a small sofa attached to a platform. Each man took a corner of the platform and carried her in effortlessly.

It was quite a show.

The woman, who had a feathered fan covering her face, lowered it as the men placed the sofa on the ground.

"Fuck a duck," I whispered.

It was ChaCha. She was dressed as a Greek goddess. She, of course, introduced herself as Aphrodite.

I watched her performance. It was a skit of sorts, a cross of stripping, drama, and humor. I didn't want to admit it, but she was a good actress. She had the men eating out of her shimmer-covered hands and staring at her glittered bosom. It finished when ChaCha was down to her pasty-covered ChoCha.

The men cheered as the curtains fell. The music was turned up, and two other women took to the stage to perform a very average pole routine. I'd seen better at Bleeding Hearts. Half an hour later, another skit took place.

I was beginning to see why men were flocking here. It was different. The laughter the skits provided was infectious and improved the overall atmosphere in the club. It wasn't seedy, and it made the environment easier, less sleazy.

Unfortunately, I was starting to see why they had a winner.

I'd seen enough. Standing, I moved to leave, but was almost bowled over by a man. I squeaked, steadying myself before I fell. The man turned. "Shit, I'm sorry." He smiled apologetically.

Oh, dear God.

My heart sank so deep it ended up in my stomach.

Sandwich bar guy's eyes narrowed at me. "Hey, I know you." He looked me over. "You're the homeless chick."

I shook my head, trying to look angry at his calling me homeless. "No, I think you have the wrong person. Sorry."

I moved to walk away, but he caught my arm, pulling me back. It was obvious he'd had some to drink. He laughed loudly. "Oh, come on, I know it's you, girl. No man forgets a face like that." He leered down at me. "You're looking much better."

"Get your hands off me," I sneered.

He tsked. "Too bad you're not hungry anymore." He shook his head in regret. "Damn, you're a pretty one." He leaned down to speak directly in my ear. "I'm regretting not taking you up on your offer that night. My cock craves your mouth, baby." He added, "What would it take for the offer to be reinstated?"

"Hell to freeze over, you dirty asshole." I shoved him away as hard as I could. He lost his balance, fell back, and all attention fell on me.

Hundreds of eyes turned to me. I flushed, looking toward the security guards that had just stepped forward to intervene. I snapped at them and spoke brashly, "Is *that* how you let men in your club treat women?"

Then I made a huge mistake.

I walked away, calling back loudly, "No, thanks. I'll be taking my business to Bleeding Hearts."

CHAPTER TWENTY

Laredo

My mouth parted in shock. I watched the woman leave, my heart beating fast.

Alessio came to my side. "What should I do, Pop?"

My eyes turned to focus on the man she had argued with. "Ban him."

My son stilled and I felt Alessio's shock. "What? *Why*? They had words, that's all. No big deal."

I shook my head. "This is a safe environment, *figlio*. He brought that shit into my club and killed the mood. I won't tolerate it." My mind made up, I repeated myself, "Ban him."

Alessio left to do my bidding, but I was still focused on the exit. I was sure I'd seen a ghost.

"Clara," I whispered to myself. I needed to see her again, see her up close, with my own eyes.

And I knew just where I'd find her.

CHAPTER TWENTY-ONE

Mina

We drove back to Bleeding Hearts in silence. Vik caught the panicked look in my eyes and rushed me into the car. Lev was driving before the passenger door even closed.

"What happened?" Vik asked as Lev kept his eyes on the road.

I unhooked the button-disguised camera and handed it back to him. "Nothing."

It was stupid to lie. Vik would see what happened when he watched the footage. I suppose part of me was hoping he wouldn't watch it to the end.

No. Hope was too weak of a word. I *prayed* he wouldn't watch it to the end.

Had I known that sandwich guy was going to be at Aphrodite's Kiss, I would never have offered to play spy. The man had humiliated me now on two occasions. He would go to sleep tonight without giving me a second thought, and he would haunt me for a time to come. I knew I was giving him power by doing that, but *crap*, it was hard to stop myself.

As we arrived back at the club, Lev helped me out of the car and, without meaning to, I attached myself to him, wrapping my arm around his waist and looking up at him, a pleading look in my eyes, asking for silent permission.

He didn't disappoint. He gave me what I needed, his arm tightening around me, pulling me into his side.

A soft sigh escaped me. When Lev held me, I felt as if nothing could touch me. He played the protector role well, and although I fought the fact that I needed it, it made me feel worth something, and that was more than I'd had in years.

We walked inside and down the long hall to Sasha's office. Vik opened the door and Sasha paused, mid-pace. He looked up from his pensive state, and as his eyes settled on me, his lip curled.

I was getting real tired of his shit. I couldn't figure out what it was he had against me. At first, I thought it was the whole wallet debacle, but as time went on, I saw it was more. I just couldn't put my finger on *what*.

Sasha looked from me, to Lev's arm that was fastened around my shoulders, then over to Vik, who he asked politely, "Got it?"

Vik held up the button camera, shaking it lightly before moving around Sasha's desk to plug it into his laptop. He worked quickly, bringing up the file. Before he pressed play on the media player, Vik looked to me. "I think Nas is going to want to see this."

This is going to be a group viewing?

My heart sank, but I took the hint and found Nas sitting in the dark corner of the bar, sipping a whiskey sour. As soon as she saw me, her face brightened. She stood, walked over to me, and took my arm. "Finally," she muttered. "While you've been off playing Maxwell Smart, I've been dying of boredom. Why do you get to have all the fun?"

"Who the hell is Maxwell Smart?" I asked and she huffed out a laugh, ignoring my question.

A single glance around the floor and I knew what she meant. We had almost no patrons at all.

I walked Nas down the long hall, but before following her inside, I pause, pulling back. My nerves sizzled. "I'll just leave you to it."

"What?" she asked, a frown distorting her pretty face. "Sit with me."

It wasn't a request. Nas did not ask.

She *ordered*.

Hesitation held me back until, finally, I swallowed hard, walked into the office, and shut the door behind me. Lev sat on the guest chair, opposite Sasha. Vik stood, while Nas sat on the arm of Lev's chair.

I huddled into the back corner by the door, feeling cold and hugging myself.

The footage was skimmed over until the show started. The second ChaCha was revealed, Nas spat out a string of outrageous and clever cuss words. Sasha looked ready to shoot someone. Namely ChaCha.

Twenty-five minutes into the footage, I piped up from my corner. "That's it," I stated. "I get up to leave in a minute."

Vik turned to Sasha. "It's a show," he uttered with a small shrug, like he didn't know what the big deal was.

Nas got it though. "Yeah, it's a show," she began. "But did you see the way the men reacted to it. It was positive and light. Not sordid. And the way they've done up the place." She looked to Sasha. "It looks nice."

Sasha nodded as if he were answering an unasked question. "We have to improve our show, improve our image. We're gonna lose more business if we don't give 'em something to talk about."

As this conversation was happening, I was watching the media player, still playing the file, with my body cold with anxiety. On the screen, I had just stood from my table at Aphrodite's Kiss and was walking away when...

"*Hey, I know you*," was heard loud and clear. "*You're the homeless chick.*"

All conversation stopped. All eyes turned to the screen.

"Please turn it off," I begged on a whisper, my voice trembling.

But no one listened. They were too enthralled in the altercation happening on the screen.

"*Too bad you're not hungry anymore.*" I bit the inside of my lip, my heart racing. "*Damn, you're a pretty one.*" My throat closed and my arms tightened around my body. "*I'm regretting not taking you up on your offer that night. My cock craves you mouth, baby.*" Tears filled my eyes and I closed them tight, not giving him the satisfaction of crying over his actions one more time. "*What would it take for the offer to be reinstated?*"

"*Hell to freeze over, you dirty asshole.*"

I heard the low whine of someone standing from a chair. I knew he was in front of me before I even opened my eyes. Instead, I squeezed them closed tighter. "I'm sorry," I told him.

I heard myself on the laptop. *"Is that how you let men in your club treat women?"* I cringed, slapping my hands over my face, knowing what was coming next. *"No, thanks. I'll be taking my business to Bleeding Hearts."*

Speaking through my hands, I let out a muffled, "Oh, God."

I heard someone chuckle quietly. Nas spat out, "It's not funny!" shutting them down before they could humiliate me anymore.

Sasha spoke. "I know it's not funny. I'm not laughing out of humor." His voice held a key note of derision. "Not only did she cause a scene, but her crazy ass announced that she'd be coming here." He scoffed. "Yeah. There goes the rest of our customers."

"Shut up, Sash," Nas hissed. Her voice softened a great deal when she asked, "Mina, you know that guy?"

I shook my head.

When Lev spoke, I felt his fury. "You said nothing happened. That wasn't nothing."

It was then that I opened my eyes and, sad as they were, they settled on Lev. "I didn't want you to hear what he said."

"Why?" he asked, bordering irate.

I bit the inside of my lip and spoke through the thickness in my throat. "Because what he said..." Oh, God, I was so ashamed. "It's true." I sniffled, the first of many tears trickling down my flaming red cheek. "He owns a sandwich bar. I asked him for food. He told me to suck his dick. At first, I refused, but," a ragged breath escaped me, "but I was so hungry, Lev. *So* hungry," I stressed. "And when I finally agreed, he told me it was too late and left me crying out in the street." I looked down at the ground. "He didn't get his blowjob. And I didn't get anything to eat." My voice turned to a whisper. "That was the day before I met you. That was why I stole Sasha's wallet." I looked up through my blurry eyes to lock eyes with Sasha. My whisper was hoarse. "I was *desperate*."

No one spoke for a while. I didn't want anyone to speak. I didn't want looks of pity. I didn't want sympathy. I wanted to go home.

"Okay," Lev murmured in that soft way of his, and it was almost as if he'd read my mind, because he turned to the others in the room and stated, "I'm taking Mina home."

Even though he wasn't asking for permission, Sasha gave it in the only way I imagined he could. "Yeah, whatever. It's not like we got customers to serve."

We drove in long, comfortable silence, holding hands over the center console.

When we arrived home, we went about getting ready for bed. Lev undressed all the way down to his boxers, no longer afraid of dashing my mild sensibilities, and I dressed in my 'hideous' yellow pajamas. Lev locked the bedroom door, pulled out the sofa, climbed in, and turned off his lamp. My lamp followed suit as I climbed into the ginormous king bed.

I lay there a long while, unable to get comfortable or find sleep.

It took a long, stern, mental pep-talk, but I made my decision.

Sliding out of bed, I shuffled over to the sofa bed, climbed onto the mattress, and wasn't a little bit surprised that Lev had predicted my move, lifting the sheets to let me under. He spooned me, wrapping an arm around my waist and pulling me back into his warm, strong body.

His scent was warm and manly. He was toasty, and his hard body cocooned mine. It calmed me. Comfort hit me immediately and I yawned.

I felt Lev's lips press lightly at the base of my neck. "Goodnight, Mina."

"Night, sweetie." My eyes turned heavy, and soon, I was lost to slumber.

We slept that way until dawn.

⚓

The next morning, as I walked out of the bathroom dressed in my black yoga pants and white off-the-shoulder tee, I was brought to a stop by Lev sitting on the edge of his bed, waiting for me.

Brushing out my wet hair, I smiled softly at the sight of him in his sweats, tee, and hoodie. "Morning."

LEV

A frown at his brow, he stood and came forward, a small turquoise box in his hand. He strode forth, a decisive gleam in his eyes, and when he stopped an inch in front of me, I knew what was coming next.

Lev leaned in low, close, and breathing in his warm, manly scent, I closed my eyes, awaiting the kiss I had been waiting for my entire life.

I stood on my tiptoes, my face turned up, ready to receive it.

This kiss would be the kiss I judged all others by. I felt it deep in my bones. This kiss would be groundbreaking. This kiss would push me over the edge and would finally fall for Lev Leokov.

This kiss…

Never happened.

His hands worked swiftly, fastening something behind my neck.

I looked down.

A silver anchor on a long, delicate silver chain sat just above the valley of my breasts. The disappointment from my non-kiss faded, but only marginally.

"It's not my birthday," I told him.

Turns out, I didn't need a groundbreaking kiss to fall in love with Lev Leokov. I knew this, because what he said then settled the matter. "This is for all the birthdays you missed out on." He reached out to brush the anchor pendant, his finger sweeping across the top of my breast accidentally. "For the birthdays that were never acknowledged when they should have been."

My eyes began to sting.

Ugh! Not again.

I was turning into a blubbering mess. I didn't want to cry, but the moment was more than I ever expected in this lifetime, and Lev's sincere delivery hoisted me over the edge.

The man had no idea how dreamy he was, and proved it when he drew me close, wrapping me up and speaking softly, "Please don't cry, Mina. I'm sorry. I'm not good with words."

I laughed through my tears at the absurdity of his statement. Cupping his cheeks, I pulled his face down, pressing a soft lingering kiss to his mouth. Pulling back, I noticed his slack look of shock, but chose to ignore it. I fingered the pendant and beamed, "I love it, Lev. Thank you. I'll never take it off."

⚓

Later that night, after another night at the club with only a handful of loyal patrons, Lev and I left a little after two a.m.

I noticed a theme happening.

During the car ride home, we held hands over the center console, and once home, we undressed and went to our separate beds. We turned off our lamps and settled in.

Fifteen minutes passed, and sleep had not found me.

I bit the inside of my lip before I called into the darkness, "Lev?"

His immediate grunt of response told me he hadn't yet fallen asleep.

I went for it, the whole hog. "You know, there's plenty of room in this bed for the both of us."

A long silence followed, and I wanted to slap my forehead.

I pushed too hard.

Just as I opened my mouth to blurt out an awkward goodnight, I heard the sheets rustle. I saw the outline of him approach the bed. He came around to the left side and slid under the covers. My relief evident, I scooched toward him before tucking myself into his side, my head at his chest and my arm resting on his abdomen.

"This okay?" I asked, knowing full well it was perfect.

His strong arm came around me and he sighed, "Perfect."

I smiled into Lev's bare chest, breathing in the warm scent of him, and fell asleep hoping I would find myself smiling my way to sleep more often.

CHAPTER TWENTY-TWO

Mina

Finding a moment alone wasn't hard to do between the hours of ten and twelve. Those were the hours Lev disappeared to workout. He always left at ten and he was always back by twelve, if not twelve on the dot. I did not know what he did during his workout. I do know, whatever the activity, he came back dripping with sweat.

I made myself clear on more than one occasion that I found Lev attractive. He was, by far, the most handsome man I had ever seen. With his golden eyes, harsh angles of his face, dark hair worn styled, and his tall, built frame, I found myself wondering what it would be like to be bare under that body, naked and sweating from a different type of workout.

Whenever Lev came home, his sweatpants and tee damp and sticking to him, my tongue would swell and I'd barely contain my panting.

Lev was sexy, plain and simple.

With our changed sleeping arrangement now becoming a permanent thing, it didn't escape my notice that I woke with a long, thick erection pressed up against my butt, or thigh, or wherever it happened to be pressed in the mornings.

We both played it cool, not bringing attention to it, but we both knew it was there. It was obvious, painfully so.

This morning went a little different, however. Having barely woken with that hard cock pressed into the crack of my ass for the third day in a row, I acted unconsciously in my sleepy state, arching my back and letting out a sigh of ecstasy as the solid length rubbed me in a most delicious way.

For a moment there, I thought Lev was a dream.

I was (obviously) wrong.

My body, acting of it's own accord, ground back into him one more wonderful time, and Lev let out a soft growl of approval. The hidden cleft between my legs pulsed gently, and suddenly I was hot all over. A want spread through me, and before I knew it, that want had increased to a desperate need.

I needed more. I was desperate for contact. I wanted that hard cock inside me, filling me, stretching me.

That was the moment Lev gently extracted himself, and a second later, I heard the bathroom door close behind him. The shower started, and that was when I woke fully, realizing what had just happened.

My neck itched with heat and my face flamed.

I had dry-humped Lev in my sleep.

That wasn't very polite, Mina.

I thought about apologizing, but knew that would be as awkward as the situation itself. So I did the next best thing, the thing Lev and I did well.

Feigning sleep, I pretended it never happened, breathing as heavily and evenly as possible as Lev exited the bathroom.

The shuffle of clothing sounded, the bedroom door was unlocked, and I found myself alone in a bed built for two.

I turned to lay on my back and sighed. My hand glanced my breast over my pajamas, slid down over my stomach, and my fingers slipped under the elastic of my panties to where I needed them most. Closing my eyes, I thought about Lev's long fingers, his full lips, and his taut butt as I brought myself to release. But it was hollow.

The satisfaction I craved never surfaced.

I waited for the sound of the back door to close before I arose. I showered quickly, opened the bedroom curtains, and sat in the center of the rumpled bed, legs crossed. My phone in front of me, I stared down at the business card and thought hard about making the call.

My stomach turned as I picked up my phone and dialed. It rang twice before he answered with a swift hello.

"It's Mina," I began. I bit the inside of my lip and told him what I needed. "You know that contact you have? I'm ready to see them."

Silence followed, then he told me where I needed to go.

"Okay." I wanted to smile, but couldn't because my heart was caught in my throat. "Thanks, Pox."

Without a moment's hesitation, I called Nas and asked her a favor.

I needed a ride.

⚓

The clinic was small but clean, and a small woman dressed in scrubs saw me to an empty room. I didn't want to go alone. Nas sat in one of the chairs, going through her phone.

I swallowed hard. "Hey," I called, my tongue sticking to the roof of my dry mouth. "You coming?"

She blinked at me, searching my face a moment before seeing the fear in my eyes. She stood, and I breathed a sigh of relief as she followed me into the exam room.

We waited in complete silence. A few minutes later, a willowy woman with a messy bun and pink scrubs walked in, smiling. "Mina?" She looked from Nas to me, unsure of which woman was her patient.

"I'm Mina," I said, sitting up straight and raising my hand like a schoolgirl.

Her smile widened as she sat. "Hi, Mina. I'm Dr. Henley. My brother called ahead. Told me you needed an IUD." She paused then asked, "May I ask why you've chosen the IUD over the implant?"

Wait...Pox was her brother*?*

They looked nothing alike.

I wrung my hands together in nervousness and told her, "Lasts longer."

She nodded in understanding then started to type on the open computer screen. "We don't have them on hand, of course." My face fell, but she went on. "I wouldn't worry about that. I'll hand you a script and send you next door. The pharmacist always has a ton of them." She sighed lightly. "I have to tell you, Mina. I don't like doing these rush jobs. In a normal scenario, we'd do an internal exam, a pap smear, and test for STDs *before* we inserted an IUD." She glanced at me kindly and asked, "I don't suppose you'd come back in a week?"

My voice weak, I spoke quietly. "I'd prefer not to. Doctors make me nervous."

She nodded in sympathy. "Okay then." Her face compassionate, she spoke gently as she told me. "I can't do much without doing an internal first."

I knew it was coming. Of course she'd have to look down there. It was where the darn thing was going.

Dr. Henley led me behind a curtained area, instructing me to remove my jeans and panties before pulling the sheet over my lower half. I did as ordered and found it easier knowing that Nas was only a yell away.

The exam was short and relatively painless and, satisfied with the results, Dr. Henley let me dress, leaving a glass of water and two painkillers on the tray table. I swallowed them down, stepped out, and she scribbled on a piece of paper before handing it to me. "Go on next door and ask for Marianne. She'll have the order filled in a few minutes."

Marianne was a stout woman who looked as though she didn't smile a whole lot. As Dr. Henley advised, my order was filled within minutes, and soon after that, I was back on the exam table, my lower half naked and covered with a sheet.

Nas stayed on the other side of the curtain. Dr. Henley and I were soon joined by Jane, the nurse who originally showed me to the exam room. Jane held my hand tight and told me to breathe deep as I was opened up with a lubed plastic speculum. Dr. Henley warned me when my cervix would clench on its own, causing my stomach to cramp painfully. She was honest and open, and it seemed as though she knew what she was talking about. The pain didn't last long. In fact, the birth control device was inserted in less than five minutes, and as soon as the speculum was removed, the pain receded to nothing.

"That's it?" I asked, stunned at how good I felt after having something inserted into my uterus.

Dr. Henley pulled the sheet down to cover me. "That's it," she stated. "Don't be fooled. You'll get some wicked cramps later on as the device settles. I'd advise you to take ibuprofen every four hours, even if you think you won't need it. It'll help the inflammation."

She and Jane left me to dress, giving me a pad to wear. I dressed quickly and stepped out to join the others.

Nas looked up. "You all suited up, sunshine? You know what they say. No glove, no love."

I glowered at her. "Shut up, Nas."

She grinned. "Oh, hush now. You love me."

I did love Nas. She was fast becoming my best friend. It didn't matter that she was my *only* female friend. She was supportive and funny and listened to me. I was thankful for her friendship.

Dr. Henley warned, "You've got the glove, but no love for a week though, okay? Not without a condom."

My face turned beet red. "I don't even have a boyfriend. There will be no love." I turned to Nas. "There will be *no* love."

Dr. Henley smiled. "I'll have the results of you pap smear and STD test by Monday. I'll have Jane call. Also, I'll have you booked in for a follow up in five weeks. I expect you to keep a diary in that time of how often you're spotting." I opened my mouth to protest, but she must have seen it coming, because she raised a hand and cut me off. "It's standard. I have to make sure the device has settled well." She threw a fear tactic out there. "If it doesn't settle well, it can become embedded in your uterus and you'll have to get it cut out. Come to the checkup, Mina."

Her fear tactic worked, damn her. I agreed to the appointment.

From the moment Nas and I left the clinic, I felt better than I had in a long time, and something told me things would only get better.

⚓

I should have listened to Dr. Henley, but being the badass I was, I didn't.

Her advice not followed came back to haunt me as I almost doubled over from pain, a sharp stabbing sensation throbbing throughout my belly. I thought I was going to be ill from the pain alone.

Holding onto the railing of the stairs, I made my way down slowly, one stair at a time. I found Lev in the kitchen. The second he saw me, he dropped the newspaper he was reading and shot up out of his chair. "Mina, what's wrong?"

I groaned, clutching my stomach. "I need painkillers. Ibuprofen."

He helped me sit before searching through the medicine cabinet. "I only have acetaminophen," he said as he brought it over with a glass of water.

I shook my head. "No. Ibuprofen. It needs to be anti-inflammatory."

"What's wrong?" he asked again, but I ignored him.

"Call Nas." I grimaced as another cramp took hold, causing me to grit my teeth.

He did, and she arrived soon after holding a white box of tablets in her hands. She shook her head at me. "Didn't listen to the doc, huh?"

"What doc?" asked Lev.

I moaned in agony, my forehead beginning to bead with sweat, doubling over. "Do you have the meds or not?"

She sighed. "Yeah, yeah. I got 'em right here." She placed the box down. I opened it with shaking hands and threw two into my mouth, swallowing them dry. Nas clicked her tongue at me. "Look at you? You didn't listen, and now you're useless. You're not working tonight. Go to bed."

But Lev was stuck on, "What doc?"

Nas took pity on me and lied to her brother. "It's Mina's time of the month. I took her to a clinic to see if they could do anything about the cramping."

I was hoping he'd shy away like most men. I didn't like lying to him. Instead, he knelt by my side and placed a hand on my knee. "Why didn't you say so?"

"It's embarrassing," I croaked, massaging my temples in a slow, firm circular motion like my mom used to whenever I had a headache. It never felt the same after she'd gone. It only felt better when someone else did it to you.

He shook his head, frowning at me. "No, it isn't. You're a woman, Mina. You can't help menstruating. It's what women do." Then he shocked me further. "Do you need me to go to the store for you?"

He was willing to go to the store and buy me feminine hygiene products like it was no big deal.

LEV

Lev Leokov was the definition of the word *man*. He'd earned it. He certainly acted like one. Not like those pussy boys who shied away from the word 'period.'

The thing was, I had used the only pad I'd been given and I needed more, as the spotting had been quite heavy. I looked to Nas. "Do you have any pads?"

She shook her head. "Sorry, doll. I'm a tampon girl."

Miserable, I turned to Lev and nodded. "I need pads."

His eyes softened. "Okay." If I didn't know better, he seemed pleased that I let him be of some help to me. "Tell me what you need."

I prattled off the single item I needed and Lev helped me to bed before leaving. He returned a half-hour later with the box of pads. He didn't seem squeamish by the situation. Rather, knowing what I needed, he lay next to me, holding my hand until I fell asleep.

Later that night, I woke for a single moment, long enough to feel Lev's warm body slide in next to me. He worked gently to pull me in close and tuck me into the space that was made for me and me alone. He rested his chin atop my head and sighed softly.

No longer in pain, and in the place I felt most at home, I found my smile before sleep took me once more.

CHAPTER TWENTY-THREE

Mina

Waking up alone but refreshed and well rested, I dressed quickly and rushed downstairs to have breakfast with Lev. Only when I got to the kitchen, there was no one there, the newspaper neatly folded in the center of the table.

Silence in this house didn't always mean it was empty, but today, it seemed it was.

That made me sad. I wanted to wake every morning by greeting Lev, putting my arms around him, and taking warmth from him as his giant frame enveloped me.

The time on the oven read eight twenty-three. Too early for Lev to have gone for his workout.

Where is he?

I wouldn't be that girl.

I wouldn't text him. No sir-ee.

I would go have breakfast with Nas instead, and try to fish out information from her.

It was a nice day. The walk did me good, now that I wasn't having phantom labor pains. The air was cool and the sun was warm. I smiled up into the sky.

Making my way up the steps, I rang the bell and waited.

And waited.

And waited some more.

Lifting my hand, I knocked. "Come on, Nas. Get up!"

She answered the door, blinking away sleep, her face bunched and hair all over the place, wearing a flimsy nightie. "What the fuck, dude?"

I beamed at her, and not waiting for an invitation, I slid by her. "I'm hungry and I need coffee."

Her expression dampened. I turned to her and stared, beginning slowly, "I actually came here to find out where he'd gone."

She shrugged, yawning. "I don't know. I'm not his keeper."

I bit the inside of my lip, my nose bunching. "Yeah," I muttered, sounding disappointed. "Me either."

Nas rolled her eyes. "Whatever. Go wait in the kitchen. Let me excuse myself from my company."

As she walked back up the stairs, I called out a little too loudly. "*Morning, Vik!*"

I turned on the coffee pot and poured two mugs full as Nas came back into the kitchen, her hair tied in a high ponytail. She'd dressed in sweat pants and a loose sweater, with last night's makeup still smudged under her eyes.

Handing her a mug, I smiled slyly. "Have fun with your *company* last night?"

She glared at me over the rim of her mug before lifting her nose. "He snores."

Just then, a low, gravelly voice came from the open doorway. "She lies. And yes, we had fun. We *always* have fun. Played *Yahtzee* until just after dawn." Vik grinned, his eyelids low from sleep. He wore his dress pants and not a stitch more. I was too amused to check out his taut and gorgeous tattooed body.

I snorted, almost choking on my coffee. "Is that what the kids are calling it these days?"

He winked at me before doing something that surprised me.

He made his way behind Nas's chair, placed his hands on her shoulders, leaned in, and pressed his lips to the space just under her ear. She closed her eyes and smiled happily. He whispered something into Nastasia's ear and her face turned soft. She lifted a hand to cup his cheek tenderly before turning her face to press a soft kiss to his lips.

These were not the actions of two people who merely slept together. These were the actions of two people very much in love. My mind went back to the moment Nas told me that Viktor didn't love her back. Was she mental? It was clear as crystal, written all over his face. In his smile. The way he looked at her. Viktor Nikulin was head-over-heels for Nastasia Leokov. And he loved her in a way that most women dreamed of.

My heart smiled for the two of them. They had something special. Even if Nas didn't know it yet.

Vik poured a cup of coffee then moved around the table, stopping to kiss my head before seating himself at the head of the table. "You feeling better, wifey?"

I smiled at his nickname for me. It was clearly designed to make Nas jealous, and from the way her nose bunched, it was working. "I'm feeling much better, thank you. Damn virus," I lied.

Vik's brow rose. "I thought it was period pain?"

I blinked at him before turning to Nas. "Is no man in this family squeamish?" I fluttered my lashes at Vik. "I was trying to protect your delicate sensibilities."

He sipped his coffee. "That's too many big words for morning, Mina."

"So," I dug. "Where's Lev?"

Vik blinked at me, eyeing me curiously. "What's it to you?"

My cheeks heated. "Nothing," I uttered, dipping my chin.

Vik grinned, the shit stirrer. "Okay, then if it's nothing to you, he's gone to have breakfast with Anika."

"What?" My head shot up, eyes blazing, unsure of whether he was lying to get a rise out of me.

"Oh," Nas muttered, suddenly remembering. "Yeah, he is." She shook her head then cringed, "Sorry. I forgot."

Why was he having breakfast with Anika? Why wasn't he having breakfast with *me*? More importantly, why didn't he tell me?

Because it's none of your business!

My mind's statement hurt, because it was true. I *wanted* Lev to be my business. I wanted him to think about me when he made decisions, like having breakfast with a tall, gorgeous redhead who clearly wanted him for herself.

I shrank down in my chair and Vik's smile fell. "You're upset."

"I'm not upset," I blatantly lied, my cool tone giving me away. "Lev can do what he wants. He doesn't owe me explanations."

Nas tilted her head. "What's going on with you and my brother?"

LEV

I shrugged, unsure about how to answer. "I don't know. One second, he's all protective and caring and giving me necklaces, and the next, he's off hiding inside himself. I thought we had a thing, but it's like he's afraid to talk to me."

Vik stretched. "He *is* afraid to talk to you. Well, not you, but people in general."

Nas shushed him, but I reached out for all the information I could get. "What do you mean? He's so confident at the club." I was confused. "Why would he be scared to talk to me?"

Vik lightly nudged Nastasia's arm. "Will you talk to your girl? She thinks she's the issue. Give her a break, Nas."

She looked down at the table and muttered a low, "We don't talk about it."

Vik shook his head before leaning across the table to me and asking, "You ever wonder why Lev locks his bedroom door at night?"

I nodded enthusiastically. "All the time."

Nas spoke quietly, "Enough."

Vik ignored her. "He does it to protect himself. He doesn't feel safe at night, in the dark." He shook his head in disgust. "He was just a little boy."

"I don't understand."

Nas got up, walking over to the kitchen sink, trying to get away from the conversation.

"She used to beat him at night, after everyone had gone to sleep," Vik explained.

My heart broke, raced, and wept all at the same time for Lev, the little boy. Part of me wanted to know, but the other part wanted to let sleeping dogs lie. "Who beat him?"

Nas, looking out the kitchen window, whispered a dead, "My mother. She hated him."

Vik sneered. "Fuck, I hated that bitch. Always knew those smiles a'hers were fake."

"How could she?" I spoke quietly through my thick throat. "How *could* she?" I turned to Nas. "Why?"

Nas lowered her head, shaking it. She couldn't speak. She looked about ready to lose it.

Vik told the story. "No one knows how long she'd been doing it. The only reason we found out was because Lev stopped talking." He pinned me with a stare. "Just stopped talking, for a whole year. He was nine." He sighed in frustration. "Now, if that were any other kid, you'd think it was weird, right?"

"Yes," I agreed immediately.

"Not with Lev. Their pops, Anton, was a good man. He loved all of his kids equally. Was one of the good guys. He married into a good family, and Lev's mother, Talya, was a nice woman. Until Lev was born."

"Why would having Lev change that?" I pried.

Vik smiled at the thought of his friend. "Lev is different."

That he was.

"Anyone with half a brain could see that he didn't think like a kid. It's almost as if he was born with the mind of an adult. He was so serious. Barely laughed. He was smart as a whip. Didn't have any friends, apart from Anika and me. You could have hit him with a hammer, and he wouldn't show pain. Something about his mind doesn't work the way yours and mine do. He doesn't show emotion often, and when he does, it's mostly anger that's built up past breaking point."

Vik swallowed hard. "There was an incident. Lev's dog was run over. He didn't understand why the dog was gone. I mean, he knew she was dead, but the emotional build up was too much for him." Vik laid it on me, hard. "They found him in his room, rocking back and forth, beating his head against the wall. The wall was covered in blood. He was covered in blood. Had to go to the emergency room to get his head stitched up."

"Oh, my God." I covered my mouth with my hands, my stomach rolling in revolt.

"It was after that incident that Talya got weird. She'd curl her lip whenever Anton hugged Lev or showed him any attention. She ignored Lev when he spoke. She showered all of her attention on Nas, forgetting about her sons. And Lev started to pull away. He stopped looking people in the eye. Stopped talking to people. Didn't leave his room. That kind of thing. The one person who was meant to love him treated him like he was invisible, so he became invisible." Vik turned to Nas. "What no one knew was that Lev would talk to Nas. He didn't say much, but she was the only person he spoke to in that time."

"He talked to you?" That was a big deal. "What would he say?" I asked Nas gently.

LEV

She let out a long, shuddering breath. "That he was afraid of the dark. So I snuck into his room one night and slept beside him, holding him. He shook so bad, Mina. I thought he was having a fit. Finally, he fell asleep and the shaking stopped. I fell asleep too."

Oh, God. My stomach turned again. I knew what was coming.

Nas turned to face me, her eyes shining. "One second, I'm asleep. The next, the covers are being ripped away and she's dragging me out of bed by my ankle." She lifted her hand and touched a spot at the back of her head. "My head hit the ground hard. It all happened so fast that I couldn't think...couldn't scream. All I could do was lift my hands and hold them out as she beat the shit out of me with her bare fists."

A tear fell down her cheek and she swiped it away. "I just remember being so scared, and for the first time in my life, I believed in monsters living under your bed." She sniffed prettily. "The monster was my mother, of course, and she only stopped when she heard me crying. Lev didn't cry, ever. When Lev switched on the light, my mother looked down at me, shock on her face. She turned to Lev, pointed a finger, and screeched at him that he did this."

My eyes closing, I doubled over, my face paling. "Jesus, Nas."

"Yeah." she nodded gently. "I hadn't perfected the fetal position that Lev had, so I took more damage than I he ever did. Sasha must have heard me crying, because he walked into Lev's room and saw her standing over me. I was shaking and crying. I was five years old. Sasha walked back into his room, calm as ever, and he came back a few seconds later, pointing a loaded 9mm at our mother's head. He was twelve.

"His lip curled and he said, 'Touch 'em again and I'll blow your fucking brains out, bitch'." Nas laughed humorlessly. "Sasha never did beat around the bush. He called for my father, went over to Lev, and stood in front of him. He motioned to me and I ran to him. He held me tight while I cried. And Lev...he did nothing, because he couldn't function." She burst into tears, covering her face, her voice breaking. "And I finally understood why my brother was the way he was."

I stood so quickly that my chair screeched. I wrapped my arms around her and she accepted what I was offering. Her slim arms came around me and she spoke quietly. "My father removed Lev's shirt and looked him over. He was bruised all over." Her breath stuttered. "Lev spoke again, and his first words to my father in an entire year were 'I'm sorry'. Father cleaned me up, hugged me tight, and then put Sasha and me back to bed. Lev slept by Father's side, and we never saw our mother again."

God, she was hurting. "I'm so sorry, Nas. I'm so sorry."

She pulled back and looked down at me, dejected and teary-eyed. "No. I had one night of it. Lev probably endured years of it. I'm sorry it didn't happen sooner."

Sadness enveloped me. "Why did she hate him so much?"

Nas explained, "He was inferior, in her opinion. She couldn't believe that she, a high-class woman, could produce something so flawed. She hated that he wasn't normal. Went so far as to get a DNA test to prove he wasn't hers, that they'd made a switch at the hospital. When the results came back that he was indeed hers, she hated him even more. He was the worst thing that happened to her." Nas frowned. "But she didn't even know him. She didn't want to know him. He was so sweet and kind. And she broke him."

No. No, that wasn't right.

"He's not broken, Nas," I told her. "He's in there. I see him. He's just…stuck."

"Yeah," she agreed then sighed long and slow. "Don't give up on him, Mina. He doesn't trust easily, but once you're in with him…you're *in*. Put in the effort and you'll be rewarded." She added, "Just talk to him and be patient if he makes you do all the talking. He might not respond a whole lot, but he's listening to every word. He'll speak if he thinks something is worth saying."

I left soon after, walking home and waiting for Lev.

I didn't understand all of him, but what I knew of him, I understood a lot better.

A piece of my heart I had hidden long ago opened right then.

Lev was a clink in my armor, a crack in my wall, and I just knew that if he really tried, I would open myself to him completely in the hopes that he would do the same.

I would do that for him.

I would do that, because he was worthy.

CHAPTER TWENTY-FOUR

Mina

The sound of one-sided chatter aired as soon as the front door opened. I listened in from the kitchen as I went about my business, making toast and pouring myself a glass of orange juice.

"Lev, all I'm saying is that she probably feels awkward here," stated the familiar melodic voice.

I stilled mid-pour and my stomach boiled with liquid hot lava rage.

She was stooping to an all-time low. If Anika had an issue with me, she should have the balls to tell me to my face, not go behind my back and try to remove me from the picture.

Lev sighed. "This is none of your business, Ani." He sounded tired.

"Okay," she muttered in defeat. "Don't say I told you so when she leaves though."

Lev walked into the kitchen, and as soon as his eyes landed on me, the lines on his forehead softened. That was enough for me. My jealousy over his morning outing left me in a rush.

"Morning, sweetie," I said through a smile as I made my way over to him. I wrapped an arm around his middle and gave him a squeeze. He returned my embrace, leaning down to kiss my hair.

"Good morning, Mina."

We separated, and Anika stepped into the kitchen wearing an easy but false smile. "Morning, Mina." She looked me up and down. "You look...comfortable."

I glanced down at myself.

Confusion went through me. What offended her? My black tank, or my overly long grey sweats?

Perhaps it was the fact I wasn't wearing a bra under said tank.

When I looked back up at her and found her glaring at the small indents my nipples were making in the material, I almost smiled. I wanted to tell her it was okay, because Lev had already seen them in real life. But I didn't. Instead, I shrugged. "Sure, I guess so." I smiled, teeth gleaming. "So, how was breakfast?"

Anika frowned. "How did you know we were at breakfast? *We* didn't know we'd be out for breakfast."

I bit into my toast, fighting the urge to throw my juice in her face. I chewed slowly then shrugged. "Vik told me."

Anika straightened, her face paling slightly. "When did you see Vik?"

Lev poured himself a glass of orange juice. His brow furrowed. "Yes, when *did* you see Viktor?"

Oh my.

Is that jealousy I smell, Lev Leokov?

It certainly seemed so. I decided to experiment with that. I lowered my lashes. "This morning. We did coffee." I smiled secretly, biting the inside of my lip. "It was…nice."

"Does Nas know?" Anika glowered.

Yes, I wanted to yell. *Because I would never do that to my friend, you turd*!

Rather, I nodded slowly. "Sure does." I turned to Lev, nibbling on my toast. "On another note…Lev, how would I ask a guy out?"

He swallowed at the wrong time, choking on his orange juice. Coughing, his face turned red and he spluttered in disbelief, "You want to date?"

My head tilted in thought. "I do. I really do. But how would I get his attention?"

My intention was to make Lev jealous, but what he said next had Anika shrinking into herself.

He sighed, running a hand through his hair. "Mina, if the man hasn't noticed you yet, he's not worthy of you."

Light rose up, warming me from the inside. My blush was very real. I swallowed hard. "H-how would I let him know that I liked him? That I wanted to go on a date with him?"

He leaned back against the fridge, looking mildly disappointed. He spoke evenly. "I suppose telling him would be the most straightforward way." He crossed his arms over his chest, his speech turning into a growl as he spoke through gritted teeth. "Ask him out to dinner." He straightened and walked out of the kitchen, uttering, "He won't refuse you, Mina. He wouldn't be so stupid."

Oh, my Lord.

He *was* jealous.

Hallelujah!

My eyes on the open doorway, I heard Anika's saccharine sympathy. "Mina…Vik won't date you, honey."

I laid a glare on her before raising my brow. "Who said anything about Vik?"

I followed Lev upstairs, allowing Anika to find the door on her own as she'd done many times before, and found myself standing outside the en suite in our bedroom. I raised my hand, knocking lightly. "Lev?"

"A moment," he growled back.

I fought my smile, but my smile won. He opened the door and I jumped back from the force of it. It looked like he had just thrown water on his face, dew droplets still lingered at his jaw, and I wanted to lick them away.

"What is it, Mina? I need to get ready for my run," he muttered unenthusiastically.

I stepped forward, reaching out with my hand. Lev took the offered hand, his shoulders slumping in relief, and he grasped at it like a lifeline.

I did that to him.

I did that *for* him.

Not Anika.

Me.

Smiling, I ran my thumb over his, looked up into his cool whiskey eyes, and asked, "Would you like to have dinner with me tonight, Lev?"

For a moment, he looked confused. "We eat dinner together every night."

I nodded. "I know. I was hoping we could go out to eat. Together, just the two of us. Somewhere nice." I kept going, because he didn't seem to understand, just kept staring down at me, his brow low. "I'll wear something pretty. You'll wear something dapper." My smile turned into a soft laugh and I shook my head in dismay. "You're not making this easy on me, sweetie. Can't you see I'm asking you out on a date?"

His brows rose. He didn't speak a while, but then he confirmed, "You're asking *me*, not Viktor."

I blinked innocently. "Why would I ask Vik out? I'm not attracted to Vik."

"You're attracted to me," he uttered, almost to himself, as if he needed the reassurance.

I didn't bother with a response. I already told him he was the most handsome man I knew. I didn't tell him he was sexy as hell and that I'd masturbated to the memory of his naked body as he stepped into the shower, but I was sure I would, eventually.

"Yes," he responded quietly. "I would be honored to have dinner with you, Mina."

I took our entwined hands apart and held his open palm at my cheek. My smile grew wider as I asked deliberately, "Lev," I lowered my lashes. "Are you going to kiss me tonight?"

He ran his thumb over my lips. His eyes on the prize, he asked hoarsely, "Do you want me to?"

I landed a light peck to the pad of his thumb and he pressed it gently into my kiss as I whispered huskily, "Yes. Very much."

"Me too," he admitted. "And yes, I think I will."

It was too much. I wanted to squeal from excitement, but had the sudden feeling that I would be sick, so I played it cool. Taking his hand from my cheek, I pressed a soft, lingering kiss to the center of his palm. "Can't wait. What time?"

For the first time since I'd met him, Lev looked lost for words. "Um..."

"Six?" I prompted.

"Yes. Six."

"Great." I beamed and moved to leave the bedroom, stopping at the open door and turning. "Lev?"

He lifted his head to focus on me.

I leaned against the doorframe and admitted, "I've been imagining what you'd look like in a pair of jeans." I straightened and winked. "Who knows? Maybe you'll wear a pair tonight." I looked down at his long legs. "For me."

No hesitation. "Okay."

My smile wide, I blew him a kiss from the door, rushed down the stairs, and ran all the way to Nastasia's.

What was the process before one went on a date?

I didn't have a flipping clue, but I knew Nas would.

⚓

Nas dressed me in a black dress with a pencil skirt that went to my knees and a high neck that showed none of my non-existent cleavage. Although I was close to my goal weight, I wasn't quite there yet, but my knees were no longer knobby and I had flesh where flesh should have been. My breasts had yet to catch up with the rest of my body. My butt, however, was doing well.

Knowing how I walked in heels, Nas hooked me up with a pair of black leather strappy sandals, and I wore my white blazer over the top. My hair was left wavy but tamed, flowing down my back. Nas lent me a white clutch to put my phone and lip-gloss in, and I was ready to go.

I waited until five fifty-five before I walked back down to the house. Using the key Lev had given me, I unlocked the front door and stepped inside just as Lev was making his way down the stairs.

My breath left me in a whoosh. I was lucky that I held onto the door handle, or else I would've found myself sprawled on the floor in a dead faint.

Lev had found his jeans.

Oh, did he ever.

Jesus Christ, they fit him like a glove. His hair styled nicely, as always, he hadn't shaved, leaving a nice five o'clock shadow playing at his jaw. The grey sweater he wore, pushed up to the elbows, was formfitting and stylish, and those black jeans...

Oh, God. He looked *incredible*.

My heart beat faster and my tongue began to swell.

It was hot in here. I fought the urge to fan my face.

I smiled shyly. "Hi."

His eyes smiled back. "Hello." The second to last step down, his eyes roamed my body. "You look stunning, Mina."

"And you…" It was sweltering in here. "In jeans." My eyes widened as I smiled and breathed, "Wow."

His cheeks took on a pink tinge. He cleared his throat and asked, "I'm not underdressed, am I?"

Sweet cupcakes, if he changed out of those jeans, I would cry throughout dinner, spilling tears into my meal, and eating them up because I was hungry and not very picky.

I stepped forward and rushed out, "No, not at all. You look…" Sexy as fudge. "…very handsome, Lev." I went on, "Don't change." I was slightly embarrassed when I said, "I like you in jeans."

He met me at the door, holding his hand out. I took it, entwining our fingers. He looked down at me. "Ready?"

Lev led me out of the house and down the front steps. I let out a restless sigh. "Ready as I'll ever be."

LEV

Dinner was a quiet affair. Lev brought us to a little Russian place down an alley in the city.

I was touched. It seemed like he'd made an effort, wanting me to experience some part of him, however small it was.

We held hands until after we seated. Lev asked questions about me, and I answered each of his questions with enthusiasm, only asking him the most basic of questions. I didn't want to spook him. I'd learned that both his mother and father were Russian immigrants, that Lev liked to play sports but not watch them, that he preferred blackberry jam to all others, that he had cousins in New York who he adored, that he liked to read rather than watch TV, and that he had a double degree in business and mathematics, which he completed at the ripe old age of twenty-one.

We ordered a few different dishes and shared them. Lev insisted we get the *stroganoff*, which was light and creamy, and the beef was cooked till beautifully tender. Next we ordered the *blini*, which were thin crepes filled with an array of fillings, from smoked salmon and cream cheese, to sour cream and caviar. Lastly, we got the *pelmeni*, and they were delicious dumplings filled with minced lamb, garlic, and herbs.

We cleared all the dishes, even though we ordered for six people. And, *damn* Lev, but even the way he ate was sexy!

Lev reached for the last *pelmeni,* but must have spotted the forlorn look on my face. He shook his head, his lip might have twitched (or maybe I imagined it), and he placed the last dumpling on my plate.

I ate it with nothing more than a smile, and Lev continued to watch me, a soft look on his face. Once our dishes were cleared, he reached out across the small table, and with a shy smile, I placed my hands in his.

He held them in silence, stroking his thumbs over mine.

Oh, boy. I was ready for that kiss.

He checked his watch. "Shall we head off? We start work in forty-five minutes."

I stood quickly. "Yeah, I'm ready."

Ready for you to kiss the shit out of me!

Lev took care of the check, cocooned my hand in his own, and then walked us to the car. "Our date...it was nice."

"Yeah," I murmured in agreement. "We should do it again."

He let go of my hand, helping me into the car.

Hmmm.

No kiss.

He drove in silence, my fingers playing with his across the center console. Before long, we were at the club and stepping out of the car.

This was it. I could feel it.

I waited for him to open my door, stepping out gracefully. I smiled up at him and his eyes returned the sentiment. He placed his arm around my shoulders, pulling me into his side. "Come on. We have work to do."

I understood that. I wouldn't dream of being unprofessional, not when I had been handed this opportunity when I *literally* had nothing. And yet, as we walked on into the club, disappointment filled me, and one thought circled my mind.

Where's my damned kiss, Leokov?

CHAPTER TWENTY-FIVE

Mina

Service was slow this evening. Although we only had four of the smaller tables empty, we were all feeling the tension. Were the customers we'd lost to Aphrodite's Kiss lost to us forever?

The thought scared the crap out of me, being that it meant I would be out of a job. I couldn't afford to be out of a job. I had a very delicate subject to bring up with Lev. That subject being me moving out.

I had secretly been going to Nastasia's in the mornings and house hunting. There were a few good options, but I didn't have enough saved in just over six weeks to warrant me blowing all my dough at once. I needed at least another two or three weeks to get into a comfortable position. I didn't want to mooch off Lev. He had done nothing but support me since he found me, and I was beginning to think I was becoming a nuisance.

Damned Anika and her comments from this morning!

They were playing on me.

When Lev and I walked into the bar and separated to head off in our designated areas, Nas stopped me before I headed behind the bar. "What did you do to my brother?" It was an accusation if I ever heard one.

My brow creased. "What do you mean?"

She turned, throwing her arms out in his direction. Then she leaned toward me and whisper-hissed, *"He's wearing jeans!"* She shook her head, eyes wide. "What the fuck?"

Oh, *that*. I rolled my eyes. "I asked him to wear them. I'd never seen him in jeans. He looks great in them, don't you think? Much more approachable." I turned to look over at him at the very same moment he turned to look at me. I smiled and lifted a hand in a timid wave. "That ass, though. *Grrr*."

Lev winked at me.

He freaking *winked* at me.

And my stomach flipped.

"*Ewww*," Nas muttered, then her voice gentled. "I can't believe he's wearing jeans. I don't know what you're doing with him, but keep doing it. He's loosened up a whole lot since you got here, *kukla*."

I was too sad to register that she had paid me a major compliment. Instead, I pouted. "He said he would kiss me tonight." I turned to look at her. "He hasn't kissed me yet. I want it so bad it hurts."

Nas's eyes widened. "I'm going to pretend we're not talking about my brother here for a second and tell you that if you want something, you're going to have to fight for it." She leaned against the bar. "Those are the rules."

My mouth parted in shock as I glared at her. "There are *rules*? Why didn't I know this?"

She shrugged. "You were homeless. I don't think homeless people are down on the rules."

I clicked my tongue and bit my thumbnail. "Damn being homeless to heck."

Nas nudged me with a chuckle. I liked when we joked around like this. It was soothing. It felt so normal to have a friend to kid around with, and yet, it was so foreign to me.

I joined Birdie behind the bar and, with a quick hug in greeting, we started to work. It wasn't long into my shift before Brick told me that Sasha wanted to see me in his office.

Sasha made me nervous. He always looked as if he had an ulterior motive. Perhaps it was hidden to the general eye, but I'd known many people like that on the streets and could spot them a mile away.

I knocked before stepping inside. "You wanted to see me?"

He stood by the side of his desk, going over some paperwork. He was dressed in a black tailored suit and white shirt. Sasha was tall, and I was sure that whatever he was hiding under his suit was close to the perfection I had seen on Lev. His dark brown hair cut into a faux-hawk, his frosty brown eyes looked up at me. "Shut the door behind you."

He would be so handsome if only he smiled.

I couldn't help it. Sarcasm was the language I spoke with Sasha. "Yes, sir. Cap'n, sir." I closed the door and sat on the guest chair.

Sasha moved around the table and sat behind the desk, looking at me in the eye. "It's been six weeks."

I nodded. "Yes, it has."

He tilted his head slightly and waited. When he realized I wasn't going to add anything, he lifted his hands. "Don't you think it was time you moved on?"

My heart shrank three sizes. My throat seized in panic. I couldn't speak for a long while. Finally, I found my voice, shaky as it was. "I wasn't aware my position here was temporary."

"It's not," he said in complete calm. "But between you and me, it always was." His eyes bore into me. "You knew that." He searched my face, and whatever he found there, he wasn't happy with it. He sighed, irritated. "You didn't know that."

I shook my head.

Sasha leaned back in his chair and I squeaked under his weight. "Lev likes pretty girls." My eyes snapped up. "Extra points if they're damaged." His lip curled. "Like you."

"I'm not damaged," I whispered.

He smiled then, but it was harsh, cruel. "You're a pretty girl, Mina. But Lev's choices in women don't lie. You might not be damaged, but you're damaged goods."

He was being unnecessarily insensitive. This was all I knew of Sasha. Nasty looks and cruel taunts. It was tearing me down emotionally. And that stunk, because I was finally in a good place with myself. "Why are you being so mean to me?"

At hearing my question, his brow furrowed in confusion. "You misunderstand me, Mina. I'm not being mean. I'm being honest. Sometimes the truth hurts."

My self-esteem had taken a major hit. I was about ready to burst into tears at the humiliation. "So, I'm fired then?"

"No," he uttered sincerely. "No. Not fired. But you're going to leave us. Quit. You're going to go far away and leave my brother alone."

No. I wouldn't. "No. I won't."

Sasha exhaled, long and slow. "I know you guys have some little flirtation happening. It's cute. But you're something he doesn't need right now."

"Who are you to say that? Maybe you should ask him what he needs."

He scowled at me. "Listen to me. Irina will tear you apart, girl. She doesn't want Lev, but she doesn't want anyone else to have him. Her objective in life is to make him miserable. As long as you're in the picture, he'll never get Lidiya back. It's her way or no way."

"I don't believe you," I told him, even though part of me did.

He shook his head at me. "I didn't want to insult you. You seem like the type of woman who would be insulted by an offer, but here." He handed me a check. "A hundred grand. Two years of wages. You'll be able to set yourself up from scratch, find a new job, and an apartment far, far away."

He knew it was coming. How could he not? I took the check between my fingers and tore it straight down the middle.

Fuming, I stood and walked toward the door, pausing as I opened it. "How does it feel, Sasha?

How does it feel that the homeless chick, the woman who has nothing, wouldn't take your money?" I looked him up and down, shaking my head in revulsion. "Your brother is ten times the man you'll ever be, and if you want me gone, you'll have to take me away in a body bag."

He grinned, amused at my sudden stand. "Calm yourself, viper. That won't be necessary."

I lifted my nose. "Is that all, Mr. Leokov?"

He waved me off. "That will be all."

⚓

It was hard to concentrate after Sasha's intervention on my relationship with his brother. Why was it any of his business anyway? What happened between Lev and me should stay between the two of us. It was none of his concern.

As the night came to an end, Birdie and I finished loading up the dirty glasses onto trays and took them into the back area to load up the industrial dishwasher. We wiped down the countertops and tables and lifted the non-slip mats for the cleaners, who would come in after we had left. We chatted amongst ourselves and waited for the others to be done so we could leave as a group.

Anika had disappeared halfway through service and I didn't see her again. My guess was that she'd taken ill.

Birdie and I chatted away. I laughed at something she'd said when I heard, "Mina?"

Lev stood behind me. I smiled back at him. "Just a second, sweetie."

Birdie continued her story and I listened intently.

"Mina?"

I turned around and bunched my nose. "Hold on, Lev. The story's almost done."

Birdie took me to the crescendo of her tale and we both burst into laughter. Then suddenly I squeaked as I was being lifted off the ground and my ass hit the bar counter.

I was quickly coming to realize that if Lev wanted your attention, he'd fight for it. I blinked, face-to-face with Lev, his hands on either side of my thighs. "Hi."

He winced. "Hello."

It was then that I noticed he was in pain and my heart panged. "What's wrong?"

He shook his head but spoke through gritted teeth. "Headache. I'd like to leave now."

"Okay." I lifted my hands and touched his neck lightly while running the other over his forehead. He was a little warm. "But first, can I try something?" I ran my hands through his hair, gently using my thumbs to circle along his temples. He groaned out loud. When I thought he could stand more pressure, I pressed harder. His eyes closed and his lips parted as I massaged his temples.

Without warning, he stepped closer, a frown at his brow, fitting himself into the space between my knees, snaking his arms around my waist and resting his forehead in the center of my chest, moaning as I went about my ministrations.

He greedily snatched my attention, and I loved every moment of it. I loved that he took what he needed from me.

I placed soft kisses at the crown of his head and held onto him, my legs wrapping around his waist. After five minutes of massage, I released his temples and wrapped my arms around his shoulders, trying not to think about his crotch being so close to mine.

We stayed in that embrace for a long while after, just relishing in the warm glow we had created in each other.

After a minute, Lev lifted his head, his arms still holding me. His eyes sleepy and his hair messy, I couldn't wait anymore. There would be no other moment as perfect as now. "Better?"

He grunted while nodding.

I smiled, cupping his cheeks. "Good." Then I drew his face toward me, meeting him halfway and pressing my lips to his in a soft but deep kiss.

The arms around me tightened and pulled me closer. Our places of desire met full force.

I moaned, sliding my arms around his neck and pressing myself up against him, needing more of him. My head was swimming. This was the kiss I was hoping for and so much *more*. It was Lev in his purest form.

His hand came up and he gripped my chin between his thumb and forefinger, lifting my face to take more of my lips. His tongue, warm and sweet, dipped into my mouth and met mine in a delicious greeting.

That was when the wolf whistle sounded, followed by a rowdy bunch of hoots and chuckles.

We parted, looking around us, finding almost everyone looking over at us from all around the room, laughing at our private show. Including Anika. And she looked ready to burst into tears.

My cheeks flamed and, burying my face into Lev's collar, I groaned in discomfiture. Lev's chest shook in what I did not believe to be silent laughter as he ran his large hands soothingly down my back. After all, Lev didn't laugh.

Hell, he barely *smiled*.

"Can we go home yet?" I muffled into his shirt.

Strong hands at my waist lifted me down to the ground, and I wrapped an arm around Lev's waist, still embarrassed. We made our way to the car, saying goodbye to the people around us, when someone stepped out of the shadows.

Lev pushed me behind him in a harsh way and it frightened me. "Laredo," he growled.

Sasha rushed forward, reaching into his pocket to retrieve a pistol. My eyes widened. Sasha barked, "You got some nerve, old man."

Vik came rushing over, ever the peacekeeper, throwing his arm in front of Sasha. "Put that away. You're going to kill someone."

Nas came closer to stand beside me. She lifted her nose at the man who stood in front of Lev's car. "Uncle Laredo."

The older man smiled at her. "You haven't called me that in a long time, Nastasia." He looked saddened. "I've missed you." He looked around to Sasha and Lev. "All of you."

I peeked around Lev to the man named Laredo, and from the way he looked at me, he was as curious about me as I was about him. When his eyes met mine, I pulled back to hide behind Lev's broad back before hissing to Nas, "Laredo is your *uncle*?"

"By marriage," she explained. "Laredo married my father's sister, my Aunt Alina. She died young." She grinned, but it was harsh. "Then he had an affair with my mother."

I peeked around Lev, gasped, and spoke to the man himself. "You did? That's not cool!"

He shrugged weakly. "We were both lonely." He looked to Nas. "And if you'll remember, I was the one who ended it and brought the matter to your father." He shook his head. "I never meant to hurt anyone. Talya was there for me in the saddest time of my life. We both took advantage of the attention, and we both regretted it sorely. Your mother especially."

I stepped out from behind Lev and stood by his side. "She was an awful woman."

Laredo looked up at Lev and nodded compassionately. "Yes. She was deeply troubled."

Sasha had lowered the gun, but still held it in his hand. "Oh, boo-fucking-hoo. It's your regular family reunion." He sneered. "What do you want?"

He lifted his hand and pointed to me. "To see her."

Shit. He *knew*. I reached up and held onto Lev's hand. "I'm sorry. I won't do it again."

Lev, thinking the same thing I was, gripped my hand tight. "It wasn't her idea. You're stealing our customers. We needed to know what we were up against. If you have an issue, take it up with me."

Laredo laughed then. "I see. *That's* what you were doing at Aphrodite's." He took a step closer, but Lev pulled me away from him. Laredo shook his head but smiled. "I'm sorry. This is rather surreal." He spoke directly to me. "You look like someone I used to know."

"I don't know you."

He sighed gloomily. "No, I suppose you don't." He looked at me then, really looked at me, and whispered, "It's like looking into the face of a ghost." I wasn't prepared for when his eyes took on a faraway look as he uttered a hushed, "Clara."

My lungs seized.

My mother.

He knew my mother.

Nas was as shocked as I was. "Mina, wasn't that your mother's name?"

I nodded, looking into Laredo's astonished but hopeful face. "Yes. Clara was my mother."

Laredo stepped forward under the streetlight, and I had the opportunity to look at him. He was average height. Not very attractive, but his smile was lovely. He had average brown eyes with plain brown hair cut into a business do. He wore a nice suit, and had a gold tooth in the bottom right side of his smile.

He looked me in the eye and said genuinely, "I loved your mother very much. She was my world. We were going to get married a few years after my Alina passed away, but..." He shook his head.

Lev asked the question I had wanted to ask since my mother was mentioned. "Are you saying you're Mina's father?

Sasha muttered an annoyed, "Figures."

Laredo chuckled, but shook his head. "No." He looked me in the eye and he looked sad. "But I wanted to be. I would have given anything to be your father."

My throat was dry. I was parched. I licked my lips and stuttered, "D-do you know who my father is?"

He smiled, and it looked like something a naughty schoolboy would pull off. "No more." He reached into his pocket and pulled out a business card. "No more. Not until you agree to have dinner with me."

Lev growled, pulling me to his side.

Laredo's brow rose as he handed me the card. I reached out and took it eagerly. He stated through a smirk, "You chose the right brother, Mina. Lev's a good boy. Sasha…" He shrugged. "I don't know Sasha. I thought I did, but…" He looked over at the angry brother. "No, I don't. Not anymore."

He walked to stand in front of Nastasia and smiled down at her with fatherly grace. "I've missed my *bella boo*. May I have a hug?"

She looked like she would've given her right arm to throw herself into his embrace, but being the badass she was, she lowered her face and shook her head.

"No?" He sounded disappointed, but smiled through it. "Perhaps next time then."

Laredo took my free hand and kissed the back of it before making his way to the street. Halfway there, he turned, snapping his fingers. "Wait, I forgot." We all waited to hear what he had to say, unknowing that it would change my life forever. He grinned happily. "There's someone you need to meet. I hope you change your mind and come see us."

I was confused. "See who?"

His smile softened. "Your brother, of course."

Satisfied with my stunned silence, he turned around and went on his merry way, unaware that my world had just imploded around me, sucking me into a vortex of white noise.

CHAPTER TWENTY-SIX

Mina

"A brother, Lev," I breathed as I slipped of my dress. "A brother." Standing in the middle of our room, wearing panties and a strapless bra, I couldn't hide my delight. "*I have a brother.*"

Lev stepped out of the closet, wearing nothing but his dark grey boxers. "Brothers aren't always a good thing."

I snorted, knowing full well he was speaking of experience with his own brother.

He came to a halt, staring blatantly at my near naked body. I was too happy about the discovery of my long lost sibling to notice. "An hour ago, I was alone in the world."

"You had *me* an hour ago," Lev cut in, sounding somewhat disgruntled.

God, he was sweet. He was killing me with the *sweet*.

I couldn't deny it if I tried. I was *so* in love with Lev Leokov.

I made my way over to him and took hold of his hands. "I know, sweetie. And I love that. But…" I shrugged. "This is family. I have *family*." I could see that he wasn't sure how to react to this news. I told him, "I'm excited about this. Can we go and see Laredo together, please?" I needed Lev to know that my plans included him. "I won't go if you don't come with me." I squeezed his hands. "You're important to me, Lev. I want to share this with you. Just you."

He exhaled through his nose. "Of course I'll go with you." He brought my hand up to his mouth and pressed a whisper-soft kiss to my knuckles.

I grinned. "So, we're dating, right?"

He nodded. "Yes, I think so."

"And I can call you my boyfriend?" A goofy smile spread across my face.

His brow rose, but his eyes smiled. "I'm hardly a boy."

Oh, baby, don't I know it.

"And I don't have to wear my jammies to bed anymore?" I asked innocently.

He stilled, feigning disinterest. "Not if you don't want to."

I sighed in relief. "Thank God." I went over to the dresser, brought out a white tank top, slid it over my head, and then went about removing my bra, pulling it through my armhole. How great did it feel to take off your bra? "Ugh. *Freedom*."

Lev locked the bedroom door and we slid into bed, leaving the lamp by my side of the bed on. I turned to look at him, resting my head on my hand. "How's your head?"

He sat up in bed, his broad back against the headboard. "Better. The massage took the bite out of it. Thank you."

"My mom used to do that for me whenever I had a headache. It always worked." I smiled, moving to kneel on the bed, shuffling closer to him.

"And now that you're better..." I lifted my leg and maneuvered myself to straddle his thighs. His hands gripped my hips tightly. "I would like another shot at that first kiss, if you please," I requested, my hands resting on his wide shoulders as I lowered my face to his.

He kissed my smile until it melted away and all that was left was raw hunger. I moaned low in my throat when the hands at my hips coaxed me down to sit on his thick erection. His stubble scratched lightly while his full lips soothed the burn with kisses that rocked the foundation of my world.

Unconsciously, my hips began a dance on their own, grinding my panty-covered sex over his rigid length. He groaned into my mouth, and I panted into his. It wasn't long before he used his hands to guide me in a slow rhythm that had my panties in a knot.

I wanted to play.

I breathed into his mouth. "Take off your boxers."

The hands at my hips stilled and he pulled back to look at me. "Wait."

"*No!*" I was sexually frustrated. I needed his cock inside me now! "No, I'm tired of waiting. I've wanted this for weeks." I kissed him, pushing my chest into his. "I'm not waiting anymore, Lev. Now."

He kissed me back with all he had then pecked my lips. "I'm sorry to put a kink in your plans, but..." His brow rose. "Don't you have your period?"

"Oh." Well that freaking sucked. I buried my face into the space where shoulder meets neck and I mock sobbed. "*No.*"

He ran his hands down my back tenderly. "We can wait."

I lifted my face and shot him a look of disbelief. "For a week? A *whole* week?"

He kissed my nose. "I would wait ten years if you asked me, Mina." His eyes softened. "I feel like I've waited my whole life for you. A week is nothing in comparison."

Shit.

I was going to cry. For real.

My throat thick, I whispered, "Shit."

His expression turned panicked at the sight of my wet lashes. "I'm sorry. I told you I'm not good with words."

Wrapping my arms around his neck, I pressed my lips to his and spoke against them, "You are perfect, Lev. Your words are honest and colored beautifully. You make me feel things I thought were lost to me. And I'm in danger of losing my heart to you."

I didn't add 'and that scares the bejeezus out of me'.

He squeezed my hips with his big hands. "One day at a time."

I nodded. He was right. One day at a time.

Reaching across the bed, I turned off the lamp and lay in the center of the bed, waiting for Lev to take his place behind me. He fitted my body to his, spooning me sweetly, but the erection in the center of my back was hot and bothered. I could feel its anger.

In the dark, I whispered, "Want me to take care of that bad boy for you?"

The arm he had around me tightened and he repeated his previous words, "One week, Mina."

One week, indeed. One week of hell.

"Okay," I spoke quietly. "Night, Lev."

He moved my hair and kissed the base of my neck. "Goodnight, mouse."

⚓

I needed a glass of water. My mouth was drier than the Sahara.

On nights like this, I could walk all the way down to the kitchen in the middle of the night, or I could go into the en suite, run the faucet, and stick my mouth under it.

I chose the easy option, obviously.

Flinging back the covers, I slid out of bed, shuffled over to the en suite, and noticed a little too late that the light inside was already on.

I opened the door carelessly, unaware that I was about to walk in on something private. *Very* private.

My sleepy eyes widened and my lips parted as I took in Lev, leaning against the vanity, boxers off, his head thrown back in bliss as he tugged on his thick cock with a firm hand.

And what a cock it was.

A small squeak escaped me.

Lev's eyes snapped to me, but I couldn't take my eyes off his furious erection. It was long, and thick, and it looked as though Lev had manscaped. I was petite. I stood there a moment wondering how on earth it was going to fit inside me. Clearly, we'd have to take it slow.

"That looks painful," I mumbled sleepily, my hand still on the handle. It took a moment before I realized this was not a dream, regardless of how hot it was. I gasped, covering my face with a hand. "Shoot, I'm sorry! I didn't know anyone was in here. I'll…" I slipped back out and closed the door behind me. "I'll leave you to it."

I rushed back into bed, but my body was hot and bothered. I couldn't cover myself.

Five or so minutes passed, and finally, Lev came out of the bathroom. He slid into bed and we lay in a long silence.

My cheeks flamed. It couldn't be avoided. We needed to talk about it or it would become 'that awkward incident that shall never be named'. "I'm sorry."

He reached out and took my hand in his. "It's okay."

"Did..." *Don't ask. Don't ask. Don't ask*! "Did you finish?"

He ran his thumb over my palm, hesitation clear. "Uh, no."

My stomach coiled in distress.

He didn't finish, and it was all my fault. I gave him stage fright. I was the reason he couldn't take care of business.

I sat up and scooched over to him. Feeling around, I found his jaw and cupped his face between my hands, lowering my face to press slow, wet kisses onto his mouth.

He growled. "Mina, that's not really helping, baby."

Baby.

My heart sighed dreamily.

He called me baby.

I shushed him and kissed him deeper. "Let me help you." Without waiting for his opinion on the matter, I turned to face his feet and straddled him, sitting on his stomach, my legs open and out on either side of his.

His voice hoarse, he croaked, "You don't need to. It's okay"

God, he wanted it so bad. I could hear it in his tone. He was just playing it cool. I understood *need*. I spoke huskily, "I've been dying to touch you, Lev, and now that I've seen it, I don't think I can keep my hands off you."

That was the truth.

Running my hands down his thighs, I brought them back up slowly in a light massage. I did this over and over again until I heard Lev sigh in pleasure. I slid my hands up to either side of his length and held them there. With delicate care, my fingertips grazed the elastic of his boxers before slipping leisurely inside. The moment I came into contact with his hot, hard tool, Lev let out a long groan, and I wrapped the fingers of both my hands around it. It didn't surprise me that the fingers of both hands weren't able to meet. My hands were small, and he was *big*.

I let go of him a second to slide my thumbs under the waistband of his boxers and, thankfully, he took the hint, lifting his hips, allowing me to push them down to his knees. I quickly took him in my hands once more, worked him slowly in an up-down motion, and asked, "Lotion?"

"Don't have any," he rasped.

I slid back so that my rump was in the center of his chest and bent at the waist, stroking him all the way. I wanted to put my mouth on him. I tested the waters by gently licking around the head of his shaft and was rewarded when Lev convulsed in a way that almost threw me off.

Panting, he gripped my hips and thrust up into my hands. "Yeah, baby. That's good. *So* good."

I had to agree. He tasted clean with a tinge of saltiness, and every time my tongue passed over his slit, I was pleased to hear the sounds of his pleasure.

Opening my mouth, I held him straight and gradually took the head of him into my mouth, sucking lightly, feeling bolder and braver with every second.

Lowering onto him, I managed to take half of his length into my mouth before deeming myself at risk of gagging. My lips around him, I started an up-down motion again and sucked him deep as I could. His low groans and panting drove me.

He tasted so good that I moaned with him. I wanted to tell him that I was enjoying this as much as he was. "You taste so good, baby."

That seemed to drive him over the edge. His hips began to thrust fitfully, driving him farther into my mouth. A growl escaped his throat and he pulled my mouth away from him. I knew what was coming, pun intended.

My hands worked him in long, hard strokes until finally, his stomach clenched, his body went rigid under me, and he shouted his release. I felt it all. His cock throbbed furiously, sending warm spurts of cum shooting out onto my hands.

I held onto his softening dick, waiting for his body to catch up with the bliss his mind was experiencing. I was horny as hell, and although I could very well rub myself into an identical ecstasy, I chose not to. I felt powerful from what I had just done. I was high on the feeling. That was enough for me.

The moment I felt Lev's body melt into the bed, I moved off him and made my way to the bathroom to wash my hands and face. Before I washed it off, I examined the sticky white goop on my hands. I touched a finger to it and rubbed it between my thumb and finger. Just as Lev walked into the en suite—buck-naked—I touched that finger to my tongue, meeting his eye in the mirror.

It didn't taste bad. It was different. A little bitter and salty, but it wasn't something I would *hate* to have in my mouth.

He watched me carefully, and it forced a smile from me as I washed my hands and mouth. "It doesn't taste so bad, you know." I told him, "Maybe next time you won't have to pull out."

And still, he watched me, his soft cock larger than any I'd ever seen. I stepped toward him, reached up, and cupped his cheeks. "Better?"

He blinked sleepily. "Much. Thank you."

He was so polite, even in situations that didn't call for it. He was so silly. It made me smile. I pulled his face down to mine so I could kiss his lips. "You're welcome, sweetie. The pleasure was all mine." His brow rose. I rolled my eyes. "Okay, well, maybe not *all* mine, but it sure was fun."

After Lev washed up, he came to bed naked as the day he was born and pulled me into his side, sighing contentedly.

One dinner date, and so many things had changed. I should have been freaked out, but I wasn't. It felt like a natural progression. It might have seemed it, but it didn't feel rushed. It felt expected.

I fell asleep telling myself that things would only get better from here.

Oh, how wrong I was.

CHAPTER TWENTY-SEVEN

Mina

It was obvious to anyone with eyes and half a mind that Lev and I were official. If the open displays of affection hadn't clued them in, the way Lev would growl at any man who touched me would have.

It was nice to be wanted, nice to be the object of a man's affection. Of course, it was different with Lev. When he gave his attention, he gave it all. When he listened to you speak, he listened intently, no matter how mundane the subject. When he spoke, he thought carefully about what he should say, as though his words were a precious gift that he only gave to few. And I was one of the lucky ones.

When he held me, I felt as though the world could just float away, leaving the two of us locked in an embrace that would bypass anything and everything.

I loved him more than I thought possible.

And so, five days passed rather easily. Lev and I had gone to the bank to set up a savings account for me. I asked that I no longer be paid in cash, and Lev agreed that it was important that I have record of where I was getting my income.

Five nights of work ended in five nights of passionate make-out sessions before bedtime, with only one of those nights concluding with Lev getting a happy ending. During the course of those sessions, I discovered how erotic it was to undress a man, how much I loved running my hands over Lev's naked body, and how serious this thing was between us. This was not a one-night, get-it-out-of-your-system type of passion. This was more, *so* much more.

Although light petting had been the main theme, I'd never lost my clothing before, not completely anyway, until last night. My tank was pulled over my head in a lust-fueled frenzy. My small breasts were squeezed by large hands. My nipples were rolled between deft fingers. And when his warm mouth closed over one stiff peak and sucked, my back had bowed in a way that might have looked like I was being electrocuted, and it sort of felt like I was, in a way.

Lev was always the one to stop the fun, knowing I was much too irresponsible to be trusted to the task.

Sex had never felt like this as an adolescent. It was clumsy and awkward and inelegant. Even *non-*sex with Lev was fluid and flowing and graceful. If this was how mild petting went, I could hardly wait for the main event.

Things could not have been going better...until that night.

The club's crowd had not gotten all that much better, but some of our loyal customers returned after they had their fill of Aphrodite's Kiss. We were grateful. How could we not be? We treated those customers as if they were kings among men, flashing them smiles, showering them with attention, and flirting at a safe distance.

I wasn't sure what time it was when Anika came up behind me, leaned forward, and spoke into my ear, but the night was coming to an end. "Sasha wants you in his office. I'll take over for you."

Since Lev and I had made it known we were a couple, Anika had been surprisingly pleasing to be around. I thanked her and walked down the hall to the office. I placed my hand on the doorknob, turned it, and let myself in. "You wanted to see m—"

My words were cut off when I spotted the scene playing out before my eyes.

Sasha sat behind his desk, looking angrier than a bull in heat with no lady cows to funk his junk. Vik stood by the antique bookcase, leaning his hip against it, glaring down at the guest chair. The man sitting there was moaning low in his throat, bordering unconsciousness, his face bloody and swollen, hands tied behind his back, while Lev…

He held his fist up, a brass knuckleduster fitted across his fingers, his face screwed up, chest heaving. I gasped lightly, my hand flying to my mouth. That was when he spotted me.

The blood left my face, leaving me feeling cold and confused. My lips parted in shock, and my heart began to race.

The streets were not kind to me. I'd seen things that would make the regular person lose their lunch and this was nothing compared to that. What shocked me was that this was Lev.

Safe, protective, wouldn't-hurt-a-fly *Lev*.

Then all three men were looking at me.

Lev's brow furrowed and, lowering his balled fist, he moved to step toward me. "Mina—"

I couldn't look at him. Lowering my gaze to the floor, I uttered, "I'm sorry," and I saw myself out, shutting the door with a light slam. I turned to walk away, but jumped when I saw Anika standing there, her face emotionless. I licked my dry lips. "Sasha didn't want to see me, did he?" She lifted her nose in defiance and crossed her arms over her chest. My mind was a chaotic mess of puzzlement. "Why? Why did you do that?"

"You want a life with Lev? *This* is life with Lev." She looked smug and I hated her right then. "You want in. You needed to know." Her tall frame straightened and she spoke down on me, judging me for judging them. "This life isn't so pretty now, is it, Mina?"

My heart squeezed. "Why do you hate me?"

Her face softened then, but only marginally. "I don't hate you. I just don't think you can be there for Lev in the way that I can." Lifting her hand, she threw it out to Sasha's office door. "Can you handle *that*?" I honestly didn't know if I could. She stated confidently, "Because *I* can. And it doesn't change the way I feel about him."

I rushed past her, throwing my shoulder into her arm, and as I did, she called out, "You'll thank me for this one day!"

No. No, I wouldn't.

Lev attempted to approach me approximately a half-hour later, but I couldn't bring myself to answer his call. I ignored him till he physically walked behind the bar, took me by the hand, and pulled me into the dark, empty corner of the bar. "Mina?" And still, I avoided his gaze. "Mina, talk to me." His hands came up to cup my cheeks and he spoke a hair's breadth away from my lips. "Please."

My voice hoarse, I responded, "Can we talk about it later?"

He ran his thumbs lightly across the apples of my cheeks. "Okay." Then he brought his lips to mine and kissed me in what I believed was an attempt to make me forget about what I had just seen, but the memory played on a loop. I turned my head to the side, disconnecting our lips, heartbroken.

Who was that version of Lev in Sasha's office?

Certainly not the man I fell in love with.

I didn't know that man, and it petrified me that our relationship may have been built on assumptions and lies. I asked myself if I knew Lev at all.

I would find out later that night.

⚓

We drove home in silence. Lev pulled my arm across the center console and held my hand, but my hold remained loose.

LEV

The drive felt longer than previous nights, where I would sing along to the radio, not even mildly caring about my tone deafness because I was too damn happy with my current life to give a damn. I had Lev, and that was all I needed.

But after tonight, I asked myself *which* Lev did I have? There were two of them, I had discovered.

I required an explanation.

The silence was heavy and growing thicker by the second.

We made our way upstairs, undressing, and for the first time in a week, I dressed in my yellow pajamas. Lev noticed. The distasteful look in his eye as he glanced at the *hideous* ensemble said so. I sat in the middle of the bed, my legs crossed.

Standing in front of the bed dressed in nothing more than his black boxers, he let out a soft sigh, unable to meet my eyes. "I understand you're confused."

My brow rose and I let out a soft grumble of agreement.

His hand came up and he scratched at his chin. "There are things you don't know about me, Mina."

I laughed humorlessly. "I can see that."

"He owes Sasha money."

My blood began to boil.

Lev went on, "This is how business is dealt with when you're a Leokov."

I swallowed hard, anger causing my stomach to dip.

"The man you saw tonight owes Sasha a hundred thousand dollars."

That was it. I'd heard enough. As my mouth opened, anger spewed forth, and something I hadn't planned on saying came out. "Who cares if the guy owes him money? He offered me the same amount to leave you, dammit!" I scowled. "Money is clearly of no object to *Sasha*." I snarled his name.

The moment I realized what I had just told Lev, my face blanched.

Lev's jaw steeled and his cheek ticked. His hands curled into fists and his stomach tightened. His voice was low, dangerous. "What did you say?"

No, no, no, no, no, no, nooooooo.

What had I just done? Blood roared in my ears and I heard my pulse loud and clear. My mouth dry, I attempted to bring some moisture to my lips by licking them. I pulled a pillow over my lap and hugged it tight. "I didn't take it, obviously." My voice was small. *Tiny*.

His eyes narrowed, and he spoke again through gritted teeth. "He *what?*"

Shit on a stick. Now you've done it!

The look on his face told me he was about to do something brash. So I did the only thing I could think of.

Standing as quick as I could, I took the two steps to the edge of the bed and threw myself off it in haste. Before Lev could think about what was happening, my body collided with his midair and he wrapped his arms around me, holding me up, almost too tightly. My arms went around his neck and my legs wrapped high around his waist. I squeezed him tight.

He was still mad. "Mina, let go of me. Please."

"Never," I whispered.

It must have been the right thing to say at the time, because his strong arms loosened around me, holding me lightly, and he turned his head to rest his lips at my temple, one hand moving down slowly to cup my left ass cheek.

I couldn't believe what I was about to say. "Your brother loves you, Lev. He might have a shitty way of showing it, but he does. Otherwise, he wouldn't bother to do what he did." I paused before adding on a squeeze, "I would kill to have a family that loves me. Don't be angry with him, sweetie. He's just looking out for you."

That soothed the raging beast. He carried me over to the bed and, without extracting me from him, lay down on his back, taking me down with him. He looked up at the high ceiling and breathed in deep, uttering on an exhale, "I'm sorry about what you saw."

Resting my chin on his chest, I spoke quietly, "Are you happy doing things like that?"

He thought about it a moment, his voice austere when he replied, "I don't feel when I do things like that."

It was such a sad answer that my heart ached for him. Turning my head to the side, I whispered, "You scared me tonight."

"I'm sorry."

So many apologies from this man. I wondered if he was sorry, or if it was just something to say to fill the void.

I lifted my face once more to search his face and pondered out loud, "Do you think you'd have told me if I didn't find out the way I did?"

His heated eyes averted, he shook his head. At least he was honest.

"Why can't you look at me, sweetie?"

Another shake of the head. His arms tightened around my back. What he said next broke my heart.

His voice hushed, he stated honestly, "I don't know what I'd do if I saw disappointment there."

My eyes shut and I squeezed them tight, holding in the tears I so badly wanted to shed. My lips lowered to his chest and I kissed him there, right over his heart.

I wasn't going to get the answers I needed. Not tonight, and not from Lev.

I would have to go elsewhere.

⚓

Waking in the morning with a hot mouth on your breast, growling into the soft flesh, suckling hard, was indeed a fine way to be roused.

My good morning came out something like, "God, *yes*, honey. Suck harder," as my arms cinched around the back of his head, pulling him closer.

Where did my pajamas go?

He removed his mouth, grinding his erection into my hip, and asked, "It's over?"

I went blank. It was over already?

Well that was quick.

Sad face.

I couldn't help but feel a twinge of disappointment. But then he asked again, clearer this time, "Your period, baby. Is it over?"

Oh!

You're such a dick.

I almost snorted, but I was too busy panting and running my fingers through Lev's sleep-mussed hair. "Yes, it's over."

The light spotting had ended three days ago, thank the Lord above.

His thumbs hooked into the waist of my silky white panties. They were yanked down with a harsh tug and I helped by kicking them off my ankles. He knelt above me. The light sunshine coming through the cracks between the curtains helped me see Lev's cock jutting up and out of the waistband of his boxers.

He was as ready as I was.

He gazed down at me, taking in the sight of my nude body for the very first time. I was glad Nas had talked me into getting another bikini wax the week before. Although I kept myself neatly trimmed, I refused to go hairless. I just didn't like it. And, right now, I was grateful for it. It kept me from feeling overly exposed as Lev's eyes slowly trailed every inch of me.

It was making me anxious. I needed contact. Reaching up, I gently ran my hands down his arms, and when our hands brushed, he entwined our fingers, bringing my hands to his lips, pressing slow, precise kisses to my knuckles.

His hands released mine and then he was on top of me. We were caught in an embrace, and we were kissing.

These kisses were not wild or passionate or lustful. They were the warm, gentle, lazy kind. The dangerous kind. The kind that made me wonder why we couldn't do this forever. Be this way forever. Be each other's forever.

I had hope that it was possible.

His lips trailed my jaw, down to my neck, stopped to greet the valley between my breasts, and then skimmed my stomach, pausing just below my bellybutton to breathe warmly at the quivering flesh there.

The tip of his nose marked the journey down lower still, and then his hands were on my hips, squeezing as he buried his nose into the soft hair of my sex.

I swallowed hard. My eyes were wide open. The apples of my cheeks burning hot. I panted lightly.

He wasn't going there…was he?

This was all so sudden. I didn't have time to chose a sexy pose to present myself. I didn't even know if I was ready for this. It was so much more intimate than intercourse. There was no hiding when you had a face all up in your love glove.

Then his hands were at my knees and he was spreading me wide open, peering down at my most intimate place. Part of me wanted to see his reaction, but my self-conscious mind wouldn't let me. My eyes snapped shut and my hands came up to cover my face.

I let out an embarrassed groan. That embarrassed groan quickly turned into a passionate moan, my hands falling away from my face as Lev's tongue came out to swipe me firmly from ass to clit.

Slow and precise.

Deep and adoring.

Wet and warm.

His tongue was a weapon, and it was killing me in his leisurely attack.

He placed his mouth over my pulsating button and sucked it lightly, pulling back as he did. My hands tangled in the sheets as a ragged sigh was ripped from my throat. Lev knew how to pleasure a woman. There was no faking my reaction. It was raw and genuine and so blissful that it bordered painful.

His fingertips played at my entrance, rubbing and kneading, but never taking the plunge inside where I needed it most, leaving me feeling bereft. And just when I thought I was going to go insane from the sweet torture, he gave me what I needed. One finger slipped inside with excruciating slowness.

And my body lit up like a Fourth of July fireworks display.

No longer in control of myself, my thighs tightened around Lev's head as I whimpered in need. I was so close.

He placed open-mouthed kisses on my pussy, lapping at me, eating me up. Every now and then, his tongue would stiffen and make the dive into me. There was no pussyfooting around. He did to me exactly as the act was termed. He was performing oral sex.

Well, no. Not quite.

He fucked my pussy with his tongue.

The thought drove me wild. The act made me senseless. Combined, I was lost.

My thighs clenching either sides of his head, my hands fisted in his hair, my head thrown back in uncontrollable ecstasy, it wasn't long before I was grinding myself into his clever mouth. His hands slid under my body, lifting my hips clean off the bed.

He pulled me into him, groaning, the vibration doing wonderful things to me till I wasn't entirely sure we were separate entities.

My body wrung tight, rigid in every way. My eyes shut of their own accord, lights dancing behind my closed lids. His mouth sent waves of pleasure up my spine to the point of no return.

I was lost to him. And he knew it.

"Come for me, Mina. Come in my mouth, baby. Give me that honey," he growled into my inner thigh.

Oh, shit.

An explosion of light discharged through me. My heart raced. I was numb.

Then, nothing but bliss.

My pussy quivered and clenched, giving him exactly what he'd asked for. My teeth snapped together, gritted tight, and a long, low moan was pulled from me without my permission as my body fought for control through release.

Holy hell. Sweet Jesus. Sweet baby Jesus.
I was a limp noodle.

Panting softly, Lev kissed his way back up my body, gathering me up and holding me tight. My flaccid arms held onto him the best they could, but my eyes would not open. I held my face into his neck. "Wow," I croaked. "That was...*holy shit.*"

His body shook lightly, but he remained quiet. When he spoke next, he spoke frankly. "I've never tasted anything like you. You're mouthwatering. Ambrosia."

I smiled into his collarbone, feeling sleepy. "And all yours, baby."

He kissed my forehead, his lips lingering. His hand came down to knead my ass cheeks. "All mine, baby."

Exhaustion took me soon after. I vaguely remember being cleaned up and tucked in. When I woke next, I woke completely alone, but sated and smiling.

CHAPTER TWENTY-EIGHT

Mina

The spring in my step was a sure sign that although I'd had an average and somewhat alarming night, I'd had a good morning. A *very* good morning.

As I made my way to Nastasia's around ten, I was 90 percent sure she would be awake. If not, I'd just have to get my knock on. When I arrived on her doorstep, I lifted my hand to pound it on the door, but thought better of it. Instead, I pulled my cell phone out of my pocket and sent her a text.

Me: Are you awake? I have brownies.

The door was thrown open a minute later. Nas blinked down at me, awake, dressed, and wide-eyed. She smiled, but when she glanced down at my empty hands, she scowled. "There are no brownies, are there?"

I pushed my way inside and snorted a laugh. "No. That was all part of my dastardly scheme to get you to let me in."

She sounded insulted. "Not cool, shorty. Not cool." She watched me climb the stairs. "Hey. Where are you going?"

"I'm going to say good morning to my hubby." I smiled to myself. "Do you mind?"

I opened the door to Nastasia's room and let myself in. The curtains had been drawn and clothes were flung around the room. Vik was sitting up in bed, a sheet pulled up to his waist, arms folded behind his head, watching the morning news on the TV Nas had on the wall. The moment he saw me, he beamed. "Damn, wifey. You lookin' good today. You're all glowin' and shit." He grinned cheekily. "You got lucky, didn't ya?"

I loved Vik. I actually had a hard time believing that he and Anika were made from the same sperm and egg, that they shared DNA. Sometimes I wanted to give him my condolences on the fact that his sister was a giant asshole.

Today, I smiled at him. "I'd come over there and hug you if I wasn't so sure you were buck-naked under that sheet."

He gave his hips a light thrust to show me he was indeed bare under there, and I held a hand over my eyes, groaning.

He was such a pig. A lovable pig.

Nas walked into her room with a tray of coffees and I took one from her, giving her waist a light squeeze. She knew me too well. She winked at me, and I took a seat on the farthest edge of the bed, while Nas sat cross-legged next to Vik. She handed him a coffee, and he leaned over and pressed a soft kiss to her cheek. And, *God*, it made me smile.

I loved how much he loved her.

"So," Vik began. "How are you feeling about what you saw last night?"

Nas' brow bunched as she trained an eye on me. "What did you see last night?"

Vik shrugged. "Business. Dealing with the Moretti prick." Vik threw me a sympathetic look. "Mina saw Lev doing his thing."

Nas' shoulder slumped and she sighed. "Oh, Mina. I'm so sorry. I didn't know."

They acted like it was a simple misunderstanding. It was the kind of reaction I'd have expected if they'd made an appointment with me they had to break, like it was so easy to understand and forgive, and yet I was still so confused. I held both hands around my coffee mug, warming them. "I don't know how I feel about it. Lev didn't exactly tell me much when we got home last night. I'm just really confused. Which is why I'm here."

Nas reached across the bed to place a hand on my knee. "I wish I could have warned you." She looked disappointed with herself. "I've been wanting to for weeks, but held back. Then when you started dating Lev, I thought he'd tell you about it." She rolled her eyes. "Yeah, as if he would, right?"

I didn't get it. "Why wouldn't he tell me?"

Nas looked to Vik and he answered for her. "You know, Lev's no stranger to female company, Mina." *Why do I need to hear this?* I scowled at him. He grinned and carried on quickly, "But those women were there for one reason, and he made sure he spelled it out for them. Something about you has him treating you differently. He's never let a woman sleep in his room before. Not ever."

Nas smiled at me. "Not until you."

My heart beamed and my belly fluttered, but I kept my game face on.

Vik added, "You're the only person he's locked into a room with him since he was ten years old. I don't know why, but he's included you into his small circle of protection. You're part of his sanctuary."

"Okay," I muttered, elated by the information, but still confused. "What does that mean?"

Nas spoke gently, spelling it out. "He didn't tell you because he's scared to lose you, doll."

I sipped my coffee, barely tasting it. "Right, okay. That still doesn't explain what I saw last night." I looked from Nas to Vik. "Either one of you want to enlighten me?"

Nas lifted Vik's left arm and pointed to a tattoo there. A large, bold tattoo that read XAOC. "It all starts here, with Chaos."

"What is that? Like a gang or something?" I asked carefully.

Vik chuckled. "Whoa there, small stuff. You call it a gang and you'll get yourself shot." He explained, "They call themselves a firm. We were a firm."

Nas sat up straight. "Let's rewind twenty-one years back." She cleared her throat. "*Bratva* were the Russian mafia, the brotherhood. They're still around, but they're not advertising, you know. They're a remote, private group. The only way to get in is to be the son of a member or have two of their members vouch for you. It doesn't happen often. They don't want people, cops namely, up in their business, so they started firms all around the world to throw off the scent of their business dealings. As far as the cops knew, the firms weren't involved with *Bratva*." She paused. "In come my father, Anton, and his brother, Ilia. Both men were members of *Bratva*, as their father and grandfather before them, but when they moved to the US from

Russia, they were asked to start a firm, recruit some of the finest Russian-American crims known to man and do what firms did."

I almost didn't want to ask. "What did firms do?"

Vik pursed his lips. "The usual. Drug running, racketeering, extortion, arms dealing, fraud, smuggling." He shrugged like it was no big deal. "You know."

Nas went on. "So dad becomes president of the firm. Uncle Ilia became vice-president. Vik's dad, Yuri, was account keeper. The firm was tight. The warehouse where they ran things was almost impenetrable. Then it comes time for the sons to be initiated."

Okay, I was getting answers, but I had so many more questions. "What does that mean? Why did they need to be initiated?"

Vik smiled. "You say it like it was a bad thing, but to us, to the sons, it was an honor. We were enforcers. Me, Sasha, their cousins, Nik and Max, and their adopted brother, Asher. We all joined at the same time." He grinned wickedly. "We were out of control. It was fuckin' manic, baby. We had guns. We had women. We had money. Best years of my life."

What about Lev?

I had to ask. "What about Lev? You didn't mention him."

Nas looked sad. "The men in the firm decided against Lev. They voted no. Said he was too unpredictable. Said they couldn't trust him." She added quickly, "Which was a total load of shit. They didn't even give him a chance."

It sounded screwed up to feel bad for Lev for him not being allowed into a group of thugs, but my heart squeezed painfully. He was always the odd one out. I hated that.

Nas continued, "So the boys are off getting their Chaos tattoos, leaving this one guy, Maxim, to enforce on his own for the night. None of the boys knew shit was about to hit the fan. No one but Lev." She sipped her coffee. "The tattoo parlor that belonged to Chaos had its door busted in. A rival firm of Italians had been on our backs for getting in on their turf. One of their men decided to send a message. Comes in, guns raised, ready to shoot whoever got in his way."

My heart started to beat faster. "What happened?"

Vik answered, "Lev happened. He came from behind, out of the shadows, threw the fucker down and let his fists do the talking." Vik smirked. "We're talking a grown-ass man with not one but *two* fucking guns, being overpowered by an unarmed fifteen-year-old boy, and being beaten so badly that he needed surgery to fix his ugly mug."

Whoa.

Nas cocked her head to the side. "The Italian was disgraced. They were a laughingstock after that. Chaos was pleased. Well, you can imagine what happened after that."

Let me guess. "They wanted Lev in the firm."

"Yep," she confirmed then smiled. "But he wouldn't join. Said that he would protect his brothers, but he would never be Chaos. My father was disappointed. He wanted Lev to be a brother in every way, but he agreed that Lev should have a choice. He respected that."

"What happened then, if he didn't join?"

Vik clarified, "We were the enforcers, but Lev had our backs. He was our muscle. We did the collecting. He did all the fighting." He hesitated before telling me, "It's like he was born to battle, Mina. It comes so naturally to him. He can get lost in here." He tapped on his temple. "You're helping him find his way out of that prison."

I uttered, "But he's enforcing now, right? How did that happen?"

Nas spoke. "My dad was getting older, as was my uncle. Both had families. They wanted to settle down, but you just don't *leave* a firm. It's for life. When my Uncle Ilia died suddenly of a heart attack, my father took it hard. They were close. Dad's health declined and he withdrew his responsibilities from Chaos. *Bratva* agreed that he was in no shape to lead." She shook her head lightly. "Long story short, *Bratva* weren't happy with the way things were being run down here without my father on board. The men were fighting amongst each other, fighting for power. People took sides. Loyalty fled. Eventually, *Bratva* forced the firm to disband. Everyone went their separate ways."

Vik drawled, "You can take the boy out of the hood, but you can't take the hood out of the boy.

You get me?" I didn't. He must've seen this, because he explained, "Most of the disbanded members formed their own illicit firms. We didn't do that. We opted to stay neutral, start a business, go clean on the straight and narrow."

My brow rose. "Doesn't look like it to me."

Nas raised a hand. "Listen, the boys, they're not doing anything too crazy here. Sasha is a broker. He loans large sums of money to people at high interest. When they don't deliver on the set terms..." She tried to smile, but it came out a wince.

I spoke for her. "They get the shit beat out of them. By Lev."

Vik scoffed. "Well, of course it sounds bad when you say it like *that*."

Ah, Vik. I couldn't help but smile at him.

I spoke softly, "Well, that explains things. I still don't know how I feel about it, but now I know."

Nas eyed me. "Let me ask you something, Mina. Does Lev doing this affect how he treats you?"

No. It didn't.

I shook my head.

She had another question. "Do you *really* want to know every time he thrashes someone? 'Cause *I* don't. Vik and I, we don't talk about it. Or are you just sore that you found out by accident?"

I was sore about how I found out. It was all Anika's fault.

Nas added, "Yes, he roughs those losers up, but those idiots know exactly what they're getting into when they make a deal with Sasha. They're not so innocent, you know. There's a reason they can't go through legal channels to get the money."

I understood this. It didn't make it any better though.

I shrugged.

Her hand came down on mine and squeezed. "Do yourself a favor. Put it out of your head. It'll cause problems where there are none." She stressed, "It's a job, Mina. Just a job. Think about it as debt collecting."

Vik nodded in agreement then uttered, "You can judge, Mina, but remember," his eyes softened, "Lev didn't judge you when he busted you stealing his brother's wallet. He gave you a job, a place to live, and fed and clothed you when you had nothing."

That statement hurt so much, because it was true. Lev didn't judge me. Sure, he didn't trust me at first, but he didn't judge me. He was there for me when I was alone, without a friend in the world. And here I was questioning him.

My heart sank. I was a terrible person.

Vik went on gently, "This is the life we were dealt. It's all we know. We might not be churchgoing, god-fearing men, but we're not bad people, babe."

He was right. Who was I to judge what was normal?

I was angry with myself. Lev was a sweet man. He was kind to me in a time when I did not deserve it. My mind made up, I went against what I had been taught about all that was good in the world. As far as I was concerned, I never saw what Anika planned for me to see.

It was not important.

It was long forgotten.

CHAPTER TWENTY-NINE

Mina

"Sunday *Funday*?" I bunched my nose with a small smile. "Do I even want to ask?"

Nas chuckled as we walked into the mall, Vik rushing up behind us and putting a protective arm around both of our waists. He grinned, biting the tip of his tongue. "It's really just an excuse so we can see our women in swimsuits."

It was warm and all, but it wasn't beach weather. "And where is this funday held?"

Nas threw me an apologetic smile. "Sasha's. He's got a heated pool 'round back."

Oh, fuck that. I wasn't interested. "Well, you all have fun at your funday then."

Nas groaned, extracting herself from Vik's arm to walk next to me. Putting her head on my shoulder, she whined, "*Mina*. Come *on*. I know you guys have issues and all—"

I snorted. "He tried to *bribe* me to stay away from Lev!"

Her brows rose and she pinched my arm lightly. "In an attempt to weasel out a gold digger, which, by the way, did not work, so you're all good. You passed his test!" She waved an imaginary flag and let out a weak and poor attempt at a cheer. "Hooray."

I stopped walking and turned, staring her down. She shriveled under my firm look.

She was lucky I loved her.

Vik pushed into the middle of us, wrapping his arms around us. "Ladies, ladies. You don't need to fight over me. There's enough Vik to go around. Now," he spoke matter-of-factly, "these swimsuits aren't going to try themselves on."

I peeked past him over at Nas. "Why is he here?"

She rolled her eyes. "He heard 'swimsuits' and *insisted* he come to," she did air quotations, " '*protect* us.' "

"I see." I eyed Vik, looking him up and down.

He grinned hard, blowing me a kiss. I turned my head to the side and bit his chest. He jumped back, holding his nipple and glaring at me. "*Ow*. That hurt. You're physical acts of violence are harming the love I have for you." He moved to lift his tee up over his nipple and stepped closer to me. "Now kiss it better."

I burst into laughter and ran away from him, hiding behind Nas. She rolled her eyes at the two of us, but she did it smiling. My friends were kind of awesome.

I hooked my arm through hers. "Okay, I'll come, but if Sasha so much as looks at me dickishly, I'm leaving."

"Whatever," Nas muttered under her breath. "You guys are going to have to get over it. Both of you. Sasha loves Lev. You love Lev. You both need to cool down and get along."

I was immediately defensive. "It's not my fault. I could easily get over it and I would, for Lev, but

Sasha won't let me. Every opportunity he has, he says something nasty or gives me that freakin' look, like I'm lower than him, like I'm scum. For some reason, I don't think you'd let that fly if it were you, Nas."

She agreed, "No, I wouldn't. I'd call him out on it."

"Oh, yeah. He'd love me for that," I mumbled.

"No, he wouldn't," she paused a moment, "but he might respect you for it. We're a funny people, Mina."

We walked into a lingerie store and headed straight for the swimwear. As we were walking, Vik called out to us, holding a clothes hanger. "I think you'd look great in this, Mina."

I blinked down at the hanger. "There's nothing on it."

He smirked. "I know."

Nas groaned painfully at the stupid joke. When I picked up a folded towel and threw it at him, he burst into laughter. Nas shook her head. "I don't even know why I waste my time with you."

Vik sauntered over to her slowly, as if he were on the prowl. "Because I'm the best you've ever had." He dipped his head to kiss her lips, nipping them gently. He spoke quieter, "And because you love me."

Nas closed her eyes and slumped into him, kissing him back with all that she had. The display was so brash, so hot, that I had to turn around to hide my blush. They looked good together.

I looked at some of the bikinis when, from behind me, came, "I think you're better off going for a one piece, darlin'." I spun around to see a young woman around my height, perhaps a smidge taller, with long blonde hair and bright pink lips smiling at me.

She didn't work at the store. She seemed to be browsing.

I cocked a brow. "You think?"

Her blue eyes popped. "Oh, I *know*. Look, we short women need to stick together, and I'm being honest here...we look like children when we wear bikinis."

She was kind of funny. I chuckled. "Yeah, I guess so."

Without permission, she took my arm and led me to the rack behind. "This here is the petite section. There are some sexy one-pieces you can try, or even a tank/bikini bottom combo. Maybe a sarong or kaftan." She shook her head. "I'm sorry. I get so caught up." She put her hand out. "I'm Cora."

"Mina," I said as I took her hand. "Nice to meet you." I admitted, "I'm grateful for the help. I'm not much of a fashionista."

Nas approached from behind. "Those are hot," she said, keeping a close eye on my new friend.

I made introductions. "Nas, this is Cora."

Nas stared, unblinking at the girl, and spoke in deathly calm. "I know who she is."

Cora was no longer sweet, not to Nas anyway, and her lip curled unkindly. "Just helping out."

"Corinna." Nas stepped forward. "You're not following us, are you?" She looked down her nose at the woman. "You know I don't have issues with beating your ass into the ground. And on that note," Nas smiled cruelly, "I see your nose healed fine."

Uh oh.

What was happening here?

Cora shrugged. "Okay, so maybe I heard about the gypsy and wanted to see her for myself." She glanced at me and her lips pursed in thought. "She's cute."

I didn't see Vik approach, but I most definitely heard him when he growled, "You out of your fucking mind, Corinna? What don't you understand about 'stay the fuck away from us'? Do you know what Lev will do if he finds out you've even looked at Mina?"

She crossed her arms over her chest and smirked, looking full of herself. "What? It's not like I haven't been playing nicely." Cora...or Corinna...or whoever the frick she was, spoke directly to me and quietly. "No hard feelings, whatever happens." She lifted a swimsuit off the rack and handed it to me. "Try this one." She smiled kindly. "It'll look good on you."

Then she walked away and out of the store.

Still watching the spot she'd exited from, I asked, "Who was that?"

Vik muttered, "Corinna Alkaev."

"Yeah," I started. "I don't know who that is, guys."

"Irina's sister," Nas stated then added reluctantly, "Cora was my best friend."

Oh my.

Drama, drama everywhere.

Our shopping trip came to an unexpected end and I bought the swimsuit Cora had chosen for me. We went home, and I was told not to leave the house until Lev got there. That was okay with me. I wasn't planning on leaving.

It was time I found out exactly who the Alkaev family was.

⚓

While waiting for Lev to come home, I sat in the living area and watched a rerun of *Oprah*. The episode was about women who preyed on men that were already in relationships. It made my lip curl in disgust. How women could do that was beyond me. I mean, I understood that it took two to tango, but actively tempting a man, knowing he was with someone...yeah. No.

It seemed like fate had forced me to watch that episode, because when I heard the front door open and I rushed out into the foyer to greet my handsome man, I was accosted by another sight.

Anika walked in beside Lev, her elbow laced through his and her other hand resting on his chest, leaning her head on his shoulder.

Anika looked like she was in heaven.

Lev looked indifferent, as always.

Curse words sat on the edge of my tongue, flipping her the bird, but when Lev turned to face me and his eyes smiled in that way that made me near-swoon, my heart reminded me that Lev was mine. Fortunately enough, my mind agreed.

I smiled up at him. "Hey, you. I was wondering when you'd get home." I glanced over at Anika, my brow raised. "I didn't realize you had plans."

He stepped toward me, forcing Anika to dislodge herself from him. When the tips of his toes touched mine, he enveloped me in a warm, secure embrace, reaching up to stroke my hair. "I didn't have plans." He kissed my temple and my skin burned from the contact. "Anika locked herself out of her apartment. She called me to pick her up. Nas has a spare key and she's on her way."

"Oh," I muttered, staring at the actress over Lev's shoulder. "Isn't that just…" *Convenient*. "…the luck."

Nas opened the front door and let herself in with a singsonged, "Knock, knock." She gave Anika a smile. "That's twice this month, Ani. Lucky for you I was home this time."

Anika looked slightly crestfallen. "Yeah. Lucky." She was digging herself into a hole. "I thought you guys were at the mall."

It sounded like an accusation, and luckily for me, I wasn't the only one who picked up on it.

Nas's eyes narrowed at her friend. "We were. Something happened. We came home." Her tone implied that she did not like explaining herself, especially not to her friend.

Lev pulled back to look down at me. "What happened?" At my light shrug, he looked to Nas, eyes flashing. "*What happened*?"

Nas leaned against the wall, crossing her legs. "Corinna wanted to meet Mina."

"What?" he hissed, his arms tightening around me to the point of pain, then he did something stupid. He aimed his anger at the situation on Nas. "*Where were you?*"

That didn't *sound* like an accusation. That *was* an accusation, plain and simple.

The air in the room grew thick around us.

"Hey," I soothed, placing a hand on his chest.

Nas straightened, looking furious, then spoke on a hush. "I know you're upset because I am too, so I'm gonna let the way you spoke to me just now fly. But do it again, Lev, and see what happens." She spoke through gritted teeth. "You're not the only one who cares about Mina."

I was surprised at what happened next.

Lev released me and went to his sister. He stood in front of her and, seeming lost, awaited her next move. When she looked up into his eyes, her anger faded as quickly as it came. She put her hand on his arm and spoke quietly, not a reprimand, but a reminder. "Watch your temper, *moj brat*."

He nodded, looking relieved that she was no longer upset at him, and pulled her in for a quick one-armed hug. Lev truly loved his sister. She was the one person he sincerely wanted on his side. I didn't blame him. Nas was a good person to have on your side.

He dipped his head and spoke directly into her ear. I didn't hear what he said, but at her response of "It's okay," I guessed he had apologized.

Anika decided then was the best time to speak. "Well, I'd better be going now." She looked to Lev, eyes wide. "Can you take me home?"

Lev looked from Anika to me, deciding where his priorities lay, and I liked that he didn't give her a straight yes. But Nas, she was on to Anika. "Vik is showering at my place. He can take you home."

But Anika looked down at her watch to hide the pink stain of her cheeks. "Oh, well, I really have things to do. I'd like to head back now. Lev?"

Nas wasn't having it. Her tone quiet but firm, she told her, "You can wait." Then Nas leaned in and uttered, "Ani, you're my friend and I love you, but I know what you're doing and I don't like it." She paused a moment then warned, "Stop. You're going to get hurt."

Anika's face flushed the brightest of red. Her lips thin, she glared at Nas and spoke through gritted teeth, "Guess I'll go wait at yours then."

Without waiting for a response, she dashed out the door and made her way to Nastasia's house.

I huffed out a long breath. "Okay, so it wasn't just me then, right?"

Nas sighed, running a hand down her face. "No. Definitely not just you."

Lev, clueless as ever, asked, "What are you two talking about?"

Nas scoffed out loud as I rolled my eyes. I stated calmly, "Anika is in love with you, sweetie."

"No, she isn't," he immediately denied my claim.

Nas nodded. "Yes, she is, Lev. Always has been."

His brow bunched in confusion. "What?" Then he shook his head. "No. We're friends. Just friends."

I wasn't ready for what Nas would say next. She sounded pissed. "Oh yeah? Then why'd you take her virginity?"

My breath left me in a sudden exhale. "Excuse me? You slept with Anika?" My head spun with this new information.

"Yes," Lev replied calmly then turned a glare on his sister. "I didn't know she was a virgin."

Nas stalked over to him, lifting her hand and poking him in the chest with her finger. "Don't play dumb. She saved herself for you. Planned your whole fucking lives together up until the time where you'd grow old together and have matching side-by-side tombstones. Then you fucked her and gave her *nothing*. She's been mooning over you since." She glowered up into his face. "You fucked up. You fix it. I am so done with this shit."

Lev's face lost all expression. He blinked, dumbfounded. "She loves me?"

I was worried by the way he said it, like he couldn't believe that Anika could feel something for him. My heart began to race. It hurt to acknowledge the facts. Overall, she was the better option. She was Russian. She was prettier than me. Her family had been a part of Chaos. She had already told me that she could be there for him in a way that I couldn't and she was probably right.

What did this mean for me? For *us*?

Slow as can be, a crack began to form through the center of my heart. This could be it. I could lose him. And so soon after I finally got him.

His gorgeous honeyed eyes met mine. "Wait. Has she been making you feel uncomfortable?"

Fear and anger had me spitting, "Only *all* the goddamn time." Panic had me revealing it all. "She flirts with you. She touches you. She made sure I saw you beating on that idiot Moretti guy." If it was over, it was over. My shoulders slumped. "She loves you, Lev." I whispered this in a way that said *If you want her, now's your chance*. "And she'll do anything to get you."

Lev held out his hand, waiting. I blinked down at it a long moment then sighed in relief, placing my hand in his. His fingers twined through mine and it felt like home.

He chastised me gently, "I told you I don't read people well. Why didn't you tell me, mouse?"

My heart slowed its pace. The feeling of his warm skin on mine calmed me. "Why would I? It would have caused problems. What can you do? It doesn't matter."

"Your feelings matter to me very much." His free hand came up to softly pinch my chin. He lifted my face to look into his fierce glare. "I would have told her that my affections belonged to another, that I was happiest with my mouse. That all I could ever offer her was friendship." He shook my chin lightly. "But you didn't give me the chance to do that. And now you're pouting."

My eyes narrowed and my lips puckered. "I am not."

"You are," he called me out. Then his eyes softened and he kissed my pouting lips hard. "Now stop it or I'll kiss them raw."

He let go of my chin and stomped up the stairs, leaving Nas and me alone in the foyer. After a moment, I called up the stairs, "Now, was that a threat? Or a promise?"

The sound of Nastasia's gagging had me laughing softly.

CHAPTER THIRTY

LEV

"We need to talk," I spoke into the receiver as soon as he answered.

Igor Alkaev was a hard man. Luckily for him, I understood men like him.

His Russian accent harsh, I heard his sneer through the phone. "Unless you are calling me to arrange initiation into *Zakon*, I don't want to hear it, Leokov." A slight pause. "What do you want?"

"I believe I made things clear to you. Your family would have no contact with mine. No excuses."

Igor sounded tired when he began with, "If this is about Lidiya..."

LEV

For once, it wasn't about Lidiya. I cut in with, "Corinna approached my woman today."

I heard him breathing, but he didn't speak for a long while. "So it's true then?" He sighed. "I had hoped you and Irina would get past your problems and unite in marriage."

My lip curled. "I know that's what you wanted, but I have told you time and time again that Irina and I would never be married."

He spoke quietly, but the anger wasn't hard to miss. "Who is she, the girl?"

My hand came down on my desk, the harsh slap reverberating through the room. I stood and snarled into the cell, "*None of your concern.*"

Igor enjoyed my sudden outburst and tried to feed it. "Some of my men say she looks like an angel. That her beauty is unmatched. Perhaps I will have to meet this woman." I growled, but he went on, "Are you sure you wouldn't prefer to marry Irina?" He came across as bored. "You would do well to remember my promise, Lev. It would be a shame for Lidiya to disappear with her mother. You know how Irina can be. So flighty. All she would have to do is board a plane with her daughter and—"

My fury rose and I cut him off with a shout, "*My* daughter. Lidiya is *my daughter*. Irina was nothing more than a vessel." My voice shook with anger. "Irina is not fit to call herself a mother, and I will bide my time until the day Lidiya is returned to her home, here with me."

Igor clicked his tongue. "Such animosity." Then he sighed, "I understand your concern, Leokov, but Irina is not the monster you make her out to be. She may not be very maternal, but she does love Lidiya. We all love Lidiya."

My eyes closed and I swallowed hard. I had to remind myself that Irina was a good actress and could lie so well that even Sasha was shocked by the sudden turn in her character. Igor didn't know his own daughter.

If only he knew.

He would know soon enough. They all would. Mirella was good at her job. I didn't want to rush the situation. When you rushed, you became sloppy, and if Irina thought for one moment that I had a plan, she would disappear into the night with my baby.

I couldn't let that happen. Lidiya was my world, and if she were taken away from me, I don't know what I would do.

This conversation was giving me a headache. "Tell Corinna to stay away."

Igor responded with an uninterested, "I'll talk to her." Then he hung up.

My heart pounded in my chest. Every day away from my little girl was a painful death on it's own. I needed her. She was the only thing I had done right in my entire life. She was proof that even the most damaged person could produce something special.

Wait. Just wait.

I closed my eyes and shook my head. No. I was done with waiting.

It's too soon.

If I felt I had the strength to wait any longer, I would, but too much time had passed already. I needed my daughter.

I dialed the number and held the phone to my ear. Mirella answered with a happy, "Hello, Mr. Lev. What can I do for you?"

"I need you to speed things up."

At my tone, she spoke quietly, "How much time do I have?"

"A week," I responded. I couldn't wait much longer.

She said confidently, "I'll get it done, Mr. Lev."

"Give Lidi a kiss for me, will you?"

She whispered her response. "In a week, you can give it to her yourself."

CHAPTER THIRTY-ONE

Mina

It was the third night in a row that Lev and I would be sent home early from lack of customers. It was worrying. If things kept on the way they were, half the staff of Bleeding Hearts would be out of a job.

Was it so terrible that the only thing on my mind was sex?

Lev and I had become thoroughly acquainted with each other's bodies. There was not a place on his tall, strong frame that my lips had not grazed, a place I had not sucked, licked, or sighed against in pleasure. But the main deed...it still had yet to happen. From the intense stares Lev had given me from across the floor during the night, I had a feeling that tonight would be the night.

As it turned out, I was not wrong.

Hooray!

As we undressed for bed, I watched in awe as Lev stripped down to nothing, his muscular body bare, sauntering over to where I lay in nothing but a pair of white panties and bra. His eyes hooded, he climbed over me, sitting up, reaching down to unclip the front hook of my bra.

The material fell away and my small breasts reacted to his adoring gaze, my nipples taut with arousal. His hands glanced my waist then up past my ribs until he gave me the contact I so needed, running his thumbs over the tightening buds.

At my small gasp, his hard cock jerked lightly in response, the dewy precum at the head of him all but begging to be licked away. He towered over me and I loved it, the feeling of being so small under him, the feeling that he could overpower me, but knowing he never would.

It was a powerful thing to cause a want so fierce in the person you loved.

His head dipped and he took one sensitive nipple into his mouth. It was something he did often. I wasn't sure if it was because he knew how wet I got when he did it, or if it was just because he liked my nipples in his mouth. Either way, it worked for the both of us.

He went to town, nipping then laving the peaks of my breasts, and doing it over and over again until I was whimpering from need. My body felt hollow and begged to be filled.

His deft fingers worked quickly to remove my panties. One quick tug and they were history, nothing but a scrap of satin on our bedroom floor.

"Bend your legs. Knees up, baby," he commanded, and I obeyed, bending my knees and allowing him an unrestricted view of my wet core.

Lev's gaze flashed with heat. He ran his big hands down my knees and smoothed them across my inner thighs until his fingertips lightly grazed my outer lips.

His middle finger teased me, gently running over my needy entrance, coating itself in my arousal. My cheeks stained pink as my heart beat harder, faster. I needed it. "Please," I whispered.

He granted my wish, the tip of his finger slipping inside me in a deliberately slow pace. Bit by bit, he worked himself inside me. A whimper escaped me as I gripped the sheets, twisting them in my hands. My pussy clenched greedily, sucking him in, begging for more.

His low growl sent shivers over my body. "You're so small, baby. So tight."

When I felt the tip of a second finger attempting to join the first, I moaned softly and my knees fell outwards, allowing more room for Lev to work. He removed the first finger from my body and I whined, begging for it back.

His eyes alight, he spoke softly, "More?"

"*More*," I uttered firmly.

Two fingers played at my folds, working themselves up and down through my wetness, preparing to enter me. I held my breath as they paused right *there*. They were pushed inside of me slowly until I was full.

It was perfect. I was so turned on. I wanted more, but wasn't sure I could take it.

Lev stated, "I'm bigger than this, baby. I need to try for three, okay? I don't want to hurt you."

Three fingers sounded like one too many, but he was right. He was big, and that big cock could do damage if I wasn't prepared well enough. My voice soft, I gave him permission. "Okay."

The fingers pulled out and in came a third. This time, I was grateful for the slow pace he liked to tease me with. Three fingers an inch inside of me became painful. I winced and moaned out loud, and not in a sexy way.

Lev removed the digits and rubbed his thumb across my clit. My body reacted immediately. "Okay," he said. "We can wait, mouse. No rush."

Was he freaking kidding me?

My head shot off the bed. "*No*! I'm done waiting. I want you inside of me, Lev. Please." I whispered, my eyes begging, "Honey, please."

He shook his head. "You're so small. I'm going to hurt you."

I didn't care by that point. I wanted us to be together in every sense of the word. No more waiting.

"Lev, I'm a big girl. I can handle i—" My protest was cut off when his head descended between my leg, his mouth sucking on my clit. His fingers came back to where I needed them, two fingers pushing inside then pulling out slightly.

He was finger fucking me while his mouth did delicious things to me, and I was in heaven.

My head fell to the mattress, my eyes rolled back, and a long moan was forced out of me.

I was wetter than ever before. Someone would be sleeping in a damp patch tonight. And at the incredible assault I was enduring, I would not complain if it were me.

I wasn't prepared for the third finger to join in, but when it was pushed inside of me, Lev nibbled at my clit. And I just about lost my mind with desire.

It didn't hurt so much this time, and with every time he withdrew then pushed back inside, I could feel myself accept what was given. My body was grateful.

Out of nowhere, it started.

My palms began to sweat. My legs went rigid. My eyes widened, and my lips parted in a silent moan. I whispered, "Oh, God. Yes. *More*."

Lev didn't need me to ask. He finger fucked me harder, his digits trying desperately to work themselves past his fingers' halfway point. His tongue came out to play, flicking me where I needed it most then suckling my throbbing bud.

My stomach tightened. I panted harshly and whimpered a hushed, "Shit. Oh, shit. I'm coming, baby."

The moment it hit me, my back bowed off the bed, my body convulsing in a rigid display of pleasure. It was an overload. Lev's fingers did not leave me, rather fought me to stay inside my pulsing channel, his hand gripping my thigh tightly, pulling me down.

My breath hitched as I continued to pant. One last tremor and my body broke out in goosebumps. I lifted my head to peer into Lev's eyes. "I need you."

Something about the way I said it must have told Lev that I meant it, because his fingers retracted slowly and then he was on top of me, his lips worshipping mine in a wet, deep kiss that I felt to my toes. He reached down to grip himself and guided the head of his cock to my hot, swollen core. The moment the tip of him kissed my waiting slit, he pulled back to look at me. Reaching across the bed, he opened the drawer to pull out a condom.

I licked my lips. "Can we go bare?"

He pulled back, blinking down at me. "I don't know. Can we?"

I nodded. "We can."

He hesitated. I soothed his doubt. "You remember when I had those wicked period cramps I had?" He nodded. I felt sheepish exposing my lie. "It wasn't period cramps. I had pain because Nas took me to see Pox's sister. I got a birth control device put inside of me." I smiled softly, reaching up to run my fingers over his lips. "I'm clean. No babies for me. We can go bare." I quickly added, "If you want to, I mean."

That was what I said. What I meant was: *If you trust me, that is.*

The condom packet was flung across the room and Lev smiled down at me.

He fucking *smiled* at me.

It hit me with so much force that I forgot I needed oxygen to live. I breathed out a shaky, "Oh my. Your smile."

I was overwhelmed.

He smiled. And it was aimed at me.

It was all for me.

His smile came down over me and I felt his grin at my lips as he kissed me. It was all I ever wanted, and now that I had it, it made me realize I would do anything to keep it.

He adjusted himself at my core, rose up on his elbows to look down at me, and pushed. The head of him went in smoothly, but soon I was being stretched and it was hard to stop myself from flinching. I gritted my teeth and closed my eyes, breathing deeply. Lev faltered, unmoving a moment, but I smiled up at him, nodding. "Lev, I want this."

His hands slid under my body to wrap around my lower back. He looked me in the eye. "Slow and steady, baby."

I braced. "Slow and steady."

He thrust lightly and my body fought to accept him. I was wet, but his cock was thick and long, and I wondered if this was going to work out the way I'd planned in my head.

I closed my eyes and breathed through the initial lunges. The more he worked me, the easier it became. My body no longer fought, and the friction of Lev driving into me was sending sparks down my spine. I opened my eyes to look up at him and his hips jerked fitfully.

He spoke through gritted teeth. "You feel incredible, mouse. Just a little more."

My hands gripped his forearms, my nails digging in as he plunged into me, no longer afraid of hurting me. He kept his pace for a long while before I reached up and laid my hand against his rough cheek, pulling him down for a long kiss.

I felt hot and stretched, and his warm touch sent me into a frenzy. "I'm ready." The naughty words sat on the tip of my tongue until I finally breathed out against his lips, "Fuck me, Lev."

It became clear that Lev would not be able to get the entire length of him in me. Not tonight, anyway. My guess was that it would take multiple lovemaking sessions to get there. Luckily for him, I was up for the challenge.

Gripping my hips, he drove into me, thrusting as hard and deep as he could go without hurting me. My chest heaved with unsteady breaths. He was driving me crazy. My pussy throbbed around him and he tipped his head back, groaning.

His arms went rigid, the veins in them sticking out, his brow furrowed as he tried to gain control over himself, but I didn't want Lev to be controlled. I wanted him to feel as helpless as I did. I wanted him to lose himself in me as I did him. I wanted Lev in all the ways I could get him.

I wanted him in a way that no others had him.

My core convulsed once more and Lev let out a shout, his hips jerking wildly. "*Mina.*"

Seeing Lev turned on this way had lights dancing in front of my eyes. My pussy tightened and tightened. My nails found a home in Lev's shoulders. I panted harshly until a soft cry flew out of me, sending my body flying as my sex throbbed uncontrollably around him.

Lev's thrusts turned erratic. He lowered his head, his nose pressed into the side of my neck, and he let out a long animalistic growl. My arms wrapped around him, holding him close as he neared his crest. He stilled, his body turning stiff, and his cock jerked inside of me, bathing me in wet heat. His release was harsh and prolonged. He nipped my neck as he gained control of his rigid body. His breath hot at my neck, he kissed me there and I smiled.

Lev was mine now in every way.

I wanted him to know I was his in every way, too.

I ran my hands down his damp back as his erection softened inside me. Turning my face, I pressed a soft kiss to his forehead and spoke quietly, "I love you, Lev. Very much."

He stopped breathing a moment. His response came in the form of those strong arms tightening around me, pulling me further into him. I smiled, my eyes closing contentedly.

I didn't expect him to tell me he loved me back. I wasn't even sure if he did. I merely needed him to know how he made me feel and that I needed him.

I was looking for long term, and, my Lev...he would give me long term.

My heart belonged to him.

Lord help the person who tried to get between us.

CHAPTER THIRTY-TWO

Mina

My head resting on Lev's chest, I listened to his heartbeat. It was almost four a.m. when I whispered, "Tell me about Irina."

Lev's hand, entwined with mine over his right pectoral, stiffened. The thumb caressing my hand stilled. "I don't like to talk about her."

I knew this. I had seen his reactions to her name being mentioned. But this was important.

I had to tell him in a way he would understand. "I'm around, Lev. I'm bound to meet her one day. It's your duty, as my man, to inform me what I'm up against." I let that sink in. "I love you. I love Lidiya. I'm a part of your life now and I know it's hard for you, but give me something, sweetie. *Anything*."

He remained quiet a long while, but I heard the beat of his heart increase. He let out a long sigh. "She was beautiful."

Ouch. Not a great start.

He went on. "She was also untouchable. It was widely known the Alkaev girls were off-limits until such a time that their father chose who they would marry. So when Irina approached me, I was cautious. We formed a friendship of sorts. I liked to listen to her talk. A month went by and she kissed me. I told her I wasn't looking for a relationship; she told me she wasn't either and that what we did together would remain private so her father wouldn't know."

Nothing too sordid so far. I listened on.

"Imagine my surprise when we made it to the bedroom and I found out Irina was well acquainted with sex. It stunned me. She knew things even I didn't know. It should've tipped me off that something was wrong, but I told myself that Irina was my friend. We had sex multiple times over three months, always using protection." He sounded dejected. "She *insisted* on protection. I never assumed we were at risk. I never thought she would be the one to tamper with the condoms."

A small gasp came from me. "You're saying she *tricked* you into getting her pregnant?"

"Yes and no," he said calmly. "Her father forced the situation on her. He planned it from start to finish. It all came out after the pregnancy was confirmed. Her entire family met with Sasha, Nastasia, and me at Sasha's house. Her father, the smug bastard, told me I would marry Irina and come work for him, with his firm, Zakon." He shook his head. "He didn't know me well enough to guess that my answer would be no. Irina was certainly surprised. She told me that she would never marry a retard like me anyway."

A louder gasp escaped me. "She didn't!" I growled. "*The bitch!*"

He kissed my forehead. "She did, but I don't think she meant it. It was only after she found out I didn't want to marry her that she got nasty. I think she expected we would have Lidiya together, raise her together, and stay friends. When I told Irina that I wanted the baby but not the marriage, her father went to plan B. Told us that Irina would have to terminate the pregnancy if she were to remain husbandless. I told them they'd do that over my dead body." He huffed out a harsh breath. "I paid them a lot of money to prevent Irina from getting an abortion. I moved her in here, hired Mirella to care for her, and to make sure she wouldn't harm the child. As long as the money kept coming, Irina's father, Igor, remained happy with the situation."

"Why?" I asked. "Why did he want you in his firm? Didn't he know you refused your own father's firm?"

He nodded. "Yes, he knew. Igor Alkaev was a part of Chaos. He worked under my father. He knew all too well that I wouldn't join. He tried to force my hand because he knew how well my family had benefitted from my knowing the stock market like the back of my hand."

My brows rose. "You have stocks?" Then they furrowed. "Wait. Just *how* rich are you?"

His body shook silently. "Rich enough to provide for my child. She will never want for anything."

"Okay, so he wanted you because they're hard on money."

He shrugged. "Far as I know, they're extremely well off."

Bastards. "Just greedy then."

"Yes, I'm afraid so. It's how the rich stay rich, mouse."

Some people were rotten to the core. "And now?"

"I pay them money they don't need, and Irina doesn't disappear with my daughter." His voice came out a growl. "It makes me so angry. She moved to another state just to spite me. Just to make things difficult, so I couldn't see my Lidi." He spoke quietly, "I hate her."

I didn't blame him. He was right to hate her. He told the story of a girl who was a victim to her father's cruel antics. I didn't buy it. She went along with it knowing full well what she was doing. Irina Alkaev was an asshole.

"I miss her," I stated, realizing full well I was not helping. "I miss Lidiya." Lev didn't say a word, just ran his warm hand down my arm and back up. "She has a home here, Lev. She belongs *here*."

He lightly pinched my chin, forcing it up to look him in the eye. "Do you trust me?"

"Yes," I whispered immediately, because I did trust him.

He planted a soft kiss to my lips, speaking against them, "Then *trust* me."

His words caused a shiver to go down my spine.

It sounded like he had a plan.

It sounded like a promise.

CHAPTER THIRTY-THREE

LEV

"Mina," I whispered into the dark.

With her back to my front, she fit me perfectly. No one had fascinated me like this little creature.

My Mina. My mouse.

She said she loved me. She seemed sincere. I wanted to believe her.

I *did* believe her.

Her light grunt told me that she was falling asleep fast. My arms around her waist tightened a little. I never wanted to let go. "I don't know what love is," I started quietly. "But if I could love anyone..." I pressed a gentle kiss behind her ear, pulling her close. "I would love you. Very much."

LEV

I didn't know how to be what Mina needed, but I vowed to try my hardest to be a man she would be proud of. The thought of disappointing her made me anxious.

She had faith in me. She believed in me.

Disappointing Mina was not an option.

CHAPTER THIRTY-FOUR

Mina

My eyes fluttered open and I was greeted by Lev's handsome face. I smiled, stretching. "Don't you ever sleep?"

His lip twitched. "On occasion." He smiled softly and it gave me chills. I would never be desensitized to Lev's gorgeous smile. "You're beautiful." Then he frowned at his compliment. "I'm sure you get told that a lot."

I laid my hand against his rough cheek. "Not the way you say it." I ran my thumb over his lips. "*Never* the way you say it."

He reached up to hold my hand, biting the pad of my thumb. "You're important to me, Mina."

I blinked. This was a little deep for first thing. "And you're important to me, sweetie."

"I want to go with you to meet your brother."

Everything stopped.

I had been trying for a solid week to get Lev to speak to me about my brother. Every time I brought it up, I was shut down before the conversation even began. I was desperate to meet my brother, but I needed Lev to be okay with it too. I gave him time and space away from the subject. And it looked like my patience had paid off. "Really?"

"Really." He stroked my shoulder, trailing down my arm. "We'll organize a dinner with Laredo. It's not like Sasha will miss us for one night, not with the way the club's going."

It was harsh but true. "Okay. I'll call today." I grinned.

"No." He shook his head. "*I'll* call today. I don't want you speaking to Laredo without me." At my defiant look, he added a placating, "It's not because of you, mouse. He can be rather manipulative."

Did I even care? Um, no. Now was not the time to be indignant.

I was going to meet my brother.

I grinned. "Set it up."

⚓

I lay my head back in the passenger seat of the Camaro, listening to the radio as Lev drove. I tried not to hyperventilate, but it was hard to breathe regardless. I was on the way to meet my brother for the very first time.

I had so many questions—about my mother, about my father. I was in Laredo's debt. I was pretty sure that was a situation not many people wanted to find themselves in.

We drove for a long while before Lev pulled up to a house big enough to rival the Leokov complex. With giant wrought iron gates, intricately designed to look as if black vines and golden leaves covered them, I sat up straighter as my heart skipped a beat.

Whelp...no backing out now.

Nas helped me dress for the momentous occasion. We settled for something understated, with high-waisted black pants and a loose white shirt tucked in. I wanted to wear heels, but Nas objected. She said it was no use wearing heels when your face would be planted firmly on the ground.

The bitch.

I found my black ballet slippers and slid them on while Nas straightened my hair before putting on my makeup. My long lashes held four coats of mascara, and with my lips glossed, I deemed that was enough. I didn't want to look like I was going to a club. I wanted to look like I was making my way to a casual family dinner.

I managed to talk Lev into wearing his jeans—*Hooray!*—with a white shirt under his black V-neck cashmere sweater. He rolled his sleeves up his forearms and I was ready to call the night off, almost preferring to undress him slowly and devour his body with my glossed mouth. But my brain reminded me there would be time for sexy fun later.

Lev pressed a button and his window descended. He leaned outside and pressed the button on the small speaker box. A loud buzz sounded before a man spoke through the speaker, "Yes?"

"Mina Harris and Lev Leokov."

The speaker buzzed again. "Of course, sir. Come right in."

The gates rattled before they parted in the middle and slowly opened wide, allowing us entry. I swallowed hard. "How rich is Laredo?"

Lev clicked his tongue before shooting me a look. "Richer than me."

Well, that was just great. Now I'd never get comfortable here.

It took us five minutes to arrive at the house. I wondered if we'd ever get there. It looked as if Laredo owned the entire block. I felt faint. The house was enormous. It made me wonder how one person could live in something so large. My brow furrowed. "Does Laredo live alone?"

Lev tilted his head to the side. "I'm not sure. When we were children, he always had people staying with him. When one went, another came. But he doesn't have a significant other, no."

Lev helped me out the car, and as we walked, the front door opened and out came a smiling Laredo. He was followed by five other men. And four of those five men smiled at me. The other did not smile, and he had scars all across the right half of his face.

I immediately knew who that man was. That man had to be Alessio, Laredo's son. The man who lost his wife to Sasha's bed then was made to bear the scars for life, all for loving a woman.

With his near-black hair and soft green eyes, his cheekbones high and a full mouth, it didn't take much to see that Alessio had been an attractive man. Perhaps, even stunning. But all that had changed.

My heart hurt for him. I didn't take it personally that he didn't want to smile in greeting. Why would he? I was part of the enemy's side. One thing was evident. He scared the bejeezus out of me.

The closer we got, the bigger Laredo's smile got. We walked up the stairs and Laredo held his hand out to Lev. He hesitated only a moment before he took it, shaking it. "Laredo."

"Lev," he sighed. "I had doubts. I figured this meeting would never happen." He looked down at me, releasing Lev's hand and taking mine in both of his. "I'm glad you changed your mind, Mina dearest."

I smiled gently. "I," then I peered at Lev, "*we* just needed time for all this to sink in. Thank you for having us."

His smile fell as he held my hands tightly. "You look so much like her. It still gives me chills." He held my eyes a short while before he took my hand and placed it in the crook of his elbow. "Come, meet my boys." He lowered his voice. "They insisted on being here tonight."

His *boys*?

More like his smoking hot *men*.

They were all as tall as each other. The solid walls of their bodies had me mentally laughing. No, they were definitely not *boys*. Those smiling men made my stomach dip in a bad, *bad* way. I was half glad Lev didn't read cues too well or he might've seen my sudden blush.

The first man, blond-haired and dressed in a light grey suit, his shirt open at the collar, I'd already met, but Laredo introduced us anyways. "I believe you've met Philippe Neige."

Philippe took my free hand, planting a swift kiss to my knuckles. His French accent was delightful. "'Allo, Mina. Nice to see you again."

The next man had light brown hair and hazel eyes, and a smile that stunned. It was bright and wide, and when he spoke, his rough tone had me swallowing hard. *"Howzit, liefie?"* If his accent wasn't enough to shock the words right out of me, the fact that I hadn't understood a word of what he said sure would have. He wore dark jeans, a white V-neck tee, and a black blazer. He grinned harder. "That was my native tongue, Afrikaans. I just said 'how are you doing, lovely?'"

"Oh," I uttered, flushing. "I'm doing just fine, thank you."

He shook my hand like a man would another man. "Nicolas Van Eden."

"Nice to meet you, Nicolas." He seemed fun.

"The pleasure is all mine, *bokkie*." He leaned forward and told me, "That means doe. And with eyes like yours, I think I'll be calling you *bokkie*, little one."

It took everything I had not to burst into laughter. He was funny without meaning to be, and super sweet. I very much liked Nicolas Van Eden.

The third man shoved his friend out of the way. "My turn." He had short dark hair and green smiling eyes, and he took my hand, shaking it lightly. "Mina, we've heard so much about you." He looked gorgeous in his tailored black suit. He only had a slight accent, but it was hard to miss. "Roman Vlasic, at your service."

"Hello," I said kindly as I shook his hand.

The fourth man stood patiently, awaiting our arrival. He had skin an olive skin tone, dark hair long enough to curl behind his ears, and green eyes framed with dark lashes. The gunmetal grey suit he wore fit him nicely. He looked as though he'd made an effort to look nice. His smile was secretive. Laredo led me to him, and he held out both hands to take both of mine. "Mina," was all he said. And he said this softly, almost sweetly.

This man, I felt, could have been my brother.

Laredo made introductions. "Davi Lobo. Mina Harris."

Davi lifted both my hands and held them to his mouth, pressing the softest of kisses to them. He released my hands, smiled down at me, and motioned to the person standing behind me.

Lev took my hand, entwining our fingers.

Oh, that's right.

My boyfriend was here, and although this gaggle of men had my mind abuzz, Lev's touch soothed the tension right out of me in the way only he could.

Alessio stood in the doorway, his eyes searching me in a way that felt intrusive. I don't think he meant it. I don't even think he knew he was doing it. Laredo looked to his son and made introductions from afar. "Alessio Scarfo. My son."

"Hi," I breathed, trying my hardest not to hide behind Lev.

Alessio jerked his chin at me with indifference.

I turned back to look at Davi, who winked at me. I smiled in return. Oh yeah. I had a strong feeling about Davi. He was the one I felt most familiar with. It was kind of strange.

Laredo clapped his hands together. "Come. Dinner will be served in half an hour. We have some time to talk and get to know each other."

We followed Laredo into the foyer and two staff members waited for us to approach. The second we were close enough, they opened the double door simultaneously and held them open with straight, emotionless faces. Laredo swept his arm out to allow Lev and me entry first. Lev helped me sit to the left of the head of the table, where Laredo sat, and took a place next to me.

Davi sat across from me and I grinned like a schoolgirl. I was *this* close to my brother. All I needed was for Laredo to confirm my suspicion. I wanted to ask right this second, but told myself to be patient. All would be revealed in due time.

For twenty-four years, I didn't know I had a brother. What was another hour's wait compared to quarter of a lifetime?

The rest of the men seated themselves around the table and Lev spoke first, addressing Alessio, who took a seat at the end of the table, away from the rest of us. "Are we going to have a problem?"

Alessio grinned cruelly at my man, his face distorting as his scars pulled and stretched with the movement. "I don't know, Leokov. Are we?"

Lev's brows narrowed. "Don't do that. Don't hold me accountable for something my brother did."

Laredo raised a hand. "Now, boys. This is not the time nor the place."

Lev shook his head. "No. You're right. I'm here for Mina. We're going to be civil. But we need to get this out of the way before your son decides to attack the wrong brother."

Alessio leaned forward and growled, "Civil?" He stood and hissed. "Look at my fucking face. That look *civil* to you?" His hard eyes landed on me. "Your woman can't even look at me. She's fucking scared of me."

My eyes turned down to look at the table, my face paling. So he'd noticed that, huh? *Crap.*

Laredo stood slowly. "Sit down, Alessio."

Alessio snarled, "I'm not done yet, old man."

Laredo spoke quietly but firmly, "Yes, you are." His eyes gazed at me sympathetically before turning on his son. "Your face doesn't frighten Mina. It's your temper that upsets her." Then he finished tiredly with, "Sit down, Alessio. You're scaring your sister."

CHAPTER THIRTY-FIVE

Mina

What what now?

Alessio was my brother?

Holy crap on a cracker.

I did not see that one coming.

My body jerked in my chair, causing my knees to hit the table and my cutlery to clink loudly. Lev's hand covered mine in quiet support, kindly ignoring the way it shook. My mouth went dry. I forced myself to breathe deep.

No one spoke.

I didn't look at Alessio when I asked quietly, "You said you weren't my father." I was confused.

Laredo let out a soft sigh. "Alessio is not my biological son. He was my brother's boy. Making me your…"

My brow bunched. "Uncle."

He smiled. "My dear niece. I can't tell you how grateful I am that you happened across my path. I thank you for giving me this night. I loved your mother very much."

Oh, my God. My head started to pound. I reached up to rub my temples. "Maybe we should start at the beginning."

Laredo chuckled. "Clara used to do the same thing when she got a headache."

My fingers stilled. I opened my eyes to look over at him. "Yes. She did."

"Don't look so surprised, Mina. I knew everything about her."

I doubted that. I knew my mother better than anyone, thank you very much. Alessio kept quiet. I was grateful. I needed time to adjust.

"Okay," I uttered. "Your brother is my dad. Alessio's dad. Where is he?"

"Dead," Alessio sneered. "Trust me, you're lucky you never met him. He liked to kick my ass whenever the fuck it suited him. Fuck knows what he would've done to you."

To my surprise, Laredo agreed. "Yes. Enzo was not a kind man. So when I pursued your mother, it was only natural that he made it a competition." He shrugged. "Clara danced like a dream. She was an angel. After my wife passed on, I thought I would never feel love again until she came along."

But I was stuck on something he'd said. "My mother was a server, a waitress. Not a dancer."

Laredo seemed taken aback, as if he didn't know how to tell me something important. "Mina," he started. "Clara worked at my first club, Sweet Blood. She was a dancer, my dear. One of the best." At my blinking stare, he added, "Did you never wonder how a waitress could afford the home you had? Did you never notice that she only worked nights?"

Shit. He was right. Our house has bigger than average and I never went without. We never had money problems. Our bills were paid on time. I had the best of everything. Every night, she put me to sleep and went to work. She would come home just before I woke to get ready for school, smelling of stale beer and...

"Oh, my God," I breathed. "My mom was a stripper."

Lev turned to me and stated, "There's nothing wrong with that. People need to work, Mina."

"I'm not judging her," I lied. "I'm just wondering how I never saw it."

Laredo smiled. "She was your mom. She was your world. You were a child. How could you have known?"

Nicolas Van Eden spoke then, "My mum was a street lady. She sold her body to all the men in our neighborhood. Some of my *boykie* friends even had a go at her." He shrugged and smiled widely, "Still love my mum, God rest her soul."

God, he was adorable.

Roman Vlasic added to the conversation, "My mother was a doctor." His eyes dimmed. "She was a terrible person. Cold and bitter." He eyed me good. "Just because my mother had a respectable position, it didn't make her a good person, *lutkica*."

Davi Lobo spoke rapid-fire in a language I couldn't understand. Laredo listened intently, nodding before turning to me. "Davi understands a little English, but only speaks Portuguese." Well, that would explain why he was looking at me so fixedly. He probably didn't have a fracking clue what I was saying. "He said that sometimes people do things that are beneath them to provide for the ones they love."

A soft smile graced my lips and I held Lev's hand tight, running my thumb over his fingers. I spoke gently to Davi. "Yes. I suppose sometimes they do."

Philippe sipped at his crystal glass of water. "I didn't have a mother." He smiled sadly. "Count yourself lucky to have had one, no less a mother who loved you so."

They were right. My mother was wonderful. I suppose it just hurt knowing that perhaps I hadn't known her as well as I thought. But all the important things...I knew those. Memories of her took me back to my youth.

I don't know why, but I felt I needed to share. "My mother, Clara, was a sweet woman. She smiled all the time, and laughed almost as much.

She was like a ray of sunshine, pretty as can be, and she always had time for me." I smiled to myself. It was nice to talk about her. "She sang to me before bed. We always had dessert. She helped me with my homework." I turned to Lev. "She was smart."

He squeezed my hand, smiling softly at me, and I went on. "Whenever I was in a bad mood, she would take me down to the store and tell me to fill the shopping cart with anything I wanted. We'd eat ourselves into a food coma." I chuckled. "She always had the corniest jokes just to make me smile. She was on the PTA. Made my Halloween costumes from scratch. Took me to the beach on the coldest days just to sit on the sand and take in the air. She was a great mom." My heart panged with guilt. I turned to face Alessio. "And I'm sorry you missed out on that."

Alessio's expression remained hard, but when he turned to avert his eyes from mine, I could see he was affected.

Why didn't Alessio live with us? Why was he left to a father that didn't want him? I didn't understand.

I faced Laredo. "Why were we separated?"

Laredo ran his tongue over his teeth. "Because it hurt Clara, and my brother liked to punish her." He frowned, almost lost in thought. "My brother was married. He didn't have children with his wife. Clara was nothing more than a plaything. I tried to make her see reason so many times, but," he sighed, "she loved Enzo."

Oh, Jesus.

My heart sank. She was the other woman? Who the hell was this person?

"Enzo was good to her for a while. Treated her well. She loved the attention, of course." He raised his brow as he made his point. "He was the better looking brother."

I see.

"Clara fell pregnant only a month after sleeping with Enzo. The entire club knew who the father was. Clara asked him to leave his wife. He refused. She told him she would leave him. Just disappear. Told him her baby needed a father." Oh, God. She sounded a little like Irina. My stomach dropped. I was so embarrassed. "He told her that after she had the baby he would leave his wife. But I knew he way lying." He shrugged. "It was no surprise to me that after she had Alessio that he stayed with his wife. Clara was heartbroken. She planned to leave town. Enzo caught her packing her things. He went ballistic."

Laredo glanced at Alessio before turning back to me. "He beat the shit out of her. Said that if she tried to leave him again, he'd kill the boy. I had no doubt that he would. She wasn't stupid enough to try again. At least she was allowed to see her son."

"He beat her?" My voice shook. "She was the sweetest person in the whole world, and he *beat* her?"

Laredo leveled me with a stare. "Enzo used whatever means to keep her by his side. When Clara realized she'd picked the wrong guy, she turned her affections on me." He smiled. "I was good to her. I loved her. I wanted to father her children. It wasn't fair that Enzo had that. He didn't deserve any piece of her. She found that out a little too late. But I took care of her as much as she let me."

My view of my mother was dimming fast. "Yeah, she sounded like a real peach."

"We grew careless," Laredo ignored my snide comment and went on. "It didn't take long for Enzo to grow suspicious. He walked in on us one night and I was caught with my hand in the cookie jar. I fought my brother tooth and nail. I fought so hard that I broke his bones as well as mine. But Clara...she'd had enough of us. She took off, leaving Alessio behind."

Poor Alessio.

My throat thickened at the harsh fact.

How could she?

"My brother tried to take Alessio's life a week later. He attempted to drown him in the bathtub. But he couldn't see it through." He turned to look at Alessio. "He didn't want to love the boy, but he did. A month later, Enzo was found in his home office stone-cold dead. He'd died of an accidental drug overdose that I presume was not so accidental. Enzo's wife didn't want Alessio. She knew he was the product of an affair, so I adopted him. He should have been my son in the first place. I love him very much. I tried to find Clara, but she hid well, funnily enough, right under our noses. I didn't even know she passed away until two years ago." He eyed me. "I didn't know she had a daughter."

Hope beamed from somewhere deep inside of me. "How can you be so sure you're not my father? You said you were intimate..."

But he was already shaking his head. "No. I'm sorry, Mina. I'm not your father. We never took our affair that far. It's just not possible that you're mine." He huffed out a breath. "But I would've killed to be your dad, sweet girl. Know that."

Tears prickled my eyes as I nodded solemnly.

Alessio had heard enough. He sneered at me from across the table. "While you were out picking flowers with your ma, I was hiding bruises from my friends."

"I'm sorry," I whispered, my eyes shining.

"What are you sorry for? You had a good childhood. I was forgotten. That's life." As I looked down at the table, he spoke into the silence. "What? You don't want a brother any more?" My heart broke. He huffed out a laugh. "Yeah, I didn't think so. Not good enough for you, am I? Just like ya mom."

Lev gripped my hand so tight it hurt. "Shut your mouth."

He said this at the same time Laredo called out, "Don't speak out of anger, my son. You best be quiet, Alessio."

"No," Alessio went on. "How about we tell her about the time my father kicked me so hard in the chest that I stopped breathing? Or about the time when he came home from the club, pulled down his pants, and pissed all over me while I slept."

Tears were trailing my cheeks now. My chest ached with every beat of my heart. I fought desperately not to sob out loud.

Lev growled, "I'm warning you, Alessio."

"While she had sunshine and lollipops," Alessio began to shout, "I had cigarette burns across my fucking arms."

The men around me had started to object angrily at Alessio's outburst. All I could do was blink through my tears and speak quietly. "I didn't know."

Alessio stood. "How could you know? Living your perfect fucking life in your perfect fucking house with your goddamn whore of a mother." He pointed at me hard. "You got the life I shoulda had." He clapped slowly, humiliatingly. "Congratulations, Mina." His lip curled as he whispered, "You got it all."

By this point, Lev had enough. He threw his chair back so quickly that it flew to the ground. He was quick, but I anticipated the attack before it began. Alessio laughed viciously, his arms wide, welcoming the impending attack. The men stood, Nicolas and Roman rushing to pull at Alessio while Davi and Philippe moved to see what Lev would do.

My arms wrapped around his waist and I gripped him tight, digging my feet in as he dragged me. "I'd like to leave now, sweetie." Something in the quiet way I spoke must have warned Lev against this fight, because, his chest heaving, teeth gnashing in fury, he slowed to a stop, turning to wrap his arm protectively around me.

Lev turned to my brother and whispered in deathly calm, "You're going to regret your words." He panted. "I'm going to make sure of it."

Alessio hooted loudly. "*Oooh*. I'm so scared."

There was no way to sugarcoat it. My brother was a jerk. A cruel, nasty jerk. I didn't want to know him. I wanted to pretend this night never happened.

Turning to Laredo, I kept my eyes on the ground as I stated, "This was a bad idea. I'm sorry for the trouble."

He sounded miserable. "Mina, please don't go."

"Enjoy your dinner," I replied as Lev walked me to the double doors. Before we made our exit, Lev paused mid-step and turned to face Alessio one last time. What he said made me cry all over again.

"Mina might have had a decent childhood, but she's been dealt her share of hardship. She's been without a home for seven years. She spent that time on the streets, sleeping in alleyways, eating trash to stay alive. Where were you sleeping two months ago, Alessio?" He spoke quietly, "I found Mina sleeping next to a puddle of piss, so emaciated that she was on the brink of death having not eaten in days."

"Mina," Laredo muttered, shaking his head with sadness. "Sweetheart."

Lev eyed my brother, who lifted his chin in defiance. "Don't assume to know her. You don't know anything about her, you sack of shit."

I cried into Lev's sleeve, tired of people seeing my tears. Lev rubbed my arm as we let ourselves out. As he opened the front door to let us out, I heard Nicolas Van Eden speak, his accent thick and harsh.

"That girl is your sister. She was sweet. And you…you are a fucking asshole, *boykie*."

To which Alessio responded a hushed, "Shut the fuck up, Eden."

CHAPTER THIRTY-SIX

Mina

I initiated sex with Lev as a distraction. It was a shitty thing to do, but I felt I needed it. I needed him. At first, he fought me, trying to tame my lustful kisses to the sweet ones I viewed as dangerous. I climbed him, nipping the taut skin at his neck, sucked at his tongue, and ground myself into his hardening length until my panties were soaked through. I'd said it before, there was just no faking my reaction to Lev. I pulled my panties to the side and slid down on him, impaling myself on his thick cock as far as I could. He'd lost this round, and with it, his control. With his back to the headboard, he sat up taller, thrusting up into me, his strong arms wrapped around me, holding me firmly, and the sex was no longer a distraction, rather a place of refuge for me.

Lev's hands on my body calmed me like a prayer. He had proved time and time again that he was everything I needed.

God...I loved him so.

My body begged for release. I wanted so much to not feel numb. I wanted to feel him release inside me. Nothing satisfied me like that feeling.

His hand came around me, gripped my wrist, and then brought it down between our joined bodies. "Rub your clit, baby. Nice and slow." Then his head dipped down to take my nipple into his warm mouth. I did as he ordered and he suckled me. Within a minute, my body went rigid, my head flinging back as my pussy clamped around him, and I whimper through my orgasm. It took less than ten seconds for Lev to follow. He released my nipple with a pop and let out a long groan as his arms tightened around me, holding me in place. His cock pulsed inside me, and I felt that wonderful wet warmth drip down, out of my core.

I felt better, and I blinked sleepily at him, cupping his cheeks and taking his mouth in a tender kiss. "God, I needed that."

"I know you did," he said quietly as he stroked my back. "How are you feeling?" he asked, keeping us joined at our most intimate places.

I leaned my forehead onto his shoulder, accepting his embrace. "I didn't have a brother before. I'll be fine without one now."

"Mina," he started. "You must be hurt."

I was hurt, but I wasn't going to let it affect me. "I'll be fine, sweetie. I promise." But my heart ached for Alessio. "I'm just sad that he suffered like that by the hands of his—*our*— father. I wish he'd been there with us. I wish Mom had taken him with her."

"You're too kind," he huffed out. "He was rude and obscene. He was a dickhead. You shouldn't care about him at all. He certainly doesn't care about you."

"Yeah," I muttered as I turned my neck to breathe him in. "Still, I don't blame him for being bitter. Sins of the father and all that crap."

His lips landed at my temple. He kissed me there and whispered, "It's okay to feel wounded, mouse. It's okay."

The first sob escaped me so painfully that I felt like my chest was ripped open and my heart was falling away piece by piece. More tears followed, and as I let out my sorrow over losing the brother I'd never had, Lev kept his arms around me and his lips at my temple, holding me until there were no more tears to cry.

The truth was, I wanted a brother, and now that I knew I had one and he rejected me, it hurt worse than the agony I'd felt when my mother passed away.

My brother hated me.

He didn't know me, yet he hated me.

The jury was in.

Life just wasn't fair.

⚓

Two days passed, and although it was a short time, it was long enough for almost everyone at Bleeding Hearts to find out I had a brother, more shockingly that it was Alessio 'Scar Face' Scarfo. Sasha found it particularly funny. And I hated him for it.

He found every excuse to tell people about the brother who didn't want a sister, and gloated while I shrank into myself.

It surprised me that Anika took me aside, and with a sympathetic look in her eye, she hugged me tight as she stroked my hair, telling me she was sorry. I despised her for that too. I could never figure out if we were friends or not. She made it hard to hate her when I so desperately needed the comfort.

Nas asked me about Laredo, feigning disinterest, but I could see she wanted to know about him. I smiled at her. "You want to come with me next time I see him? He's our uncle, after all."

She blinked down at her coffee mug and nodded. "Yeah, that might be okay." She quickly added, "I mean, I wouldn't let you go alone anyway. Not after Alessio pulled that shit." She nudged me lightly. "I got your back, *kukla*."

"I know he had an affair with your mom, but it's okay to admit you miss him," I muttered gently.

"I don't," she said all too quickly. At my unmoving stare, she shrugged and squawked, "I don't!"

I let it go. She didn't want to admit it, but I knew the truth.

Saturday morning came, and Lev and I lazed around in bed, making love with aching slowness, in no rush to leave our bubble-o-love when the buzzer sounded. Lev got out of bed, in all his nude glory, went to the wall, and picked up the receiver. "Yeah?"

I watched from across the room as his shoulders stiffened and he hissed, *"You got some nerve, asshole,"* then he hung up. When he turned, his jaw was tense and he looked over at me.

A frown marred my brow. "What is it?"

He opened his mouth to speak, when the buzzer went off again. He picked up the receiver once more and held it to his ear. He held it there a long while and closed his eyes. "You've got five minutes.

Not a second more." With a sigh, he hung up the receiver and told me, "You might want to shower. You have a guest."

"Who is it?"

He leaned against the wall and spoke quietly, "Your brother."

I pulled the sheets higher up my body, my shoulders stiffening. "I don't want to see him."

Lev watched me closely. "Are you sure?" I didn't respond quickly enough, so he threw on a pair of pajama pants. "Okay. I'll send him away, mouse."

Just as he unlocked the bedroom door from the inside, I called out, "Wait." If I didn't hear him out, I would forever wonder what he'd come to say to me. "Okay, I'll see him. Give me a minute."

I rushed across the room into the en suite and had the quickest shower of my life. I didn't bother with makeup, just brushed out my wet hair, threw on a pair of blue jeans and a loose white sweater, and slipped on a pair of flip-flops before making my way downstairs.

Lev stood there in his pajama pants, his arms crossed over his chest, glaring at Alessio in complete silence. The moment he heard my footsteps, he spoke to my brother who stood a few feet away, his hands behind his back. "You've got five minutes. Make the time you have worth it, because you'll never get another chance."

He kissed my head as I passed him, and I watched him walk into the kitchen. I stopped a long way from my brother. He was dressed in a pair of brown khakis, a white tee, and a black jacket. He also looked extremely nervous.

"Hello," I mumbled.

He raised a hand in greeting and sighed as he spoke, "Hey." He stepped forward and held out his other hand. He did this so quickly that I stepped back with a flinch. Alessio's face twisted as he held out the bunch of pink tulips, his hand falling slightly. "Shit. I'm not gonna hurt you, Mina."

I hugged myself, my voice flat. "You already have."

His hands found his hips, the bunch of tulips hanging upside down. He dipped his chin, nodding to the ground. "Yeah," he admitted. When he lifted his head, he spoke sincerely, "I shouldn't have said what I said. I thought about some of the things I told you later on, and I..." His lips thinned. "I shouldn't have said those things. It wasn't your fault he was a mean bastard, and I mean it when I say I'm glad I took all that shit from Enzo so you never had to. So,"—he shrugged awkwardly and spoke quietly—"sorry."

He seemed genuinely sorry—or at least he acted it.

"Okay," I muttered under my breath.

I didn't know what else to say, so I didn't say anything.

Alessio, looking more and more uncomfortable by the second, swallowed hard. He moved to place the bunch of tulips on the hall table by the door and stepped back. "Okay, well, that's all I wanted to say, so I guess I'll see you around." He thought about that then sighed, "Or not."

He was being civil, and something told me that was a big deal for Alessio Scarfo.

Alessio moved to leave when I called out, "Would you like some coffee?"

He stilled, spun back around, and then reached up to rub the back of his neck. He nodded uneasily. "Sure. Coffee would be great."

We took our coffee in the living room where we could speak alone, but where I wouldn't have to be far from Lev. I wasn't sure how this would end. It seemed Alessio could be unpredictable when provoked.

I kept my first question simple. "How old are you?"

"I'll be thirty this year," he told me as he held his coffee mug tighter than he should have. "How about you?"

"I'm twenty-four."

A long silence followed.

"And you were homeless," he added quietly.

"Yeah." I nodded slowly. "I don't really like to talk about it."

"Sure. Okay," he said. "And you're working at Bleeding Hearts?"

"Yeah. I'm bartending."

"How are you liking it?" he asked politely.

I smiled down into my mug. "I like it just fine."

Oh, God, this conversation was so freaking *painful*.

It was like eating chalk. Cheap and tasteless.

LEV

I sighed, running a hand through my damp hair. "You don't have to be so polite, you know? You can ask me real questions. I promise I won't get freaked out."

He nodded, but his hesitation was clear. "Clara..." He cleared his throat. "She was nice, huh?"

"She was," I said genuinely.

He bit the inside of his lip. Just like I did when I was nervous. And the act made me smile. "You got any photos of her?"

"No," I told him with deep regret. "I left my photo album with my foster parents when I ran away. I was seventeen and stupid. I didn't even think." I huffed out a long breath. "I'd do anything to get it back."

He must have really wanted to see that album, because the next thing he said was, "I'm good at finding people. If you give me their names and whatever other info you can, I'll see what I can do."

I smiled at him then, and I grinned wide. "Lev's already looking for them."

Alessio shrugged. "Can't hurt to have two people looking." His lip twitched. "Many hands make light work, you know?"

The conversation was getting easier. My heart warmed.

But my smile fell. "You've never seen a picture of Mom?"

"Yeah, I have, but those were at the club. Laredo has a stack of 'em. She was all dolled up for the stage. I guess I wanted to see how she looked in real life, you know?" His lip twitched and he caught my eye. "Those photos at the club...I've seen our mother's tits."

A bark of laughter came out of me so hard that I had to cover my mouth. "Oh, man. *Ewww*."

His body shook with silent laughter and the scars around his mouth stretched. "Yeah, not cool." His smile stretched as far as it could and he winced, reaching up to rub the thickest scar at his lip.

I noticed.

He noticed that I noticed, and his smile fled.

He lifted his hand and ran it in front of his scarred face. "I wish I could change this." He paused a moment before adding, "I haven't always looked this way."

I tried to smile. "I haven't always looked this way either."

Alessio pinned me with a stare. "You're beautiful though." He shook his head. "You don't scare kids with your ugly mug."

His words were pained, and it hurt to listen to them, but he was my brother, and if he wanted to talk about it, I would listen attentively, because he needed me to.

"I know about what happened. I know about your wife and Sasha." I reached over to lay my hand over his, the hand that rested on his knee. "I'm sorry."

He shook his head. "Don't be. She was a fucking lunatic. We married in Vegas after a drunken night out. We met a few hours before. I didn't even know her. I sure as fuck didn't love her. She was beautiful though." He shrugged. "My own fault for thinking with my cock."

I removed my hand, flushing at his crude admission. "I see."

He glimpsed down at his wristwatch. "Shit. Is that the time? I..." He looked up at me, wearing a hesitant look on his face. "I gotta go."

Disappointment filled me. "Oh." I stood and he followed suit. I forced a smile. "Well, it was nice talking to you, Alessio." I wasn't sure how my next request would go. "I know it might sound crazy, but if you have any pictures of Enzo, I'd really like to see them. I know I can't call him my father, but I was made from part of him. I'd like to see how he looked."

His face brightened. "Yeah, I got a few. I can bring 'em down one day."

A breath of relief left me. "That would be great."

Alessio grinned then. "I'll bring 'em down if you let me find your foster parents."

I narrowed my eyes at him, but did it smiling. "You really want to see that album."

His smile softened. "I know I can't call Clara my mother, but I was made from part of her."

Without permission, I reached out and took his hand, squeezing. I released it quickly and walked into the hall for a pen and piece of paper. I returned with the written details and handed it to him. "Here. These are all the names of the family members and where they used to live. I can't remember much more than that." I pointed out the phone number on the corner of the page. "That's my number."

Alessio looked down at the details before folding it up and slipping it into his pocket. "This is a good start. I'll let you know if I find anything." He looked up at me. "I'll call."

I held out my hand and he took it, not shaking it, just holding it. And my heart ached. Today had gone well. I didn't want him to go. I wanted to know more about him. I wanted to talk from dusk till dawn until there was nothing left to say.

My eyes bright, I asked on a whisper, "Can I hug you?"

He blinked down at me. His response came in the form of him tugging the hand he held, pulling me to him until his arms wrapped around me, and his warmth blanketed me. Reaching up, I gripped the sides of his tee and rested my head on his chest, closing my eyes, just taking in this special moment.

He was tall and warm, and it felt right. I felt safe with my big brother, just as I should have.

His voice thick, he spoke quietly. "I'm so sorry, Mina."

"It's okay, Alessio," I reassured. "It's over and done with. Forgotten. We're good."

He squeezed me tight until someone cleared his throat. We pulled back from each other to find Lev standing in the open doorway, wearing a stoic expression. "Time to go, Alessio."

I glared at Lev before turning to Alessio and softening my face. "Text me so I have your number, okay?"

Still, he held my hand, almost unwilling to release it. "Yeah, okay."

Finally, he let go, and I walked him to the door. I picked up the flowers that had been left there forgotten, and smiled. I waved off my brother and stood there, watching him leave.

Strong arms came around my waist, hugging me tight. I lifted a hand and laid it on Lev's forearm as he asked, "How'd it go?"

My smile was bright. "Good. Really good."

He sighed softly. "I suppose we're going to be seeing more of him then." I turned in his arms to look up at him. At my confused look, he stated, "I don't like the way he spoke to you that night. I'd like to break his nose."

I patted his chest. "He apologized. I think meeting me overwhelmed him. I don't think he was ready to for it." He grunted and I smiled slowly. "I'm suddenly very tired." His brow rose. I uttered, "I think we should go back to bed."

He blinked then smiled. And my heart stuttered.

I squeaked as he lifted me over his shoulder and took the stairs two at a time. The afternoon found our room was filled with the sounds of my moans and Lev's groans of pleasure.

Really...how better to spend a Saturday?

CHAPTER THIRTY-SEVEN

Mina

Saturday night at Bleeding Hearts, with yet another sparse room of men, had me going to offer advice to a person who did not want it. Perhaps my opinion was unnecessary. Unwarranted. But Lev was invested in this club, and seeing it fail would kill me.

There had to be an alternative.

Sasha sat at his desk glaring at me. I was starting to think he had no other way of looking at me. "Burlesque," he repeated, and I nodded.

"Yeah. I mean, you wouldn't have to change much. The girls already know how to dance. The only difference would be that they'd keep some of their clothes on, but be a little flirty with the patrons, tease them. They want to keep their jobs, so even the ones who might not be on board will come around...I think."

His glare had not evaporated. I didn't know what his problem was. It was clear things were not going well.

I thought it was a good idea.

I stepped forward. "Listen, I've been online. Burlesque is so in right now. And it's not just men who love it. Men find it sexy, and women don't find it seedy. I found that a lot of women won't go into a gentleman's club, but they would a burlesque joint." I paused to let that sink in. "You could double your audience."

"Mina, we're a gentleman's club—" he started with that *I-know-more-than-you-do* tone of his.

I cut him off with a calmly said, "A gentleman's club that is *failing*." His jaw ticked. I added quietly, "We can change this. We don't have to let Bleeding Hearts fall."

Sasha picked up a pen, tapping it against his hardwood desk. "What do you care if we go bust?"

I didn't need to explain anything to him. He was baiting me. He knew why I was invested. I loved his brother more than life itself. I simply stated, "I care."

My heartbeat increased and I waited patiently to be told to go away. You could say I almost shit myself when Sasha opened his desk drawer and flicked a credit card over the table at me. "You've got a month to show me this could work. Otherwise, I'll be doing it my way."

"What's my budget?" I asked as I took the shiny black credit card.

"There is no budget," he muttered, but added on a smirk, "but know this. Whatever you buy that doesn't get used is coming out of your pay. So spend wisely."

Did he know whom he was speaking to? I was the queen of thrifty spending! I had this in the bag. Failure was not an option.

After the club closed that night, Sasha called everyone over to the bar to tell them there would be some changes being made. The dancing girls came forward, faces drawn. I wasn't sure, but it was kind of obvious they thought the club was closing.

Sasha spoke. "I think it's time we talked about where this club is heading."

One of the girls' shoulders slumped. She looked about ready to cry.

Sasha went on. "Things aren't working the way they're going. Aphrodite's Kiss has stolen our customers. They took a chance and it paid off." He paused before he added, "It's time we did the same."

He leaned back against the bar and asked, "What do you know about burlesque?"

Birdie chimed in, "I know about burlesque. I danced burlesque before I moved here. I tried to find an act to join when I first came down, but I couldn't find anything." She looked to the girls. "It was popular in Chicago. It's more of a show than a strip joint."

"Right," Sasha nodded in agreement. He looked to his dancing girls. "You want to keep your jobs?"

A collective murmur went around. What a stupid question. Of course they wanted to keep their jobs.

Sasha nodded. "We shut down Monday through Thursday this week. I need to get some shit done. When you come back on Friday, I want to see what you can do."

My face fell, along with my heart. "Sasha, that's not enough time."

He turned his hard stare at me and repeated, "Friday. I expect you here early. No later than five p.m. Show me what you got."

My stomach dipped. It wasn't enough time. I felt Lev's eyes on me. I turned to my left and looked up into his warm honey eyes. "It's not enough time," I muttered.

He searched my face before calling out, "Birdie," and when she approached, he stated, "You want to earn some overtime?"

Birdie grinned. "Hell yeah, baby. I got two little mouths to feed at home."

His eyes softened at her enthusiasm. "Mina is going to need your help with the girls. Can you show them how it's done, how to dance?"

She placed her hands on her hips and puffed out a long breath. "My guess is most of these girls started by doing some form of dance." She stepped forward and hollered, "Yo, chicas. Who here has a background in dance?"

To my surprise, almost all the girls raised their hands. Birdie grinned. "Well, all right. We're gonna need to buckle down and come up with some choreography before Friday. Who's with me?"

The smiles on the girls' faces were priceless. They were excited, which in turn excited me, taming the fluttering butterflies in my belly. I turned to Anika and Nas. "I'm going to need help with handouts and advertising." I looked over my shoulder at Sasha. "Free drink with flyer?"

He nodded. "Okay." Then he frowned then added, "One per customer though. You better write that shit down."

Lev's hand enclosed around mine and I smiled. "I will. I promise."

A hand squeezed my shoulder. Birdie spoke quietly, "Mina, I don't know if this can be done, but I'm going to try my hardest."

I stepped forward and wrapped my arms around her, hugging her tight. "Thank you so much for your help." I pulled back, looking frazzled. "You need to tell me what the girls are going to need."

Birdie's brow rose in thought. "You got time to go to the mall on Monday?"

I shrugged. "Sure. What are we shopping for?"

"The most important part." She grinned. "Costumes, baby."

Oh my.

What the hell had I gotten myself into?

⚓

Sunday funday had arrived at the Leokov complex.

This meant that I not only had a chance to wear my new swimsuit, but it would give me an opportunity to see Lev in one.

I mean, I know. What's the big deal? I've seen him naked. Right?

Wrong!

It was awfully sexy to see a man in clothes that fit him right, and with the body Lev had, I wasn't sure how anything could fit him wrong. I was dying to see him in a pair of swimming trunks.

When I stepped out of the bathroom after dressing in my new, uber sexy one-piece, I mentally thanked Cora for her assistance. It was beautiful, with small slits of material cut out at just the right spots, across the ribs, in the center of my breasts, and above the thighs. It was revealing without looking skanky. I loved it.

My hand on the door handle, I paused, blinking at the sight of Lev's bare butt as he pulled up his swimming trunks, if you could even call them that.

He turned around and I choked on my tongue.

They were different. Not like board shorts. Not like boxers. They were tighter, like boxer briefs. Very European.

I liked.

But then I remembered Anika would be there. "You're wearing *that*?"

Somewhere along the lines, I'd unknowingly turned into an alpha male.

Lev frowned, looking down at the navy blue short shorts. He turned his face up, brows raised. "I...yes."

I crossed my arms over my chest, lips thin. "They're tiny, Lev. You can see everything." I bent at the waist and whisper hissed, "And I mean *everything*."

"They're the only ones I have, mouse. They're going to have to do."

My lips pouted as I blinked down at his impressive junk. I muttered, "Oh, I bet Anika is going to *love* that."

He stood, legs apart, and smiled cunningly. "Is this jealousy, my mouse?"

"No," I lied swiftly. "It is not." I feigned boredom with a cool shrug. "I just wanted you to know that everyone is going to see your frank-and-beans."

Then he did something miraculous.

He tipped his head back and barked out his laughter. And it was beautiful.

I watched him laugh, and my mind was fried by the rough barks of merriment coming from him. It sounded freeing, and I was overwhelmed. I was unsure how to react.

Was it appropriate to burst into tears of joy when you heard your man laugh? I thought not. So I kept quiet, watching closely, committing this moment to my memory bank. I would keep it there for a rainy day, when I needed it most.

"Frank-and-beans?" he muttered, way too amused, wiping away tears of mirth. Then he straightened, holding out a hand. "Mina, come here."

I pouted the entire way over. His hand enveloped both of mine and he bent to look into my face as he smiled softly. "I am dangerously close to falling in love with you," he tilted his head in thought before adding, "if not already there."

Oh, my God.

Did he just say that? Did he *really* just say that?

Oh, *God*.

He lifted a hand to run his thumb across my cheek. "Do you think I care what Anika thinks?" He laid his hands across my shoulders and pulled me in, kissing my stun-slacked lips with a smack. "She isn't you." He pecked my lips once more. "She will never be you."

My heart beat fast and hard, pounding in my chest.

I reached up to wrap my arms around his neck. His arms came around me and he straightened, lifting me right off the ground. He held me like I weighed nothing at all.

"Who sleeps in my bed at night, mouse?"

I buried my nose in his neck and mumbled, "I do."

"You do," he confirmed. "And who makes me smile?"

I smiled against the stubble on his throat. "Me."

"Exactly." He turned to kiss my cheek. "No one else. It's you, Mina. It's always been you." He spoke softly, "I just needed to find you. Now that I have you, I won't be letting you go. Okay?"

"Okay," I whispered, feeling my jealousy slip away.

He let me down, threw his robe on, and slipped on his leather flip-flops before sliding on his aviators. I quickly stopped to throw on a white sundress before slipping my feet into a cheap pair of light pink flip-flops. Then we made our way to Sasha's.

By the time we walked around the house to the glass pool house, the others were already there in their swimwear, chatting, eating, and drinking cocktails. I stopped just inside the door, my wide eyes looking around, taking in the awesomeness.

This pool house was amazing.

It was built around the gigantic, circular pool. With stones paving around the outside of the pool and rainforest placed strategically around the perimeter, it looked as though we were outdoors. My heart almost burst with excitement when I saw the slide. You needed to walk a flight of stairs to get up there, but I needed to get up on that thing. I felt like a five-year-old at a waterpark.

A glance to my left saw a stern looking man in a black polo shirt, standing behind the bar, mixing drinks.

Okay, so maybe not a setting for a five-year-old, but still amazing.

This pool house was more of a pool mansion, with sofas, a dining setting, and the biggest TV I'd ever seen in my life on the wall, a fully functional bathroom, and an outdoor shower stall. I would've happily lived here forever.

"Whoa," I muttered under my breath.

Nas was in the pool already, wearing a black bikini. Anika lay reclined on a deck chair in a 1950s-style leopard-print bikini with a high waisted bottom, her eyes closed in relaxation. Sasha and Vik stood by the bar, waiting for the bar man to finish mixing drinks. Both of them wore black board shorts that came above the knee.

I would dub this pool house *The House of Sexy*.

Nas spotted us first, smiling hard. "Wicked. You made it. I thought you'd never leave your bed."

I choked out, "Nice, Nas. Real nice."

She feigned complete innocence as I heard a mild, "Hey" from Anika.

I turned to smile at her, but lost my fake smile as her eyes landed on Lev just as he was removing his robe. I wanted to seem inconspicuous, so before his big reveal of Sir Frank and The Twin Beans, I stepped in front of him, standing right in her view. Then I lifted my head and smiled. "Hi, Anika. How are you?"

She watched Lev closely as she responded, "I'm doing well, thanks."

"Come on in," Nas called out. "I swear the water's beautiful. Like a warm bath."

I wanted to guard my man's delicate sensibilities, but couldn't resist the pool calling my name. With a grin, I threw my sundress off over my head, ran as fast as I could, and then jumped, landing in the warm water with a loud splash. Once I reached the surface, I lightly paddled next to Nas. "Oh, God, that's amazing."

Lev took the deck chair next to Anika, took off his sunglasses and lay back. She watched him with a keen eye, turning on her side to face him. She smiled and spoke quietly. He didn't turn to her as he responded, placing his hands behind his head and closing his eyes. She spoke some more, and I couldn't help but notice how she was holding herself. On her side as she was, her boob was dangerously close to falling out of her bikini.

I was about to open my mouth, when I heard Sasha say, "Ani. You're tit's about to say hi to me." I spun to look at him. His eyes fierce, he handed her a cocktail and said, "You need something to cover up with?"

She blinked up at him, seeming confused. "No. I'm fine. Thanks."

I had to turn to smile at Nas. She smiled back, rolling her eyes. It seemed I wasn't the only one who'd had it with Anika's flirting.

I would hate to make a scene today, but totally would if I needed to. She needed to watch herself around me. I might have been small, but I could be vicious when triggered.

Vik sat on the edge of the pool, handing both Nas and me a fruity cocktail each. I smiled in thanks as he lifted his beer to us. We raised our drinks in cheers and sipped in the relaxing setting.

I was beginning to think I was a major douchebag for not wanting to come here today. Sasha even came across as civil. I was glad to be here.

Nas turned to me. "So," she started. "You speak to Alessio yet?"

I beamed. "Yes. He messaged me yesterday so I'd have his number, and we've been texting ever since." My smile softened. "He's actually not a bad guy."

Sasha snorted as he slipped into the pool. "Yeah, well, you never seen him go at your throat with a fucking blade the size of King Kong's dick."

I turned to scowl at him. "You fucked his wife."

Sasha sipped his beer and shrugged. "He shoulda kept her on a closer leash."

I groaned. "God, you're a pig."

He grinned in that slimy way I hated. "You know it, Mina."

"I seriously pity the girl who ends up with you," I muttered as I shook my head in sympathy for the poor unknowing girl that would marry Sasha.

His face fell, but he probed. "So, Scar Face Scarfo is your brother. He's shouting that shit from the rooftops." He eyed me. "How'd you talk him into claiming you? Said he didn't want no sister. Now he does. I'm curious. What did you have to do?"

He wanted me to take the bait. He wanted a fight.

He wouldn't get one.

I sipped my cocktail and shrugged. "He regretted treating me the way he did. He apologized and I got over it. I'm not discussing private details with you,

Sash. All you need to know is that my brother and I are working to repair our relationship."

He titled his head slightly. "You tell him shit about the club?"

My face flushed. I had told him some, but nothing important. "Not really. He asked why we're shutting down. I told him something big is coming." I grinned. "I might've told him to expect his competition to return with a bang."

Sasha's eyes searched me. "Oh yeah? What did he have to say about that?"

I pinned him with a stare. "He wishes us good luck. And he meant it."

Nas piped in. "That's nice of him." She muttered sincerely, "That's really cool, Mina."

I smiled. My brother was actually a decent guy. It made my heart warm.

Vik spoke matter-of-factly, "Yeah, but it's not like he still doesn't want to slice Sasha up into chopped liver."

I was in full agreement. "We haven't talked about it much, but I'm sure he does." I glanced at Sasha before turning my eyes away, wanting to make my point in perfect calm. "What Sasha did to his face changed him. He's a shell of the person he used to be." I shrugged. "I don't really blame him for wanting revenge, to be honest." A shiver went through me. "Can you imagine how that must feel? To have your wife cheat on you with not just another man, but a rival, then to have to wear those scars forever, reminding you daily of something you'd rather not recall?" Silence passed through the group. "He can't forget it, no matter how hard he tries." I spoke quietly, "What Sasha did won't let him."

The silence encompassed the group for a short while as we sipped our drinks in quiet. But soon enough, Vik had us laughing about something stupid, and when Lev joined me in the pool, carrying me on his back, I was quickly reminded this unlikely group of people meant something to me. I might not have a complete family, but I was a Scarfo by blood and a Leokov in my heart.

I felt safe in the knowledge that I had more family than what I started with.

And Lev was more than that.

He was home.

CHAPTER THIRTY-EIGHT

SASHA

She stood by the bar, head down, hiding in plain sight. Her wavy auburn hair trailing down her back in soft waves. Her tall curvy body a living fantasy. One that made my life absolute hell.

She was beautiful. Exquisite. Not like the other girls I'd had in my bed.

Anika Nikulin was elegant.

Anika Nikulin was stunning.

She was graceful.

I made a deal with Viktor when we were teenagers...my sister for his. He had yet to make his move with Nastasia, but I was tired of waiting for Anika.

Making my way to the bar, I stepped in close. Too close. Her near bare body brushing my front. And yet, I leaned in closer, wanting to feel the full heat of her back against my chest.

She turned, eyes wide, glancing down my body. "What are you doing, Sash?"

I couldn't help myself. My hands came up to rest on either sides of her small waist. "I can make you forget him," I muttered. My thumb ran over the elastic of her bikini bottoms. "I can make you forget he ever existed, Ani."

And I meant it too. Lev didn't want her. He had Mina. Her time to make a move was over. Lev was happy now. She missed out.

She glanced up at me through lowered lashes. Her melodic voice soft, she uttered a regretful, "You were never competition, Sasha. Not next to him." She glanced over my shoulder, and from the way her eyes turned warm, I fucking knew she was watching him.

Jealousy screamed through me. I hated that she loved him.

She looked back up at me, reaching up to gently squeeze my forearm as she murmured, "You never even came close."

When she took her drink and walked back to the deck chair, she lay down, her eyes discreetly watching my brother.

And there it was. The woman I loved held a torch for my brother. *Figures.*

It didn't matter though. I would use every weapon in my arsenal to have her. Anika would be mine.

I fucking vowed it.

CHAPTER THIRTY-NINE

Mina

Shopping with Birdie at a prop shop had been...well...interesting, to say the least. Halfway through our shopping expedition, I was wide-eyed and stunned at the things one could find if they looked hard enough.

Who knew nipple pasties were available at lingerie stores? Or that tiny sailor costumes and fishnets were so readily obtainable?

Birdie knew—that's who.

We left the mall with two shopping carts full of accessories, and Birdie had called the girls to meet us at the club after I'd asked Sasha for permission to meet there. Lev was busy working the books, but told me he'd meet me there later in the day.

We arrived at Bleeding Hearts just after two p.m. Most of the dancing girls had come, but two of them sent messages through the others that they weren't able to make it. Birdie was kind of pissed at that. She warned me that Sofia and Martina were kind of slack. She warned both girls that if they couldn't perform the new routines, they'd likely be let go. Both girls treated the threat with an aloofness that stunned me.

Didn't they realize they were at risk of losing their jobs? I was shocked they didn't seem to care.

Sasha watched from the sidelines as we unveiled the first box of props. Out came feathered fans, vintage silken fans, garters, feather boas, top hats, satin face masks, a large box of nipple pasties, satin gloves, retro white crocheted parasols, ostrich feathers of all colors, leather whips, and thin walking sticks, and the girls went wild.

A small woman named Lilah came forward, touching the feathers with a smile on her face. "Wow. They're so soft."

A green-eyed girl called Petra grinned as she picked up a lace garter. "And so feminine."

A tall African-American woman I knew as Shonda wrapped a feather boa around her neck. "Would you look at this stuff? Mmmm hmmm. I am liking this."

The rest of the girls came around to view the items we'd pulled out, and I counted eight women. I sighed mentally. It might be enough for opening night, but some of these girls worked part-time. If Sofia and Martina didn't show up, we were going to be in trouble.

Birdie called out. "Come around here, ladies. I got some things for you that you're going to love. Thank you for texting me your sizes; it helped a lot." She struggled with the second box and I rushed over to help her. She smiled at me and turned to the girls. "Who wants to see the cool costumes we got?"

A cheer went around and Lilah squealed out, "I'm so excited!"

Birdie took each costume out of the box one-by-one, handing them to the girls who they fit. Each girl received a different color corset-bodied one-piece with thigh-high fishnets, and one additional costume. They weren't all the same. Some girls got a teeny-weeny sailor outfit, while some were made to be bunnies. Others were French maids, policewomen, cats, and we even had a Red Riding Hood.

The way the girls chattered excitedly had me biting my lip to squelch down my smile. I was happy that they were happy.

When Lilah held up a pastie and asked, "How do we put these on?" Birdie assisted, telling Lilah to take off her t-shirt and bra. Lilah grinned as she undressed, and the other ladies watched carefully as Birdie showed them how to apply the pasties by using the glue on Lilah's bare breasts.

My phone vibrated in my pocket and I smiled down at the display.

"Hey, I haven't heard from you in a few days," I answered happily.

Alessio sounded a little shy. "Yeah, well, I'm taking enough of your time. I didn't want to bug you."

I grinned. "To what do I owe this pleasure?"

He made a light grunt. "Not sure if I should've called or not, but after I spoke to Dad, he told me I should." He was hesitating.

My smile dropped. "What is it?"

Alessio sighed. "Just had two of your girls down here asking for work."

I closed my eyes. "Let me guess: Sofia and Martina, right?"

"Yep." He went on. "We told them we didn't need them."

My brow furrowed. "Why would you do that? You had people approaching the club to steal our workers away from us."

He clicked his tongue in annoyance. "Yeah, well, shit's changed. We're not doing that no more." He stated, "Tell your girls they're not welcome here, all right?"

A small smile graced my face. "Is this your way of telling me that you're not going to fuck with my work?"

He stayed silent a moment before saying, "That's exactly what I'm telling you."

"Thank you, Alessio," I responded quietly.

His reply was just as quiet. "You're welcome, Mina."

I immediately made my way to the bar and approached Sasha. "So I just had an interesting phone call from my brother."

Sasha's brows rose. "Why the fuck you telling me?"

I bunched my nose at him, and raising my hand, I poked him in the chest. "You know, you could be nicer to me. I have important information to tell you."

He sighed. "Whatever. Shoot."

"Alessio told me that Sofia and Martina were at Aphrodite's Kiss just now applying for work."

Sasha's jaw ticked, but as always, he spoke evenly, "Fucking bitches. They're fired. Soon as they come in, tell 'em to come see me in my office."

I nodded, perfectly happy with both girls' dismissal. "You know we can't work with just nine girls. We're going to need at least three more at a full-time level."

He glowered at me. "How the fuck do you know that?"

LEV

I bit my tongue, but I really wanted to tell him to eat a thousand dicks. "I've done my research; that's how." I huffed out a breath. "Listen, I probably wouldn't have been able to do any of this without Birdie. I think you should put her in charge of hiring the next few girls."

For once, he didn't disagree, looking over at the woman. "She surprised me with all this shit. I didn't realize she was management material. I could've used her a few months back." He nodded. "I'll talk to her."

Thank the Lord for small victories!

While I was on a roll, I decided to push my luck. "You wouldn't happen to have a professional camera lying around, would you?"

His drab stare told me that no, he did not. His brows furrowed. "What do you need a camera for?"

"I always had a thing for photography and..." my face flushed... "and I was good at it. I thought if you had a camera, I could take photos of the girls for the flyers. I have something in mind, but I just need the tools to do it." I waved my hands in dismissal of the idea. "It doesn't matter. I'll make do without it." As I walked away, I turned and started to walk backwards while I told Sasha a genuine, "Hey, thanks."

He frowned. "For what?"

My shrugged. "For giving my idea a chance. It means a lot. So thanks."

I went back to the girls and listened as they projected their ideas for dance routines and solo performances. We worked out that each act would need to be between three and five minutes a piece, with two intervals during the night. I was impressed with these women. They were taking it all in stride and contributing. I was proud of them.

An hour later, a delivery came to the club and it was addressed to me. I signed for it with confusion written all over my face. When I opened the package, I gasped.

Inside was a brand new Pentax professional digital camera. My lips started to quiver. I knew who had done this.

From behind me came a stern, "You break it, you bought it."

LEV

I gently put the box down on the bar before turning and asking, "Why? Why would you give this to me?"

Sasha looked down to the ground, clearly uncomfortable. His response was curt. "I didn't buy it for you." His voice softened. "I did it for the club. I bought it for the club."

A small smile tugged at my lips, and soon I was beaming. "I'm going to take the best photos you've ever seen."

His brows rose at the conviction in my tone. "The best photos I've ever seen?"

I grinned. "The best *goddamn* photos you've ever seen."

He smiled then, but it was small. He sighed to himself. "For your sake, I hope you're right."

Sasha Leokov didn't know who he was working with.

He didn't know who Mina Harris really was. I needed to show him, and I fully intended to do just that.

I would win him over.

I would.

⚓

Lev called just before five to tell me that he wouldn't be coming to the club as planned. He got caught up in those numbers of his and totally lost track of time. Luckily for him, I'd had a good day; otherwise, I might not have been so accepting.

After seeing some of the photos I intended to put on the flyers, Sasha was impressed. He didn't show it, but I knew he was. Why else would he have offered to give me a ride back home?

Sasha and I were now your regular BFFs. Well, not really. But he would succumb to my charm. Eventually. I was sure of it.

Sasha drove up into Lev's drive long enough to mutter, "Fuck me."

I lifted my head to see what had brought out the curse to find my brother's car already in the drive. And he was sitting inside.

"Thanks for the ride. I'll see you later," I muttered distractedly before stepping out, walking over to Alessio's car and knocking lightly on the window.

He was scowling down at a piece of paper in his lap, but as soon as he lifted his head to look at me, his face gentled. I opened the passenger door and sat inside, smiling, leaning over the seat to give him a light squeeze. "Hey. I wasn't expecting you. What are you doing here? And what are you doing outside?"

His arm came around me to hug me back, and he uttered, "I gotta talk to you. Alone."

Crap.

I pulled back. "That sounds serious."

He shook his head. "I don't know. It might be nothing, but," he passed me the piece of paper, "here, look for yourself."

My fingers worked quickly to unfold the paper. When I read what was on it, my chest squeezed. "You found them," I whispered. "You found the Petersons. Already?" I smiled and chuckled. "You do work fast."

"Mina, that's the thing," he started cautiously. "How long ago did you ask Lev to find them?"

How long? I thought back. "About six weeks ago. Why?"

He cursed, running a hand down his face. "I don't want to cause no trouble, you hear, but I think you need to know that someone contacted the Petersons a few weeks back, asking all sorts of questions about you." I frowned. That couldn't be right. He added quietly, "And I think it was Lev."

"What?" I laughed humorlessly. "No. That can't right."

Alessio lifted his hands in a helpless gesture. "I don't know for sure. I don't know. Maybe you should talk to him about it. If it wasn't him, I don't know who could've been asking about you. It's a creepy coincidence though." He continued, "And I don't believe in coincidences."

My heart twisted.

Lev wouldn't do that to me.

He wouldn't.

I blinked out of my thoughts, moving on. "You spoke to them then? To the Petersons?" He nodded slowly. I was suddenly nervous. "What did they say?"

Alessio spoke calmly. "I spoke to Maggie. I told her I was your brother. That we didn't know about each other until just recently and that you were looking for them."

My throat tightened. I asked a hushed, "What did she say?"

His eyes widened comically. "Well, first she fucking cried like a baby." My hand came up to cover my mouth as my face crumpled. Alessio laid a hand on my knee, patting it, and went on. "Then she wanted to know how you were and where you were staying. She asked if she could see you. I didn't tell her where you were, but I said I'd take her details and that if you wanted to meet, you'd call."

My voice quivered. "How are they? How's James?"

Alessio smiled. "They're good. They live pretty close to where they used to. I don't know about James. She didn't mention him."

"Wow," I muttered, looking down at the paper in my lap. I swallowed hard then huffed out a long breath. "Thank you." I turned to him. "Thank you so much."

Then he said something wonderful.

He shrugged. "You're my sister. I'll help where I can."

Before I burst into tears, I threw myself over the seat, wrapping my arms around his neck and pulling him close. "Same goes for you...brother." I released him, smiling. "I'd better go."

He checked his wristwatch and nodded. "Yeah, me too. Gotta get ready for work." His face changed then and he clicked his fingers. "Wait, before I forget." He reached into his pocket and pulled out an old photograph then handed it to me. "Meet Enzo Scarfo."

The face that looked back at me was handsome. Very handsome. With high cheekbones, a sharp nose, and low brows, he looked dangerous. He didn't smile in the photo, his near-black eyes staring back at me. A shiver ran through me. "He was very handsome."

Alessio sneered. "He was a cruel bastard."

If the things Alessio had mentioned were anything to go off, I agreed wholeheartedly.

So when I took the photograph and gripped it tight between my fingers, tearing it down the middle, I muttered, "I've seen him now. My curiosity is sated. And I hope he's burning in hell for what he did to you." I tore the photo to pieces, holding them tight in my hand so I could throw it all in the trash.

Leaning over to kiss my brother's cheek, I said my goodbyes. "Come by this week. We'll have lunch."

He didn't hesitate in his quick response. "Yeah, okay. I'll call."

"Thanks again." I smiled.

He winked. "Anytime."

The moment I walked inside the house, I knew something was wrong. I found Lev sitting on the bottom stair, his head in his hands.

I dropped everything and rushed over to him, wrapping him up in my arms. "Lev? Sweetie, what happened?" I asked in panic.

He lifted his head to look into my eyes. "Irina's dead."

Out of all the things I expected to hear, that was not one of them.

My heart pounded. "Oh, my God."

He ran his hand down his face and spoke in distress, "Why couldn't she just give up? Why did she have to fucking push the way she did?" He looked up at me in anguish. "I just wanted my daughter."

Confusion passed me. "What are you talking about, Lev?"

"It's my fault she's dead," he spoke raggedly.

I sighed. Of course he felt it was his fault. He wanted his daughter so badly that he likely thought he was the cause. "No, sweetie." I held his hands and spoke softly. "This was not your fault."

He nodded firmly. "Yes, it was."

I spoke sternly, "No it wasn't."

"It was." His face turned pained. "I had Mirella plant cocaine in her house." He closed his eyes, distressed. "She died of an overdose."

Oh, shit.

We were in big trouble.

CHAPTER FORTY

Mina

It was a sad day at the Leokov house. After Lev had confessed his part in Irina's death, although my heart was aching, I calmly asked him to tell me the whole story.

Lev explained that he'd been planning something big for months. Mirella had been waiting for the right time to plant the drugs, preferably after Irina had been out on an all-night bender, which just happened to be the night before. Mirella had called the police to the house just after seven a.m., and when they arrived to the house, Mirella had escorted them through the house to the living room, where Irina slept on the sofa.

When Mirella tried to wake her, she knew something was wrong. Her body was stiff. Irina was already cold.

A confounded Lev told me he never intended on this happening. He hated Irina, but he didn't want her dead. He just wanted child services to remove Lidiya from Irina's care so she could come home.

Igor Alkaev called Lev soon after to tell him that Irina had passed away. Igor was devastated. Lev was genuinely shocked.

That wasn't part of the plan.

The police contacted Lev, and he told them he would be there as soon as possible to collect Lidiya. He asked that Mirella stay with the child until he was able to fly down so Lidi would not be stressed by the situation.

When Lev asked to speak to Mirella, he was advised that she was being interviewed and that Lidiya was currently playing with a child services officer.

Lev panicked.

He was going to lose his daughter.

Lev asked me to go with him to get Lidiya, and I told him that even if he didn't want me to go, I would have. Four hours later, we were flying out to bring Lidiya home. Either that, or for Lev to be arrested.

My chest squeezed the entire way over. I knew in my heart that if Lev was the cause of Irina's death that it was accidental. You just couldn't fake the shock Lev wore on his strained face. I planned to be there by his side the whole way. I chose to believe Lev didn't have anything to do with Irina's death. Thinking otherwise was too damn painful. And until such a time that the police had evidence to suggest that he did, I would be there, holding his hand.

He didn't speak the entire way there, just held onto me like a lifeline. When we reached the police station, it was close to three a.m. Lev was asked for ID and, once his identity was confirmed, a kind policeman escorted us through. "I'm sorry for your loss, Mr. Leokov."

Lev replied quietly, "Miss Alkaev and I were not close. The only thing we had in common was our daughter, but thank you."

The policeman nodded in understanding. "Still, it's awfully distressing when someone takes their life."

I squeezed Lev's hand tight and asked, wide-eyed, "I'm sorry. What did you say?"

The policeman blinked, surprised. "I apologize. I thought you'd already been briefed on the situation."

Lev shook his head. "I was told she died of an overdose."

The man nodded. "Yes, we believe so. We found three empty pill containers close to the body, as well as a note. We believe this was a suicide caused by intentional overdose of prescription medication. But the family has requested an autopsy. Toxicology reports normally take four to six weeks, but the cause of death has been listed as suicide."

I looked up at Lev. He looked down at me.
We had a silent conversation using just our eyes.
Oh Lord.
Oh, thank you, God.

He had nothing to do with this.

Lev was innocent.

We were led to a small room where we were told to wait. We waited in complete silence, and when the door opened, in came Mirella holding a sleeping Lidiya, followed by a woman in a suit. Mirella tried to smile, but she looked tired. She handed Lidiya over to Lev and he held his sleeping daughter tight.

The woman, who introduced herself as Detective Maria Palmer, asked Lev to tell her a little about his relationship with Irina. Lev told her that he didn't have a relationship with Irina Alkaev.

She nodded in understanding. When she asked if he knew Irina had been undergoing counseling for depression, Lev replied he didn't.

Detective Maria Palmer had told us Irina's death would not be treated as suspicious, that they had reason to believe Irina had been planning this for a while. When the police had searched Irina's computer, they found an open search engine titled 'easiest ways to kill yourself'.

She looked down at Lidiya and shook her head sadly. "My deepest condolences to you all. You're free to take your daughter home. We don't want to cause any undue stress. If we have any questions, we'll call."

Lev thought about catching the next flight home, but I advised against it. Instead, we got a hotel room at the airport, and once inside the suite, he laid Lidiya down on one of the double beds, covering her. Lev then turned to Mirella and asked quietly, "Did you do this?"

Mirella shook her head wearily. "No."

"How did this happen?" he questioned.

"I don't know," she responded. "Irina must have been planning this for a while. She was clearly unwell."

"Then what happened to the drugs you planted?"

"Confiscated, along with all the others." Mirella looked up at him. "The bag was untouched, Mr. Lev. I swear."

He sat on the bed with a sigh. "Shit. Then I didn't kill her? She really offed herself?"

Mirella spoke softly, "Yes, I believe she did."

I sat down on the bed next to him, resting my head on his arm before turning to kiss his shoulder. "What now?"

He looked from Mirella to Lidiya then back to me. "Now we take Lidiya home and give her the life she was meant to have." He looked up at Mirella. "You coming?"

Mirella smiled weakly down at the little girl sleeping on the bed. "Where Lidiya goes, I follow."

The next morning, we flew home. Lidiya held onto her daddy the entire way.

CHAPTER FORTY-ONE

Mina

Nas and Sasha greeted us at the door, hoping to get some Lidiya love, but sadly, she'd fallen asleep in the car.

Mirella took her to her room to nap in peace, and Sasha hugged his brother, clapping him on the back tightly. "Everything okay?"

Lev sighed. "Yeah. I think so."

Nas asked gently, "What happened?"

Lev looked down at me before turning to his brother and sister. "Irina swallowed a bunch of pills." He huffed out a breath. "Left a note saying *I'm sorry.*"

Nas gasped softly and Sasha's brow furrowed. "She killed herself?"

Lev nodded. "Yeah, the cops aren't treating her death as suspicious, so I guess, yeah, she did."

Sasha got down to the main point. "And Lidiya?"

Lev sighed tiredly. "She's home for good."

Nas smiled sadly at that. "I know you wanted her home, but I'm sure you didn't want her to come home this way." She wrapped her arms around Lev's waist. "I'm sorry, Lev."

He gave her a light squeeze. "Thanks."

When Nas released him, Sasha squeezed his shoulder. "We got you. You need anything, you let us know."

With their kind offer, they left, and taking Lev by the hand, I led him upstairs to our bedroom, locking the door behind us. I pulled Lev toward the bed and he took the hint, lying down. I curled into his side and waited.

He stroked my side a long while before he whispered, "I thought I killed her."

I kissed his tee-covered chest and spoke softly, "You didn't, sweetie."

"I know," he drew in an unsteady breath, "but I thought I did."

I didn't respond. He'd tortured himself enough over the passed twenty-four hours. It was haunting him that he could have been the cause of Irina's death. He needed time to come to grips with the fact that he didn't do anything wrong.

And I would be there, even in silence, if that was what he needed.

⚓

A week passed rather quickly.

Under the unforeseen circumstances, Sasha decided to close the club up until the following Thursday, re-opening next Friday, giving us all time with our little Lidi bear.

She had adjusted well, if the shrieking giggles were anything to go by. We all fought for her attention, but the place she seemed most comfortable was in Lev's arms, just watching the world from way up high.

The change in Lev was incredible.

He was smiling more, laughing more, and not even just at Lidiya, at everyone. My sweet man was trying hard to be the daddy Lidiya deserved, but Lev was Lev. He was special that way, and one day, I knew Lidiya would see him for the man he was.

Bunches of flowers started to arrive at the house. Letters of condolences followed. Igor Alkaev politely asked Lev to attend Irina's funeral, but Lev respectfully declined. He told the man, "I'm sorry for your loss, Igor, but let's not pretend here. Irina made my life hell in any way she could. I'm sorry she's dead, but I won't be coming to her funeral. Neither will Lidiya."

It was a sad moment, but I was proud of him.

Igor asked Lev if he and his wife would be able to see Lidiya on occasion, and Lev told him he would need to think about it. We spoke about it at length, and Lev called Igor back to tell him that if they wanted to see Lidiya, they would have to come to the house and do so under Lev's supervision. The old man was offended at the offer and hung up on Lev.

Two hours later, his wife called back and accepted the offer.

We understood they were grieving, but after all the shit they pulled, they were lucky Lev was offering even that. Igor Alkaev did not deserve to see Lidiya, but we both understood they genuinely loved Lidiya, and she should not be punished because their families didn't get along. The fact Lev was giving them an opportunity to see her at all was a miracle, in my opinion.

I walked into the living room, smiling wide at the sound of Lidiya's wild laughter. I found her on the floor, kicking through her laughter, with Sasha noisily pretending to eat her belly. "Stop, Asha!" she cried through her mirth. "No mo! No mo!"

It was hilarious to see a man in a suit reduced to this.

Sasha lifted his head. "No more? Are you sure? Because I'm still hungry."

Another peal of giggles. "No mo. *No*. Asha pay a me?" she asked as she stood up and ran to the corner, where I set up her tea set.

Sasha checked his watch. "Baby, I would love to play with you, but I need to go." He walked over to her. "Come here."

Lidiya was already holding her arms up. I watched from the door as Sasha lifted her and cuddled her tight, holding a hand at the back of her head tenderly. "I love you," he told her quietly.

She pulled back, puckering her pouty lips. "Kiss?"

Sasha smiled, smacking a loud kiss to her lips before putting her down. "Bye, princess. Be good."

She sat on the carpet, waving in that way an almost three-year old did, up and down and super floppy. I smiled at Sasha as he went past. He jerked his chin at me and let himself out.

I walked into the room and sat by Mirella. "How are you doing?" I asked quietly.

She let out a long sigh. "I'm doing okay." She was clearly lying.

"You need a break," I told her honestly. "You're exhausted."

She shook her head, but her mouth betrayed her by yawning. "I'm fine."

I stood, pulling her up by her arm. "Go. Shoo. Get some sleep. And don't you dare come down until tomorrow morning. You're off duty."

She smiled, blinking tiredly. "If you're sure..."

"I'm sure," I uttered, gently pushing her out the door. "Now scoot."

Mirella shuffled down the hall to her room and closed the door behind her. It was nice having her around, but the poor woman needed a break every now and again. It was only natural that she was bound to succumb to fatigue.

Lidiya pulled on my hand, and smiling, I reached down to pick up my chubby bubby. "Hey, you," I said, smacking a kiss to the plump cheek. "You want to play with me?"

"Pay a me, Eena." She kicked her little legs, trying to get down. I chuckled and let her feet touch the ground. She ran to the tea set and I followed. She poured pretend tea and we ate pretend cookies, and she said the same thing she'd been saying for a whole week.

"Mama sweeping."

It broke my heart every damn time. My expression sad, I repeated gently, "Yes, baby. Mama's sleeping."

How did you explain to a two-year-old that her mother was dead?

You didn't. It was distressing enough as it was that she would be permanently separated from Irina, and regardless of how many times I had been told Irina was a bad mother, I was sure Lidiya didn't see it that way. I liked to believe Lidiya loved her mother. Children were funny that way. When they gave an emotion, they gave it all. I wanted to believe that even Irina was not immune to her daughter's love.

Lidiya soon got sick of playing and grabbed her blankie, throwing her thumb into her mouth. She approached me like it was no big deal to come on over and curl up on my lap, her legs dangling and her head resting on my chest.

I loved these moments, where it was just me and Lidi, where she gave that love so freely, almost as if she knew I needed it. I knew she wasn't my daughter by blood, but she was the daughter of my heart.

Ten minutes passed, and the little angel was definitely asleep with all dangly limbs. I kissed her forehead and held her tight. I didn't need any more than this.

I whispered into her hair, "I would have given anything to have a child like you, my Lidi. I'm glad you're home."

From behind me, in the open doorway, came, "You want children?"

Turning my head, I saw Lev standing there, a soft expression on seeing his two favorite girls. I smiled. "I love kids." I quickly added, "I thought you were meant to be working, mister."

He leaned his tall body against the wall. "I find myself distracted."

I understood. Lev's attempt to bury himself in Bleeding Hearts' books was not working.

"Come here," I told him.

He didn't hesitate. I knew what he needed.

Once he was seated next to me on the sofa, I gently passed Lidiya over to him. The chubby little girl was hefted effortlessly onto Lev's lap. She snuffled in her sleep, but quickly got comfortable on her father. He breathed a sigh of relief and pressed soft kisses into her hair.

He loved her so damn much. I found myself getting choked up over it.

Resting his cheek on her little head, he turned to me. "I make a good kid, if you're interested," he finished with a smile.

I chuckled and shook my head at his terrible joke. My smile wavered, as I knew it was time to bring up something I had been dreading. I'd been holding it in for a full week. It felt cheap to bring it up after Irina had died.

"Lev, sweetie," I started, "I need to ask you something, and I need you to not get angry with me about it, okay?"

He frowned, rocking Lidiya. "Okay."

My mouth dry, I tried to explain the quick way. "Alessio found the Petersons for me." From the way his body stiffened, I had my answer. But I had to ask. "I need to know if you found them first. I need to know if you lied to me."

Disappointment flooded me when he responded quietly, "I wasn't ready for you to see them." He went on, "I wasn't ready for you to leave me."

My eyes closing, I uttered a gentle, "I love you, Lev, but this...this was not about you." My eyes prickled behind my closed lids. "I begged you to find them. You told me you would. Knowing I could have seen them over a month ago...it hurts."

"I'm sorry," he said in that robotic tone of his.

My eyes snapped open. "I don't think you are." I shook my head. "I think you're sorry you got caught." I stood and spoke gently, "I'm going to see them this week, and I'm taking Alessio with me. Don't try to stop me." I paused a moment. "I'm pissed at you, baby." There was no heat in my saying that, only disappointment.

He blinked up at me, almost as if my quietly spoken statement shocked him. He repeated with more feeling, "I'm sorry, Mina."

My voice flat, I walked out of the living room, muttering, "So am I."

⚓

He found me lying on our bed an hour later, staring up at the ceiling.

My frustration was there, evident, but I wasn't going to make Lev drown in it. That wasn't my style. I forced a smile. "Hey. Where's the princess?"

His eyes didn't meet mine. "Nas stole her away."

I checked the time on my phone. "She's going to be hungry soon."

"Yeah. Nas is keeping her for dinner. Ada made spaghetti." He sighed, stepping into the room. "I need you to understand something about me." I waited carefully. He opened his arms wide and stated, "I'm selfish."

My brow bunched. "No, you're not. You're not selfish at all."

His jaw tight, he sat on the edge of the bed and nodded. "I am. And I'm ruthless. When I want something, I will do whatever I can to get it."

That didn't sound like the Lev I knew. "You're being dramatic."

His warm eyes met mine. "I didn't want you to see the Petersons for two reasons." He held up a finger. "I wanted to punish Maggie Peterson in the knowledge that you were looking for her, but she couldn't find you. I wanted the salty words she spoke to you the day you ran away to rot in her mouth like maggots. She hurt you. I wanted her to suffer the consequences of her actions that day."

Whoa. That was kind of ruthless. I cleared my throat and asked, "And the second reason?"

He lowered his face and ground out, "The son, James, is recently divorced."

I didn't understand. "What does that mean?"

His expression fierce, he stated, "I wasn't going to lose you to a man you once loved. It wasn't going to happen."

My irritation sparked at that. "Don't you trust me?"

He pinned me with a knowing stare. "When Anika is around, is it me you don't trust, or is it her?"

"Her," I squawked in disbelief that he'd even ask me that. Then I realized he had made a point. "Okay," I began, "I understand your stupid reasons for not wanting me to see them, however invalid they are. But," I sighed, "things have changed. *I've* changed. I think I've made it clear that I love you. *You*. Not James."

Lev reached up to unbutton the collar of his shirt. "You don't know that seeing him wouldn't bring up old feelings."

"That's true," I admitted. "But those feelings you're speaking of were that of a sixteen-year-old girl who was shocked that a guy would actually notice her, not a twenty-four-year-old woman." I reached over to wrap my hand around his. "I don't swoon at every guy who throws me an appreciative look, do I?"

He sighed, fighting to loosen his tie with his free hand, jerking it roughly. "You loved him."

He was not wrong. I did love James. But that was an age ago.

That love had faded and made room for a bigger love. A mature love. A *real* love.

Taking his hand, I placed it in his lap as I worked on loosening his tie gently. I spoke softly, "I love you." I undid the silken tie, draping it over his shoulders. "I want you." Pulling on both sides of the silk, I drew him close and got right in his face. "Do you understand me?"

His hand came up to rest high on my waist and he huffed out a long breath. "I can't lose you."

I leaned forward just enough to capture his lips in a warm, loving kiss. "Do you trust me?"

There was no hesitation in his rough response. "Yes."

I laid a hand against his stubbled cheek then threw his words back at him. "Then *trust* me."

We spent the afternoon in bed, holding each other and kissing like a couple of sixteen-year-olds.

It was tame and exactly what we needed.

Any day spent with Lev was perfect.

Just perfect.

CHAPTER FORTY-TWO

Mina

When Nas wanted something, she played hard at getting it.

Around six, Lev walked over to her house to fetch Lidiya, but came back empty-handed with a scowl on his face.

I fought my smile. "What happened?"

He shut the door with more force than necessary, grunting, "Sleepover. No boys allowed, apparently."

I did laugh then, making my way over to him and wrapping my arms around him. "You're not the only one who missed her, you know?"

He frowned down at me. "I just want her here with me." His face softened. "With us."

"It's only been a week, sweetie. They're excited. It's going to take time for them to get it out of their systems. They love her to death."

He lifted his hands to unbutton his shirt. "They're going to be the *death* of *me*."

My brain grinned. I had the perfect distraction. I squeezed his waist. "Hey, can I get your opinion on something? I need you to be honest though."

He looked tired, but was ever obliging. "Of course, mouse."

I was going to remedy that exhaustion. I smiled innocently. "Great. You get comfortable, and I'll be back in just a second." I rushed over to the en suite, grabbing the black garment bag on the way. I closed the door just in time to see Lev throw himself back on the bed, resting an arm over his eyes.

It took less than five minutes to dress, and when I opened the door, Lev was in the same position I left him in. I walked slowly, careful in the heels, so as not to embarrass myself by face-planting. When I made it a few feet from the bed, I cleared my throat.

Lev lifted his head with a sigh, and when his eyes landed on me, they widened comically. Unconsciously, he kept his eyes on me but reached for his dick, gripping it firmly in his hand.

I stood tall, legs apart, expression pure. "Honest opinion, sweetie." I turned for him slowly, and asked a sultry, "Is this hotter than boobs and butts?"

His eyes trailed the teeny-weeny navy blue and white sailor outfit. The skirt frilled prettily and added no coverage at all, revealing my navy satin and lace panties. The white shirt coming just under my breasts, I wore it open but tied at my cleavage. My cute sailor hat pinned high up on the left side of my crown, I watched as his eyes trailed my legs and the thigh-high fishnets that covered them then down lower to my white peep-toe heels.

Grinning, I spread out the feathered fan and waved it in front of my face. "Sweetie, I need your sincere opinion."

Lev's full lips parted lightly and he squeezed himself tight. He muttered distractedly, "Much hotter than boobs and butts."

"So this burlesque thing could work?"

He nodded slowly before standing and stalking slowly toward me. I swallowed hard and took a wobbly step back in my heels. "Lev?"

I squeaked when he pounced on me, tackling me to the ground. I moaned when he turned me on my knees, pulled down the scrap of satin covering my pussy, and drove into me from behind. I sighed when we released moments apart. I smiled sleepily as he carried me to the bed, laying me down with gentle ease, wrapping his arms around me.

Oh, yeah.

This burlesque thing could actually work.

⚓

"Slow down!" I hollered, lightly hyperventilating.

We were going to get there too soon. I didn't want to be early. What kind of loser showed up early?

Me. That's who.

Lev reached over to squeeze my hand. "We're going *under* the speed limit, mouse. We're not going to get there early."

We were on our way to meet the Petersons. It was a forty-five-minute drive from where we currently lived, and with Lidiya in the back seat, singing to herself, I made every excuse in the book to pull over.

The first one had been that I thought Lidiya was cold, but when Lev checked the rearview mirror and saw Lidiya smiling back, waving her wobbly wave and saying her sweet, "Hewwo, Papa!" he turned to me, brows raised. I shrank into myself.

I was not going to admit I was nervous. No way, no how.

The second time, I tried to tell Lev that I needed to pee. He told me I didn't. I yelled that I did.

So he smiled at me.

The asshole.

The third time, I told him that I thought we'd gotten the dates mixed up and should go home to check. By that point, Lev was straight-up ignoring my hysterics and whistling along to the radio, while

Lidiya watched her dad closely before putting her lips together as if she was going to whistle, but making a horrifying shrieking noise through the tiny hole her mouth was making.

I didn't want to laugh. Why was she making me laugh? It should have been illegal to be that cute. Really.

My face felt hot and I breathed deep through the knot in my stomach. I dressed nicely, wanting to impress, but not too much. So I wore black jeans and a white blouse with my white blazer over the top. I slipped on my black ballet flats, applied a little makeup, and then tied my hair up into a high ponytail.

And now? Now I was sure I was going to blow chunks all over the Camaro's upholstery.

We got there a little after two p.m., and while Lev got Lidi out of the car, I waited inside, gathering my thoughts. After a minute to myself, Lev opened the passenger door, looking gorgeous in his jeans, tee, and dress jacket, holding an adorable Lidi in her pretty pink dress and white cardigan, her curls a chaotic mess at the top of her head.

With these two by my side, I was ready as I'd ever be.

I took Lev's offered hand and stepped out of the car. He locked it, put his arm around me, and lead me to the modest-looking house. Then suddenly, the knot in my stomach faded to a pinch. A second later, it was gone completely. Another moment, and I wasn't afraid anymore. I had once loved these people dearly. There was no reason to be afraid.

We approached the front door together, and Lev's arm tightened around my shoulders. I stepped forward to press the doorbell.

A loud chiming sounded, and not ten seconds later, the door opened.

The woman who stood there looked different, but under all the lines on her face and salt-and-pepper streaked hair, I found Maggie Peterson.

Her brows drew low and she placed a trembling hand to her mouth in stunned disbelief. "Mina, is that you, honey?"

At my smile, a gasp escaped her and she didn't ask permission. She wrapped her arms around me and drew me in for a tight, warm hug, her body quaking the entire time. I lifted my arms to hug her back and listened to her shaky whispers of, "Oh, Mina," and "My little girl."

I swallowed through the thickness in my throat and squeezed her tight. When she pulled back, her eyes were wet, but she was smiling. "Where are my manners?" She motioned to us all. "Please, come in. John and James are out back."

I swiped away the stray tear I didn't know had fallen and followed her inside, with Lev and Lidi trailing behind me. As we walked down the hall, I saw pictures of new family members of all races and backgrounds. I smiled and asked, "More sons and daughters?"

She smiled weakly and shrugged. "We only do temporary fostering now. No more than six months at a time."

She didn't say much about that, but I had a feeling that was my fault.

Maggie held my hand as we entered the backyard. "John. James. Look who's here."

A much pudgier-looking John than I remembered stood from his place at the table. He smiled wide and didn't waste time; he came forward and wrapped me up in a bear hug. "Oh, Mina, Mina. What am I going to do with you?"

We separated and I smiled kindly. "You look good, John."

He chuckled and patted his belly. "Yeah, sure do. I'm surprised you haven't asked when I'm due." He laughed good-naturedly.

But the man who stood by his chair, looking at me as though I'd betrayed him in the worst possible way, caught my attention. "James," I breathed.

He was still handsome as ever in that All-American way. His sandy brown hair cut neatly, his blue eyes clear, he looked harder than I remembered. There were no smiles spared for me that afternoon. He uttered offhandedly, "Mina. Nice to see you."

The way he said this indicated that his statement was a lie. A big, fat one.

"Yeah." My voice was small. I absently rubbed at my forearm. "You too. Where are the twins?"

John rolled his eyes but he did it smiling. "At a friends house. Teenagers." There was a thick moment of silence before John cleared his throat.

"Well, are you going to introduce us to this fine-looking fella, or are we going to have to guess?" He smiled wider. "Because if I had to guess, I'd give him the name Thor."

My smile returned full force. John hadn't changed a bit.

I stepped back, allowing Lev to place his arm around me. I looked up into his warm cognac eyes and announced. "This is my...my..." My smile softened. "This is my Lev." His arm tightened around me. He bent down to kiss my forehead. I leaned into him and added, "And the little princess on Lev's hip is his daughter, Lidiya."

Maggie came forward, took one look at Lidiya, and beamed. "Hello, princess. Would you like a dolly to play with?" She looked up at Lev and explained, "I've got tons of toys if she wants to play with something."

Lev stared at Maggie a long moment before placing Lidiya on the ground. My heart pumped hard before it slowed in relief as Lidi took Maggie's hand and blinked up at her. "I pay a dolly?"

Maggie looked down at the cuteness that was Lidiya before announcing, "Of course you can play with a dolly."

That was the good thing about Maggie. She spoke fluent baby.

As Maggie disappeared inside with Lidi, John gestured to the table and we sat. "What are you having, Mina? And Lev, was it? What can I get you to drink?"

I smiled. "I'll have a glass of juice."

"Same," Lev responded.

John clapped his hands together. "It will be done. Give me a second."

He left us with James and, the coward I was, I refused to look him in the eye when I asked, "How are you, James?"

I felt his eyes on me. I felt his anger at my small talk. Truth was, I wasn't ready to discuss what happened. Not just yet.

After a long pause, he responded a low, "Just fine, thanks."

I nodded. He didn't ask about me. My guess was he wanted to throw me out of this house and gladly never see me again.

I suppose I expected things to be awkward, but he was angry with me. Furious, even. And I didn't understand why.

We were both to blame for what happened. The sex didn't just happen. I didn't seduce him. We were an item. We loved each other. I'd be damned if I was going to take all the blame for what we were caught doing.

Maggie opened the back door and returned with Lidiya, holding a Barbie doll at the very same time that John returned with our drinks. He placed three glasses of juice down for Lev, Maggie, and me, while he and James sipped on beer.

Well...this was going to be fun.

About as fun as pulling teeth, I thought.

"So," Maggie started, raising her shoulders in a light shrug. She held a firm smile, but her brows pulled down in a would-be frown. She asked quietly, "Where have you been, honey?"

I opened my mouth to respond, but nothing came out. Gaping fish was a good look on me.

Instead, Lev replied calmly, "Up until three months ago, Mina lived on the streets."

Silence. Thick as concrete.

"What happened three months ago?" James asked icily.

Lev uttered, "I found her." His message was implied. I was his. His hand came down on my thigh, squeezing lightly.

John surmised, "You chose being homeless over living with us?" He sounded hurt.

Maggie's eyes shone brightly. "We would've taken care of you, honey. You were our girl."

It was funny what seven years could do to a person. In listening to all of this bullshit, I found myself bitter. I scoffed, "Oh yeah? I thought I was nothing but a little whore, Maggie? Isn't that what you called me? Oh wait, no. That's not right. Apparently, I was a little tramp."

Maggie drew back, her expression pained, but I wasn't done.

"You were angry with me." I turned to a somber John. "You both were." I looked at James. His jaw clenched tight. "And you..." I shook my head. "You said nothing." My heart clenched. "You said you loved me, but when we were caught, where were you? Hiding with you tail between your legs, that's where." I shook my head. "Don't tell me I had a place here. I considered you my parents up until that day." I glared at James. "I wasn't the only one to blame."

John spoke quietly, "I think we all handled the situation poorly."

Maggie shook her head. "No. *I* handled the situation poorly." She blinked away tears. "I know it doesn't mean much now, but I regretted saying those things to you the second they were out of my mouth." She tried to force a laugh, but it came out a whimper. "I don't even know why I said it. But I've regretted it for seven years."

Her emotion hit me hard.

I felt like an asshole. "It wasn't just you, Maggie. The whole situation was out of control." I sighed. "There was no way you would have let James and me be together. Even if somehow you were okay with it, which you weren't, child services would have placed me in a different home when they found out. I was seventeen. I didn't want to go to another home." My breath caught as I let out a broken, "This was my home."

At my sudden distress, Maggie broke down. She placed a hand over her face and cried silently. The mood at the table had dampened a notch and a half. John sat quietly while James frowned down at his hands.

This was something I caused. I needed to do something, *say* something. "For what it's worth, you guys were the best. I loved you, and I never thought badly of you after what happened. I just needed to go. Be on my own. I was sick of being someone else's burden."

At that, James stood suddenly. "I'm out." He didn't look at me. "Glad you're not dead, Mina."

Before anyone could respond, he was gone. I stood before I realized what I was doing and followed him. He was not going to make me feel guilty, dammit.

When I stepped out the front door, he was already unlocking his car. "What is your problem, James?"

He opened the car door. "Go back inside, Mina."

He tried to sit and close the door on me, but I caught it before it shut, pulling it open. "No. We're going to have it out. What is your deal?"

James scoffed. "Go back to your man, Mina. Forget about us. Again."

Oooh. We were finally getting to the point of things.

"Why are you so mad at me?"

His expression turned vicious. He stepped out of the car and stood a foot away from me. "Why am I mad?" He glowered. "*Why* am I mad?" He blinked a moment before throwing his arms out and shouting, "*You left me!*"

Uh...what?

His jaw ticked. "You didn't even say goodbye, just packed a bag and ran. You left me. You left us," he panted. "I loved you."

My heart sank. "I loved you, too. But when push came to shove, you didn't show me at the time I needed it most. Your mother said some vile things to me, and you said nothing."

He dipped his chin, shaking his head. "I was a kid, Mina. You were my girl. She was my mom. We both knew what we were doing was wrong. Why else would we have kept it hidden? We knew we shouldn't have been doing it, but we loved each other. Nothing else mattered." He sighed. "If you'd have just given her some time to cool down... She was shocked."

I gritted my teeth. "I was seventeen years old. She called me a tramp. She had hate in her eyes. And you...you wouldn't even look at me." I told him the honest truth. "You were a coward."

His hands came up to rest on his hips. He nodded slowly. "Yeah, maybe I was. But I would've given up everything for you. I loved you that much. I would've dropped everything. My football scholarship, my family, none of it mattered. If you just asked me to pack a bag, I would have come with you. We could've been together," he finished on a whisper.

"You don't know what you're saying," I told him. "I would never wish the life I've lived upon someone I loved. I wouldn't even wish it upon someone I hate." I leaned against his car and looked out into the street. "I was starving, James. Literally starving before Lev busted me stealing his brother's wallet. I wasn't ready to die. I just wanted to get something to eat. Stealing that wallet turned out to be the best thing that happened to me. It changed my life."

James huffed out a breath, leaning on the car in the space next to me. "I would've always provided for you. You never would have gone hungry if we'd done that together. But you didn't give me the opportunity."

I changed the subject. "I heard you got divorced." I turned to him. "What happened?"

He looked at me, those baby blues full of sadness. "I was still in love with another woman. My wife resented that so she left me." He blinked slowly, reaching out to take my hand. "It's only ever been you for me, Mina. Only you."

His hand was warm on mine and a sudden rush of emotion hit me. I squeezed his hand and spoke quietly, "You need to move on, James."

"Like you've moved on?" he uttered sternly as he released my hand.

I nodded. "I moved on seven years ago."

He puffed out a long breath. "That sucks."

No, it didn't suck. It was wonderful. I had Lev, and he gave me things no other man could, not even James.

There was nothing more to say. I held out my hand. "I hope you find what you're looking for, James."

He took my hand, shaking it lightly. "I already have, but she doesn't want me anymore." He shrugged. "That's life, I guess."

It was life, unfortunately.

Just when I moved to let go, James pulled me forward so quickly that I was thrown into his body. His arms came around me and his lips came down on mine hard.

Wide-eyed and my body rigid, my mouth remained slack as he groaned into my lips.

Well, that certainly brought a new definition to the saying 'stealing a kiss'.

CHAPTER FORTY-THREE

Mina

The rest of the afternoon went off without a hitch. Maggie and John apologized for James' abrupt departure. They apologized even more so for what happened that night seven years ago. I told them that it was long forgotten and that I wished them well. And best of all, Maggie left a moment and came back with the leather-covered photo album I'd left behind. Flicking through, I could see it was untouched apart from some new additions at the end where Maggie had added some photos of us as a family. I couldn't wait to show the photos to Alessio. We left close to five p.m., and Maggie asked if we could get together sometime for lunch. I hugged her tight and told her that I would love to, even though I was somewhat sure that wasn't going to happen.

As we drove home, Lidi fell asleep, which gave me the perfect opportunity to speak to Lev without distraction. "What did you think about Maggie and John?"

He thought about it. "I think they regret causing you pain. They seem like nice people."

"And James?"

His jaw tensed. "He was an ass."

I agreed in a sense, but now I had to tell him the awkward part.

"He kissed me today." I turned to look at him. His hands had tightened around the steering wheel so tightly that his knuckles turned white. "After I followed him out, we had it out. He was angry with me for leaving. He told me he was still in love with me. That it was why he got divorced." I paused before landing the biggest blow. "He told me to leave you today and asked me to marry him."

At the last part, Lev turned to me, his face slack. He gathered himself before clearing his throat and asking, "And what did you say to that?"

I feigned indifference, "Well, after I slapped him for that rude kiss he planted on me, I told him he needed to get a grip. I explained that I only wanted to marry one man, and I was already with that man." I let out a breath of frustration. "You called it, baby. I was wrong. He definitely wanted a slice of Mina pie."

Lev uttered an irritated, "I'm not sure whether to find him and beat the shit out of him, or just sit here and be thankful in the knowledge that you wish to marry me one day."

I grinned saucily. "How about a kiss of gratitude?"

He glanced at me and his hard face softened, a small smile gracing his lips. He leaned over and I pulled back. "Not on my lips."

He looked confused. "Then where?"

I smirked, turning to look out the window. "I'll show you when we get home."

His low growl caused goose bumps to trail up my arms. And when we got home, he kissed me well and good.

In fact, he kissed me boneless.

⚓

It was the night before the club reopened, and Sasha called together a dinner meeting before the grand affair. It was held at the main house. Ada had prepared a wonderful banquet in celebration, and I was salivating at the look of it all.

We ate. We talked. We laughed.

Everything was going well. Almost too well, if you know what I mean. So when Anika turned to me and said what she did, it was hardly a surprise. It was expected. "So, Mina, what's happening? Are you looking for your own place yet?"

The entire table went silent.

"Ani." Nas stared at her. "Honey, don't."

Anika had been drinking since we arrived. She was currently on her fourth glass of wine and she looked rather mellow. She waved Nas off and blinked slowly. "What? We're all friends here."

We were?

I wasn't so sure of that.

I cleared my throat and responded, "Well, actually, I have been looking online at apartments."

Nas sounded taken aback. "*What*?" While Lev stated a firm, "No." And Sasha… Oh, Sasha. All he said was, "Good." They did this simultaneously, stopping to look at each other after they heard the others' response.

Lev cleared his throat, putting his napkin down. "Not that it's your business, Anika, but there would be no point in Mina moving." He lifted his glass of wine and sipped at it. "Mina proposed to me two days ago." The table went silent. He placed his glass down. "And I've accepted."

What?

What what what*?*

Where the heck was I when this proposal was happening?

I was surprised that Lev's pants hadn't caught fire, because he was clearly a liar.

"Um..." I started as everyone turned to stare at me.

But Lev helped me out. "Remember? In the car. You told me that you planned to marry one man, and that one man would be me. I agree with you. I think you should marry me."

I leaned forward, forced a light laugh, and then whisper-hissed, "That was hardly a proposal, *sweetie*." I said sweetie like it was sticky and needed to get off me, like, now.

"Sure it was," he uttered conversationally. "And I accepted." He looked around the table. "We're getting married."

Nastasia chuckled, and that chuckle turned into a laugh. Viktor grinned, and soon, he was chuckling too. Sasha looked to Anika, and Anika looked as though her world was ending. I hated that for her, but she needed to understand Lev and I were together. That we loved each other. And that I was not going anywhere.

I turned to him, a smile spreading across my lips, but I did this shaking my head.

He winked at me.

I drew my face toward his shoulder, resting my lips there. "You know, we probably should have done this in private."

He kissed the tip of my nose. "Nonsense. Like Anika said, we're all friends here."

I grinned. "So we're getting married?" He nodded, smiling down at me, his tender expression softening his hard face. I asked on a surprised laugh, "And when will this wedding of ours take place?"

He shrugged lightly, looking all too pleased with himself. "I'll leave that up to you, mouse. A day from now, a week from now, a year from now, I don't care. As long as you wear my ring and promise to one day be my wife, I'll be a happy man."

His lips came down to kiss mine in a slow, warm kiss. When we separated, I looked around the table and announced with a smile and a shrug. "Looks like we're getting married." I finished by putting a hand over my mouth and laughing out loud, my disbelief evident.

It was surreal.

LEV

Three months ago, I was living in an alley, *my* alley, and struggling to keep myself alive. Today I was engaged to be married to the most handsome, thoughtful, kind man in the world. A man who saved my life. A man I loved with every beat of my aching heart.

It was finally happening for me.

Life was happening.

And I loved it. Every hard, trying, demanding second of it.

Right now, life was good. And although I wanted more out of it, I didn't need it. My happiness was restored by the faith of one man.

One imperfectly perfect man.

⚓

My smile was bursting to show itself, but I had told myself that I needed to be cool. "Birdie?" I called. When she turned, I motioned with my fingers for her to come to me. She looked worried when I told her, "Sasha wants to see you in his office."

"Is everything all right?" she asked slowly, carefully.

I forced a sigh and gave her a grave look. "Not really. Come on. We'll talk about it."

Down the hall, she paused before we went into the office. "Have I done something?"

I threw her a sad smile, opening the door, and she went inside. I followed and closed the door behind us. While Birdie moved to sit opposite Sasha, I stayed by the door, hiding my giddiness.

Sasha sat back in his chair. "How you doing, pretty bird?"

Birdie frowned. "F-fine, I guess."

"Good." He sat forward. "I've noticed you working with the girls. And after today's rehearsal, I gotta tell you…" He paused for effect. "…I'm wondering why you never gave me an opportunity to give you a management position. Because I gotta say, Birdie…I need you."

"Wha…?" She turned to look at me before facing Sasha. "What is this?"

Sasha grinned then. "This is you getting a promotion. A well-deserved promotion, if you want it."

Her eyes bugged out. "Are you playin', baby? Because that ain't funny. I got two babies to feed and I need the money. So if…"

Sasha slid over a piece of paper. Birdie picked it up with shaking hands and she whispered, "What's this?"

Sasha smiled softly. "That's your base wage. Underneath that is the bonus you'll be getting for last week's overtime."

Birdie stuttered, "But…but…but…" Then rasped, "But that's double what I'm getting now."

He narrowed his eyes at her. "You saying you're not worth that? Because I can adjust it to—"

She cut him off with a firm, "Don't you dare! You hush now."

And Sasha laughed. "Does this mean you'll accept my offer?"

She raised a brow. "Slow down, sugar. You haven't even told me what it is I'm gonna be doing. How about you start with that?"

I stepped forward, moving to stand by Sasha's desk. I smiled down at my friend and told her, "Sasha was hoping you'd be the stage manager. Which puts you in charge of the girls, ordering new costumes, helping to choreograph their dance routines, setting up nightly rosters...that sort of stuff."

Sasha nodded in agreement. "It also means you'll have to work longer hours. Not too many, but at least another five hours a week."

Birdie thought about it for a long moment then smiled up at Sasha. "I'll make it work." She held up the paper that Sasha had scribbled down her management wages on and waved it around. "For *this*, I'll make it work, baby. You got yourself a stage manager."

She squeaked excitedly as she stood and hugged the both of us, leaving Sasha and me for a moment alone. I smiled after her, clapping my hands together at the feeling you got from seeing someone you cared about succeed in a way they never thought possible.

I took a seat in the chair that Birdie had vacated and sighed lightly, "That was awesome."

Sasha's eyes narrowed at me.

My eyes widened. "What?"

He searched my face before muttering, "Who the fuck are you, Mina Harris?"

I rolled my eyes at him and his goddamn dramatics. "You know who I am, Sasha." I mumbled, "I'm just a girl."

He shook his head. "No. You're not."

I wasn't sure what he meant by that, but he said it softly, and there was less acid in that statement than I had ever heard from Sasha. My brows bunched. "Hey. Are you okay?"

He ran a hand down his face. "No. Not really." I wasn't prepared for that admission, nor when he, suddenly looking weary, confessed, "If this doesn't work, we're going to have to shut down. We're losing too much money."

I knew this. It hadn't been said, but we all knew it. It was one of the reasons the girls were working as hard as they were, and when Sasha surprised us all with an all-new interior, our excitement for opening night doubled.

The club looked classier than ever. While the stage remained the same, new flooring had been put down, and gone were the red velvet drapes, replaced with heavy black curtains that looked elegant and stylish. Most tables were replaced with booths with black leather seats and white pins. The bar stools were exchanged for high-back chairs. The walls had been painted black, and Sasha had paid a man an exorbitant amount of money to have the photographs I took of the girls in playful and provocative positions spray-painted every few feet.

Our flyers were a hit. Lev, Vik, Nas, Anika, and I made our way all over, posting posters on the walls of popular hangouts and handing out flyers. It had been a long few days, but the hype was showing. Our social media page—which was Nas' idea, God bless her—skyrocketed overnight, with people tagging their friends in interest. Women who wanted to dance for the club had contacted us via email and expressed how thrilling it was to have a local burlesque act.

The current reaction was a positive one. Now we had to wait and see if our hard work had paid off.

"It's all going to work out," I told him, my confidence flaring.

He reached up to pinch the bridge of his nose, shutting his eyes tightly. "If it doesn't, we're fucked. We invested everything into this place."

I stood, walking out the door. "Ugh. No negative Nancy's allowed." I called back, "We're going to make it work, dammit."

As God was my witness, we were going to make it work.

⚓

When I got home that night, I told Lev I would be up to bed in a minute, wanting a moment alone before I picked up my cell and dialed the number.

I was calling in a favor.

CHAPTER FORTY-FOUR

Mina

I sat on the sofa, my legs curled up under me, sipping my coffee while watching Lidi dance to one of the many catchy Wiggles songs that was playing on the TV. She put her hands in the air, clapped when prompted, stomped her little chubby feet, and sang along, although I wasn't really sure what language Lidi thought The Wiggles sang in. It sounded like she was going with Swahili.

Lev walked in, coffee mug in hand, looked at his little girl, and smiled, shaking his head. I grinned, and my shoulders shook in silent laughter. He was in the middle of getting ready for his workout, checking his watch, walking around in sweat pants and no tee, and my gut clenched at the sight of his bare torso.

Those broad shoulders just did it for me. And when we had our time alone, I held onto them, hanging on for the ride like nobody's business.

The faint red mark on the left shoulder had me flushing hard. I might have used that shoulder to ground me after my orgasm by biting into it and clutching at him, my nails embedded in his upper arms as I moaned through my release.

The front door opened quietly and Sasha let himself in, still looking sleep-mussed in his blue jeans and black tee, making his way right for the little girl dancing in front of the television. He didn't bother with hellos. He snatched Lidiya up and she squealed excitedly, "Asha, putta down. Putta *down*."

His voice croaky, he told her, "Ada made pancakes. You want pancakes, princess?" She stopped fighting and cinched her arms around his neck. He cocked her high on his hip and, with a jerk of his chin, strode out the door.

This happened more often that not. I was wrong when I suggested that Sasha and Nastasia fighting for Lidiya's attention was just a phase. Truth was, they treated Lidi as if she was the daughter neither had, and they loved her to pieces.

Lev checked his watch again, and I knew it was time for him to go. As soon as we woke, I made him his tasteless oatmeal and he ate it in silence. I mean, how else would you eat oatmeal that possibly tasted like cardboard? There were no 'mmmm's and 'yum's to be had. Let's be honest. It tasted like trash. I wasn't sure how he could stomach it.

Correction. I'd eaten trash that tasted better than unsweetened oatmeal.

Blech.

He came forward, his eyes soft, and towered his large body over me, reaching down to grip my chin as he planted warm, gentle kisses to my lips. "I have to go."

He went to move back, but I snagged him, my fingers dipping into the waist of his pants. "You can play hooky. We can go back to bed and play patty cake." I bit the inside of my cheek. "We've got at least half an hour before Sasha brings Lidi home."

"But I always work out between ten and twelve."

I nodded. "I know. But one day off won't kill you, right?"

He looked confused. "But I always work out between ten and twelve."

My eyes rolled a little, but I straightened quickly with a smile. "I know, but—"

He cut me off, his voice quiet, anxious almost. "I always work out between ten and twelve."

This was one of those moments. One of those moments where your head tells you not to push, but you're not sure if you hold back. I came to realize rather quickly that messing with Lev's routine was a big no-no. Nothing made my man more irritated than someone screwing with his schedule.

I understood the underlining issues. He craved a semblance of normal in a world where he felt different. His childhood had done things to him that made him the way he was today.

Did that frustrate me? At times, yes.

Lev could not be *fixed*. And I didn't want to repair the broken part of him. He was perfectly imperfect, and I was his in heart and soul.

More importantly, he was mine. And that was a big deal. Lev did not give himself to people. They merely borrowed his time. And here I was, his attention given fully to a person who probably didn't deserve it. I was grateful though, and I often reminded myself that he had compromised a lot of himself for me and I needed to do the same.

Releasing the elastic at his pants, I reached up to finger the swinging anchor pendant he had bought me and I smiled gently, knowing I'd have to pick my battles. "Okay, sweetie. Have fun."

His shoulders slumped in the immense relief I imagined he felt at my quick out. His hands came up and he laid them on my cheeks in gratitude. When his lips descended, I found myself leaned up, into him, needing his lips on me. He kissed me softly once, twice, three times, then whispered against my lips, "I love you, Mina."

It was the first time he had said the words. I *felt* his love, but hearing the words...wow. It was breathtaking. I'd come to realize the saying was true. Patience was a virtue.

I kissed him again. And again. And before I could drag him down onto the sofa with me, I pushed him away gently. "Go. Now. Or I'll tackle you to the ground."

His eyes smiled and he chuckled lightly. He threw me a wink before he left, and I threw myself back on the couch and blew out a long breath. "Have mercy."

My man was a serious case of sexy.

The front door opened again, and just as my excitement flared at the thought of Lev disregarding his routine and spending the morning in bed with me, Nas stuck her head through the crack and called out, "Pancakes at Sasha's. Move your ass, *kukla*. I'm starved."

I rose of the sofa with a sigh. "Yeah, yeah. I'm coming."

I'd rather have been doing a different type of *coming,* but pancakes were still pretty awesome.

Nas and I walked side-by-side, taking in the morning sun. I couldn't help but ask, "Where's Vik?"

Nas slipped on her giant sunglasses and shrugged. "I don't know. It's not like we spend every waking moment with each other."

I frowned. "Uh, yeah you do."

She scoffed. "No. We don't."

It sounded like there was trouble in paradise.

We walked on a while, and she asked quietly, "If Lev wasn't committed to you, but you loved him, what would you do?"

My haunches rose. "I would kindly tell him to fuck a duck." She sighed softly and I stopped in my tracks. "What's going on, Nas? What happened?"

She paused a moment before she threw her arms up and rushed out, "I don't know. You and Lev are getting married." I threw her a look that said 'yeah, so?' and she shook her head gently. "I want that. And I'm not going to get that with Vik."

My brow furrowed. "Who said? He loves you, Nas. Anyone can see it. He *loves* you."

Her lip trembled. "No. He doesn't." She took in a deep breath and let out a long exhale. "He sleeps around, you know." My face must have conveyed that I did not know this, because her eyes widened and she nodded. "Yeah. And then he comes to me at two, sometimes three in the morning, and sleeps in my bed. Because I let him." She let out a humorless laugh. "He doesn't love me, Mina. He loves that I'm a willing booty call, that I'm a sure thing. That's all I'll ever be to him." Her eyes watered and she whispered a broken, "I can't do it anymore. It hurts too much."

"Okay, so he has commitment issues," I started, but she shook her head.

"Don't make excuses for him, Mina. Please," she begged then pleaded, "I need you on my side for this one. I need a friend who gets it. Okay?"

She sounded beaten and desperate. I found myself offering her what she needed. "Okay, Nas," I told her. "I get it."

Her face dejected, she nodded lightly. "Thanks, shorty."

I smiled. "Anytime." Then I hooked my arm through hers and pulled her along. "C'mon. It's too early for this crap. I need pancakes."

We arrived at Sasha's not a minute later and murdered those freaking pancakes.

Opening night arrived quicker than any of us expected, and I glanced around the room, taking in the new sights and familiarizing myself with the new layout. Everything was different. It was exciting.

Birdie helped the girls prepare, giving last-minute instruction and helping with their costumes, hair, and makeup. I was a little surprised when Sasha instructed Nas, Anika, and me to change when we got there. Apparently, it had been decided that bar staff would dress like the dancers, but at a subdued level. When I alerted Sasha to the fact that heels and I were not friends, he told me Birdie had taken care of it. I was pleasantly surprised by the low-heeled peep-toes she got for me.

We changed into our new uniforms that consisted of thigh-high fishnets, garters, black and red corset-busted one-pieces, and frilled micro skirts. One of the girls lent me a long pair of satin, fingerless gloves, and they were just gorgeous. I thought it would feel weird. It didn't. It felt sexy. I felt sexy, and I was dying to see what Lev thought.

LEV

Once dressed, Anika, Nas, and I made our way out of the stage area, only to be howled and wolf-whistled at. I covered my face with my hands, blushing furiously, but laughing hard. Before I even had time to recover, I felt a warm, hard body crash into mine. I wrapped my arms around him with an *oomph* and blinked up at him. "Lev? What's wrong, sweetie?"

He glared down at my pushed-up breasts. "What the hell are you *wearing*?"

A smile formed. "Didn't you get the memo?" I waved my arm back to Anika and Nas. "These are the new bar uniforms."

He shook his head profusely and made small grunting noises that said 'no' then a growl escaped him that said 'oh, *hell* no'.

I placed a hand over his shirt-covered taut stomach and reasoned with him. "This is all part and parcel of changing things up. We want the experience to be genuine. Do you understand?"

His jaw tight, he growled out, "I don't like this." He snuffled an annoyed, "Everyone can see your goodies."

I grinned up at him. "And only you get to unwrap me later." I went up on my tiptoes to nip his chin. "Isn't that just wicked?"

I heard the girls walk away and I was glad for it. When Lev reached down to palm my ass through my new costume, he took my earlobe into his mouth and sucked then whispered into my ear, "You're naughty. And naughty girls get punished."

My eyes rolled back at the feeling of his tongue on my lobe, but when it registered what he just said, I pulled back, wide-eyed. "Punished how?"

Oh, God, my voice was hoarse. Like, pack-a-day-smoker hoarse.

His lip twitched. "What am I going to do with you, mouse?"

"I have a few ideas," I muttered as my eyes hooded and I pressed my lips to his, loving the way his tongue dipped in to stroke mine.

And then he was gone. Nas, rolling her eyes, pulled me away and called out, "Geez. Break it up. We've got shit to do. You can eye-fuck each other from across the floor, *capisce*?"

I took my place at the bar. The deejay Sasha had hired played soft RnB throughout the club until things got started. Sasha made his way into the bar, smirking to himself, and came straight for me. He looked excited when he stated, "The line is already three blocks down." He chuckled, shaking his head in disbelief. "Three fucking blocks down." He pointed a finger at me, smiling as he inclined his head, and then walked away.

I wasn't sure what that meant.

Sasha was weird.

Half an hour later, and we all took our places, the door opened, and the club began to fill. Once we reached capacity, the door closed once more, and Nas, Anika, and I were run off our feet with flyers for free drinks on entry. We no longer served people at tables or booths. If you wanted a drink, you needed to come to us.

The lights dimmed. The deejay turned down the music, and then he spoke, "Good evening, ladies and gentleman, and welcome to the grand opening of Bleeding Hearts Burlesque."

The crowd cheered, and I was surprised at the amount of women in the crowd. The deejay waited for the cheer to die down before he went on, "We hope you enjoy what we have to offer. Our girls are dying to meet you."

The spotlights beamed front and center, and we waited with bated breath.

The deejay's voice deepened huskily as he announced, "Ladies and gents, I give you…" He paused for effect. The curtains began to open. "…The Diamond Dozen!"

The twelve girls on stage looked like dolls sitting on wooden chairs. Each dressed in a different color of the same costume, the same costume the bar girls were wearing. The bass boomed as The Weeknd's "The Hills" came to life. It was a slow, sexy song that allowed the girls to show off their moves. It was a song about a torrid affair a woman was having with an addict. The girls moved in sync, working with the chair, gyrating against them, and wolf whistles came from all over.

I saw women watch them, mesmerized, and men gaze adoringly at our girls. When Birdie hired the three new girls only days ago, I wondered if they would be ready in time, but I was proven wrong, and gladly at that.

As the song ended, the girls fell to the floor, faces cast, eyes open, like dolls that had been hypnotized into living by the music and falling as it ended.

The spotlight's shut off and the curtains closed.

Then…silence.

My breath caught in my throat.

Oh no. Crap, no. They hated it!

My cheeks flushed a moment before the crowd went wild, standing and cheering at the top of their lungs. Whistles and eager roars went out through the air around us, and my heart boomed in my chest. I could safely say that was the scariest moment in my life.

Nas pulled me into her, squealing in my ear and rocking me side-to-side. A chuckle caught in my throat, and then I laughed hard, clutching at her. Then something happened, and I felt tears welling up in my eyes.

My throat tight, I blinked them away.

Everything was going to be okay now. I felt it deep inside me.

Bleeding Hearts would live to a ripe old age.

As people left, others took their places. The club remained at full capacity all night long, and some time after eleven, I received guests. As soon as I saw them, I made my way around the bar, rushing over to my brother and hugging him around the middle before placing a kiss to Uncle Laredo's cheek. "You came!"

Laredo smiled, wrapping his arm around me, pulling me to his side. "I couldn't miss my niece's big night."

I reached for Alessio's hand and squeezed. "I'm so glad you're here."

Alessio looked down at me, pride evident in his eyes. "You did this?"

I scoffed, "No!" Then I looked around. "We all did this. It was a group effort. We all pitched in. Everyone had a job and they totally nailed it."

"You did good, kid," Alessio muttered, taking in the new establishment.

That was when Sasha came up behind me. "What the fuck do you think you're doing here?"

My eyes wide, I spoke up but choked on my words. "I-I invited them."

Sasha glared at me. "What the fuck for? They need to leave."

I stood between my uncle and brother, glowering up at Sasha. "No, they aren't going anywhere."

Sasha's jaw ticked before he took on a reasonable expression. "Listen, boys. You got your own club to run. You need to go."

Alessio wrapped an arm around me. "No, we don't. We closed for the night."

Sasha looked from Alessio to Laredo. "It's Friday night. One of the busiest nights of the week. Why the hell are you closed?"

My voice caught in my throat while my heart sank. *Here goes nothing.* "Because I asked them to."

Sasha's confused look had not wavered.

I shrugged and explained myself. "We needed people to get in the doors tonight. It was important, Sash. I don't want to lose this place. None of us do. So I asked them to close for the night," I swallowed hard, "to give us a fighting chance."

Sasha's expression cleared. His brow furrowed before he looked to Laredo, his voice low. "Why would you do that? You don't owe us anything."

Laredo nodded. "I know. But when Mina told me about what you had planned, I found myself curious." He shrugged. "Winning is no fun when there aren't any worthy competitors around."

Alessio agreed with a less than friendly smile thrown in Sasha's direction. "Yeah. It's no fun takin' shit from a man who's got nothin'." He added, "I'm waitin' for you to get so high up that you'll break somethin' when you fall. You get me, Leokov?"

Sasha stared at him, not blinking before he barked out a harsh laugh. "Fuck you, prick." Then he did something ballsy.

He held out his hand to Alessio.

And my heart skipped a beat.

Alessio glared at that hand a long while before reaching out slowly, taking Sasha's hand and shaking it firmly. "Nice place you got here."

Sasha smirked. "I know."

Alessio grinned and it pulled his scars tight. "God, you're a fucking asshole."

Sasha smirked harder. "I know."

Oh, my stars. Had my selfish actions just mended the rift caused by years of hatred?

I watched Sasha release Alessio's hand and hold out the same hand to Laredo. The older man smiled gently as he took it in his and shook it lightly.

Um, yeah. My small smile widened. *I think they did.*

CHAPTER FORTY-FIVE

Mina

It was a week after opening night, and news of the new burlesque act in town had tongues wagging. Our social media page had well over ten thousand followers in that single week, and although it saddened us all, Sasha had wisely made the decision to no longer open every night. Now, Bleeding Hearts was a strictly weekend establishment, opening Friday, Saturday, and Sunday nights.

This gave the girls time to practice during the week and learn new routines without the pressure of rehearsing and working on the same day.

Rumors of the girls' beauty spread fast, and soon The Diamond Dozen were the hottest girls in town. Everyone wanted to catch a glimpse. Our audience had indeed doubled, tripled even.

Sasha revealed that in our opening weekend, we had earned more than what we normally made in an entire week, and that was including all the free drinks we had given away with flyers.

The relief in the room was palpable. Shoulders slumped and people sighed out loud, others laughing happily. Lev pulled me into his side and I gripped his shirt tight, smiling into his chest.

Everything was working out. It was unbelievable. Miraculous, even.

The following Monday came quickly, and when the front gate bell went off as I passed the kitchen, I stared into the small CCTV, watching the car window open. She lowered her sunglasses, looking directly into the camera, and without a second thought, I buzzed her in.

I waited uneasily for the doorbell to chime, and as soon as it did, I threw it open.

The petite blonde in the long maxi-dress removed her glasses then smiled gently. "Hey, Mina."

"Cora," I greeted softly. "What are you doing here?"

She dipped her chin, sighing quietly. Then she blinked at me a long moment. "Can I come in?"

I thought about it. I probably shouldn't have let her in, but something about this girl screamed 'safe.' I nodded, moving back to allow her room to pass. She stepped in and smiled once more, but it was tired. "Thanks."

She moved into the living room and waited for me to enter before she sat on the sofa beside me. "Is Lev home?"

I checked the clock on the wall. He was still working out. "He should be home any minute now."

"Okay." She swallowed hard. "Do you mind if I wait until he gets here?"

"Not at all." I stood. "What are you having? Coffee? Juice?"

She smiled then sighed. "Coffee would be great, thanks."

I stood, went into the kitchen, and then returned with two mugs of coffee, both black. "I didn't know how you took it," I told her as I handed her the mug.

"Black is perfect." She sipped at her coffee then asked, "How are things?"

My lip twitched at her attempt at small talk. "*Things* are good." My smile faded. "How are you doing?" I reached over to place my hand on her knee. "I'm so sorry about Irina."

Cora shrugged. "Thanks. I'm getting there, you know? Mom called me. She asked me to fly out and pack up Irina's house, so…yeah…that was…" Her breathing hitched. "…painful." She looked into her coffee, tapping a fingernail on the ceramic of the mug. "Irina wasn't like me. She let my dad dictate her life. I never did. I told my parents I didn't owe them anything. That was why I moved out when I was eighteen."

She smiled. "I don't know if you know this, but I lived with Nastasia for two years before it all turned sour, which was totally my fault. But Irina was the golden child, you know? I was the black sheep." She frowned and muttered, "And look at where it got her." Her eyes shut tight and she admitted on a whisper, "I hate my dad. I hate him so much, Mina."

I didn't know what else to say apart from, "I'm sorry."

When she laid her hand on mine and squeezed, my heart ached for her. "Thanks for letting me in today."

I checked the clock again. "Lev will be home any minute now."

She smiled, but it was forced. "I just hope he doesn't kick me out."

I wouldn't let him. Corinna Alkaev may have said things she didn't mean to old friends, but she didn't deserve to be punished for them forever. I would make Lev listen. I didn't know how, but I would.

We made polite small talk for the next five minutes before the back door opened, and Cora stiffened. Lev walked into the living area and took one look at our guest before he stilled. He looked down at me, a questioning expression on his face, and I smiled encouragingly. He blinked at me, and then recovered quickly, making his way into the room. "Corinna," he uttered.

She smiled up at him, but it shook. "Hey, Lev."

He was sweaty and red in the face, but he sat by me in his workout gear and asked calmly, "To what do I owe the pleasure? Have your parents sent you? Because I told them—"

She shook her head and spoke, cutting him off. "No, they haven't sent me." She nearly rolled her eyes. "Since when do I do their bidding anyway?" She quieted her voice. "I haven't spoken to them since after Irina died, and don't plan on speaking to them again until they can admit they screwed up."

Lev seemed mildly stunned by what she had said. "Then why are you here?"

She took a deep, quivering breath before she laughed lightly and shrugged, placing her hands in her lap. She whispered a pained, "I miss my niece."

From the way Lev went rigid beside me, I knew he did not like that statement. It was so open. He didn't like not knowing exactly what a person meant. I needed to intervene.

"You want time with Lidi then?" I asked her gently.

"I just want to see her again. I don't care how. You name the time and place. I just—" She looked to Lev, imploring, "I know you hated Irina, but she wasn't always a hardass. And Lidiya is all I have left of my sister." Lev's jaw ticked. She sighed, dipping her chin. "I know you don't trust me, and that's fair, but I will do anything you want. I just want some time with Lidi."

The front door opened, and Nas walked in. "Yo, shorty!"

"In here," I called, suddenly anxious about Cora's presence.

Nas went to walk into the living room and fell short a step, looking directly at her ex-best friend. Cora stood and swallowed hard. "Hey."

Nas looked the woman up and down before entering the room and speaking slowly. "Hey, yourself."

Cora's bottom lip began to tremble and her eyes filled with tears. When she dipped her chin, her tears falling to the ground, Nas moved, and what she did surprised me. She placed her arms around Cora just as a sob escaped her. Nas held her tightly, whispering, "I'm sorry."

Cora clutched to her like a lifeline and let out a broken, "No, I'm sorry. The things I said to you…"

Nas shook her head, squeezing gently. "Forgotten."

The two women embraced for a little while, and when they separated, Nas sat next to Cora, taking her hand and holding it in hers. Something told me that no matter how strong Corinna Alkaev thought she was, she had reached her breaking point.

Nas looked at me. "So, what are we talking about?"

Lev responded, "Corinna wants to see Lidiya." He paused a moment before he said, "And I am considering it."

The look of relief on Cora's face was evident, but she masked it with excitement. "Really? Because I don't even care if we stay here the whole time. I could have a picnic with her in the front yard and stay out of your hair. I promise not to get in your way or anything."

Lev looked down at Nastasia's hand, which still held Cora's. "You were once like family, Corinna."

Her lips trembled again and she uttered quietly, "I know I fucked up. And I'm so sorry."

Lev stood. "I see no reason why you can't see Lidi every now and again." He looked at the little woman and told her, "She doesn't have her mother anymore. I'd like for her to have access to someone who knew Irina when she was a child. Someone who can show her the good side of Irina."

Cora's face sad, she responded quietly, "I can do that. I can be that person."

Lev nodded. "I know you can." He checked his watch and muttered, "Mirella took her to the park. They'll be home soon enough. You're welcome to wait."

He didn't say another word, just turned and walked away.

My heart warmed, and that warmth spread throughout my entire body.

God, I loved Lev. He was a good man.

I stood too, looking down at a stunned Cora. "I'm guessing it's been a while." I turned to Nas and smiled. "I'll give you guys time to catch up."

My feet took the stairs two at a time—no small feat for a short girl—until I made my way into our bedroom, opening the door to find Lev in a state of undress. He looked up at me then threw down his boxers, leaving him in the nude.

My voice soft, I told him, "You're a good man, Lev Leokov." Then I started to undress.

His eyes landed on my bare stomach and he watched as I undid my bra. His voice came out husky. "I need to shower, mouse."

"No," I told him, hooking my thumbs into my panties and lowering them. They fell to my ankles. "You need to get me dirty." I stepped out of my panties and moved toward him. When I reached him, I looked up into his face, the picture of innocence. "And *then* we'll get clean together. Okay?"

His hands came up to rest on my hips and he squeezed lightly, his eyes hooded with lust. "Who am I to argue with my betrothed?"

I grinned as his lips descended. "Suck ass."

We spent a long time in the shower.

And when we were finished, I was far from clean.

I was deliciously mussed.

CHAPTER FORTY-SIX

Mina

I watched in quiet amazement as the extended Leokov family met, hugging and kissing and chatting as laughter burst out of people left, right, and center. Normally, in situations like this, I would have felt out of place, yet somehow this amazing group of people included me like it was no big deal.

I didn't care what they thought.

It was a big deal, for me.

We had made the half-hour drive to attend the small wedding that Lev explained would be held at his cousin's club, The White Rabbit. I'd never heard of the place, but when we got there, I immediately understood the appeal.

I got it. I did.

It was freaking hot.

Who wouldn't be taken by an Alice in Wonderland themed club? From the giant bronzed Cheshire cat, to the whimsical, artistic paint on the walls, my chest panged with regret from not bringing the *good* camera Sasha had bought for Bleeding Hearts. It didn't matter; I whipped out my phone and snapped away happily at almost everything in sight.

Lev told me I'd need to dress up for the night, and when he sent me to buy an appropriate evening gown with Nas, the two of us came back arguing. I still couldn't justify spending hundreds of dollars on something I'd only wear once or twice.

We compromised in the end, buying me a stunning black dress that cost a hundred and fifty dollars. It was a cocktail–style dress, and although it wasn't what I was sent to buy, I could see myself wearing this little number again and again, totally getting my money's worth. When I came home and modeled it for Lev, he agreed that it was lovely.

He dressed in a black suit, a white crisp linen shirt, and a black tie. Mirella dressed Lidiya in a pale pink number, a pastel pink bow holding her curls together. I sat in the back seat with my chubby little angel, and wasn't at all surprised when she fell asleep during the drive. It was so relaxing being a passenger that I felt I could have joined her.

It might have seemed strange to hold a wedding on a Wednesday night, but after Lev explained that it was only to be a small affair and that the club would likely be open to the public on the weekend, it kind of made sense.

We arrived at the club, parked, and made our way out. Lev pulled me into his side and held a sleepy Lidiya's hand as we entered the party.

I was nervous, meeting more of the family. But I shouldn't have been.

Lev's cousin, Nik, greeted us at the door, grabbing Lev and heaving him into a long man-hug before pulling back and kissing both his cheeks. When Nik spotted Lidiya, his face changed. It seemed the guy was a sucker for kids. He got to his knees, smiled, and held his arms out to Lidi. Lidi, knowing a good thing when she saw one, didn't hesitate to hug the man, and he lifted her, kissing her cheek. When Lev introduced us, I could have fainted dead away.

Why, you ask?

Because it went something like this.

"This is Mina. She was homeless. I found her. I'm keeping her. She loves me. So we're getting married."

And I *died*. Embarrassment seeped out of me like oozing slime. My gorgeous fiancée had unknowingly made me sound like a freaking gold digger.

I choked out a laugh. "He doesn't mean that," I told Nik, my cheeks flaming.

Nik grinned, and his single dimple came out to say hello. Lidi poked it with a small finger, and Nik gently nipped it.

Oh, my Lord. These Leokov men were stunning, every single one of them.

Lev frowned down at me. "That's exactly what I mean, mouse."

I glared up at him, stepped on my tiptoes, and whisper-hissed, "Maybe *ixnay* on the *omelesshay*, sweetie. Okay? Thanks."

His face softened a degree. "I'm not ashamed of you, Mina."

Nik coughed out a laugh before coming over and wrapping his free arm around my shoulders, leading us in. "Whatever, Mina. I'm not judging, sweetheart. Come meet the family."

I spotted Nas and Sasha talking to another man who looked remarkably like Nik, and when we approached, the man spotted me, separated himself, and came at me like a bull going at a rodeo clown, only happily. He reached us, bent a little, wrapped his arms around me, and lifted me in a giant bear hug. I squeaked as he shook me around like a doll a moment, set me on my feet, and pulled back, beaming. "Lev's woman! I'm Max, groom, cool dude, cousin."

I couldn't help but smile. This guy was crazy.

I looked him up and down. He wore a sophisticated three-piece suit with white Chucks, and still looked heavenly. When my eyes reached his face and landed on his smile, another Leokov dimple came out to play and my stomach flipped. Max put his arm around me and pulled me into his side, shaking me a little. "Don't be shy, short stuff." He grinned, and I swear his teeth sparkled. "We're family."

That was when Lev approached and Max pulled back, opening his arms wide. Lev smirked, walking into his arms. More hugs and kisses were exchanged then suddenly a gaggle of pretty women appeared, along with two other men—who were both sexy as hell, mind you.

What the heck were they putting in the water up here?

A brunette with a wide smile and green eyes stepped forward and eyed our gorgeous little princess, who was now resting her head on Nik's shoulder and sucking her thumb. Smart girl. The woman smiled gently. "Hi there, honey. And who are you?"

"This little angel is Lidiya." Nik jerked his chin to Lev. "Lev, this is my wife, Tina. Tina, baby. Lev, my cousin."

Her face brightened and her excitement was completely genuine. She came forward and hugged a rigid Lev, rubbing a hand up and down his back. "Oh, wow. Hi!"

She pulled back and without an introduction, she came forward and put her arms around me. "I'm Tina!"

I hid my surprise the best I could and hugged her back. "Mina."

She laughed softly. "No. *Tina*. With a T."

I smiled at her. She was cute. "I know. I meant my name is Mina."

She gasped. "Mina!" She pointed to herself. "And Tina!" She looked at her husband with wide eyes and spoke slowly. "Mina and Tina. That's so cool."

Nik chuckled under his breath and then laughed, shaking his head. Tina wrapped her arm around mine. "We were going to bring our girls with us, but," she cringed, "we don't get much time alone anymore. When Nik's mom offered to babysit all the little ones," she huffed out a laugh, "I almost threw them at her." Her smiled faded, she stopped mid-step, and her face turned pained. "That sounded terrible." Her lips pursed. "I'm a horrible mother."

I laughed. She was adorable. "No, that sounds kind of reasonable, actually."

"Really?" she asked, genuinely concerned.

I nodded. "You need time for yourself too."

She smiled at me before turning to Nik, who was glaring at his brother and reluctantly handing Lidi over to Max. She went willingly, and Max pretended to eat her chubby cheeks. God, these men were destroying my ovaries, one sweet act at a time. She smiled and laughed through the sucking of her thumb. Tina told me, "Gosh, she's beautiful, Mina."

I grinned, pushing down the fact I had no right to feel proud of Lidi. "I know. And I think she does too."

Tina rolled her eyes. "Oh, I know. Little girls know how to play their daddies. And it only gets worse as they get older, trust me."

I mentally took note.

Tina brought me over to the other women, who all smiled up at me. "This is Mina. She's Nik's cousin's wife."

Another brunette spoke, but her head had a tinge of red to it, and her green eyes were brighter than I'd ever seen. "Which cousin?"

"Lev," I told her, then I added, "And we're not married. Not yet anyway."

Tina's face went slack. "Oh, I'm sorry. I just assumed."

I waved her off with a smile. "That's okay. Really. Lidiya is Lev's daughter."

An olive-skinned man uttered, "I'm Trick." He pulled a short woman with chocolate brown hair and big brown eyes into his side. "And this is my Lola."

The reddish-brown brunette smiled. "I'm Nat." She pointed to the tall ashy-blond man rocking a sexy five o'clock shadow. "And that's my husband, Asher." She lifted her hand and pointed to the gorgeous arctic blonde woman next to her. "This is Mimi." She leaned forward and mock-whispered, "She's our resident dyke."

I choked on a laugh as Mimi winked at me. "Hi. Nice to meet you all." This was a wedding reception, wasn't it? I asked cautiously, "Where's the bride?"

Nat rolled her eyes. "Helena, my sister. Max knocked her up good. She's only a few months along so, you know." Only, I didn't know. My confused expression must have given me away, because her brows rose and she grinned before explaining, "She's in the bathroom, yacking."

Tina smiled happily then shrugged. "Happens to the best of us, right?"

Max approached with Lidi, and all the girls made cutesy noises as he spoke. "Tell Helena I'm leaving her." He placed his cheek on Lidiya's head, and the little girl smiled around the thumb she was sucking. Max sighed then smiled, "There's another woman in my life."

Mimi blinked at the little girl. "Would you look at those lashes?"

Nat grinned. "And that curly hair?"

Lola stepped forward and ran her fingers down Lidi's cheek. "Oh, my God, she's freaking *adorable*." She looked to me with a pucker. "I'm in love."

But Lidi blinked over at the hard-looking Asher, smiling hard. Nat clucked her tongue. "Of course she chooses to like the broodiest mofo in the group."

Probably reminds her of her dad, I thought.

Lidi leaned forward, holding her arms out to Asher. He smiled then and his face transformed. He was smoking *hot*. He came forward and took her from Max's arms. He pulled back to look down at her as she rested her head on his shoulder. His voice was low, rough. "It's 'cause she's got good taste."

I narrowed my eyes at her. "It hasn't escaped my notice that she's only going to the men." I turned to Tina. "Only gets worse as they get older?" Tina nodded solemnly. I huffed out a breath. "Crap. I'm going to have to watch this one with a hawk eye."

The girls laughed as the men grinned, and then someone was wrapping their arms around me. I didn't have to look. I sunk back into him and smiled, placing a hand on his at my waist. Tina happily announced, "This is cousin Lev."

"Hello," he muttered from behind me.

A few greeting were exchanged before Tina sighed contentedly, her face turning soft. "You guys look good together."

Lev spoke an amused, "I think so too. Thank you."

A young woman with long dark brown hair and green eyes came out of nowhere. She wore an elegant and fitted wedding dress in off-white lace that showed off her small baby bump. "Ugh, sorry, guys." She sighed tiredly, but looked ridiculously happy. "Stupid Max and his mighty sperm."

Tina chuckled. "Helena, this is Lev and Mina. Lev is Max's cousin."

The bride turned to us. "Whoa, hey. We don't know many from the other side of the family. It's nice that you could be here." She smiled kindly as Max put his arms around her and kissed her head. "Thank you so much for coming."

Max explained, "My dad and Lev's dad were brothers." He grinned at Lev. "Remember the shit we used to get up to?"

Lev shook his head. "No. But I do remember the shit *you* used to get up to and blame on *me*."

The group of people burst into laughter and Max shrugged. "That's 'cause you were an easy target, bro."

Nik shook his head. "Nah. You were just an idiot."

"Yeah." Max puffed out his chest. "Idiotically *awesome*."

I laughed to myself. These guys were a hoot.

After all the fuss, I wouldn't admit it, but I was glad we came. It was nice to hear about Lev amongst family that obviously loved him.

Sasha and Nas strolled by, and Nas handed me a drink. I took it gratefully and Max jerked his chin to Sasha. "Lev's gettin' married. Nas has Viktor wrapped around her pinkie." I was sure I was the only person who noticed Nas' expression turn sour, but Max went on, "When are you gonna settle down, Sash?"

Sasha smiled slyly. "Who knows, man?" He paused before adding a rather cryptic, "You never know what's written in the stars."

Nik nudged Sasha. "Yeah. Who knows?" He grinned at his cousin. "Even Sasha might find a woman to put up with his broody ass."

Tina scoffed. "Excuse me, mister, but I remember meeting you, and you were the broodiest son of a gun I'd ever met." She looked around at us and uttered a sincere, "I almost wet myself. He was so cold. He scared me."

Nik pulled his wife into him and squeezed her tight. "Yeah, well, it took meeting you to thaw me out, baby."

Nawww.

They were stupidly cute. I kind of loved them.

Nastasia cleared her throat and forced a smile. "I don't know about marriage. It's so… final." She tried to cringe, but I saw the haggard sadness on her face.

Goddamn Vik. What was he doing to her? I was going to wring his damn neck.

Nat sighed. "Wow. You sound like me." She pulled Nas over and threaded her arm through hers, smiling all the while. "Come here. You just became my new best friend."

The conversation flowed effortlessly throughout the night, and my cheeks started to hurt from how much I was smiling and laughing. I felt at ease with these people. They were a good sort, women who had met their matches and men who had learned to love.

I held onto Lev and imagined where I would be if I hadn't met him. A hard shiver went down my spine and my stomach knotted uncomfortably.

The thought was far too painful to consider.

⚓

We arrived home from Max and Helena's wedding just past one a.m., and the funny thing about it was I didn't want to leave in the end. I had a blast hanging out with the girls, and Tina had invited me down to her boutique to do some dress shopping. She promised that ninety percent of her garments were reasonably priced, with the other 10 percent being exorbitant purely because they were shipped from Italy.

The girls were lovely, and I couldn't remember the last time I connected with a group of people as quickly as I had them. I promised I would come down with Nas and check out Safira's Boutique.

Was tomorrow too soon?

CHAPTER FORTY-SEVEN

Mina

They say all good things must come to an end, and I was afraid our good thing was close to breaching the safety barrier.

It happened three days later when I had just walked into the house to hear Lev let out an animalistic roar from the kitchen. My heart pounded and I rushed over to him.

I found my him hunched over the kitchen table in his sweats and tank, looking about ready to break the table in half.

"Sweetie," I asked cautiously. "What's wrong?"

It was then that I noticed a piece of paper scrunched in his fisted palm. He breathed so hard that his chest heaved. I took another careful step forward, placing a hand on his back. "Baby?"

His eyes closed and he rumbled out, "Igor Alkaev wants custody of Lidiya." He let out a long breath. "He's taking me to court."

My brow furrowed. "On what grounds?"

Lev barked out, "I don't fucking know, Mina. *Shit*. When are they going to leave me the fuck alone already?"

I tried not to take his anger personally. I knew he wasn't angry at me, after all. "Have you called your lawyer?"

He squeezed his eyes shut and muttered a cold, "No. I want to talk to Igor."

"I'm coming with you," I told him, and I was not asking.

Lev shook his head. "No. I'm going alone."

I didn't want to be the voice of reason, but if I didn't take that role, who would? "Sweetie, you know how you get when you're angry. You can go a little cuckoo," I uttered quietly. "Let me come. I won't say a word. Just let me be there for you."

Yeah, okay, let's be honest. I was worried that Lev might kill the asshole.

I came up behind him and placed my hands on his hips, leaning in to press my body to his, kissing the center of his spine. "Let me come, baby. Please. I'll stay out of the way. I promise."

He turned in my arms and looked down at me. "I don't want you out of the way. I want you safe, here with Lidiya."

I blinked up at him. "And if it were me, would you let me go alone?"

His brow furrowed. "Of course not."

"And that's why I'm coming with you," I stated.

Although Lev didn't like it, he conceded, and we made a quick stop to Nastasia's where Lev called Sasha, and then we were on our way to the Alkaev residence.

I pitied the fool.

⚓

Igor Alkaev answered the door, and I had to admit he didn't look at all as I pictured him. I imagined a short, rotund man with a bulging belly, dark hair, and maybe a beard. What I got was a tall, slim man with greying blond hair, a sharp nose, cold dark eyes, and a constant expression of distaste.

Igor showed us inside without a word and told his apparently voiceless wife, Vera, to bring in some coffee. She left without a word and Igor smirked. "So, you got the letter, I see."

Lev was too tightly strung to sit. Instead, he stood by my side as I sat on the leather lounge. "I did. I want to know what the hell you're thinking, Igor, because you're not getting my daughter. I had two long years without her, and I'll be damned if I give her up now."

Igor watched Lev closely. "You've changed," he stated. "Something is different about you. I can't put my finger on it. You're"—his brows rose—"poised or something."

Lev grunted. "Tell me what you want."

I watched both men carefully. I had pepper spray in my bag and I was not afraid to use it. I was no shrinking violet when my loved ones were involved.

Igor sniffed. "You have nothing I want, Leokov." His face shuttered. "Not anymore."

Lev gritted his teeth. "You're not getting another dime from me, not ever again."

The older man's face blazed bright red. "My daughter is dead, you imbecile. You impregnated her then decided you didn't want her. She loved you. Of course she became depressed. She dealt with your cruelty for years before she took her life." He took a breath and let out an arctic, "And it is all your fault." He sat up straight, adjusting his tie that did not need adjusting. "You're toxic. Lidiya is better off with us. We love her."

Lev swallowed hard, his jaw tight. "Think about what you're doing. It may be the last thought you ever have."

Igor smiled then, and it was slimy. "Is that a threat, Leokov?"

Lev replied calmly, "No threat. Accidents happen."

Igor stood just as his wife returned with coffee for us all. "It seems we have nothing left to discuss. Please leave."

I stood and took Lev's hand as he said, "See you in court."

We turned, and Lev's hand gripped me tight enough to hurt. Just as we moved to open the door, it was thrown open and Corinna stood there. She looked as though she was on a mission and didn't have time to stop and say hi. She strolled in like she owned the place, and with a snarky smile, muttered, "Mother." She looked to her father and couldn't hide the look of disgust. "Inconsequential sperm donor."

And there she was, our teeny, tiny angel of vengeance. They say the best things come in small packages. We were about to realize just how true that saying was.

Igor went rigid. "I told you never to come back here."

Cora scoffed. "As if I would willingly. Get a clue, old man." She smiled slyly. "I'm here for Lev."

Igor jerked his chin toward Lev. "Take him, then. We're done."

I watched in amazement as Cora chuckled lightly. "Wow, you really are a tool." She walked over to the leather lounge and sat. "You don't want

Lidiya. You're just pissed that your golden child is gone. And I get that. I miss her too, but what you're doing is disgusting." She sat up straight and looked Igor dead in the eye. "You want to play hard, Papa?" She smiled a Mona Lisa smile. "Maybe you should check your safe spot; find your ledger."

Igor's face went slack.

Cora's smile faded and was replaced with mock-concern. "Your search will probably be futile though." She shook her head in uneasiness. "So many thieves out these days. It's a shame, really."

Igor's face paled as he whispered, "What have you done, Corinna?"

Cora stood. "I'll tell you what I've done. I've made four copies of that ledger." She paused momentarily. "You can have the original back, but if you want to go ahead with this petty custody battle for a child you don't want," her voice lowered a notch, "I will air all your dirty laundry, all over. Every news network will know the ins and outs of Zakon."

Her father stepped forward and looked like he was ready to strike, but he stopped himself. "I'll be killed."

She shrugged. "So you'll be a martyr to the cause."

I wasn't sure I was seeing right, but Igor's forehead began to glisten with sweat as he choked out, "*You'll* be killed."

Cora folded her arms over her chest. "Yeah, I thought about that already. See, if anything happens to me, I gave strict instructions to release a copy of the ledger to the FBI. The other three copies..." She looked so pleased with herself as she sighed, "Who knows where they'll go?"

Igor looked ready to roar.

Cora leaned forward and stage-whispered, "By the way, does Mama know you were the one supplying Irina meth?" At her mother's pained gasp, Cora turned to us, cringing. "Shit." She spoke through the side of her mouth, "That's awkward."

A thick silence enveloped us. We stood there, soaking in what Corinna Alkaev had just dealt her father, when finally, she clapped and stated, "Okay, so we're leaving now, and you're not going to see us again. Not ever. If you even try to look Lidi's way, I will crush you like the fucking insect you are, you sad, bitter man." Her harsh expression wavered a moment to reveal a deep sadness. "I loved you once." She turned to her mother. "You need to leave him, Ma. He's insane." She warned her mom, "Get out while you still can."

Igor's fists balled and he uttered through gritted teeth, "You disrespectful whore."

Cora ignored him, still looking at her mother. "Call me if you need me. I'll support you in whatever you choose." She smiled at the quiet older woman who now had tears in her eyes. "I love you, Mama. Always have. Always will."

She turned on her heel and motioned for us to leave. "Come on. Let's go."

Cora walked us to our car and murmured, "Go. I'll meet you at Nastasia's."

Lev didn't stop to ask questions.

We got in the car and drove.

⚓

Cora and Nas were waiting for us as we stepped out of the car. I held out my arms. "What the hell was that?"

Nas turned to Cora and nudged her shoulder. "That's what you call having *game*."

Lev approached cautiously. "Please tell me that was not a bluff."

Cora smiled at him. "No. Nas has a copy, and so does Sasha. My lawyer has one, and the last ledger is in a secret location." She sighed. "Pappy will be royally fucked if he messes with you again."

"Why?" he asked. "Why are you helping me?"

Cora looked down at the ground before speaking softly. "You said I was like family once. And families look after each other, have each other's backs." She paused. "I always felt more at home here than I ever did over there."

Then Lev did something odd.

He stepped forward, wrapped his arms around Corinna, and hugged her. And this was no short hug. It lasted a full minute, at the very least. Cora slumped into him, reaching up and gripping his jacket tightly as she accepted the rare show of affection from a man who seldom gave it.

And I stood by, smiling like a loon.

He pulled back and cupped her cheek. "Thank you, Corinna. I'm in your debt."

But she shook her head. "You don't owe me anything. I just want Lidiya to be happy, and she's happy here."

That she was, the little munchkin.

A thought crossed me. "Are we sure Igor will heed the warning? He's so cocky. Doesn't seem like the type to worry about a threat."

Cora's brow rose. "Oh, he'll listen." She chuckled. "I emailed him back a copy of the documents just so he knows I'm not playing around."

"Whoa," I stated in awe. "You're a badass motherfucker, Cora." I smiled in appreciation. "I like it. It's a good look on you."

Nas cut in then, "Cora's going to be staying here for a while, just until she gets back on her feet."

Cora blanched. "Unless you don't want me to."

Lev replied sincerely, "Stay as long as you like. We have plenty of room."

Nas nudged Cora and whispered, "Ask him."

Cora's brows bunched, and she shook her head discreetly.

Nas rolled her eyes. "Just ask him."

"Ask me what?" Lev enquired.

Cora shook her head, looking mildly embarrassed. "It's not important."

Nas sighed loudly. "You realize she's officially cut off now, right?" Lev nodded, but shrugged. Nas muttered uncomfortably, "She kind of needs a job, you know, to *live*."

Lev looked down at Cora. "Can you serve drinks?"

"I don't know. I never tried," she replied.

Ooh! Ooh!

I raised my hand like a first-grader, not even bothering to mask my excitement. "I can teach her." I looked to Cora with a smile. "I can teach you." I shrugged. "If I can learn, so can you. And I was terrible when I started."

Nas tilted her head in thought, half-chuckling at the memory. "You really were." At my indignant, "Hey!" she then turned to Cora and shrugged. "She really was."

Lev nodded. "Okay, it's settled then. You'll work at the club."

Cora's shoulders slumped in relief and she let out a sincere, "Thank you."

Lev merely responded, "We're family. We look after each other."

Oh, man, he was so getting laid tonight.

CHAPTER FORTY-EIGHT

Mina

Cora's first night went off without a hitch. She was a natural, and thanks to the two of us being the same size, she was able to wear the Red Riding Hood outfit Birdie had bought for me. I told Birdie to put in another order for costumes in my size, but different to the ones I had. Birdie told me that it would take a couple of days, and that was okay. I didn't mind sharing with Cora until then.

When I went to tell her about the subtle flirting for tips, I noticed she'd already been doing it. When I thought to mention the house blend bottles full of iced-tea, Cora had already figured it out. And when I saw her lean over the bar to place a kiss on a big spender's cheek, I was a little miffed. It was clear I wasn't needed.

The girls on stage were dancing out a routine to Rihanna's "Bitch Better Have My Money", and I was mesmerized. They swayed their hips delicately, their breasts hidden behind sparkling pasties, and their expressions were sultry. They really were beauties, our Diamond Dozen.

Halfway through the night, I turned to find my brother sitting at the bar right in front of me, wearing a slight grin. I squeaked in surprise then threw myself over the bar to wrap my arms around him. I laughed in his ear, "How long were you watching me stare into space?"

He hugged me back then kissed my cheek. "Only a minute." He pulled back and began, "I need to t—" But he stopped midsentence, losing his focus when his gaze landed on Cora. His brow furrowed. "Who's that?"

I turned to blink at Cora then turned back to him. "Corinna Alkaev. She's new. Started tonight. She's a friend of the family."

But Alessio was lost to her, and I hid my grin. He shook his head lightly before starting again. "Can I talk to you for a minute?"

I looked around the bar. There were a lot of people waiting, and with Nas, Cora, Anika and me all working our tails off, I grimaced. "Any chance you could wait five minutes, just until I help with this crowd?"

Alessio smiled at me, and I could've sworn I saw pride there. "Take your time. It can wait."

He waited ten minute without batting a lash, and finally, when the intermission crowd slowed, I motioned to Nas that I was stepping out. She winked at me and I walked around the bar, linked my arm through Alessio's, and made our way to the only free space in the club by the bathroom walls. "What's up?"

He hesitated, and when he started to talk, it was cautious. "So, you have to know that Enzo was loaded, right?"

I thought about this then shrugged. "I didn't know that, no."

What did that have to do with me?

Alessio nodded. "He was. And I got his inheritance."

I looked up at him. "And so you should have."

He shook his head. "But I'm not his only kid. You're his kid too. And I want to share it with you."

Oh. I understood. He felt an obligation to me.

My heart swelled and I warmed with happiness. I smiled up at him, reaching up to cup his scarred cheek. "You're sweet, Alessio, but no. I don't want it."

He took my hand from his cheek and squeezed it. "Too late, Mina. It's already in your bank account."

I pulled back, my brow furrowing. "What?"

Alessio held onto my hand, refusing to let go. "I spoke to Lev last week. He agreed that you could use the money, and the freedom this kind of money brings. He wants you to be set, and so do I." His grip on my hand gentled. "He was a shitty father, Mina. The money isn't everything, but he owed us at least that much."

Okay. He wanted me to have the money. He was adamant about that.

"How much money are we talking here?" I asked quietly.

Motioning with his fingers, I brought my head close to his and he whispered the figure into my ear. My eyes widened and I pulled back with a gasp, shoving him in the chest. "Get out!" My mouth gaping, my head swam. "Oh, my *God*. Shut *up*!"

And Alessio's body shook with silent laughter. "Yeah."

My mind was a mess. That was more money than one person would ever need in a lifetime. I couldn't think. I was a mess.

Then suddenly, I blurt out, "What if I wanted to donate it to charity?"

Alessio's brows rose. He clearly wasn't expecting that response. He thought a moment before answering, "It's your money, Mina. You can do what you want with it. If you want to donate it, then go for it."

"Hey, Mina?" someone spoke from behind me. I turned to see Cora staring patiently up at Alessio, her eyes grazing over the scarred half of his face. She didn't look at me when she spoke again, but remained fixed on the tall, brooding man. "Lev's looking for you."

"Cora, this in my brother Alessio. Alessio, this is Cora, our new bar girl."

That broke Cora out of her state. Her brows rose and she smiled. "You have a brother?" Then suddenly, it was as if Alessio's scars had disappeared and she only had eyes for the man behind them. She stepped forward and held her hand out. "You're a lucky guy to have a sister like Mina," she finished with a wink.

Alessio stared down at the pocket-rocket that was Cora then slowly, carefully, he took her hand, shaking it lightly. "I know."

She bunched her nose adorably. "I'm sure you're not so bad yourself though."

I added on a chuckle, "He's not." I smiled softly up at Alessio. "He's kind of awesome."

Alessio released Cora's hand and she placed that hand on his arm. "Would you like a drink? I can bring it over."

Oh my.

Cora was giving all her attention to Alessio, and he looked as if he wasn't sure how to handle it. He lowered his gaze and shook his head. "I'm fine. Thanks."

I was sure it had been a long time since Alessio got the kind of attention he used to, and from the way Cora was looking at him, he'd just gained an unlikely admirer.

I didn't want their one-sided conversation to end, so I did something I probably shouldn't have. "Hey, Cora, you've done so well this evening. I don't want to push you too hard. You're off for the rest of the night."

Cora's brow furrowed. "Oh, okay. So what do I do now?"

"Sit. Have a drink. Enjoy the show," I told her.

"By myself?" she questioned, looking a little uncomfortable.

"No," I stated then blinked up innocently at my brother. "Hang out with Alessio."

They both went silent.

I had made my move; it was time for them to connect four. Alessio spoke first, and he glared at me while doing it. "I should go."

I blew him a teasing kiss. But then Cora looked up at him with wide eyes. The regret she wore was genuine. "You need to go?"

Alessio's neck flushed. "I don't need to go, but I should."

Cora looked mildly devastated, but she played it off coolly. "Oh, okay. Sure." She laughed quietly, and uttered graciously, "You have better things to do than babysit."

Alessio looked down at her and blinked, his brows furrowing in confusion, and he asked slowly, "Unless...do you want me to stay?"

Her shoulders slumped in relief and a real smile appeared. "Would you?"

No hesitation. "Fuck yeah."

And that was how it was done, people.

Cora beamed, stepping forward to link her arm through Alessio's, and I watched them walk away to find a table.

I watched them for the rest of the night, and when Nas questioned where the oompa loompa was, I pointed out to the floor, and we both spotted them laughing together, sitting thigh-to-thigh.

Alessio turned his face to talk directly into Cora's ear, but she turned to him at the same time. They stared into each other's eyes a second before Cora closed hers and leaned forward a little. Her lips connected with Alessio's, and after his moment of stunned disbelief, he closed his eyes and let it happen. They kissed so sweetly, so tamely, that my heart skipped a beat.

Nas wore a look of shock, and I seconded that expression.

Well, that was fast.

Cora reached her hands up to cup Alessio's cheeks, and Alessio pulled back as if he'd been electrically shocked. He lowered his face and said something before standing and leaving Cora sitting there on her own.

She slumped into her chair and shook her head, looking miserable. Alessio was a proud man. She needed to give him time. His scars were a plague on him.

I looked to Nas, and she returned my sad look. I hoped Alessio would give Cora a chance.

After all, time healed all wounds. Or so they said.

CHAPTER FORTY-NINE

Nastasia

I stood by the windowsill looking out at the moon, lost in thought. Dressed in the black and red kimono Vik had bought me, my gut clenched from nerves.

It was time.

I turned to where he lay on my bed, naked as the day he was born, and reached up to grasp the gold cross hanging around my neck—another gift from Vik— before I swallowed hard and spoke quietly, "Vik...honey...I need you to do something for me, okay? No questions. I just need you to do it."

His face turned up to look at me and he frowned. "For you, baby? Anything."

And he meant it too.

Goddamn it.

My lips quivered. I took in a deep breath before exhaling slowly. "I need you to go home." The first of my tears fell and I inhaled brokenly. "I need you to go home and not come back here, okay?" My chin dipped and my arms tightened around myself. "It needs to be you. *You* have to leave. Because I'll keep doing this." I averted my eyes when I looked up again. "Because I'll keep loving you, and I can't do it anymore." I swallowed hard, swiping at the tears on my cheeks, and tried to pull off calm. "So you need to go." When he made no move to leave, my face crumbled and I begged through a whisper, "*Please.*"

There it was, out in the open, and I was shocked by how shitty it felt. There was no relief, no weight off my shoulders. If anything, the weight had tripled.

I was losing myself.

He blinked at me a long moment before he sat up. "What are you talking about, baby?" He held his arms out and my heart cried out to be wrapped up in them. "Come back to bed," he uttered.

I shook my head. "No." My voice was rougher than I wanted it to be.

I walked over to the bed, sitting with my thigh grazing his. I looked him in the eye and uttered the words I dreaded to say. "Tell me you love you, Vik." My hand shot out to grip his and I almost pled, "Just tell me you love me."

His thumb grazed mine for a long moment before he muttered, "What's this all about?"

At my silence, he asked, "For real, baby? You gonna let me go? Just like that?" His brow furrowed in confusion.

I understood the confusion. I'd never done this before. I wasn't a drama queen, and I never demanded anything from Viktor Nikulin.

He was my heart and soul, and I loved him with everything I had, but I was officially worn out by our non-relationship. I wanted more. I needed more.

It was all or nothing.

My face impassive, I stated, "I can't do this anymore, Vik. I can't be the woman you call at three a.m. for a nightly booty call. I deserve better, like a man who isn't afraid of loving a woman." I shook my head. "I don't understand you. One minute, you're hot, and the next, you're cold." My voice shook. "I'm almost thirty years old. I can't wait forever."

His arms came around me. He pulled me close and I let him. He lifted me onto his lap, wrapped me up tight, and held me close when he stated, "I want you to think on this, okay? Don't make any rash decisions. Just...just think on it. And if this is what you really want in the morning, I'll go. I'll leave you alone. Deal?"

One more night.

Holding onto him, I nodded against his chest.

My heart broke at that very moment.

Come morning, we both knew what my decision would be.

CHAPTER FIFTY

LEV

"Have you decided?" I asked as I approached my mouse from behind, watching her scroll restlessly through charity websites.

With her fist under her chin, she grunted, "No." Then she sighed. "There's too many of them. I have no idea how to decide which are worthy enough to donate to."

I thought about that.

It would be a hard decision to make. I stepped forward, pulled back the desk chair, and lifted her. I sat in her place and lowered her down to my lap. "Even if you only give half of your inheritance, there is a lot of money there. Why not split it up into four or six and donate to multiple causes."

Mina melted into me, resting her head on my chest, curling up on my lap like a cat. "That's not a bad idea. I might do that." She let out a breath of frustration. "But that doesn't make the decision any easier."

"You could always draw them out of a hat," I uttered, just enjoying the feel of this little creature in my arms, not serious in the least.

I held onto her and the world slipped away. She calmed my mind and my soul lifted when close to her. Mina Harris was the better part of me, and I would keep her happy for the rest of my life.

She stilled in my lap and looked up at me with wide eyes, wearing an expression that said '*Now why didn't I think of that?*'

"That's a great idea," she whispered. A small smile graced her beautiful face and she leaned up to kiss me. I took her lips gently, dipping in to taste her, and she sighed softly. "I love you, Lev."

It was time to explain something to Mina, something about who I was. "I have never belonged, Mina," I started. "I have always had a feeling of loneliness inside of me, and I never understood it, not when I'm constantly surrounded by people. I do, however, understand I differ from the masses. In a constant state of confusion, misunderstanding plagues me." My brow furrowed. "I'm always thinking, 'What did I say to make Nastasia mad?' or 'Why did Sasha look at me that way?' Why doesn't my brain work the way it should?"

I paused a moment, and Mina listened intently. "I would've given anything to be normal. And around you, I feel normal." I laid my hand against her cheek and ran my thumb over her jawline. "I've never had ordinary. You gave me that. I plan on repaying you what I owe you for the rest of my life."

She leaned into my hand and closed her eyes. "We saved each other." She opened her eyes and glanced at me lovingly. "I think we can call it even, sweetie."

Perhaps she was right. Perhaps we were destined to find each other. Either way, I would do everything in my power to make sure Mina had a full and happy life. Just as she'd given to me.

⚓

My phone chirped and I pulled it out of my pocket to read the message.

Nas: Get over here. We need to talk. PRIVATELY.

I turned to look over at Mina and Lidi, who sat on the floor watching a children's movie on the television. They were apart but holding hands.

My throat constricted.

I didn't want to leave, but Nastasia was my sister. She was important to me and when she called on me, I would be there.

Standing, I stilled when Mina turned to look back at me. "Be back soon. Nas needs me."

Mina blew me a kiss and I took it with me as I walked out the front door and made the short journey to my sister's house.

LEV

She was waiting for me at the front door, holding it open. With a wave of her arm, she said, "Get in here."

It sounded serious. Nas was rarely short with me and right now, she seemed annoyed. I made my way up the steps and as I crossed the threshold of her home, I stated, "Something's wrong."

She puffed out a long breath, walking through to her dining room and taking a seat. "Yeah, something's wrong, Lev." She jerked her chin, motioning for me to take a seat, so I did.

"What is it?" I asked carefully.

Nas sat back in her chair and uttered softly, "Do you love Mina?"

My face turned hard. What an idiotic question. "Of course I love Mina."

What was this about?

My heart pounded. When things came to Mina, I didn't mess around. "What's going on, Nas?"

Then she said something I wasn't expecting. Here eyes sad, she muttered, "I'm a little disappointed in you."

The pounding in my chest increased. "Why?"

My sister shook her head. "The public proposal was cute, Lev. It was you down to a T." She shook her head. "But I was hoping you'd step outside your box, get down on one knee and ask Mina in a way that would make her feel special."

I lowered my face, momentarily lost in thought and when I raised my head to look at her again, I asked, "Do you think Mina would like that? A proposal?"

Nas smiled gently and told me, "Every woman wants a proposal she can tell her kids about."

Children? With Mina?

I liked that idea.

Yes. A proposal.

I could do that.

My mind made up, I leaned forward slightly and queried, "What do I need to do?"

Nas grinned then. "I thought you'd never ask."

CHAPTER FIFTY-ONE

Mina

Something was up.

I wasn't sure what exactly but Lev was acting distracted and kind of off, even for him.

When I asked him what was wrong, he shook his head and muttered something about having too much on his mind. I told him he could talk to me and when he turned to me and smiled, he stated that he would talk when it was needed.

I trusted Lev with every piece of me and if he told me not to worry, I would try my hardest not to. But I loved him, which meant I would go ahead and worry anyways.

It was Sunday and after having a predictably late Saturday night at the club, Lev woke to get his workout in and although part of me wanted to be the early bird, the other part of me didn't give a flipping flip if I got the worm or not.

I was tired and because of that, I slept my way through to eleven thirty, and Lev would be arriving back from his run at anytime now.

Walking my sleepy ass down the stairs, I shuffled into the kitchen to pour myself a cup of coffee. I'd taken the first sip when Lidiya came into the kitchen, an empty Sippy cup hanging from her hang while the other one rubbed her tired little eyes, and she whined. "No nap. No *nap*." Then she stomped one little foot.

Mirella followed her in. "Lidi, sweetheart, you're tired. And when you're tired, you need a nap." Mirella rolled her eyes slightly and smiled in a way that read 'kids, huh?'

Lidi was already at my side, holding up her arms and without hesitation, I picked her up, rocking her from side-to-side and kissing her forehead lovingly.

Her eyes were already starting to close when Lev walked in from the back door. And when he spotted me, holding Lidi, rocking her grumpy self to sleep, his eyes went warm.

He made his way forward and kissed her chubby cheek before turning to me and kissing my lips, feather soft. A now sleeping Lidiya dropped her sippy cup to the kitchen floor with a clang and clap and she jolted but didn't wake.

Lev pulled her out of my arms, held her close and walked her to her bedroom where she could nap in comfort. I followed him upstairs so I could watch him undress and when I arrived back to our bedroom, he already had his tee off.

"We have the night off," he threw out into the silence.

My nose bunched. "What? Why?"

Lev looked over at me, his hands on the waistband of his sweat pants. "Because you deserve it."

I liked the club. It was my home away from home. I enjoyed it there.

With a light shrug, I uttered a sincere, "That's okay. I don't need a night off. I love club nights, besides, it's only three days a week."

He blinked over at me, seeming surprised that I wouldn't want a night to myself. "I thought we could go to dinner. To that Russian place you like."

Ooh.

Blini and *Pelmeni*. I didn't think I could pass that up but it was a work night. We could go anytime.

The he added something that would have me giving up my fight. "Like on our first date."

My smile was slow to form and catlike. "You want to have a date night?"

He nodded. "Yes. Just the two of us."

Shit, that was sweet.

How can I say no to that?

"Okay." I smiled harder. "But, just so you know, for you, I'm a sure thing, baby. Always."

His lip twitched and he threw down his sweats, leaving him in the nude. I let out a low whistle of appreciation and his body shook in silent laughter. Then I followed him into the bathroom to watch him bathe because... well... I could.

LEV

⚓

Arriving at our dinner destination, Lev talked to the woman at the counter, speaking in rapid fire Russian, getting more and more frustrated with every additional word, he slapped his hand down on the counter and turned to me, his face hard, his lips thin, "They're booked for a private function."

It didn't bother me that the short journey was wasted. I was just happy to be there with Lev. "That's okay, sweetie. We'll go eat somewhere else."

He looked down at me, his voice clinical. "No, it had to be *here*."

I blinked at his unlikely tantrum. "Well, *here* isn't available. So we'll go somewhere else." I took his hand and led him out of the restaurant, running my thumb along his knuckles. "It's no big deal, Lev. We'll come back another time."

His jaw tight, he nodded but I could tell he was upset, and I didn't understand why. I couldn't believe I was saying it but, it was just food.

When we got into the car and Lev asked me where we should dine, I was brutally honest with him. "Honey, all I want to do is go home, watch movies and eat pizza with you. Follow that with getting naked for playtime and that would be the best date night ever."

He looked over at me a long moment before he took my hand, lifted it to his mouth, pressed a soft kiss to the back of it and sighed, "If that is what you wish, mouse."

We came home to an empty house and I kicked off my shoes, holding them and walking them up the stairs with me. Halfway up, I squeaked as Lev hefted me up into his arms and walked me the rest of the way and into the bedroom.

Someone had cleaned up the mess I'd left in the form of a pile of clothes by the sofa, the bed was made immaculately and the bathroom light was on, a wonderfully sweet smell coming from inside.

Lev took my hands in his and looked down at me, his eyes warm. "I wanted tonight to be special. So far, it hasn't been but I'll make it up to you." He walked me over to the bathroom, opening the door all the way, revealing what the sweet smell had been.

A bubble bath had been run, smelling of vanilla with rose petals scattered throughout it.

My breath caught. "Oh, sweetie. It's beautiful."

His hands came down on my shoulders from behind and he rested his chin on my head. "Why don't you soak for a while? I'll call for pizza and when you're done we can find a movie to watch."

I turned, forcing his arms to dislodge. I looked up at him and stated fiercely. "This is the best date night ever. I know this and it's barely even begun, but I know this." I reached out to squeeze his hand. "This *is* special."

His eyes softened even more and he reached for the bathroom door handle. "Go. Soak. Relax," he uttered, closing the door behind him.

I did as I was told and, undressing and slipping into the tub, I soaked in the warm water in the tub for a long while, until the water started to take on a slight chill to it.

Where had all this romance come from?

It sounded like Lev was feeling the need to prove himself or something of the like. I would need to set him straight. I didn't need romance, not like this. I just needed Lev to be himself and I'd be forever happy.

I let the water out, wiped myself down then dressed in my white robe. When I made my way out of the bathroom to tell Lev to cut it out, my breath left me in a whoosh.

Why, you ask?

Because standing in the middle of the bedroom was Lev, with the lights off, hundreds of tea candles lit all over, the room glittering in the soft illumination. The bed turned down, he swallowed hard, taking in my expression of shock as my gaze flittered across the room. Still dressed in his three-piece, Lev shifted his weight on his feet and held out his hand.

I hesitated only a moment before I came to him, reaching out to place my hand in his. "What is this?" I asked quietly, awestruck.

He took a step back, away from me and reached into his breast pocket. When he pulled back, he looked down at what he's just pulled out of his pocket and when my eyes settled on the cue cards he held, my brow rose.

Lev cleared his throat, once, twice, a third time. "Mina," he read. "The way we met was highly unusual and I admit I was most relived when I found out you were not a thief."

My brows rose higher but he didn't see, so he continued.

"And I"—he looked around the room, down on the bed, over at the sofa before he got distracted and announced—"I forgot the flowers. Hold on."

He whizzed past me and out of the room, leaving me in the middle of the bedroom, mouth gaping. He returned in under a minute and held a beautiful bunch of flowers in his hand. Clearing his throat again, he went on. "And I am grateful for having met you." He thrust out the flowers and read robotically, "Here in this bouquet you will find vines of Ivy, Lilac and Camillia."

He switched to another cue card and went on. "Ivy symbolizes fidelity. Lilac symbolizes first love. And Camellia symbolizes thankfulness and appreciation." He pushed the flowers out farther into me and I took them. He looked relieved when his shoulders drooped. In the candlelight, I saw a sheen of sweat beading his forehead. Reaching up to loosen his tie, he swallowed hard and read on, "With this bouquet, I give you a promise. A promise that I will always be faithful to you, adore you and never take you for granted."

Waving the cue cards across his face, he lifted his gaze to me and asked, "Is it hot in here?"

I shrugged, holding my flowers but he didn't see it. He was in presentation mode. Switching cue cards, he spoke clinically but his voice croaked, "They say penguins mate for life." He reached up again and jerked hard at his tie. "And I want to be your penguin." He jerked the tie harder until it came undone, hanging from his neck. He quickly undid the top button of his shirt and glanced across the room, glaring at the nightstand and muttering, "Damn candle went out."

Wait? He wanted to be my penguin?
Huh?

He moved to relight the tea candle but I stopped him.

It was obvious. He was distressed.

Holding onto his arm, I pulled him back in front of me and asked, "Honey, what is all this?"

Lev closed his eyes and he shut them tight. Sitting on the edge of the bed, he let out a long sigh, using his forearm to wipe the sweat from his forehead and reached into his pants pocket.

He pulled out a black velvet box and set it on his knee.

Breathing deeply, he opened the box, brought his eyes to mine and shook his head, "Can't you see I'm trying to ruin a proposal here?"

I looked down and blinked down at the ring sitting inside its beautiful box. "But we're already engaged. Sort of."

He held the box, running a hand down his face and he uttered a hushed, "I just wanted this to be romantic."

Getting on my knees in front of him, I crawled between his open legs and looked up at him tenderly. "Oh, sweetie. I don't need romance," I told him. "I just need you exactly how you are."

His jaw tight, he couldn't even look at me. This meant something to him. So I tried something else.

I spoke softly, "Lev, it's just me and you right now. Although your presentation was very informative, I was never one for flowery words. Just give me words from the heart, baby."

He looked down at me, a sad frown etched on his features. He took a deep breath and when he opened his mouth, beauty came out. He started on a whispered sigh, "You're everything to me."

My eyes were already watering.

"I would give my life rather than disappoint you and I would hurt anyone who tried to remove you from my side. I have never met a kinder woman. You're wonderful with Lidiya. I want to have children with you, as many as you'll allow, so we can experience parenthood together."

I bit my lip but it didn't stop the tears from coming. They blurred my eyes and trailed my cheeks.

"I'll be a good father to them. I pray that our babies will be like you but if they are like me, I don't want you to worry, because I'll guide them and show them they are loved even if they don't understand what that means. I will teach them."

My eyes closed as broken sobs escaped me. I held onto Lev's knee for support.

"I will spend my life loving you and you will spend your happy life making me a better person, as you already have, from your mere presence." He held out the box and whispered a nervous. "I will be the man you deserve. I'm not quite there, mouse, but I'm working on it. Marry me and my sole purpose in life will be to take every action so you don't ever regret it." He took my hand and with shaking fingers, slipped the ring in place. It fit perfectly. "Will you marry me, Mina?"

I stared at the ring, gleaming in the light, blinking away tears as a broken laugh escaped me. "Yes." I laughed again, reaching up to throw my arms around Lev's neck, kissing his stubbled cheek. "A thousand times *yes*."

And Lev breathed again, his chest heaving, his arms coiled around me tightly. His only response to that was a whispered, "Oh, thank God."

We laughed together, making love into the night and I couldn't remember a time I was happier.

CHAPTER FIFTY-TWO

Mina

Lidiya's birthday came the following week, and Lev wasn't sure if it was appropriate to do anything for it. I, however, disagreed. While I understood her mother had recently died, Lidiya was a child. She didn't understand that. I explained to Lev that by having a party for her, we were giving her our love and showing our support.

She deserved a party.

With Nas, Anika, and Cora on my side, Sasha and Vik were won over soon after, and finally Lev came around to the idea of doing something to make his daughter happy.

Honestly, I think being a father came naturally to Lev, but being a *daddy* was a whole new thing for him. He wasn't used to needing to provide something more than monetary support for Lidiya, and now that the role had freed up, he was falling into it like a dream, enjoying it immensely.

When Lidiya got a boo-boo, she ran to Lev. When Lidi needed kisses, she puckered her lips up at Lev. And when she needed to go potty, although Mirella was around, she wanted Lev to stand by the door so she could sing to him.

Smart man that Lev was, he quickly got used to putting Lidiya to bed at night, singing her songs and reading her stories, and I wondered if Mirella was even needed as a full-time caregiver. Part of me was sure she was kept around as a grandmother figure. She was family, after all. And she said it herself—where Lidi went, so did she.

I happened to stumble across Lev singing Lidi to sleep the other night. And when I say stumble, I mean I creeped like a goddamn stalker to get a glimpse of how he handled her. His version of

"Twinkle, Twinkle, Little Star" went something like this:

> *Twinkle, twinkle, little star,*
> *Burning gas is what you are,*
> *Up above the world so high,*
> *You'll burn gas until you die,*
> *Twinkle, twinkle, little star,*
> *Burning gas is what you are.*

With my head titled in thought, I was impressed. And kind of turned on.

Who knew nursery rhymes could be so informative? And sexy?

I sent invitations out for Lidiya's third birthday. I was almost cruel enough to make it a dress-up party, but decided to be kind to our guests and scrap the idea. Although, seeing Lev dressed up as a cowboy, in chaps and wearing a Stetson, was almost enough to change my mind.

When the day came, our home was overrun with people. We rarely got one guest a day usually, and that was normally family, but seeing the house full of smiling faces, pink balloons, and purple streamers was heartwarming.

Lidi, dressed as a princess in a bright pink dress with a silver tiara arranged around her curls, was overwhelmed with glee. Every time a person would arrive, she would smile, take their hand, and lead them inside, muttering, "Dank you a coming."

Her 'thank you for coming' was a little off, but she was so adorable that even Alessio was won over by her. She reached her arms up to him and, hesitantly, he lifted her onto his hip. She prodded his scarred cheek with gentle fingers and looked up into his face with her doe eyes. "Owie?"

He turned to me, desperate for a translation. I smiled into his 'help me' expression. "She wants to know if it hurts."

Alessio shook his head. "No owie," he uttered, taking her little chubby hand and putting it against the puckered flesh there. "It doesn't hurt, angel. Not anymore."

From the corner of my eye, I saw Cora standing against the wall, holding a glass, and she looked at Alessio like he was the sexiest man alive. Her lust-filled eyes were giving her away, and when she caught me looking, I smirked.

Cora bunched her nose and discreetly flipped me the bird.

It was going to happen—mark my words. I would do what I had to for them to hook up. She wanted him. He wanted her. Why was that so hard to understand?

God, people were dumb.

Nas looked at Vik from across the room, and when he felt her eyes on him and lifted his head, she lowered her glance. It wasn't the first time in the past two weeks that I saw them do this. It also didn't escape Lev's notice that Viktor had stopped coming around. They hadn't spoke in that time.

Something had happened between them, and Nas was not opening up, probably because it was still too painful to talk about.

All I knew was that Nas was miserable and Vik had developed the temper of a T-Rex with itchy balls.

Relationships were collapsing around us, but Lev and I were going stronger than ever.

I smiled to myself and gazed down at my sparkling white gold engagement ring. It was chic with only three small diamonds, but I loved it more than anything I'd ever owned in my entire life. And what was more...Lev had chosen it.

The hardest thing I ever had to do was tell Lev that I decided on a long engagement. I shouldn't have been worried. He simply responded with an, "Okay," then added, "But we're still going to marry, right?"

I emphatically assured him we would, but I just wasn't ready for that right now. There was so much going on, first with the club, then with my newfound inheritance, and finally with the photography course I was doing. When I was ready to get married, I wanted to be selfish and have it be all about us as a couple, and I didn't want to rush that, because we deserved more than a pressurized wedding full of stress.

But it would happen. Eventually.

I glanced around the room just in time to witness Anika raising her hand, rearing back, and slapping Sasha across the face so hard that it echoed through the room. The tall redhead stood there a moment, chest heaving, eyes shining bright before she looked around the room at enquiring eyes, blushed furiously, and whispered a hoarse, "Excuse me."

She left the room, and Sasha, looking unaffected with a blazing red mark on his cheek, turned to the people watching and glowered, "What? You never seen a woman slap a guy before?" He looked to me and muttered, "I think it's time for cake."

I looked over at the time. "No, it's not." At Sasha's fierce scowl, my brows rose and I called out, "Um, I mean, it's cake time everyone!"

Lidiya, who was now being held by Uncle Laredo, was brought to the table where Ada had placed the pink-sprinkled double layer cake with white chocolate butterflies around it. A chorus of "Happy Birthday" started, and Lidi sat on Lev's lap, smiling, clapping, and singing, even though she didn't know the words.

When it was time to blow out the candles, she leaned forward and blew with all her might, her tiny fists clenching from exertion. The candles were extinguished and a cheer went out around us.

I was smiling so hard it hurt.

More cheers were heard after Lidi had conned Lev into lighting the candles again and again, just so she could blow them out.

Nas called for pictures to be taken, and lifting Lidiya off Lev, I sat in his lap and placed her down on mine. I hugged Lidi tightly, and Lev wrapped his arms around my waist. Lidi pointed to the camera just before the photo was taken and a laugh escaped me. The photo was taken that way, Lev looking at me lovingly as I closed my eyes and laughed, and Lidi smiling wide, pointing at the camera.

This picture would be the first of many. It was enlarged and framed, and Lev hung it in the living room for all to see. Anyone with a pair of eyes could make out what we were.

We were a family.

EPILOGUE

Mina

Arriving from the club just after three a.m., Lev and I went about our nightly routine, changing out of our work wear, showering, and getting ready for bed. As I passed a very naked Lev, he struck out like a snake and snatched my hand, pulling me to him.

I was expecting it. He did this every night.

I went with a light laugh, loving the way he bent down, his lips conquering mine with nothing more than a simple connection. I was his in every which way, and Lev was mine. Mathematics be damned...Lev plus Mina equaled *one*.

One heart. A shared soul.

One love.

When he released me, I went over to the bed and slid under the covers. When Lev approached the bedroom door, he paused, looking down at the key that remained inside the lock. He stared down at that key a long time, and reaching out, I watched as his fingers closed around it.

My heart skipped a beat when he removed it, holding it in his grasp.

I swallowed hard, looking over as he made his way to the bed, key in hand, and he sat. He opened the top drawer of the nightstand and dropped the key inside. When he closed that drawer, he did it slowly, with determination and finality.

Pride rushed through me, and without another thought, I shuffled over to him, wrapped my arms around his neck, and placed my cheek against his from behind, turning my head to kiss the stubble there. He leaned into my kiss, taking all that I was offering along with it.

Our bedroom door remained unlocked the next night, the night after that, and every night thereafter.

And, finally, Lev felt as I did.
Safe.

As I had many nights since I met Lev Leokov, I fell asleep smiling.

LEV

The End

LEV

A Note From Belle

Hi there,

Thank you so much for taking the time to read **LEV**. I hope you loved Mina and Lev, and all the rest of the crew, as much as I do. It would help a great deal if you would please take the time to leave a review :)

Thanks again,

Belle x

Printed in Great Britain
by Amazon